THE HARVESTERS

THE HARVESTERS

*To Sean,
Hope you enjoy
this story.
best wishes*

ANTHONY SPARROW

Copyright © 2015 Anthony Sparrow

The moral right of the author has been asserted.

Apart from any fair dealing for the purposes of research or private study, or criticism or review, as permitted under the Copyright, Designs and Patents Act 1988, this publication may only be reproduced, stored or transmitted, in any form or by any means, with the prior permission in writing of the publishers, or in the case of reprographic reproduction in accordance with the terms of licences issued by the Copyright Licensing Agency. Enquiries concerning reproduction outside those terms should be sent to the publishers.

Matador
9 Priory Business Park
Kibworth Beauchamp
Leicestershire LE8 0RX, UK
Tel: (+44) 116 279 2299
Fax: (+44) 116 279 2277
Email: books@troubador.co.uk
Web: www.troubador.co.uk/matador

ISBN 978-1784621-742

British Library Cataloguing in Publication Data.
A catalogue record for this book is available from the British Library.

Typeset in Aldine by Troubador Publishing Ltd

Matador is an imprint of Troubador Publishing Ltd

This book is dedicated to all the people I have known throughout my life, they have helped create the person I am today.

1

Present Day Harvest

The alien mother ship approached Earth using the Moon as a shield against being detected, effectively avoiding all the instruments designed to search the skies for unnatural heavenly bodies or listen for little green men from outer space. From the world's largest radio telescope in Arecibo Puerto Rico, to all the laser and gravity wave-scanning devices pointed towards the heavens by SETI scientists the world over twenty-four hours a day, it managed to evade them all.

However, these particular aliens were far from little and far from green. They also didn't want to be seen by any of the inhabitants from Earth for very good reasons.

Stealthily, the approximately fifty-kilometre-diameter spaceship, on its journey from its starting point out near the edge of the solar system, attained high synchronous orbit on the dark side of the Moon without so much as a twitch on any Earthly scanner printout or deep space listening device.

Also, the inhabitants of Earth would not have noticed that Pluto's third small moon had vacated the orbit around its host planet, something it did once every Earth year. Nix had travelled across the solar system, cunningly using planets to conceal itself on its annual voyage.

Only the Hubble Telescope, had it been looking in the direction of Pluto, could have noticed something missing from its normal place in the solar system.

Fortunately for the alien inhabitants of the hollow moon, the accurate cosmic stare of the most powerful telescope ever devised by man was trained on the galaxy NGC 4710 at that particular point in time.

The adult alien inhabitants were approximately three metres in height. They were bipod in form, not too dissimilar to human in appearance. They stood on long gangly legs. Arms rippling with tight knotted muscles that flexed every time they moved. They had pale skin that was covered by a fine mouse like fur giving them a grey sheen appearance.

They were almost totally naked except, from the fine fur and a very small covering of underwear to hide their modesty. Their sparse garments were worn purely for practical reasons as the genitals of both male and female were proportionally larger in comparison to equivalent human reproductive organs.

Roaming the cosmos for thousands of years, this species had decided that clad only in what could be described as loin cloths, was the most practical way to travel among the stars.
Having a totally automated atmosphere, why bother with covering materials that harboured bacteria and needed constant cleaning and drying.

Their heads were also large in comparison to the rest of their bodies. A large oval mouth in the centre of the face was filled with two rows of razor sharp, shark-like teeth. They had two large round eyes high up on the skull. These were complemented by small flat ears set far back against the sides of the head, almost reaching the start of a fat neck that increased in size, until it fanned out onto broad shoulders.

On the dark side of Earth's Moon, the alien occupied moon hid in constant shadow, skulking, like some beast of prey, waiting to pounce on an unwary victim. They didn't wait long. Simultaneously, from round portholes, three much smaller spacecraft exited their mother ship. This trio of vessels were disguised as lumps of rock, designed to fool the people of Earth into thinking they were nothing more than small meteorites that would plunge into the Earth's atmosphere, burning up to nothing.

On the B729 in Dumfriesshire, a lonely stretch of road, Samantha Long drove her aged Ford Fiesta through the autumn twilight. The car showed its age, flecks of rust peeked through the dull unpolished blue paintwork. Whilst driving, she was technically breaking Scottish law as she chatted on her mobile phone that was firmly wedged between shoulder and ear.

Samantha was in her early twenties. She had dyed blonde hair beginning to show dark roots. It would need colouring again soon she had thought that very morning, whilst looking at her reflection in the bathroom mirror applying her daily heavy makeup.

"Hi Tracy, we still on for the gig tomorrow night in Kirkpatrick?" she asked her old school friend. Tracy's positive reply could only be heard by Samantha.

"That's great, really looking forward to it. Yeah, just on my way over to Tynron to see my mother, try to go at least once a week," replied Samantha, in answer to the question Tracy had asked. Just then the car started to splutter and cough.

"Okay, I'll pick you up around... Oh shit, sounds like the car is playing up again, I'm gonna have to go now Tracy, I'll speak to you later, bye."

Tracy was cut off abruptly as she was midway through saying cheerio in return. Samantha managed to pull over to the side of the road as the engine gave one last wheeze and died.

"That's the third time this month. It's high time this piece of crap went to the knacker's yard," she muttered to herself out loud.

Pulling up a number from her contact list, she stabbed the call button.

"Hiya Dad. Guess what? Broken down again, I'm gonna have to get something more reliable than this old rust bucket!"

Samantha went on to explain to her father her exact whereabouts on the remote road hoping he wouldn't be too long in coming once more to her rescue. It was cold outside, and the cold was creeping into the car's cabin now the warm air blower had died along with the engine. She wrapped the fur trimmed coat she was wearing closer to conserve body heat.

Unbeknown to Samantha whilst she was busy chatting to her lifelong friend, one of the three small alien spaceships had been tracking her, following at a discreet distance.

It was now stripped of the rock like exterior disguise, which had burnt off during the descent through the atmosphere, giving a false appearance of a shooting star. The design was the classic Unidentified Flying Object oval rugby ball shape as seen in so many science fiction comics and films. Although they tried to avoid being seen, it was impossible to carry out their yearly task without being observed from time to time. However, without any hard proof apart from an occasional blurred photograph, visiting alien sightings reported on odd occasions to the authorities, were normally dismissed as hoaxes.

Quite small in relative size to the mother ship, the spacecraft was still an impressive two hundred metres in length and one hundred metres across the girth at the midpoint. Without a visible blemish on the smooth copper-coloured body, it was very sleek and very fast. Unless it was moving, it was also impossible to tell the front from the rear. Drawing on the power of Earth's magnetic field gave it terrific speed within the atmosphere. It also had the ability to hover motionless, using its own generated counter-repellent magnetic aura.

The two alien pilots on board were donned head to foot in

black tight fitting spacesuits. Their heads, covered with huge black helmets, were massively over-proportionate to corresponding human spacesuit attire.

Both were lying horizontal on couches that contoured their prone bodies. With no instrumentation visible, they were connected to the spacecraft control centre by complicated telepathic electronics inbuilt to their oversized helmets.

Both were satisfied they had found a good specimen to abduct and acknowledged to each other through thought alone. One of them had scanned Sam's body for any defects, diseases, cancers or tumours that may have been present. The scan had come back negative. Slowly the spacecraft descended towards their chosen victim. The other alien creature, using conscious thought via the telepathic link to the onboard controlling analytical artificial mind, gave instructions to launch a probe. The probe hung suspended in the air for a few seconds, a metre outside the hull of the alien spaceship, until directed down towards Samantha's car.

Spherical in shape it was exactly two centimetres in diameter. Sensors relayed images of its flight back to the mind now in command of its every move. It had a means of propulsion similar to the spacecraft that spawned it, using magnetic waves to pull itself towards, or push away from larger objects. It contained four microscopic robots currently compressed and dormant. When free from the miniature sphere and activated, they would be just over half a centimetre long and capable of independent movement.

The alien whose thoughts controlled the momentum of the probe guided it expertly towards the front of the travelling car, steering it underneath the front bumper up into the engine bay. It floated up behind the radiator until it reached the very top of the engine compartment, whereupon it split open, scattering the microscopic robots across the air filter plastic covering.

Unfurling, the tiny mechanical robots resembled soldier ants in stature, multiple legs on a thin elongated body, ending in an engorged head. The head was one mass of microscopic teeth lined in circular row upon circular row, like a miniature hole boring machine.

Now it took both the alien pilots all their telepathic concentration to manipulate the tiny robots, in addition to controlling the spacecraft. Without finding secure footing, one of the tiny robots easily slipped off the old greasy engine cowling. It fell, tumbling under the car to be lost.

Those that remained scattered like cockroaches in the kitchen when someone turns the light on. Their multiple legs ended in minute pincer like claws. These now bit into the surface of the oily engine block plying for grip.

Soon, two of the micro robots eventually found what the aliens had been searching for, the cars HT leads. Using their head cutting devices, they started to burrow into the cables ejecting their eyelash sized legs as they progressed further. Inside the core of the cables they easily broke through the copper connecting wire. The two micro robots exploded as they severed the electric current, but they were no longer required. With two of the four engine cylinders now inoperative, the car inevitably spluttered to a halt.

From the probe being launched, to the car coming to a full stop, had taken less than twenty seconds. Now the spaceship floated effortlessly directly above the stationary car.

After calling her father, Samantha twiddled with the radio without success before noticing a small beam of light on the bonnet. Instinctively she peered out the windscreen up towards the source. The intense bright beam shone directly into her eyes forcing her to automatically blink. She ducked back due to the magnitude of the light.

Common sense told her to stay inside the car in relative safety. However, she was fascinated to see what was giving out such a bright beam of light. Samantha was secretly hoping it was some sort of rescue helicopter, but she couldn't hear any rotor sounds. It was also slightly ludicrous that one would be nearby just as she broke down she thought. So, with the curiosity of a cat, she opened the car door and climbed out of the driver's seat.

Outside, she stood transfixed by the light with head tilted upwards. The narrow beam had become somewhat hypnotic as it moved to cover her upturned face, like a spotlight, picking out the leading actress in a stage play.

Another probe had already been launched by the aliens even before Samantha had left her car. As she stood mesmerised in the circle of light, the probe hit her left ear splitting open in the process.

One of the tiny robots to emerge from this microscopic probe quickly crawled inside her ear, ejecting its legs to become more like a large maggot in appearance and movement. The legless robot worked its way quickly down her ear canal, before slicing through Sam's eardrum, into the soft tissue beyond.

Samantha felt the pain as the tiny metal monster chewed through her inner ear. She screamed out loud, digging in a little finger, pulling out the little discarded legs in the process, wanting to rid herself of the bug. A bug that subconsciously, she concluded was a huge mosquito that had somehow managed to crawl inside her head. Deeper and deeper the micro robot burrowed, until it finally found her spinal column at the base of the neck.

Samantha jumped about hysterically in excruciating pain. Unperturbed, the tiny robot bore between two vertebrae wreaking havoc with the neural pathways inside. An instant later, she became totally paralysed, falling into a useless mass of arms and legs, unable to control any bodily functions from her neck down.

As she lay there, she was still dimly aware of her surroundings. Her head felt like it was splitting open, but beyond that she could feel nothing. All she could do was move her eyes. Her breathing was spasmodic and shallow.

When Sam fell, like a marionette that just had all its strings cut at once, the fall was without any control of downwards direction on her part. Looking directly out across the road, she could see the rugby-ball-shaped alien vessel that had moved from its position overhead. It now hovered inches from the ground a short way off. Looking back on her relatively short life, she had always been sceptical of unidentified flying objects before now. Now, here was one right before her very eyes. She speculated she should perhaps alter her doubtful stance on the existence of extraterrestrial life from now on.

The copper coloured spacecraft shimmered periodically, as the surrounding anti-gravitational forces repelled Earth's own powerful magnetic halo.

A seamless panel slid open mid way along the fuselage allowing a tall black shape with a huge helmeted head to emerge. With its long shanks, the alien didn't take long to cross the short distance to the road where her useless prone body lay.

Samantha wanted to scream again as the huge black suited figure loomed over her. Needing some respite from this nightmare, she fainted instead.

The alien bent down to attach two shackles, one to each of Samantha's ankles. The shackles were joined together with a short link of flexible metal cord. Holding the metal cord by one hand, the alien effortlessly lifted the captive leaving arms trailing causing her hands to bump along the ground as it carried her back to the vessel.

On board, the door panel slid shut behind them. The alien strode down a long corridor before rounding a corner. A little further on and a tall door loomed to one side. As the alien carrying Sam approached, the door opened inward, triggered by some automatic process. Once open, it revealed a large chamber. Misty green tinged cold air rushed out.

Inside the massive compartment, several other human bodies were hanging by ankle shackles on hooks. Their heads suspended about one and a half metres above the floor. The alien hoisted Samantha's body on the next available hook.

Samantha regained consciousness just as she was being hung upside down by the cable between her ankles. With lifeless arms and head hanging down all she could do was look directly beneath her.

The floor had an odd design she thought, it was covered in criss-cross grooves. A dark thick liquid ebbed back and forth along some of the furrows. Peering up from her current position, similar to looking down her nose whilst standing upright, she could see the head of the body hanging next to her.

As she looked at it she noticed something odd about the neck of her fellow human until, it finally dawned on Samantha exactly what was wrong. Eyes wide in apprehension, she suddenly realised what was about to happen to her. She couldn't stop the huge tears that welled up her eyes.

The alien, satisfied Sam was secure, pulled out a knife approximately half a metre in length from some concealed part of its spacesuit leg covering. It had a large handle with a small spindle to be used easily in conjunction with spacesuit gloves. It also had a razor sharp serrated edge. With one deft movement the alien slid it easily across Samantha's throat, giving the distinct appearance the alien was some sort of expert in the field of human butchery.

Samantha couldn't breathe with her windpipe almost sliced through. Blood poured from the gash in her throat running though her dyed blonde hair in rivulets. It cascaded onto the floor where it was channelled into the grooves mixing with the other dark red liquid. It was the last thing Samantha would ever see in her life.

Some days later, the three alien spaceships returned to their mother ship on the other side of the Moon. Each had a hold that was full to bursting of harvested human corpses, enough food to last the parasitic alien settlement for another year.

The statistics for human missing persons around the world would increase by a few hundred here and there. A mere drop in the ocean of the thousands of persons reported missing in countries around the globe each day.

—

Over the next one hundred and twenty-five years, as the human race started to explore the nearby planets in the solar system, the aliens would continue their covert harvest. Every year they would return, to the Earth, the Moon and eventually Mars, from their hiding place near Pluto, to conduct their ruthless bloodthirsty undertaking.

2

The European Space Exploration Travel Corporation

The sun was a bright disc on the horizon. It shone through the double paned insulating plastic roof causing Robert Goodyear to squint.

A huge clock on the wall informed him it was almost ten in the morning on Sunday the nineteenth of May in the year two thousand one hundred and thirty-seven.

He was standing on the very top of the world at the North Pole, straining to see through the refracted light, the twelfth marvel of the modern world, the Orbital Space Elevator.

Arriving at Borealis Station fifteen minutes earlier, he had been in quite a hurry. Now the forty-four year old was hesitant. Robert didn't like lifts. Elevators as the rest of the world called them. Although he was in pretty good physical shape all things considered, one of his major shortcomings was being slightly claustrophobic. In fact he was quite claustrophobic, but didn't like to admit to it.

The trip to Mars was going to start with the long ride up to Satellite Two inside the Orbital Space Elevator. He was not looking forward to the prospect one little bit. Space travel involved lots of enclosed spaces, spaces that were usually very compact.

He shook a bottle in his jacket pocket just to check it was still there. Pills would help keep his nausea in check. He just needed to remain calm, keep on top of those constricting feelings. It was all in his head, he reminded himself.

Trying to keep his mind occupied, his thoughts wandered. He remembered the last time he had made the elevator ascent. It seemed so long ago now. Four hours climbing up to Satellite Two, the staging post at the end of the Orbital Space Elevator, one hundred kilometres up in the thermosphere.

Shuttles ran between Satellite Two and the main spaceport that was just known simply as Gateway. Gateway orbited another two hundred kilometres out beyond the elevator terminus.

The Orbital Space Elevator really was a magnificent constructional achievement. It started on the floor of the Arctic Ocean, just over one kilometre below the ice pack. He had studied all the facts when he was much younger, fascinated at the complex engineering that had been used to build it. A huge hole had been punched into the ice cap allowing access to the Arctic Ocean seabed, where monstrous concrete and steel pillars were buried into the very bedrock of the planet along the top of the Lomonosov ridge, the site primarily chosen for being one of Earth's more stable tectonic plate interactive areas.

The European Government had been the main instigator of the project initially. The European Space Exploration and Travel Corporation, known simply the world over as the Corporation, then invested heavily, together with several major British financial institutions throughout the twenty-two year long construction.

Now the Corporation, by virtue of its rich and rewarding space mining operations within the Asteroid Belt, had acquired the majority shareholdings of the Orbital Space Elevator over the last thirty years. It also owned ninety per cent of the Mars Facilities.

His gaze slowly followed the structure up towards the heavens. Six triangular titanium and steel alloy girder frameworks made up the star-pointed hexagram giving the formation enormous rigid strength. This framework stretched right up to the start of the stratosphere.

The highest construction ever built by man stopped just short of ten kilometres. A dozen super slim lightweight and incredibly strong carbon cables fanned out from the top of the main structure, to rock anchor points buried in ice over a fifty kilometres away. Above the framework, the two main climbing cables continued for over ninety kilometres. At the very end of the cables, Satellite Two hung in low orbit. To retain such a low orbit it was tethered to four gigantic solar wind anchors, drifting like huge drogue kites way out in the exosphere.

A young man ran across the foyer and up to Robert, who was still staring skyward unaware of the newcomer. The new arrival had run all the way from the heli-jet pad. He was slightly short of breath. Casually dressed in denim trousers and open necked shirt like Robert, and, just like Robert, also had a small rucksack slung across one shoulder containing hastily assembled personal items.

He was quite a handsome young man, sporting short curly black hair, his emerald eyes flashed bright green catching the sunlight beams cascading in. According to the short briefing he had received from his friend and colleague Jenny Smith on the journey from London, they were short on time.

"I think we should get a move on!" the young man exclaimed to his superior.

"Huh?" Robert shrugged in reply, before his wandering mind snapped out of his daydream up in the clouds.

He gaze dropped to James Cleaver, his grade two technical

assistant. In possession of a great analytical mind he had just turned twenty-five years old. Robert hoped he would take over his Senior Analyst position in the Corporation one day. He certainly had the mental capacity for the work.

"Yes, you're right, we need to get a move on. The elevator won't wait forever."

He motioned with his hands towards the general direction of the main entrance, still feeling anxiety driven churning sensations in his stomach. Now the urgency was a thankful distraction.

They strode together across the red and white tiled floor of Borealis Station, towards the centrally-located chamber departure lounge at the base of the vertical shaft.

As the Corporation owned the majority share of the Elevator, which included Satellite Two, it would have been impossible for it to leave without them. Every ascent was costly if not a little dangerous. Today's unscheduled ascent had been quickly arranged specifically for James and Robert. The Corporation wanted both of them out on Mars as soon as possible, regardless of the expense.

"What's so important?" James asked excitedly.

The previous evening at his home in London, whilst playing a fellow chess master in Rome, he had been abruptly interrupted.

Robert's lifelike three dimensional head and shoulders had suddenly appeared in the space previously occupied by a chess board with the game in progress. James was preparing to move his queen into a check position.

"Hi James, sorry to barge in like this and spoil your evening," he started, before pausing for a second. He had been in a hurry to sit down to make the call, now he realised he was in an uncomfortable position so readjusted his posture before continuing.

"A high priority mission has come up, requires both our

presence I'm afraid. A heli-jet will pick you up in Hyde Park at eight tomorrow morning. You okay with that?" James was still a little shocked so just nodded approval.

"If you contact Miss Smith in the office on a secure link on the way up tomorrow morning, she'll brief you the basics. Sorry again for interrupting whatever you were doing."

"Okay, no problem. I'll see you tomorrow," replied James, finally finding his voice, not really knowing what to expect the following day. The chessboard re-appeared. He then went on to win the game in nine moves. After thanking his opponent and terminating the connection he packed his rucksack with some essential items.

Next morning at eight on the dot, a heli-jet landed opposite his apartment block. James couldn't help noticing it was the personal flight of the Corporation President. Not only that, you needed written permission from the prime minister just to fly over inner London these days. He was very impressed, as were most of the passers-by that stopped to gawp. He allowed himself a broad grin as he boarded the direct flight to Borealis Station. Being the only passenger, the stewardess made sure he wanted for nothing.

During the flight he opened up a secure link to his offices on a global access terminal. He had more than a soft spot for Jenny, having had the pleasure of her company on a couple of evening dinner and theatre dates in the past. He liked to think the feeling was mutual, but it was always difficult, even frowned upon, to have any sort of relationship between work colleagues.

"Hi Jenny, what on Earth's going on?" he asked.

Jenny, with cute dimples in her cheeks, beamed out of the screen back at him. "Hello James, I know precious little I'm afraid."

She went on to explain what little she did know, that he was going to be on the Orbital Space Elevator making an unscheduled ascent at ten o'clock. Also, the Mars interplanetary supply vessel *Oceans Dawn*, that had been due to depart later in the week, had been swiftly rescheduled for a flight that afternoon for the both him and his superior. After some small talk he felt a little embarrassed as she had ended their conversation with a rather sincere "… take care and return back safely."

Now, an hour later, here he was crossing the foyer of Borealis Station with his superior. Robert glanced behind them before he began to answer James's questions.

"The official version is there are a few problems at the Mars Facilities. Production quotas are falling short of Corporation predictions." Robert stopped and put a hand on James's shoulder. He pulled him round so they were standing face to face. "We need to have a look first-hand, find out what's happening and correct any faults we might uncover."

James looked surprised, that would hardly warrant both of them having to investigate he thought. "Surely the Facilities Controller on Mars should be quite capable of solving those sorts of problems," he retorted.

Robert leant closer before continuing in a hushed voice. "That's the official reason on the Corporation personnel movement log. The real reason is that some strange events have occurred that no one can explain. Now, an asteroid miner has died in very mysterious circumstances. Obviously, the Corporation bosses want to keep a tight lid on it. We need to find some plausible explanation before someone lets the cat out the bag. Rumours have already started to filter back to Earth. The press are getting nosey. More seriously, so are some Euro Government departments not in the loop, they cannot be fobbed off so easily."

"And where do I fit in?" James asked.

"The Corporation have managed to excuse the rumours so far, but they need real answers fast. I have a feeling this is going to be an intensive exercise. I may need you as a sounding board to bounce ideas off, plus, another young, more alert logical mind like yours, thrown into the mix, might spot something I may overlook."

They continued walking towards a large set of double doors guarded by an empty desk.

"Besides, I thought it was about time you experienced a trip to Mars. Look at it as part of your apprenticeship. I know you have never left the European States before. We need to find out if space travel agrees with you."

James was inwardly pleased with himself. Now he knew why he had worked so hard studying at school, college and finally university, before spending two years as an analytical trainee. This was part of his dream coming true. It would normally cost a small fortune for an ordinary civilian businessman to travel to Mars, now he got to go for free albeit, under the guise of work.

This then was the first step to achieving his ultimate goal of spending a week or possibly two, on vacation at the leisure resort of Paradise Moon in the Sea of Tranquillity. He would still have to wait quite a while until he was a fully qualified analyst, plus receive a substantial pay rise, before that day finally dawned. Perhaps he and Jenny might get there one day he added to his thoughts, but his thoughts were cut short, as a few more strides saw the two companions reach the security desk, just outside the main departure lounge.

On the sloped top of the unmanned desk in front of them they found a large imprint of a hand set deep into the surface. Robert placed his hand within the outline of the imprint. A faint light scanned his fingerprints. At the same time a scanner read the details stored on the identity chip embedded at the base of his thumb and forefinger.

The background to the recess turned a luminous green colour to show all was well. If Robert had been an imposter the recess would have snapped shut, trapping his hand in an instant. Security guards would not be far away. A voice spoke from nowhere in particular.

"Good Morning Senior Analyst Goodyear, have a safe onward journey."

James repeated the process with similar results.

"Good morning Grade Two Analyst Cleaver, have a safe onward journey."

The two security doors behind the desk opened to reveal the aircraft-hangar-sized departure lounge. Now they could see the square Elevator cabin, the extent of a football pitch above their heads. Two cables three metres across ran though the two halves of the Elevator.

Running away from the double doors to the left and right were several rows of privacy lockers. Across the floor, overall-clad employees flitted here and there. One of the team, a smartly dressed female with auburn hair in a plaited ponytail, was approaching the two men standing on the threshold.

"Good morning gentlemen," she said smiling politely. "We have been expecting you, please follow me."

Turning on her heels without waiting for any sign of acknowledgement, she led the way across the floor to one of the banks of lockers to the left of the entrance. The way she moved was almost mechanical, robotic even, James observed. Robert must have been on a similar wavelength. They looked at each other quizzically for a second, before both shrugged. They then set off quickly following in her footsteps, racing to catch up. James knew the Corporation had been working on advanced robotics for some time. Could this be the fruition he asked himself? She was very lifelike, if she were indeed an android.

Coming to a stop, she turned to face the space between two privacy lockers. She waited until they stood either side of her before offering instructions.

"If you would place your chipped hands here and here please."

She pointed her hands to the sliding locks on the front of the two upright metal cabinets. As soon as their imbedded chips were within close proximity, the locks slid back with a double click.

"Coded to match your unique genetic number from your personal implants," she smiled a somewhat artificial smile, and then continued her instructions. "Please change into the overalls provided and leave your Earth clothes, watches, wallets, all personal electronic equipment, etcetera in the cabinets, they will remain quite safe here until your return. If you would like to transfer any personal hygiene belongings you require for the voyage to these small bags, these you will be taking with you." As she spoke, she produced two small pull cord canvas bags, handing one to each of them. "Is everything clear?" She gave them a few moments to ask questions. As none were forthcoming she walked off briskly.

Swinging open the privacy locker door caused an overhead opaque laser light to form a circular column around each of them. James, inside his light-induced private changing room, quickly discarded his ordinary clothes. Standing completely naked, he took out some protective, slightly unassuming padded underwear, the neatly folded pale blue overalls and a paper and cardboard-based pair of slippers found inside the locker. He slipped on the sterile items.

Once changed and having sorted out his personal effects, James closed the locker door. The security lock clicked shut causing the screening laser light to evaporate. Almost simultaneously, the two men were released from the privacy of their temporary changing rooms. Now they stood staring at each other.

"I don't like the idea of leaving my belongings behind, especially my personal media access device," whinged James. "I feel quite lost without it," he added.

"Don't worry. There are plenty of access terminals in the

Elevator, on Satellite Two, and on board the Corporation spacecraft. You will have a direct link with the main Corporation databases. Each terminal is totally secure which is the main thing," stated Robert, before leading the way out of the privacy area towards the middle of the lounge.

There were a series of semi-circular bench chairs centred round the huge cables that disappeared into the floor like two huge tree trunks.

They sat down away from the busy operatives organising small trains of cargo containers onto cherry pickers that took the supplies up to the Elevator for loading.

There were three other individuals similarly dressed in light blue overalls, obviously taking advantage of the unscheduled ascent. The two analysts sat as far away from them as was possible.

James realised Robert had been in small talk mode for some time now, talking trivia since leaving the locker area spouting technical information about the Elevator that James already knew. He guessed it was a cover and played along nodding when it seemed appropriate.

"… also, those cables are only as thick as your arm by the time we get up to Satellite Two. Quite amazing really how the two motors on top of the Elevator cabin haul that contraption up against gravity's will."

There came a lull in his talk as if Robert had finally convinced himself there was no immediate threat from any covert listening devices in the nearby vicinity.

James observed the three other passengers sitting nearby. Two were obviously together, talking about replacing some important experimental component on Satellite Two. Suddenly they pointed excitedly to one of the crates on a cargo train crossing the hallway, as they recognised their carefully packed item.

The other person he couldn't quite make out what he was

doing there. He was male, about five foot ten with ginger hair that was quite distinctive. He had a roundish, quite dark pink blotched face that was usually associated with red headed people. He also looked quite out of place. James couldn't be sure, but it also appeared he had moved closer to them. Perhaps he was just being overly paranoid.

Sensing the pause, he guessed Robert was at last going to divulge some useful information.

"Look James, I can't really go into much detail about our mission here," Robert was unconsciously still being furtive, eyes twitching this way and that. "We have to suspect everyone is some sort of news hound or industrial spy. Also, only a handful of Corporation employees know the whole picture. News of our departure will have leaked and be widely known by now, people will be asking questions. We have to be extremely careful."

Robert and James sat in silence for a few minutes. "I'll give you a full briefing, basically everything I know, once we are underway and away from any eavesdroppers," Robert said finally.

James accepted these facts in silence before leaning back in his chair. His head rolled backwards, automatically he looked up.

Above them hung the huge seemingly innocuous rectangular box that would transport him on his first leg, of his first ever voyage into space. His mind was racing, what was this journey all about. He knew he would have to be patient, take control of his flaying emotions, all would be revealed in due course.

Suddenly, they were both aware that the auburn-haired woman, who had greeted them earlier, was once more now standing before them.

"Gentlemen, if you would like to come this way to collect your spacesuits, the Elevator is just about ready for departure."

3

Lode Drifter

Andy Hubbins surveyed the mess room. It was aptly named he thought, it was a bloody mess! He noted that some of his crew could have done with a wash and tidy up as well, even if water was a scarce commodity.

The Asteroid Belt mining spaceship *Lode Drifter* was a hard working vessel operating in harsh conditions. Little time was given or even available, to keeping the spaceship or its inhabitants clean. The small spacecraft's hard life was reflected by the scratches, scrapes and gouges in the walls, door frames and table tops. Discarded empty food packets and wrappers occupied the corners of the room.

On the long arduous journey back to the Mars Scientific, Research, Mining and Refining Facilities, it might get a bit of a spruce up, only for the next crew of mining degenerates to take it straight back out to the Belt treating it with the same contempt and disrespect.

Tidying up the mass of degradable food wrappers and cartons was usually performed when the artificial gravity gyros were switched off for the duration of prolonged space flight. During the journey back from the asteroids to Mars, the detritus floated. It was sucked onto the air conditioning inlet vents where it could be picked off into refuse sacks quite easily.

At this particular point in time, keeping the interior of the vessel clean was the last thing on Andy's mind. The task of mining operations controller on any tour was a big responsibility, especially when it was not going according to plan.

A typical mining tour out in the abundant asteroids lasted one hundred and twenty days. Thirty days out, sixty days surveying and mining, before thirty long days travelling back. There were eight crew on a conventional mining tour cramped together like sardines in a very small tin can.

Normally working in shifts, the entire crew would not usually be trying to occupy the mess room all at once, like they were at this precise moment. However, Andy had called this emergency meeting. Somehow, they had all managed to squeeze into the little room. It was rather a tight fit. In fact, that wasn't quite strictly true. Andy was leaning in the doorway watching so technically not physically in the room. As he watched them jostling for seating space, he ran through this motley crew in his head.

At the far right of the room sat Josie Carter, an American by birth who was his first officer and second in command. Josie was a highly qualified asteroid surveyor. On previous tours she had located some high-paying ore. None of the crew was disappointed with her work. Slowly chewing her way through some high-energy food bar, she carefully inspected the newly exposed contents after every bite, as if expecting to find something abnormal amongst the nuts and chocolate.

Josie and Andy had been on over twenty tours together now. They had been close once, very close in fact, having experienced a brief intimate affair that was now well and truly confined to the realms of history.

Unfortunately, there is not much room for romance and

compassion whilst on a mining tour in the Asteroid Belt. On a small, sweaty, usually smelly overworked mining spacecraft, there simply isn't the time or the physical inclination he reflected briefly, on what he considered were the main reasons for their failed relationship.

Next to Josie was Aimee Laurant who spent her tender years in France studying astrological geology at university. Now in her mid-twenties, this was only her second tour so it was still a new and exciting adventure so far. She was also under Josie's protective wing learning the practical side of the asteroid-mining business.

Aimee was chatting to Raman Tingle. Raman had West Indian grandparents which plainly showed as he had also inherited the casual laid-back attitude of the West Indian people. It looked to Andy that there was some sort of chemistry going on between them. He felt a pang of jealousy. Aimee was a very attractive young woman.

Then there was Steve Wilson a Scot through and through. Although quite short he was as hard as they come. Not one to frighten in a dark corridor late at night, especially if he had a few whiskeys under his belt.

Standing next to Steve bending down to talk to him was Deimos Wells. Deimos had to stand. He physically couldn't sit down in the cramped room with his long legs that forced him to stoop every time he walked under a bulkhead.

Deimos had been born on Mars and due to the low gravity had grown rapidly. As soon as he reached over one metre in height at the age of six, his parents shipped him backed to Earth for the rest of his childhood, hoping to halt the rapid growth. Now fully grown, he was just over seven foot tall. He was also very thin. It looked like he had been stretched out on a medieval rack.

Next, dipping a well-used tarnished spoon into a bowl of brown sludge that was supposed to be reconstituted Irish stew, with his eyes firmly fixed on Andy, was the eccentric Irishman Kieron McCabe. Andy could never read Kieron, his moods or his thoughts. Sometimes, he seemed to be away in a world of his own. However, he was a first class physician having saved quite a few lives, and limbs, in the few years since he had ventured out to Mars. Everyone was glad to have him around as accidents were quite frequent in their line of work.

What was he thinking now? Andy wondered. He started to feel slightly uncomfortable under his unflinching gaze. Maybe he was just looking straight through him, lost in his own personal reflections. Andy never asked him why he had decided to leave the comforts of Earth, maybe he would get around to the question one day. Then again, perhaps he had been responsible for some medical disaster forcing him to be struck off, discredited? Maybe, it would be better all round if he didn't ask. He let these thoughts slip into obscurity.

Lastly, keeping very quiet in the near left hand corner of the room was Mei-Lien Chin, a last minute replacement for Teunis Landry who failed to show when they took command of *Lode Drifter*. Andy had seen her work-history resume. It must have been okay, now though for the life of him, he couldn't remember one word on it.

Being a temporary member of a mining team was always hard work. It took time to integrate, to fit in, for people to measure your worth. Also, as the temporary status may only be limited for one tour, people were less inclined to get too close, too familiar. In the minds of the usual crew, they hoped Teunis would be rejoining them again on the next tour. They all liked the nostalgic Dutchman.

Quiet or not, the Chinese woman had turned out to be a tough worker, who just got on with the hard graft at the end of the day. Andy had no complaints, but he had a strange feeling there was more to this woman that was not immediately obvious.

"Right listen up you lot!" Andy half shouted. He banged his fist on the wall to get the desired attention. The hubbub of idle chat stopped, all heads now turned towards the mess room doorway.

"As you may have guessed, I didn't get you all here for nothing. I know two of you should be asleep, and the rest either at ease, working or getting ready for shifts."

"Or trying to have a quiet lunch!" Kieron quipped.

Andy cleared his throat. "The thing is, we are way down on our ore potential, we're halfway through the tour and nowhere near halfway filling our ore sack."

The ore sack was an enormous intricate wire mesh repository slung under *Lode Drifter*. The carefully cut ore was lifted from the asteroid being mined in manageable chunks to be unceremoniously dumped into the sack.

"I know it's my fault, we spent far too long looking for platinum or lithium, both in short supply at the moment so demanding a high price as a consequence…"

"And trying to find that rich cobalt asteroid we tagged last time we were out, what a waste of time that was, probably knocked out the belt and halfway to Uranus by now!" Steve exclaimed, butting in. This caused a few confirming expletives from the other crew members. Holding his hands up in mock surrender, Andy paused for a moment to allow the mumbles to die down.

"Okay, I know, I know, it was a major wild goose chase on my part. However, we have a very nice vein of titanium on the go that could see us to the end of this tour and beyond," Andy declared, waving his arms wide in the limited space to emphasize the point. "With all hands working every available second we just might get a full sack before our time is up, or we could pack up operations here and search out some richer pay dirt."

"What if we don't find anything more valuable, even less

bonus than this crap we're mining now!" Deimos said, almost shouting to stress the point.

"Come on, it's not that bad, eh, Josie?" Andy looked to support from his first officer.

"It is a high yielding ore, we should get a moderate bonus," Josie said enthusiastically, trying to boost the declining morale.

"What are the chances of finding some nice iridium Josie?" Raman asked.

Josie shrugged. "About the same chances as you finding my lost virginity," she said with a smile, causing a few spontaneous laughs.

Andy couldn't help suppress a smile before thumping the wall once again to regain some control. "Alright, settle down. As we are all in this as a democracy I suggest we have a vote on it. Then, I won't get all the blame when we get back to base with next to no bonus."

Kieron raised his hand a short way to get Andy's attention who nodded back approvingly.

"Why don't we hedge our bets a bit skipper? I know we can't afford to lose Josie from the mining ops if we want a full sack, just suppose we cut her loose for a couple of days, to see what she can find?"

"I like that idea," agreed Aimee. "We could all do a few longer shifts to make up the time Josie is away from ops."

There were nods and noises of general approval dotted around the room.

"Okay, let's vote on this new proposal then. We stay on the titanium for the time being, I'll rota in some extra time for all of us, except Josie, who will have a look about, see what's what," Andy said, raising his hand with all but one of the rest the crew following suit.

Andy turned to face Mei-Lien. "You get a say as well, you are currently part of this crew."

"I'm happy to go along with anything you all decide, I was

just happy for the work in the first place. I haven't had a tour since half my crew were wiped out last year on *Black Jewel*."

"You were on the last tour of *Jewel*?" Deimos exclaimed, more as a statement than a question. "That was a bloody disaster!"

"Bloody is about right. Very bloody, when see your one true love get smashed to a pulp against the hull half a metre away from you. Where that rock came from still haunts me. Suddenly out of nowhere and wham, it took out half the vessel and half the crew," she said softly.

"I'm…" Andy began, but didn't know the right word to say, sorry didn't seem adequate.

Mei-Lien shook her head disparagingly. "Four months drifting in that wrecked hulk, almost out of air, half starved before the rescue spaceship found us."

A stifling quiet followed before Andy broke the silence. "I should have noticed your last tour vessel. I should have realised," he mumbled, feeling very awkward, not really knowing what to say next.

He had sensed some deep unknown with this woman, now he knew why she was quiet and withdrawn. He must have read the name of the last spacecraft she had served aboard, how did he miss that? Getting through that tour would have been a nightmare to any hardened miner.

"Hmmm, well, you still get a say on where we go from here. What are you views on what you heard so far?" he added, trying to steer the subject back to the matter in hand. They waited for a few seconds, all eyes on the Chinese woman. Slowly she lifted her head up to speak.

"From what's been discussed, it sounds a very logical solution to our current predicament."

Andy let out a low stifled breath. That was a tricky moment he thought. Quick to get his crew's attention back to their current dilemma away from the ill-fated *Black Jewel*, he rushed to conclude the meeting.

"Right, that's settled then, now let's get back to work. I'll work out the new rota. It'll be up in ops control on the vid screens in under an hour, Josie, good hunting."

There followed a general melee of chatter as they got up to leave the mess room. All except Kieron, who was still trying to eat his stew whilst being jostled from both sides. A spoonful of gravy covered meat was seconds away from his mouth only to be unceremoniously dumped onto the table as someone jogged his arm.

Raman turned to Josie. "Good hunting, find my iridium, perhaps a nice enormous juicy nugget of gold yeah!" he smiled broadly, holding out a huge clenched fist.

"I'll try my best Raman, just for you," Josie smiled back. She touched his knuckles against her own, much smaller fist as a sign of respect.

—

The small one-man-scout spacecraft drifted slowly through the asteroids, panoramic three-dimensional sensors generating automatic small course adjustments to avoid the slowly moving massive boulders on all sides. Josie had come a long way from *Lode Drifter*.

She was almost at the end of her given time and her patience. The density scanners had yet to find anything exciting, certainly not enough valuable materials to up and move sticks from the current titanium-mining operation. The quiet solitude was shattered by the communications link.

"Josie, Andy here, how's it going?"

"Hi Andy, nothing to report I'm afraid. I thought I found a promising lump of zinc, but it turned out to be a trace, not enough to worry about at only a few tons."

"Okay Josie, I'm going on shift now, after my ten-hour stint I'll get back to you. If you haven't found anything by then I think we will call off the search. We'll concentrate all efforts here, sound good to you?"

"Sure thing Andy, speak to you in ten hours," she signed off, just as the bar chart readout on a seismic density scanner started showing high peaks. The scanner's particle beam had located and penetrated a smallish asteroid, fast approaching the scout spacecraft.

"Hello what's all this then?" Josie said to herself, as she started to interpret the readings. "This looks promising, very promising," she said, before letting out a long low whistle.

—

Andy made his way to the gear room that housed the main forward airlock. The gear room was the biggest room on the spacecraft. It housed the spacesuits, mining exoskeletons and the miner's rock-cutting microwave-frequency modulation lances, sitting in their recharging racks.

Andy slipped into his spacesuit effortlessly. Then he went about the task of fitting into his own personal exoskeleton that looked just like a giant metal human skeleton, its torso protection bars imitating human ribs.

All skeletal units were adjusted to fit the owner's frame and their frame alone. It needed to be very close fitting, almost becoming an extension of the wearer. His stood of its own volition alongside the other ghost-like silent metal giants belonging to the rest of the crew. They were lined up in a long row against the starboard wall. Two gaps in the line confirmed two of the crew were currently working outside.

The tungsten and titanium crystalline alloy used in the exoskeleton units gave the wearer protection against any potentially body crushing boulders. Using hydraulics, the arm and leg movements were extenuated by the unit to mimic the wearer's movements. The hydraulic system also gave the wearer greater strength lifting and pushing.

Andy stepped backwards into the skeletal frame of his unit. Standing on the two footplates the hulk of metal suddenly came to life. Console lights and pressure gauges lit up, external spotlights on the shoulders and head bars cast long straight beams of intense light.

The rib cage and crutch pad both swung round his torso along with the upper and lower leg armour. The metal arms hung free while he adjusted his waist and shoulder straps.

Once he was happy with the fit he lifted his right leg. At the same time the hydraulics lifted the exoskeleton right leg in unison. Then he tried the other leg with similar satisfactory results. Taking large strides across the gear room, he reached the opposite wall that housed the microwave lances.

The rock cutting lances looked like super-sized twenty-first century army rifles. When the extra-large trigger was pulled, instead of a bullet exiting the large nozzle, several invisible beams of concentrated microwaves emitted outward. The concentrated beams focused on an invisible cutting point, highlighted by three small guide lights that intersected approximately one metre in front of the barrel.

It took a skilled operator to handle these delicate cutting tools. Pitch the wrong frequency and instead of a nice smooth slice, the rock could shatter with disastrous results.

Selecting one showing full power, he slid it from the wall-mounted rack before attaching it to a special cradle built onto the right forearm of the metal exoskeleton.

Twisting shut his helmet, the last thing to do was to slip his arms into the skeletal unit's arms, at the same time, pulling the shoulder and head protection bars over his upper torso and headgear. Now, he was ready to enter the airlock. He double checked his air tank dials, one showed full, the other three quarters, more than enough for the ten hour shift he was about to undertake. He was ready to start work.

The transition between the gravity on board and the

weightlessness of space was seamless he was so used to it. Outside the spacecraft he clipped himself to the hull while testing his thrusters. Satisfied all his gear was fully operational, he untethered himself.

Below him, Steve was hanging in the void by the opening to the ore sack. On the asteroid twenty-five metres away, Deimos was busy cutting out another roughly-square block.

Andy gave a short blast on his downwards thrusters. He drifted slowly down towards Steve. "Hey you two, how's it going?" he asked over his intercom.

"Things are sweet here Andy, that Deimos is a master of the lance, he's cutting really fast, faster than I ever could. I'll have to get him to give me some lessons sometime. Aye up, here comes another one."

Deimos turned, giving the newly cut block of titanium rich ore a shove in the process. Slowly it floated towards Steve who operated his small side thrusters to manoeuvre around it. With a little push here and there, he gently guided it into the gaping mouth of the ore sack. Using a small gun, he expertly fired a small spike with an attached snap ring into the block as it passed him. The snap ring was in turn connected to one of a dozen cables inside the ore sac to secure it from bouncing around inside indefinitely.

"Okay Deimos, let's swop places, the power in your lance must be just about finished. Steve, get yourself back aboard, your shift's over for now."

They both acknowledged Andy, who set about the task of changing positions with Deimos. Shortly thereafter, Andy was busy at the rock face cutting out blocks and pushing them back to Deimos, who now guided them into the cavernous ore sack to join the hundreds of other similar-sized blocks.

Just over an hour into the shift an unexpected screaming noise came out of the dark. It penetrated both working men through their suits, to the very core of their bodies. Andy instantly let go of the lance, instinctively trying to cover his ears which was totally impossible in a spacesuit.

In frustration he banged his gloved hands against his helmet protection bars screaming out loudly himself. The agony lasted about ten seconds when the noise abated just as swiftly as it had appeared.

"What the hell was that?" Deimos shouted.

"Dunno, but it nearly ripped my damn eardrums out!" Andy shouted back, before turning from the working face on the asteroid looking back at the spaceship.

The first thing he noticed was a column of gas, probably air, venting from a small hole in the side of *Lode Drifter*. His fingers flicked over the large buttons on a console attached to the left forearm of his exoskeleton.

"Emergency! Emergency!" he shouted through the now patched-in communications system, so all the crew could hear him.

"The spaceship's been holed and we're venting gases, all hands on deck, this is an emergency. Josie, get your arse back here at the double. Josie? Josie!"

Andy started to move back towards the mining vessel waiting for acknowledgement from his first officer, but none was forthcoming. He swore aloud several times. Things were definitely going from bad to worse.

4

Martian Harvest

The sky was soft pink. Teunis Landry would never get used to it even after living on Mars for over ten years. A pale pink champagne colour that was quite pleasing to the eyes, quite a contrast to the harsher colours of the surrounding landscape.

Teunis was driving an old, heavy six-wheeled explorer ground vehicle whilst simultaneously trying to read a map. He had bought the battered ground vehicle second hand a few years previously, using most of his saved-up hard-earned mining bonuses. Vehicle purchases were not cheap on Mars.

Suddenly he swerved, attempting to avoid a large boulder that he had caught sight of out the corner of his eye. The vehicle bucked as the side wall of one of the tyres caught the edge of the rock. Teunis cursed out loudly in his native Dutch, any significant damage to the vehicle out here would not be easy to repair.

The map he held was old and faint, not a very good copy at all. Reading the map whilst driving at full throttle, was probably not the cleverest idea, he thought to himself. Pulling back on the throttle lever slowed the lumbering explorer to a more leisurely crawl.

Large square areas on the map he had already searched

were crossed out. Using the stub of a well worn pencil another five square centimetres were scribbled over. Teunis double checked his position on the map with his instruments. The global-positioning monitor showed the explorer was approximately two hundred kilometres southwest of the crater Mie in the Utopia Planitia.

"Waar u mijn weinig een zijn?" he muttered to himself, all the while tapping the unshaded areas on the map with the chewed end of the pencil.

"Ik weet de overblijfsel van Viking Twee verbergen zich hier ergens!"

Being an archaeologist as well as an asteroid miner, one of his favourite pastimes was trying to find the buried remains of ancient exploratory landing craft. So far, three years of his spare time had been spent looking for remains of *Viking Two*.

By luck, four years previously, he had stumbled across various crashed pieces of the *Viking Two* Orbiter. Those remains were now safe in storage at the Mars Facilities, the next task was to find and retrieve the Lander part of the unmanned spacecraft. The problem was it had been covered by shifting sand and grit for over one hundred and sixty years.

Onboard scanning instruments were continuously sweeping a twenty-metre circle for any large metallic objects. Unfortunately for Teunis, the ancient records detailing the precise landing site no longer existed. So it boiled down to this painstaking boring sweep, back and forth covering twenty metre strips of storm ravaged shifting sands and boulders in an area where it might possibly have landed, an area that seemed infinitely vast.

Teunis decided to call a halt to the current search for a while. He was tired, in need of a break. He was also requiring sustenance as his stomach rumbled once more, reminding him it was a long time since breakfast. It would also be a good time to check his rapidly dwindling supplies.

He tapped one of the grubby old dials on the command console in front of him. Air was plentiful, according to the readout, at least enough to last a fortnight. Standing up he gave his aching muscles a good stretch before venturing to the back of the cabin. Checking the contents of several storage bins his facial features attained a more serious look.

"Hmmm," he muttered under his breath, his food and water provisions were not looking good. Another four or five days and he would be forced to return or starve. Despondently, he grabbed some cracker biscuits from near the bottom of one bin, and some food tubes containing processed cheese from another. Then he snatched out a small brown plastic bottle, one of several, from a purpose-built bottle-storage shelf.

As well as old artefacts, Teunis also liked the classics in music. A very old somewhat jittery Eagles recording was currently playing making the atmosphere in his command cabin rather relaxing. After his simple lunch, accompanied with rather too much black-market rough whiskey, he started to feel very tired. Slowly his head drooped onto his chest. It wasn't long before he succumbed to a deep sleep, his loud snoring competing with the drifting music.

While he slept, a large dust cloud suddenly billowed up on the horizon, one of the many spectacular natural Martian phenomenon. This particular marvel was a spontaneous wind and dust storm, a storm that was moving towards his stationary position at an alarming rate. At the leading edge of the fast moving clouds there happened to be a rugby-ball-shaped alien spaceship using the thick dust as a cover.

On board the vessel, two renegade alien creatures had been monitoring Teunis. They had been tracking his movements since leaving the Mars Facilities on his continuing quest, his passionate, needle in a haystack search for space probe antiquities.

These two particular aliens had recently escaped from

their mother ship, *Nix*, a satellite moon of Pluto, as internal factions of the controlling family tribes fought for supremacy over the dwindling food supplies, supplies that were now becoming much harder to obtain.

Since the Human expansion of the solar system, collecting their main protein food source had become much more difficult without being detected, some of the alien families had even resorted to cannibalism.

Eventually, after a long bloody mutiny, only two alien family tribes remained. These two tribes then fought one huge defining battle inside the colossal hollow moon. The surviving victorious tribal kin now numbered less than one hundred, from the original moons inhabitants of over three thousand.

Some members of the defeated smaller tribal factions managed to escape death by stealing some of the Human collector spacecraft. Two of these escapees were now bearing down on the sleeping Dutchman.

Even though the need for secrecy had been all but lost with the breakdown of their society, they still strived to remain undetected, now more so from being hunted down by their own kind, than being perceived by humankind. The selection process for perfect specimens was also now virtually redundant. With the dwindling access to supplies, any human body however old or disease ridden would suffice.

This storm was the perfect cover these outcasts had been waiting for. Now the hunters were rapidly homing in on their prey and they were hungry, very hungry.

Inside the explorer ground vehicle the instrument that would normally monitor imminent adverse weather conditions was broken. Teunis had meant to fix it after his last trip out. The loud speaker that should now be emitting an ear-drum splitting warning klaxon was quite happily relating that it was still a 'Long Road Out Of Eden'.

Teunis was eventually woken by the land explorer being shaken violently. It only took a couple of seconds for him to realise exactly what was occurring.

"Oh mijn god!" he shouted, as the communications dish was wrenched from its mounting. Although he couldn't see what had happened, he guessed, from that unmistakable tearing metal noise echoing into the cabin above the blasting wind. Optic cables trailing from a large gash in the outer hull, now slapped against the roof, cracking like several circus lion tamers whips.

As well as repairing the storm detector, re-securing the dish was something else he should have mended, and now deeply regretted. He formed a mental picture of the dish in his mind, its fixing bolts just about corroded right through with oxidation, caused by the caustic Martian soil slowly eating into the securing mounts.

He forced himself to focus on his immediate predicament. Outside was now just a blur of dust. Small stones whistled and rattled past the windows. Suddenly, heavy debris hit the one of the side windows with such energy it rocked the vehicle. The thick laminated window spider webbed under the force of the blow.

Teunis threw out his arms to steady himself. He quickly scooped up his helmet, pulling it over his head in one swift movement, before sealing it down on the neck of his spacesuit with panic stricken fumbling fingers.

Unseen and unaffected by the high winds the alien vessel was slowly moving ever closer. A two centimetre perfectly-round sphere, a probe launched from the alien vessel, found the gash in the outer hull that once housed the communications dish.

Four micro robots from inside the probe went to work immediately upon their release, sheltered from the high winds by jagged protruding torn metal. They started to bore with their circular teeth into the inner layer.

Teunis checked the communications console. He knew it was already dead, just another futile helpless gesture spawned from panic. Instinctively, he pushed a large red button that released a distress beacon. The flashing electronic beeping device was immediately scooped up by the wind and carried away.

That was a really stupid idea he thought, a fraction of a second after pushing the button. Now they will be searching for him wherever the beacon eventually ended up. That could be hundreds of kilometres away by the time the storm abated, and these storms could last for days, even weeks.

Just to add to his problems, the depressurisation alarm started whooping, coupled with a dozen annoying distracting flashing amber lights scattered about the cabin. Air was rapidly escaping from the interior.

Two of the tiny robots had been swept away by the initial rupture of the inner hull as they had cut through into the cabin. The remaining two waited patiently until all the pressurised air inside had escaped.

Once inside the explorer ground vehicle they soon located their target. They attacked with such ferocity it was almost as if they were in a race with each other to be the first one inside their victim's spacesuit.

Teunis didn't stand much of a chance. It was all over very swiftly. Once his suit had been punctured, the insect like micro robots made a straight line for his head. He screamed as he felt the multiple metallic legs frantically crawling up his chest.

Frenzied hands clawed at the material in vain, as air whistled out the holes made by efficient metallic robot mouths. Trying to look down inside his suit through the neck of his helmet, he couldn't stop himself shouting hysterically at the unknown terror, slowly making its way up his body.

He bashed at the side of his helmet as one of the tiny

robots found its way onto his neck before scampering up to his ear. A few seconds later Teunis slumped in his chair totally paralysed. As the last remnants of his air supply seeped out of the little round holes in his suit, it took with it all vestige of life.

The alien spaceship was now so close to the six-wheeled vehicle, the scanners looking for *Viking Two* started bleeping wildly. The wind velocity raged even higher causing the cracked window to cave in, toppling the vehicle over on one side. Dust whistled into the cabin.

An alien in a black spacesuit waited patiently by the exit door for its confederate to manoeuvre into position, effectively shielding the ground vehicle from the storm, allowing it to venture outside to claim their prize.

It had won the telepathic race to paralyse Teunis. It licked thin lips as it pondered selecting first choice of the human body parts. It was considering the heart might be the best organ, the others being a little past their prime, given the age of their victim.

The alien however never got the chance to leave the spacecraft or to have any of the desired human pickings. A second rugby-ball-shaped spaceship appeared out of the gloom of thick-billowing dust. They would never know if the newcomers were more renegade aliens or members of the surviving ruling family tribe.

It attacked employing a continuous beam of light aimed directly towards its alien counterpart below. Cascading showers of boiling metal erupted from the beam's contact point on the smooth copper-coloured hull.

Caught off guard, the aliens that attacked Teunis now beat a hasty retreat up into the swirling clouds. They were swiftly followed by the second spacecraft. Both alien vessels were locked in a deadly dog fight, firing at each other as they disappeared into the whirling wind and dust. Behind them, splashes of copper-coloured metal splattered onto the Martian sand below.

—

Three days after the thick dust first rolled across the plains, the wind dropped abruptly as the storm dissipated. The airborne sand, once suspended, fell out of the sky like heavy rain for a few minutes. In the storm's wake, the deceased body of Teunis lay in his crippled vehicle half-buried on its side, three exposed wheels uppermost.

Several days later, a search party out from the Mars Facilities, found the still active distress beacon. Tracking back on an opposite bearing to the direction the storm had travelled, the search party eventually came across his remains.

5

Oceans Dawn

Robert Goodyear and James Cleaver were swiftly ushered through the weightless central hub of Gateway. Gateway, a slowly rotating orbital space station, looked just like a giant wagon wheel rolling along at a snail's pace, against the inky-black backdrop of space.

Their shuttle from Satellite Two had been held up, as several smaller, sleeker commercial spacecraft jostled for departure slots once they had obtained their cargo and passengers from the recently arrived Orbital Space Elevator.

Much to Robert's annoyance, they had been almost the last shuttle to leave Satellite Two, mainly because, as far as he had seen, they had a great deal more in the way of transportable goods than any of the other smaller vessels.

Finally arriving at Gateway, they were manhandled, pushed and thrust through the hub's last airlock by anonymous spacesuit clad figures, to find themselves in an airless umbilical arm that joined the space station with the interplanetary supply vessel *Oceans Dawn*.

Pulling themselves through the flexible connecting tube they entered one of the spaceship's airlocks, where they could eventually catch their stale recycled breath.

The outer door had no sooner thudded shut behind them when an illuminated green triangle imbedded in the door, transformed into a red cross as air now started to rush into the surrounding void within the airlock.

The cross was a warning that there existed a difference in atmospheric conditions either side of the door. In this particular case, there was nothing except deadly empty space and vacuum outside, as the umbilical cord detached itself with an audible snap. It coiled and twisted slowly back towards Gateway like a drunken snake.

Together, the pair tumbled onto the long central bench seat where they located thin straps ending with plastic carabiner clips. They attached these D-rings to material loops located on either side of the waist belts of their spacesuits. Without warning, their strap restraints jerked taut, pulling them tight to the bench as the vessel started rotating, slowly at first, before gaining momentum with every revolution.

As the rotation increased weight gradually returned to their bodies. The hissing inrush of air slowed with the constant increase in enveloping pressure.

It took less than five minutes before the spaceship had acquired a gravity field almost equal to that of Earth. The airlock was also now full of what could loosely be termed fresh air.

Given the ability to stand upright once more breathing unaided, the two disrobed their space suits with relative ease.

Gloves, boots, bodices and helmets were stowed in two of the many vacant numbered alcoves dotted around the airlock walls. A clear plastic panel slid across and secured the alcove, to stop the contents floating out during periods of weightlessness.

Both made a mental note of the numbered alcove they had chosen for their suits. Barring emergencies, they would not need them again until they reached their final destination, the planet Mars.

So this is *Oceans Dawn* thought James. During the long

climb up on the Orbital Space Elevator he had looked up the details of the spaceship via a computer access point. He would have liked to have used his own personal media access device, but that was now sitting idle in a locker inside Borealis Station.

The access point he had utilized allowed direct entry to the main computers at the Corporation, using the correct series of passwords of course. Corporation databases were a mine of information for most things on and off planet. He called up a synopsis of the Corporation's current operational vessels. On the list he located *Oceans Dawn*.

The spaceship was shaped like the round drum of an old fashioned washing machine that used centripetal force to create an artificial gravity field. It was nothing like the myriad of small spacecraft, such as the asteroid-mining vessels or ice-gathering tugboats. These smaller vessels created artificial gravity using large magneto gyros positioned in the base of the hull. The main drawback with the hull-based system was the huge amount of power the gyros required from the fusion-drive engines. So much power in fact, it required the small spacecraft to turn off the gravity field, leaving the crew weightless, for the duration of any prolonged flight. The interplanetary spaceships using the rotational system, could maintain a constant gravity field drawing virtually zero power from the propulsion system, which resulted in almost ninety-five percent forward thrust efficiency rating.

Within the drum-like design, were three circular floor levels surrounding one large round hole, right through the middle. The gaping hole enabled the spaceship to encompass a number of universal rectangular-shaped pods, pods that could hold all manner of cargo, such as specialist mining equipment and provisions.

For a typical Mars resupply voyage, the cargo pod was a kilometre-long rectangular container carrying every-day essentials for the human Martian inhabitants.

The fusion drive propulsion unit was detachable. It slotted onto the far end of the cargo container, remotely controlled from the Bridge. The huge powerhouse, that pushed the whole vessel across interplanetary space at just over seven hundred thousand kilometres an hour maximum thrust, could easily be jettisoned in the event of any disaster. It was strategically placed to be as far away from the living quarters as was possible, even with magnetic defence fields, there was still a possibility of a flash of micro meteorites hitting the fuel cells with catastrophic results.

James was suddenly jarred out of his recollections as a wasp like buzzing sound, was followed by a loud ka-chung. The heavy looking inner airlock door began to swing open. A clean shaven head poked round the half-open door followed by one shoulder, an arm, and finally a hand. There was a swiftly spoken welcome before the hand beckoned them to follow its owner who, as fast as he appeared, quickly disappeared from view.

Exiting the airlock they found themselves walking very fast down a corridor that ran the entire one hundred and fifty metre length of the vessel. Almost jogging, they were hurrying after an *Oceans Dawn* crew member who was certainly not waiting on ceremony. There was a general sense of urgency that you could almost taste in the atmosphere around them.

Without stopping their guide spoke up above the clatter and general din that surrounded them. "Hi there, I'm Able Crewman Ian Watson at your service. I've been assigned the task of looking after you on this voyage. If you look up at the corridor walls every ten metres there are a series of what we call 'at-a-glance' location markings."

Ian carefully pointed out a set of the markings just below an unbroken hand rail as they rushed passed.

"The spaceship is so uniform, one corridor looks much

like all the others. It is quite easy to become disoriented. These markings are designed to tell you instantly where you are. They start with a number of bold lines indicating the deck level. As you can see, this is level two."

James glanced up just in time to notice the next set of marks. Two bold lines closely followed by three horizontal thin lines. Finally there were three small squares. Looking further up at the ceiling he glimpsed level three above through gaps in the metal flooring. Someone above ran in the opposite direction, making a soft vibrating noise as they went. The sound slowly receded.

"The second set of lines indicates the number of the corridor we are traversing. There are six main corridors on the spaceship running stern to aft, this is corridor three. The small squares reduce in number as you get nearer to an airlock or stairwell that will take you up or down to the next level. Consequently, they increase in number the further you move away in the opposite direction."

James noticed the small squares had reduced to one as they now approached a ladder. The ladder was a simple affair set into a semi-circular recess on the right hand wall. A semi-circular hole offset from the main corridor floor give access to the level below and the level above.

Ian indicated the two newcomers to ascend up the ladder after him. They followed closely behind. On the next level up James noticed the markings on the wall. This one had three bold lines followed by three thinner horizontal lines and one square. They were now on the inner most level three. It contained all the recreational, catering and living quarters, he remembered from recently studying the vessel's schematics.

"In the event of power failure all deck markings are illuminated as part of the emergency lighting system. They are there to guide you to the airlocks should we need to abandon the spacecraft or you are instructed to return to your cabin."

Ian paused while this information was absorbed. "Obviously you would use the hand grab rail to pull yourselves along if we lost the artificial gravity as well. Remember airlocks are situated at each end of level two. Do not worry if you can't get to the airlock where you left your own personal suit, all airlocks have an excess of emergency suits, is that all understood so far?" he asked.

The two passengers half nodded and mumbled the affirmative. Robert turned to his colleague. "Don't worry James, you'll soon get the hang of it," he assured his understudy.

James managed a slight smile, but still looked bemused by the whole experience. A voice suddenly echoed around them, the corridor giving it distinctly bass undertones.

"This is the Captain Edmund Cooper speaking. Mars supply vessel *Oceans Dawn* is now leaving the hospitality of Gateway in two minutes and twenty-seven seconds. Second Officer, Mr. Francisco Garcia, has calculated our current flight plan to Mars. The spaceship is now locked into a fully automatic countdown procedure. For your own safety, I urge all passengers and crew to kindly retire to their bed cradles for our imminent primary ignition sequence. Please ensure all airtight doors are secure."

The voice of the captain tailed off, now it became obvious why their guide had been on the hasty side.

A few moments later, they came to a halt outside an airtight cabin door. Spacecraft doors were much the same design on all vessels. The door was either pushed from the outside, or pulled from the inside, to release the seal. Once the seal was broken the door then slid sideways on two runners top and bottom.

Ian pushed a square panel on the front of the door which seemed to fall backwards slightly at his touch. Some unknown force then took over whereby the door slid sideways to reveal the interior of the cabin. He guided his newly-acquired charges over the threshold.

"If you kindly get into your bed cradles as fast as is humanly possible please, I'll return once we are underway," said Ian, before turning to run off down the corridor at breakneck speed.

Robert grabbed the inside door handle giving it a sharp jerk. The door then did the rest, sliding shut and pressing forward slightly to recreate the seal.

Inside, the cabin was cramped and compact. Taking up most of the interior space were two reclining chairs, or bed cradles as they were referred to, currently in the sitting upright position.

"Well I must say this is cosy!" Robert exclaimed, still trying to hide his feelings of nausea. He wasn't sure if he was suffering from the after effects of space sickness, the anxiety of their transit so far, the claustrophobia brought on by the cramped cabin, or more likely a mixture of all three. Standing there, he was dimly aware the very small room was looking decidedly smaller by the second.

"I suppose we ought to make ourselves comfortable," suggested James, looking over the two bed cradles in their chair-like form. Distracted, he didn't see Robert pop a pill into his mouth and swallow hard.

"Yes and quickly, we must almost be at the ignition blast point."

James walked round to the furthest cradle, both of them sat down almost simultaneously.

"I was hoping you would tell me a bit more…" James blurted out, but was cut short mid-sentence by his superior.

"Sorry James, no time for that now. I'll bring you up to speed once we are underway before they slow our metabolic rate down for the duration of the flight."

As James sat down, side panels under the cradles armrests

moved inwards, pushing his arms close by his sides so he could hardly move them. The cradle also started to level out, turning into a flat bed.

"Not that yielding are they," James complained. "And now this cradle is trying to squash me flat," he added, feeling very uncomfortable.

"This vessel can attain five G's during acceleration. If you're not used to it, you could suffer from G-LOC and pass out. If that happens, you need to be held secure to stop you slopping about," explained Robert.

They were interrupted as the captain's voice, now with more tone and less bass, reverberated round the cabin.

"Fifty seconds people, look sharp, everyone should be secure now ready for ignition."

Robert closed his eyes to shut out the room and the overwhelming unbearable feeling of nausea that now washed over him like sea spray. To James those fifty seconds seem to last forever as they waited patiently. The cabin lights dimmed at minus ten seconds.

James was unsure what to expect when suddenly he felt a slight jolt. Very slowly their bodies started to feel extremely heavy. The cradles strained as the centripetal gravity force counter acted with the forward thrust of the vessel. The room seemed to hang at a crazy angle as pressure squashed both of them long ways and sideways into the very unforgiving supporting fabric.

It didn't take long after primary ignition for the vessel to obtain full thrust. James felt a huge weight on his chest, like he was trying to be forced through the back of his cradle. With these immense forces acting on his body, James eventually passed out.

Returning back to consciousness, he found his chin was resting on his chest. He had slid down in the cradle even against the harsh restraints. His mouth was dry, it had that awful taste present, the taste you get when you come round after a catnap, the taste of stale saliva. He smacked his dry lips.

"Oooerr," he groaned, feeling groggy, "what happened?"

"Happens to most people first time," said Robert, helping James to a sip of water. "Don't worry, after a few flights you'll get used to the G-force."

Putting the cup down, Robert went back to stand in the very centre of the cabin. He held a small black box in the palm of his hand. Slowly, he turned round the room watching the device intently.

James was now fully conscious. Robert had pressed a small button on the armrest of his cradle allowing the restraints to relax releasing both his arms. Instantly he was hit with a bout of pins and needles in his forearms. He rubbed them vigorously before straightening to sit upright.

"Okay, can you now please tell…" He was cut short again as Robert put a finger to his lips and glared at him.

James noticed Roberts wash bag was open on the floor. The contents had been spilled out in a heap. He also noted that there were a few items that looked like they didn't belong there.

Robert continued to monitor the room twiddling with small dials on the black box. Slowly, he moved towards the small table pushed against the opposite wall to the cradles. He extracted a small round seat recessed in the wall and sat down. Carefully, he placed the small black box on the table between him and the wall.

"Right, that should jam the scanning frequencies, don't want them listening in. One of them must be in the very next cabin," he jerked his thumb over his shoulder at the blank wall behind him.

"Who is listening in?" James asked in a hushed voice.

"Just standard procedure, an inquisitive captain will sometimes listen in on his passengers. A good captain likes to know everything that's going on aboard his spacecraft. That includes what his passengers are up to. Forewarned is forearmed as they say," Robert explained, and then continued. "Although, here we have two distinct listening frequencies which I find most peculiar, perhaps it's not just the captain who wants to know what we are doing here."

"Won't they become suspicious if they don't hear anything, just a jamming hum or whatever that thing does," James said, almost whispering and pointing at the little black box on the table.

"No need to whisper. My little magic box has matched the sniffing frequencies of their intrusion devices, both of them in fact. They are currently hearing a recorded conversation we had in my office last week. Remember when we were discussing why Venus, now in its new orbit, the same orbital path round the Sun as Earth, is veering off course by one thousandth of a degree each day. It has to be corrected otherwise the terra forming process will be a waste of time?" James nodded.

"Well, that's what they are listening to. We have about seven minutes of the recording left to run before it switches off," Robert declared, glancing at his watch to note the time.

Extracting the other round seat on the opposite side of the table, James sat down staring at Robert questioningly.

"Right, I guess you want a full explanation then," Robert stated, his hands squarely planted on his thighs. James nodded again, even more enthusiastically.

"Okay, here we go. As you know, humans have been on the Moon and Mars for quite a number of years now. In some cases whole families now live and work off world. We have even had children born in these environments. There are nearly two thousand people working and living on both planets. Mortality rates are high, people have gone missing altogether. It has generally been put down to accidents, drifting off into space, explosions, staying outside too long, getting lost on the surface and running out of air, there are multiple reasons," he was expecting a response, but James remained silent, soaking up the information.

"There have been some developments on Mars. One of the miners was reported missing for just under a week before they found his body. No great shakes there you might think, just another accident, but when they took him back to the Mars Facilities they found something, something they couldn't explain, two small round ragged holes in his spacesuit."

Robert stood up and started to pace the small cabin in a small circle rubbing his arms. He was feeling hemmed in, walking round and round gave him the false impression of distance and cubic capacity. James's eyes followed him mesmerised.

"At first they considered it might be some sort of intergalactic worm-like creature as it looked like the holes in the fabric had been chewed. After the resident surgeon carried out an autopsy, the Facilities Controller reported her findings to the Corporation bosses. Whatever was in that report caused them to send us on this jaunt? I guess they didn't want to expose us to the full autopsy findings until we get to Mars. I'm hoping to get a complete picture from the Controller upon our arrival," Robert finally concluded.

"Where else do they think the holes came from then?" James enquired.

Robert shrugged in response. "That's what we are going to try and find out. I find it quite puzzling to say the least, any ideas?" he asked.

"There have been no previous reports like this on Mars before, therefore logic suggests a possible extraterrestrial creature has recently arrived on the planet," James announced. "There will be an almighty uproar if it turns out to be true," he added, after a strained look appeared on his face.

"That's not all. A mining vessel out in the asteroids has

had a strange misfortune. They think something unnatural holed their ship. They are on their way back to Mars and should coincide with our arrival," Robert declared. There was a dull clanging on the door before he could say any more, his mouth hanging open for a second.

"Bugger it!" he exclaimed looking at his watch, there were still two minutes left to run on the jamming box replay.

"We are going to have to risk they don't notice a break in the conversation when I switch this off. Just follow my lead James, are you ready? Remember, Venus in its new orbit veering off by a thousandth of a degree every day."

Picking up the jamming device Robert switched it off in one deft movement. Simultaneously, he started speaking urging James to join in.

"No, no, no, I can't believe that," Robert blurted out.

James was a split second behind him. "Yes! You must. After Venus was pulled into a twin orbit with Earth, its poles cannot be aligned to the exact symmetry as they are on Earth. The mass of the Northern hemisphere must be so top heavy it's pushing it off its artificial axis like some out of control spinning top."

At the same time Robert spoke again trying to confuse the snoopers. "What if the rotational speed changed due to it now being further away from the sun and is considerably colder now than…" at this point the airtight door slid open interrupting him, his voice trailing off. Ian squeezed into the room as Robert stood aside.

"Right then, ready for a quick tour of the spaceship. A bit of something to eat and then we can put you into the Dormouse Torpor State for just over eighteen days. That sound okay to you?" he asked.

"Dormouse Torpor State?" quizzed James.

"Yes, we put you into suspended animation just like the now extinct edible dormouse when it entered its hibernation period on Earth many, many years ago," Ian replied, turning to leave the room. "Don't worry, it's totally painless, you won't feel a thing," he added over his shoulder, almost chuckling.

"Does it involve needles? I bet it does. I just hate needles," James grumbled.

6

Aimee's Watch

Aimee stifled a little giggle. It had been such a long time since they had spent any quality time together. She tugged at Raman who followed behind her along the upper-deck corridor.

"Come on," she encouraged the big rugged miner, her small hand just managing to hold onto three of Raman's fingers.

"Are you sure this is okay?" asked Raman.

"Its fine, don't worry, Josie gave me the code to her cabin ages ago. She told me to use it whenever she was out prospecting. There's so much more room and it has a single bed!" she squealed in anticipated delight. "Don't worry, she's the only one who knows about us I promise," she said, answering Raman's enquiring look. She knew what he was thinking.

"I must confess bunks do make things damn awkward. Trouble is there is just nowhere on board that's private with any decent amount of room to turn round! Let alone, y'know…" Raman suggested.

"I do know y'know, that's why this is just perfect," replied Aimee.

She peered through the airtight door window that led into

the operations control and bridge room. There was no one in sight, which came as no surprise as she was supposed to be the crew member on watch.

She had taken the precaution of plugging a remote communications device in one ear, should anyone wish to contact her in an emergency or to ask for a read out on any of the control room scanners. They were both hoping normal operations would continue without a hitch for the next thirty minutes at least.

She pushed the door's central panel, it slid open sideways, ending with a jolt. Inside the control room there was a slight hum of fans cooling electronic components. The air felt warmer, a dry electrically charged tang to it, unlike the fresher, cooler air out in the recently vacated corridor.

The proximity scanner, a plate of flat glass several metres square showed a mass of foreign bodies moving slowly in and out of its maximum range. A single stationary mass sat directly in the middle of the screen. The small black object next to it was an electronic representation of *Lode Drifter*. Outside through the large viewing windows, they could see two miners working hard. One was at the rock face cutting, the other below them stationed at the mouth of the ore sack.

"Looks like the boss is cutting at the moment," noticed Raman. He recognised Andy by his distinct red and purple coloured spacesuit and mining exoskeleton. He immediately felt a tinge of guilt. Things were not going well with the tour. He should be resting now or working double shifts. Aimee wasn't interested who was working, she had only one thing on her mind. She grabbed his arm turning him round slowly. Then grabbing hold of his other arm, she backed up to the wall pulling him after her. Their faces met as his head bent forward. Kissing passionately, their hands now swiftly running up and down each other's hot bodies, Raman quickly lost all sense of guilt.

"We had better make this quick, before someone notices we're missing," Aimee said, before turning to face Josie's cabin control panel on the wall. She tapped in the four character pass code followed by a sharp tug on the central grab handle. The door pulled forward slightly allowing it to slide open. As they entered Raman slid it back behind them. It sealed them in the bedroom automatically as a standard precaution.

A dim silver beam of light entered Josie's cabin through a small porthole, faint reflected sunlight just enough to see by. Raman moved to switch on the cabin lights, but Aimee stopped him.

"It's kinda romantic like this in the semi-dark," Aimee said quietly, trying to make the forthcoming events appear to be tender moments. It would end up being a quick fuck just like all the other times, but she thought there was no harm in trying to be a little bit passionate, just this once.

They kissed again, slower this time. Aimee's tongue probed Raman's mouth. He willingly reciprocated. Aimee started feeling more aroused, tingling sensations stirring in her loins.

Raman undid two buttons on Aimee's coverall. Slowly his right hand slipped inside to find the round orb of her left breast which he started caressing delicately. Aimee's left hand dropped to Raman's crutch feeling his hard engorged member under the thin fabric. She shivered uncontrollably.

They continued caressing and kissing until they could contain themselves no longer. They pawed at each other's clothes in a frenzied haste to remove them. The paper-based disposable overalls soon disintegrated into a heap of tattered rags.

Once they were completely naked, they lay down on the bed. Their frenzy subdued slightly as they continued to intimately explore each other's bodies. Raman's tongue licked Aimee's left nipple which was now quite pronounced while his hand fumbled at the top of her inner thighs.

She opened her legs slightly to accommodate his large hand as it stoked the sparse soft tangle of pubic hair before moving on to probe her vaginal lips.

He found her very receptive sliding two of his large fingers into the moist soft tissues. She arched her back in response.

Soon his fingers were squelching in and out teasing her labia with his thumb. It didn't take long for Aimee to cry out as she reached a long-overdue orgasm.

Aimee stroked Raman's penis in return which started oozing pre-ejaculatory fluid. Either it was their awareness of limited time or the sudden pressure of the situation, foreplay had been very swift. Both of them were more than ready to copulate completely which they sensed without speaking.

Raman rolled over on top of Aimee and positioned himself between her legs. Aimee helped guide his throbbing penis into the opening of her vagina where he thrust in with a low moan. Aimee gasped and temporarily lost her breath, taken aback by the more than average physical size of her lover.

Raman settled down to a steady rhythm, but it wasn't long before he could not hold back. With a couple of deeper thrusts, he finally exploded inside Aimee, who felt the warm semen erupting from him deep within her.

They held that pose for a half a minute, Raman gyrated his hips slowly to make the most of the pleasure of his ejaculation before they both relaxed their tensed up muscles. Finally Raman collapsed exhausted.

Sweat that had built up between their stomachs and chests, now chilled as they pulled apart. They lay squeezed side by side on the single bed, breathing and heartbeats slowly returning to normal.

They didn't speak, there was nothing to say. After what seemed like an endless age, but was actually only a couple of minutes, they turned to face each other.

Aimee smiled and stroked the beads of sweat trickling

down Raman's face. Raman smiled back. They lay face to face stroking one another's features. Aimee drew circles on the dark skin of Raman's chest, a glaring contrast to Aimee's almost white flesh that glowed quite ghostly in the pale silver light.

It wasn't long before they were becoming aroused again.

"D'you think we have time?" Aimee enquired with a wry smile. Then she grabbed hold of Raman's enlarging penis with less passion and more urgency.

"Why not, what would the others do in this situation?" Raman answered sarcastically.

Aimee knelt on the edge of the bed. "Shove over into the middle," she almost ordered.

Raman complied without question. Aimee straddled him, easing herself backwards inch by inch onto his throbbing erection. Slowly, teasingly, she lowered herself then raised herself up only to repeat the process.

Raman grabbed her hips, wanting her to thrust down hard. The teasing was excruciatingly blissful, but he was feeling impatient. Any moment he expected Andy or one of the others to interrupt them and ask Aimee for some information. Aimee realised it was becoming all a bit much for Raman. She lowered herself feeling the full length of him inside her. It felt a little uncomfortable if she were totally honest with herself, but this was her game, she had started it so had no option other than to continue.

Moving up and down slowly she got used to the feeling. Raman's hands moved up from her hips to caress both her perfect round firm twenty-five-year-old breasts that bobbed up and down with her slow movements.

He gently rubbed her nipples which responded immediately giving Aimee a pleasurable feeling too, unfortunately, a feeling that was to be cut very short.

Raman lived approximately two seconds longer than

Aimee. The mining spacecraft *Lode Drifter* was struck by an object. The object was a two-metre-long cylinder of alien origin, slicing a path through the vessel in a thousandth of a second.

It was designed to cut its way through any obstacle along its flight path using a beam of intense energy projected directly in front of it. Anything in that circular beam was vaporised instantly.

As Aimee rocked back and forth eyes closed enjoying the moment, the alien projectile entered Josie's cabin. It passed straight through Aimee and continued through the outer hull unhindered. The force of the cutting beam coupled with the immense speed of the object caused Aimee's upper body to explode in a mass of blood and flesh.

Raman lay paralysed for two seconds screaming, covered in his lovers' entrails and blood. His own hands had been severed from his wrists with the force. He still had Aimee's lower torso and legs straddling his waist.

As soon as the projectile left the cabin there was a lull before everything not bolted to the floor was sucked through the perfectly round fifteen-centimetre exit hole.

Raman's scream seemed to echo and reverberate through the corridors of the vessel, long after he, and Aimee's remains had been evacuated into outer space.

7

Passage to Mars

The tour of *Oceans Dawn* didn't take that long. Soon the trio consisting of James, Robert and Ian were lounging in the canteen after the whistle-stop tour. They had just finished some reconstituted freeze-dried chicken in a sort of red wine sauce with instant mashed potatoes. James considered it was actually not too bad. It had been transformed from an innocuous frozen grey lump and dusty white powder into a tasty edible meal in less than a minute. Ian was rounding off the remains of his lunch with a few interesting statistics.

"There are twelve crew members at any one time. We can accommodate an extra twenty souls if required, for migration, replacement personnel, that sort of thing. Plus, if we have the armed forces personnel container attached, another ten soldiers complete with their fighting exoskeleton units, full body armour and weapons. This flight however, we have just the standard crew, stores and supplies to last the nice folks of Mars for a couple of weeks, oh, and of course, three passengers."

"Three! Did you say three passengers?" Robert enquired.

"Yes, you two and an experienced miner going out to join on with one of the asteroid-mining vessels, you might have seen him earlier, ginger hair, flushed face."

"Who does he work for? What's his business? How come he's on board if this flight was brought forward specifically for us? I must see Captain Cooper about this. This could lead to a serious security breach."

Robert was fuming. He thumped the desk, more out of frustration at having so many questions with certainly no answers forthcoming.

"Wooo slow down, you'll give yourself a heart attack," said Ian. "I don't think the captain will have time to see you right now, besides there could be quite a rational explanation. I'll find out what I can and let you know okay?"

Robert didn't reply immediately. After considering the situation for a few moments, he reluctantly agreed. What could he do in any case he thought? They were all in the same boat, literally, until they set foot on Mars.

"Right then, any more questions?" Ian asked.

"Yes, can you please explain what is going to happen to me while I'm in the, what did you call it, the Dormouse Torpor State?" asked James.

"Ah yes, the Dormouse Torpor State, our drug-induced suspended-animation process. Quite simple really, first, we turn your cradle from its chair-like state into a flat bed. Once you lie down, we pump you full of some concoction of drugs that the deep space expert doctors on Earth mixed together, hey presto, it slows the human metabolic rate right down to almost nothing. You get extremely cold as we drop the cabin temperature to just above freezing. Once that happens coupled with the drugs, your body is now so cold, you only take a breath every thirty seconds while your heart has slowed to three or four beats a minute. The next thing you know we defrost you, wake you up and you are in orbit around Mars. The bed cradles have been designed to perform a vibrating massage every so often just to keep your muscles flaccid. Also, you'll be monitored twenty-four seven," concluded Ian.

"Sounds slightly dangerous, what if something goes wrong?" James frowned.

"Nothing can go wrong these days. There hasn't been a fatality for over five years now. Besides, your personal implants will pass biological readings to our instruments that will let us know should anything go amiss," Ian said reassuringly.

Robert had been listening, but also thinking about the stranger in their midst, what was he up to? Having overcome his initial knee-jerk reaction to the news of the third passenger, he had calmed considerably. It must have been him trying to eavesdrop their conversation earlier, before their tour of *Oceans Dawn*.

"Would it be possible to bring us back to the land of the living before we reach Mars orbit? I'm sure James would like to see the approach to Earth's second nearest neighbour, third if you count our moon. To see the orbital manoeuvres etcetera," Robert enquired.

"I don't see why not, it shouldn't do any harm. I'll even ask the captain if you can observe from the bridge if you like. It's kinda funny, the other passenger made the same request," Ian looked bemused.

"*I bet he did*," Robert thought to himself. It was his idea to get up and have a snoop about before the strange passenger was brought out of the Dormouse Torpor State, seems like this other person obviously had similar ideas.

"Right then, I'll give you approximately twenty minutes, you need to evacuate your bowels before going into the Dormouse Torpor State, if you having trouble use these."

Ian passed them a large green-coloured suppository each. "That'll work in less than a minute so I suggest you might want to be quite close to the lavatory before you use it," he added with a wry grin.

Twenty minutes later the three of them were back in the small cabin. James and Robert were lying down on their cradles reclined into flat beds. Ian inserted several sterile intravenous needles into the crook of their left arms. He then connected these to tubes which appeared out of a metal box about a metre square that was hung from a special hook on the side of the cradle frame.

"Okay, now you won't feel a thing… Wake up now, hello, wake up," Ian's voice sounded very distant.

James was still wondering how long he would have to wait before the drugs took effect when it dawned on him he was being roused.

"Hello James. We are just about to start our approach to Mars orbit. Don't make any sudden movements, not until I check you out thoroughly."

Ian proceeded to check every inch of James's body. He gently massaged his legs and arms, fingers and toes.

"What are you checking for?" James enquired. He was slightly concerned Ian was getting a bit too familiar with him.

"Just making sure you haven't got any frozen bits of flesh, we don't want you to have succumbed to frost bite. Everything seems to be okay, you will ache for a couple of hours especially in the chest area, lungs and heart in particular."

"I feel quite hungry too."

"Ah! That's a good sign, a nice full English breakfast yes?" Ian said sarcastically.

"That would be nice, with a large mug of tea," replied James, not realising at first he was the butt of a joke.

"Sorry, only kidding. No can do I'm afraid. It will have to be powdered scrambled egg and some dry toasted biscuits to start with, with a glass of plain water. You'll want to vomit after every mouthful. Funny side-effect that and never quite understood it myself. Feel hungry, eat and then can't keep it down, but I suggest you do try."

"This is just great, now I'm going to be horribly sick. I'm rapidly going off this space travel lark," James retorted. "How's Robert?" he asked.

"He's been up a while now, I expect he's waiting for you on the..." Ian never finished the sentence as at that very moment the door slid open on its near silent nylon runners.

Robert strode in looking very pleased. "Hi, you're up at last. Well what do you think of it so far?"

"I was just saying to Ian, I could go off this space travel malarkey quite easy," replied James, slowly moving his tingling arms and legs.

"It does get easier, I'm sure you will get used to it quite quickly, the suspended animation hardly has any effect on me these days," declared Robert. "Mind you I have been on quite a few space flights over the last twenty years. I should be feeling used to it by now," he added as an afterthought.

"Right gentlemen, if you are both okay I will leave you to get on with my other duties, don't forget we are only about fifteen minutes from Mars low orbit. If you want to watch the final approach I have cleared it with the captain for you to be present on the bridge. Security will check you first so leave any weapons behind!" Ian smiled jokingly, before turning to leave the room. Robert checked his departure by placing a hand on his arm. Ian stopped in mid step.

"Ian, did you find out about our third passenger, what was his business again? An asteroid miner wasn't it," he asked politely.

"Not much more than I already told you I'm afraid. I checked out his name and details on the Corporation database passenger manifest. He has mining credentials, worked on the South American and African continents as well as the Pacific deep water gem mines. I even went as far as to casually ask him his business. He said he's on his way to Mars to join an Asteroid-mining crew if he can. He seems a likeable fellow from my few dealings with him."

"Okay, thanks for that information," Robert said, letting go of Ian's arm. He slid the door shut once he had vacated the cabin.

James managed to lift himself onto his elbow. It felt like he had failed to catch a cricket ball that had slammed into his chest.

"Come on James, let's get going. The view of the Mars Facilities in Hebes Chasma from orbit is something else. I wouldn't want you to miss it now we have come this far without any mishap."

Selecting a button on one of the arms caused the cradle to resume its chair-like shape.

"Where have you been since you've woken up? Did you find out anything covert about our mysterious travelling companion who says he's just a plain miner down on his luck?" enquired James.

"He's no miner. I'd even go as far as to put a bet on it if I were a betting man. As it happens, since waking, I have been quite busy. Our fellow passenger was in the canteen. I realised he hadn't seen me so I doubled back to have a quick look in his cabin. Guess what I found hidden there?" Robert paused for dramatic effect.

"A covert eavesdropping listening device of some description," suggested James.

Robert face dropped, he looked crestfallen. "Oh, you guessed."

"I would have been surprised if you didn't find anything. Logic dictates he is a spy of some sort, sent to keep an eye out for us," James concluded.

"And an ear," added Robert smiling slightly, trying to make light of the matter, before continuing in a more serious tone.

"Who is he working for? That's what I'd like to know."

"Why not confront him? Catch him on the back foot. I doubt he would be expecting that we've latched onto him so quickly," replied James, who was now attempting to stand upright. He winced with each movement.

"Hmmm, we could do that, however, I'm loathe to be

calling him out so soon. I think we might benefit from him thinking he is still at large to do his prying. Here, let me help you."

Robert helped James onto his feet. He walked him round the confined space a few times before sitting on one of the recessed chairs by the small table. In the centre of the table James noticed the little black box jamming device. Robert must have put it out as soon as Ian had left the room.

"So what are our eavesdropping snoopers listening to now?" James asked, as he jerked his thumb at the device on the table.

"Ah! Now then James, do you remember that little theory of mine about how our Solar System almost has an uncanny design about it, as if it was made easy for us humans to explore, to help us slowly expand into space one logical step at a time."

"Yes, I remember discussing it with you. You suggested that the act of travelling to the Moon back in the twentieth century was like mankind dipping its first big toe into the murky waters of space travel. Then we progressed onto Mars and Venus followed by the exploitation of the Asteroids. Then there are the outer planets with their myriad of moons acting like a series of stepping stones, the gas giants giving us unlimited energy resources, their moons huge stores of ice," James took a deep breath that stung the very depths of his lungs before continuing. "I asked you what happens when we get to the edge of our solar system. That was my main concern, where do we go from there? Do we fall off the end or come to a black canvas backdrop?" he laughed before wincing again.

Robert put forward his side of the argument. "I suggested that by the time we conquer the moons of Pluto the human race will have developed the means to travel to the nearest star, a star that may have another Earth-like planet."

"And in retaliation, I argued that if your logic held any

water the nearest star with an Earth-type planet would be a mere space hop away, not several light years to get to," interjected James.

"I then contradicted you by saying that we need to develop a faster than light fusion drive first, only then can we really explore the millions of stars in the heavens. We should discuss this fascinating subject again, it was an enlightening conversation. Now, we really ought to get to the Bridge. Are you okay to walk now under your own steam?" Robert asked, picking up the jamming device. He carefully slipped it back into his personal effects bag under some other items.

Using the at-a-glance corridor location markings they made a slow trek to the Bridge. James was feeling less stiff with each step, his breathing becoming easier on every rung of the ladders. He was still feeling very hungry though.

They knew the Bridge was on level one between stairwells one and two. It didn't take long to reach the airtight door to the main control room, even with them moving at little more than strolling pace.

Through the plastic glass panels at the back of the bridge they could see out through the forward observation windows. Both were struck dumb by the beauty of planet Mars hanging in space before them.

After a quick pat down by one of the Bridge personnel, who was wearing a small taser sidearm on his hip, they were allowed into the command centre of *Oceans Dawn*. An official looking man came over briskly shaking their hands in turn.

"Welcome gentlemen, I am Captain Edmund Cooper. Please can I ask you to sit over here, we are only five minutes and thirty seconds to Mars orbital insertion."

He led the way to two swivel chairs beside a dull and very dead looking console that was obviously offline.

"Weapons console. Not used these days, not since they removed the forward microwave beam and laser weapons array. This vessel was originally built equipped with military weaponry, before the Corporation had them decommissioned," explained the captain.

They swivelled in the chairs to turn their backs to the lifeless console. Now they could observe through the main viewing windows in relative comfort. There were also two large glass screens that showed reflected views of the planet's surface directly below the vessel.

It was while he was twisting round in his chair that James noticed the mysterious asteroid miner sitting at the other end of the Bridge in what appeared to be another now operationally defunct spare chair. He nodded towards James. James felt that it was only polite to return the gesture.

For the next five minutes there was a general hubbub of space chatter between the crew, the ground tracking stations and the Facilities Control Centre. It didn't take long before the vessel attained geostationary orbit directly above the complex that was the entire Mars Facilities nestling in what could only be described as one enormous gash on the Martian surface.

Robert, who had a fascination for facts, turned to James to explain what now filled their immediate view.

"James you are now looking at Hebes Chasma. It is a completely enclosed depression six kilometres deep. It is over three hundred kilometres east to west and one hundred and thirty kilometres north to south. With a large mesa, five kilometres high rising out of the middle of the depression creating two long inwardly facing banana-curved valleys either side of it. At the eastern end of the mesa, where the two valleys meet, in an arrow-head-shaped canyon, the Mars complex of refineries, laboratories and research buildings have been built on the purple bedrock of the valley floor."

Robert had pointed out the various points of interest during his detailed verbal analysis. James could see the round and rectangular buildings tucked into the V-shaped end of the mesa. Surrounding them, the near vertical high walls to the south, west and north protected the facility buildings from the wild wind storms that could kick up any time. The eastern wall was formed of gentler slopes, but still protected the complex from that direction.

Tall funnels poking out of the refining buildings expelled plumes of scrubbed hot air and steam into the thin atmosphere. The thin clouds swirled round and round right up to the rim of the valleys. Reaching the top, the faint wisps were caught by the constant gentle Martian wind, which pushed them out into space to be lost forever. Robert then pointed out the pipeline that headed down to the southern horizon.

"They go down to the polar ice wells. There was an abundance of frozen water near the Martian south pole in the early days. They use a lot of water in the smelting works both for cooling and as the primary energy source by extracting the hydrogen," he explained. "Alas, almost depleted now. They obtain water from further, much further away these days."

Small objects flitted about the buildings, some on the ground and some in the air. As Robert finished talking they witnessed four of the smallish objects becoming larger.

"Here they come, the small spacecraft to relieve of us of our cargo container," said the captain who turned to the helmsman to speak directly. "Release the holding clamps once they have a secure lock," he ordered, above the general background chatter.

"When do we get down to the surface?" James interrupted.

"Once the container has been taken away, a small shuttle has been authorised to dock and pick you up," the captain replied.

"We would normally have a container full of refined scarce and precious materials, ready to attach to take back complete with fully fuelled propulsion unit, plus any additional passengers. However, as we have arrived three days early, we will have to remain in orbit for a couple of days whilst they get things organised down there." He pointed a finger straight down towards the deck. "In the meantime, if you would like to make your way back to your cabins, please remain there until we fetch you to depart. It will be in approximately two hours. The Martian pace of life is very laid back. People and time seem to move very slowly…" the captain's voice was interrupted by a sudden klaxon sound, the whole room fell silent.

One of the crew studying a small monitor finally spoke above the klaxon din. "Proximity alert. Small meteor incoming. Approximate size two metres. It's going to be close, very close. Tracking now at one fifty three degrees, speed three hundred plus kph, impact in five, four…"

As far as James could tell, everybody on the bridge had stopped breathing.

8

Disaster in the Asteroid Belt

The asteroid-mining spaceship *Lode Drifter* was typical of all the small spacecraft that mined the Asteroid Belt. It had two decks, both upper and lower sloped outward forming a pointed ridge down both the port and starboard sides of the vessel. This design, like twentieth-century tank armour, was intended to deflect away any large slow-moving stray boulders that may penetrate the magnetic field defences.

The magnetic field protection really came into its own when the vessel was propelled forwards. However, there is no protection against small objects travelling at high velocity straight at an object that was virtually stationary.

Inside the mining vessel, the front half of the lower deck was taken up with the gear room, easily the biggest room on board. This room also housed the main forward airlock.

Leading off the gear room through an airtight door was a short corridor. This corridor ran between the galley and provisions store rooms on the starboard side, and directly opposite, the mess room on the port side.

At the aft end of this short corridor was another airtight door. Beyond this door was a crossways corridor the height of both decks. This tall open space was a firebreak between the two main internal bulkhead walls.

A full quarter of the spaceship behind the aft bulkhead contained the upper and lower port and starboard engine rooms. If the fusion engines malfunctioned, which they were prone to do on older models, threatening the safety of the crew, the entire aft section could be jettisoned with the help of explosive bolts.

Access to both the engine rooms as well as the upper foredeck was negotiated by a series of rung ladders attached to both the fore and aft bulkhead walls. A haphazard array of disjointed scaffolding combined with rung ladders culminated in suspended mesh platforms outside all the doors.

The mesh platform in the very centre three quarters of the way up the crossways corridor gave access to the upper deck via yet another airtight door.

Off this corridor that ran down the middle of the upper deck there were three small cabins containing bunk beds. There were two cabins on the starboard side, one on the portside aft of a small emergency airlock.

In this confined space there were two access points halfway down leading to two heads with integral shower units. It was all rather compact and reminiscent of a small twentieth-century sailing schooner.

Hidden in-between the jumbled maze of little cabins and washrooms were the fresh water cylinders, recycled washing water and waste cess tanks. A plumber's nightmare of different size pipes ran overhead seemingly everywhere joining up the correct tanks with the correct appliances.

A dusty battered plastic sign pointed out that in the event of artificial gravity failure or prolonged weightless periods, the showers and waste disposal units were NOT to be used under any circumstances. In smaller print, the sign described how in weightless conditions, the special faeces vacuum pumps MUST be utilized. These, as any miner would tell you, are most uncomfortable.

At the very forefront of the upper deck corridor, through one more airtight door was the very centre of the spacecraft operations, the main control room. A huge toughened plastic window gave a grand panoramic view of the mining venture outside. Cameras around the vessel relayed images to twelve glass monitor screens. These monitors could be observed at the same time scrutinizing all movements through the main airlock directly below the viewing windows.

On either side of the vessel just behind the main control room flight deck there were two single cabins. One was for the captain/operations controller, the second for the second in command, the cabin doors only accessible directly from the control room.

All cabins and corridors were airtight, doors automatically sealing themselves in the event of depressurisation on either side, even if they were occupied. Airtight doors had a large illuminated green triangle, or a red cross symbol inlaid into them, indicating if there was air or vacuum on the other side. Doors could normally only be operated if the symbols on both sides were matching.

The design was simple enough, if either deck was holed by a celestial projectile that managed to circumvent the magnetic field, those rooms not affected would still retain pressure. Either way, if a projectile pierced either deck vertically, or horizontally there would be casualties, it was inevitable.

While Andy made his slow way back to *Lode Drifter*, he watched the last remnants of air dispersing from the hole on the port side.

"All crew sound off!" he demanded.

"I'm sealed in my cabin Andy," said Kieron. "I have a red cross on the door. I guess that means the upper corridor outside has been compromised," he added.

"Okay, nothing you can do but sit tight, until we get the holes patched up. Anyone else please respond?" Andy pleaded. The silence was deafening.

"Andy, over here," Deimos called out from the port side emergency airlock. Andy slowly jetted over to join him.

"Whatever it was, it's gone in through the airlock outer door." Deimos pointed a gloved finger at the perfectly round hole in front of him exactly fifteen centimetres in diameter. Andy positioned himself to look into the hole forcefully pushing Deimos out the way. Deimos just had time to fire his air thrusters to stop him tumbling out of control.

"That's bloody weird, it's left a perfectly round hole in the inner casing too, what the hell could do that?"

"Something moving damn fast!" exclaimed Deimos, somewhat annoyed at being jostled out the way by his impatient boss.

"I'll put a patch on the airlock door Andy. I reckon whatever it was will have come out the other side with the force its hit the spaceship."

"I'll go check it out." Manipulating his exoskeleton thrusters, Andy slowly hovered over to the starboard side of the vessel. As he came up over the control room he could still see a trail of debris disappearing fast into the void. Air, water vapour and the small cabin items that had obviously exited the starboard side of *Lode Drifter*. He was expecting to see a huge exit hole, but was surprised by what he found.

"Whatever it was has gone clean through," he whistled low and long. "Its exit point must be Josie's cabin, with exactly the same size diameter outlet as the entry one. This is just impossible, almost as if it drilled its way through the metal using some sort of high-power cutting device."

"That would make it unnatural, an artificial object in fact," chipped in Kieron.

Andy located a portal in the sloping hull plating. Inside were various sizes of sheet metal. He unhooked the thermal welding lance strapped to the side wall.

"Judging by the trajectory, I calculate the object passed

through Steve and Raman's cabin plus some of our plumbing no doubt, this is going to be one hell of a messy job," declared Deimos.

Andy selected a relatively small metal plate that would cover the hole in the outer hull. Returning to the starboard breach he set about welding it in place. With their sun visors down, bright welding light flashed as both Demios and Andy set to work melting metal to metal.

"Okay, all repaired this side," said Deimos, flipping up his visor. He had welded the plate to the airlock door in record time. "As the entry and exit holes are both in the upper deck, we can assume that the lower deck is still intact? I'll go in the main airlock and find out. I take it we still have artificial gravity, eh Kieron?" Deimos enquired, as he stowed the port side thermal lance.

"Yep, I'm still standing. However, the emergency lighting is on in here. I expect the upper deck electrics have been compromised somewhere," Kieron replied.

"Okay, I'm all done here Deimos. I'll wait outside until you check the integrity of our patches from the inside, just in case they need more work," instructed Andy.

As he waited patiently, Andy looked round at the now quite distant debris trail. Instinctively he logged away a directional reading. Somehow, in the back of his mind he figured it might be important one day. After storing the readings he found himself staring into the distance. Several bright objects caught his field of vision. One he noted could be a gas giant, possibly Saturn. Without knowing at the time he was also staring at a distant satellite planet called Pluto.

"Andy!" Deimos shouted. Andy jumped. It brought his mind back to the present situation with a start.

"Mei-Lien is here in the gear room, she must have been checking her kit, getting ready for the next shift. Her bloody exo has somehow toppled over. It's trapped her, crushing the lower forearm in the process. She also appears to be unconscious, although, I can't really tell with my suit on."

"Is the arm bleeding?" Kieron jumped in.

"No, just looks like it's been flattened, her hand is quite dark, loss of circulation I guess," replied Deimos.

"Okay, as there is no actual blood, you can move the exoskeleton off Mei-Lien while you have yours on still. I really need to get down there fast though." The surgeon spoke with anguish in his voice, fearing that it may already be too late to save her arm. "Can you bring me a survival mask and a thermal jacket, it's getting bloody cold up here, and can you hurry, please," he pleaded.

Deimos moved Mei-Lien's limp body away from her fallen exo unit before he climbed out of his own exoskeleton. He left his spacesuit on as he would need it in the corridor above him. With arms full after collecting the items Kieron asked for from one of the kit lockers, he made his way to the airtight door to exit the gear room.

The airtight door showing a bright green triangle slid open easily enough at his touch. He made his way through the short corridor to the aft airtight door, before proceeding up to the upper deck entrance via the rung ladder and scaffolding. His progress was hampered by the simple fact that he was abnormally taller than most Earth-born human beings. He was totally unsuitable for easy movement within a vessel designed on a smaller scale of human form. He was also carrying the thick jacket and the mask with its small oxygen cylinder tucked under his arm. This was proving very tiresome as the tubing became snared on the ladder rungs for a second time. He cursed under his breath.

After what seemed like an age, he was finally standing on the mesh platform in front of the door that would open onto the upper deck corridor. The red cross on the door partially reflected on his face mask. It seemed to flicker faintly, like the dying embers of an open fire, its direct electrical supply somehow being interrupted.

"Kieron, I think you are right about a short out, don't touch the hull with your bare hands whatever you do. It may be live."

He punched open a panel at the side of the door revealing several large buttons. Pressing one marked EXPEL automatically started a low hissing noise as the air in the crossways corridor was extracted.

After decompression, the green triangle on the opposite side of the door turned to a red cross matching the symbol on his side of the door. He yanked at the handle, sliding the door open in one deft movement, revealing the upper corridor lit by the dim emergency lighting.

The cabin Kieron and Deimos occupied was the first on his left, aft of the port side emergency airlock. Peering through the semi-dark he located another panel next to the cabin door, inside was an override button which allowed him to decompress the cabin.

This was an abnormal procedure, decompressing a room with someone inside was very unhealthy for the occupants. However, this was an emergency now requiring necessity. He had to rescue his shipmate from an icy tomb.

"Okay Kieron, you will have to hold your breath for a couple of minutes. I'm about to decompress on your mark, let me know when you're ready."

Deimos waited for an affirmative reply before punching the button marked EXPEL. It took two minutes twenty seconds to remove all the air from the small cabin allowing the door compression symbols to match. As he rushed out Kieron grabbed the mask. Cupping the face piece over his nose and mouth he took a couple of large gulps of air before pulling the retaining straps over his head.

"I'm getting too old for all this nonsense!" he mumbled

through the plastic mask. He then spluttered gasping for air for a short while as his racing heart slowly calmed back to a normal, more sedate rate. Clipping the small air cylinder to his belt, he grabbed the coat before pushing his way past Deimos pulling it over his shoulders. He was through the aft airtight door shutting it behind him before Deimos could politely ask if he was okay.

"What's going on in there!" Andy demanded, making the startled rescuer jump.

"Right, the Doc is on his way to see Mei-Lien. I'm going to check the inner breaches."

"Get a move on will you. Let me know if there are any signs of anyone else, Aimee should have been in Ops Control."

"Nothing so far, Mei-Lien and Aimee's cabin opposite the Doc's and mine look okay. There's no one home," he said looking inside. "Ah! Just as we suspected, there is a hole in the wall of Steve and Raman's cabin which is on the opposite side of the corridor to the airlock exit hole. I'm opening their door now."

The door opened with a struggle as if its runners had been buckled. Finally, Deimos managed to get his shoulder in the gap to force the door open with a shove.

"What a bloody mess, looks like someone has exploded in here. I can't make out if it was Steve or Raman?" Deimos stifled his feelings. He felt sick as he described the death of one of his close friends so transparently. Managing to subdue his anguish, after a slight pause he continued his descriptive running commentary.

"Across the room almost waist height is another perfectly round hole. That must lead into Josie's cabin."

After a moments silent refection he made his way out. "I'm back out in the corridor now. It's taken out a bit of pipe here, could be the shower waste, it could be sewerage. I can't smell anything being in my suit. I hope it's not the crap waste for all our sakes. Still no sign of Aimee as yet."

"Where the hell is she then? What's going on in the Control room!" Andy demanded.

Deimos covered the last few feet of the corridor to stand outside the control room airtight door.

"Well it looks like we have pressure in the control room. I'm going to risk re-pressurising the corridor and the cabins, let me know if your patch starts venting."

"My patch!" Andy exclaimed. "What about your patch?"

"My patch on that airlock door is totally sound. I would trust my life on it! Don't you worry about that, I'm a demon with the thermal lance didn't you know?" Deimos said, trying to lighten the mood a touch. He was trying to alleviate some of the tension he sensed in Andy's voice along with the anxiety he detected in his own.

Deimos couldn't begin to imagine what Andy was going through right now. They trained for disaster in simulated circumstances, but this, this was for real. They somehow had to stay focused.

He reached the corridor atmosphere control panel just outside the Ops room airtight door. Locating the button marked ADMIT, he stabbed it with his gloved forefinger.

Air hissed into the corridor and throughout the holed cabins. As the air pressure continued to rise, Andy confirmed both outer hull patches were holding fast as he flitted from one side to the other.

An hour later the whole spacecraft was re-pressurised. Deimos had managed to isolate and fix the electrical short so the hull was no longer live to the touch.

Andy, Kieron and Deimos were now standing in the gear room, next to an inflatable medivac bed. They had discarded spacesuits. All the exoskeletons were in a neat line against the wall.

On the temporary bed lay the prone figure of Mei-Lien, a drip feeding her left arm. Kieron finally broke the silence after a questioning gaze from his operations controller.

"I've given her a strong sedative for now. Her radius is almost non-existent and the ulna not much better. The forearm muscles are completely wrecked. I can't do anything until we get back to the Mars Medical Path lab where we can culture grow some new bones, However, that is not the problem. The main worry is what state the muscle tissue will be in by the time we get back. We might have to replace some of the dead stuff for synthetic which will end her mining career for good."

"After the *Black Jewel* disaster and now this one, I think that might already be a foregone conclusion," suggested Deimos dryly.

"If I were her I'd be paranoid about being jinxed in some way. Even worse, word will get round, crews might make her out to be some sort of Jonah. I reckon her days as a miner are definitely numbered to the amount remaining on this tour," added Andy. They stood for a few more moments in silence while those thoughts were digested.

"Right then, let's get up top and try to figure out what's what," Andy commanded at long last.

The three men made their way through the airtight doors and corridors into the ops control room. Andy typed out the overriding master entry code for Josie's cabin on the panel next to the door. The door slid open silently.

After stepping inside, with the other two now peering round the door frame, Andy let out a low groan.

"Well, I guess we know now what happened to Aimee and Raman. I thought there was something going on between them."

It was Kieron who stated the obvious. He was instantly rewarded by glares from the other two, as if to say it wasn't a crime to want a little physical fun now and then, certainly not a crime that carried a death sentence.

Although their bodies had been sucked through the fifteen centimetre exit hole along with all the other loose articles from all the cabins, they hadn't left without making a bit of a mess. The cabins outer wall was covered in one big blood stain, starting from the mattress of the single bed, right up to the ceiling.

In silence, Andy set about sealing the inner hull breach with expanding silicon foam. He smudged some blood on his sleeve in the process. Deimos retrieved the control room thermal welding lance, goggles and a suitable-sized metal plate.

Kieron left the two of them to patch up the inner breaches. The shock of what happened was finally sinking in for all of them.

No one said another word for a very long time. In a sort of trance they set about making *Lode Drifter* as shipshape as possible.

Luckily, none of the water pipes or water tanks had been ruptured, apart from a shower waste downpipe which had emptied a small amount of residue water over the deck. There was also a pipe leaking from a joint ruptured by the impact which gave some concern as well as a foul odour into the bargain. Thankfully for them, a few turns of a spanner soon sorted out that problem.

After a few hours hard toil, the three crew members stood in a line looking out of the observation window on the Bridge. They had a variety of drinks between them, a mug of tea for Andy, a large Martian whiskey for Kieron and large Martian vodka with orange juice for Deimos.

Two of the dozen glass monitor screens were dead, they were not important enough to be fixed so they hissed quietly while displaying crackly lines tracking slowly back and forth.

They were holding an impromptu two minutes silence for their departed work friends and colleagues who had come to a miserable end. Two in what appeared to be the throws of joyous ecstasy. In silence they said their own personal prayers.

While they stood quietly in thought, all three

simultaneously noticed a small object picking its way between the asteroids in front of them. It looked like the scout spacecraft.

"Josie?" Andy enquired, squinting into the blackness. A garbled disjointed message spewed out the communications systems.

"... *Lode*... mayday... lost com... glad... ee... u..."

Deimos placed his glass on the console top before leaning forward a little.

"It's the scout!" he exclaimed, slapping his two companions on their backs enthusiastically. They both jolted forward, just about avoiding spilling their drinks.

"Josie! Thank the gods for small mercies," Kieron exclaimed, before downing the remains of his whiskey in one gulp.

9

Ganymede Outpost Two Five Three

"Ganymede outpost two five three to Mars Scientific Laboratories, come in!" Trevor Frude shouted out loudly, in his broad New Zealand accent. Trevor headed up the three-person scientific team stationed on Jupiter's largest moon Ganymede.

"That bloody telecom pick up IS working isn't it?" he asked, throwing the question in the general direction of the two other occupants in the outpost control room.

"It was the last time we called in for our weekly routine check up a few days ago," replied Leila Santos.

"Ganymede outpost two five three to any bugger anywhere in the cosmos, please respond, this is a bloody emergency for God's sake!" Trevor shouted again.

The third member of the team, Roger Taplow spoke up. "Definitely transmitting boss, you nearly went off the scale that time. There is no need to shout so damn loud though. The intercom sound pickups are quite sensitive you know," he added sarcastically.

"Oi! Less of your bloody lip! When were you put in charge? Besides, it makes me feel better shouting, and while I'm in this mood, why do we have such a large frigging number to call out, we are, after all, the one and only outpost on Ganymede. I should be shouting Ganymede outpost bloody one to anybody that can be bothered to listen in case we are all dying and would like to know the reason why!"

"Sorry boss, just trying to point out that you've no need to shout, that's all. Besides you know the reason, we are the two hundred and fifty-third outpost in the solar system since the human race began space exploration."

"I know that you imbecile, I was being ironic," scoffed Trevor.

Roger looked hurt, which had the desired effect on his female counterpart Leila. Leila Santos was second in the small chain of command although she could have been easily mistaken for being in total command. She took no nonsense from Trevor who, in turn, then took his frustration out on Roger, it was a vicious circle.

"Okay, okay, let's all calm down and deal with this situation like intelligent adults," Leila interjected, before Trevor could shower Roger with yet more verbal derision.

"After all, we are supposed to be the clever ones. I mean, we're supposedly top notch brainy scientists. As such, we all know swearing and shouting sarcastically in a loud voice will get us absolutely bloody nowhere!" Leila concluded, loudly and sarcastically.

Trevor was in no mood to calm down. He was too fired up with the current situation. He wanted the whole solar system to know about it.

"You know, you really surprise me sometimes," he stated, shaking his head slowly whilst wagging a finger in Leila's direction. "Whatever happened to that galaxy-renowned Brazilian hot temperament that is the norm for South American Latin types? You of all people I would expect to be ranting and raving too, given the circumstances."

"I like to use my Brazilian hot temperament where it can

be appreciated, like dancing the samba or between the sheets. No point in wasting my energy shouting my head off into empty outer space. Besides, talk about contrasts, you New Zealand types are supposed to be cool, calm and placid, especially in a crisis!" Leila snapped back.

"Shut up! Shut up both of you," Roger cried.

Trevor was nearing boiling point. He was halfway out of his seat. He desperately wanted to hit something, it looked likely to be the unfortunate Roger. "Don't you ever tell me to shut up, you, you upper class English…"

"Shut up and listen a second for goodness sake!" Roger exclaimed, in his perfect public schoolboy baritone.

As quiet descended on the room a faint voice could be heard. "Ganymede outpost, this is the asteroid-mining spacecraft *Crystal Star*, go ahead."

The voice cutting through the hiss was very faint but clear enough to understand fully.

"And about bloody time!" Trevor slumped back into his chair in relief, his pent-up anger subsiding just a fraction.

"*Crystal Star*, Ganymede outpost to *Crystal Star*. This is Trevor Frude, Chief Science Officer of Ganymede outpost two five three, boy, have I got a story for you. If you didn't believe in extraterrestrial life before now, you bloody well will once I've finished."

Trevor glanced again at a small three-dimensional display that relayed the pictures from a camera out on top of the main dome roof. He could still see the two rugby-ball-shaped spacecraft that lay smashed and twisted slightly buried in the surface of Ganymede just over a kilometre southwest from the outpost. He needed to do this just to remind himself that he wasn't dreaming. Just as he turned away from the display to start to relate the events of the last two hours, he failed to notice movement by one of the wrecks. A large figure clad in a black spacesuit exited one of the crashed vessels. The humanoid figure stood up, stumbled about for a minute before falling down gracefully in slow motion behind a small rocky outcrop, obviously still concussed.

The outpost on Ganymede was the typical exploratory prefab design, with a large central dome split into four sections. In one section was the Control Room. In the second could be found the canteen and recreation area. The third quarter contained the food stores, wash rooms, latrine and water tanks. Finally the fourth section contained the sleeping quarters including their individual spacesuit lockers.

Four connecting tube like arms radiated from the central dome through numerous sealed sliding doors to four smaller satellite domes.

The smaller domes consisted of two laboratories, an emergency lifeboat rocket spaceship on a launch pad and finally, the fourth dome contained a workshop with integral garage for an exploratory eight-wheeled ground vehicle. This vehicle, because of its shape and two forward arms used for collecting soil samples, was known affectionately as the Land Crab.

"So these two alien spacecraft come in low over the horizon firing some sort of energy beam at each other. Are you recording this? Confirm please," Trevor suddenly thought to ask in mid flow, but then continued without waiting for an answer. "Bloody well better be! I don't fancy repeating this lot. Anyway, these two rugby-ball-shaped vessels looked really beat up, both scarred along their flanks. One even had a bloody great hole in its side. They were both flying erratically, maybe due to the damage they had sustained. So erratic in fact they eventually collided with each other, just as they passed over our main dome. They were that close to us we instinctively ducked. Down they came with such a crash our buildings nearly lifted clean off the ground," he exaggerated.

Roger glanced at Leila, raised his eyebrows and then shook his head with disdain.

Trevor continued unabated. "We've lost two airtight seals in Lab one which is now inaccessible," he paused for a quick breath, took a small sip of juice from a beaker before continuing. "Are you getting the pics? *Crystal Star*, are you getting the video feed we shot? Confirm please." He coughed up some of the residue liquid from his mouth he had not entirely swallowed down the right way, and then wiped his moist lips with his sleeve. There was a brief silence before the reply came.

"Negative outpost two five three, your transmissions are very low powered. Has something happened to your radio antenna array? Your pictures and video signals need to be boosted, what we are getting is very blurred, almost nonexistent. If we weren't so deep inside the belt, almost at the outer rim, I doubt we would have picked up your transmissions at all."

"It might be interference from the alien spaceships, they are quite large. Maybe their impact could have damaged our equipment. Perhaps the alignment of the dish is shot to hell, I'll get onto it, try to sort something out, are you staying where you are? I'd hate to lose this connection after all the trouble we've had trying to get hold of someone."

"Outpost two five three, we are currently in the middle of a mining op, as such we are tethered to our asteroid in situ. However, we are drifting within the Asteroid Belt so could lose you at any time. All your transmission so far, along with the grainy pics, will be forwarded onto the Mars Facilities. Try to sort out your transmission and get back to us. I'd like to see some better shots myself."

"*Crystal Star*, we will do our best." Trevor felt drained sliding further down in his chair as the connection was severed.

"I think I've found the fault," Leila said. She had been using the laboratory outside cameras to check the antenna array on the main dome.

"The main dish has slipped on its mounting, looks like its pointing straight at Jupiter, no wonder Mars couldn't hear us. I bet you the self-tracking servo motors have burnt out as well trying to realign the dish," she concluded.

"Looks like someone needs to get outside in a suit, take some kit, climb up there and sort it out," Trevor said, crossing his arms looking at the other two as he spoke, making it quite clear he had no intention of going anywhere himself.

"I'll go," Roger announced. "One small jump in the very low gravity out there and I'll be on top of the dome. Obviously this job requires my high level of expertise."

"As long as you don't jump too far and disappear off into space," Trevor quipped in reply, leaving that small exchange of words a draw in his book.

"Just for once can you stop acting like little boys in the playground?" pleaded Leila. "Can we try to work together on this? I want to get outside too. I'd quite like to take a firsthand look, which we cannot do until this whole matter has been logged, recorded and sent off to base."

"Couldn't agree more," agreed Trevor, his arms still firmly folded across his chest. Roger stood up. With an understanding glance at Leila he tapped out the code to the locked control room door which opened obligingly. It slowly closed behind him as he made his way to his spacesuit locker in the living quarters.

After he had left, Leila turned to Trevor. "Why do you always have to be so nasty to him? You are always on his case, putting him down."

"You are always on my case, perhaps if you were a bit easier on me! Perhaps show me some of that Latin passion? Maybe even a little bit of Samba in the bedroom, eh?" Trevor smirked.

"Oh, so you're not adverse to a bit of blackmail now? If I sleep with you you'll go easier on Roger, is that it?"

"Well it has been a long time since we both saw any action, how long is it now? Nine months and another three before we are due to finish up and get back to some sort of civilization."

"Aha!" exclaimed Leila. "So all your aggravation comes down to pent up sexual desire. That's the real reason you go about shouting, swearing and hen pecking Roger twenty-four seven. I think, due to recent events, we are going to be relieved fairly quickly. Perhaps you'll be back to the pleasure dens on Mars before you know it. As for me, don't even think about getting me between the sheets!"

"Don't worry on that score, you're not really my type," snorted Trevor.

"I think you're suffering isolation sickness. You're going ever so slightly mad. When we get full communications back I'm going to report you for gross misconduct to the scientific council…" Leila never finished. Trevor waved his hands frantically before interrupting her.

"Do your worse, I've had it with the scientific council. I had it with this Godforsaken outpost, with you, that English twit with the silver spoon up his arse, with this whole crappy set up. I'm going back to Earth with this story. Maybe get some artefacts out there to take back." Trevor jerked his thumb in the direction of the crashed spacecraft. "I'll be famous as the man that made first contact with an alien race. I'll be rich too, so rich I'll have women clamouring after me, you'll be sorry then when you could have been as famous as me." He turned in his chair and switch on a communications link. "Roger, are you at the airlock yet?"

Trevor was becoming impatient, wanting to get out to the crash site, salvage what he could. Maybe even get a dead alien on ice? His mind was racing, working overtime on the endless possibilities to make a lot of money from what had literally fallen into his lap.

"Suited and booted boss, in the airlock now. Decompression in fifteen seconds," he replied, in his perfectly crisp English accent. He stood a foot away from the outer airlock door checking his gauges. He held a bag of tools with oversized handles for use in his spacesuit gloves.

He double checked the thermal heaters of his suit were working. It was minus one hundred and fifty outside. There was no margin for errors.

So preoccupied with all these tasks Roger failed to notice the symbol on the airlock door had lit up red to indicate zero pressure had been equalised. Automatically, the airlock door started to roll up like a medieval portcullis revealing a metre-wide opening.

The only surviving alien from both wrecked spacecraft had recovered from its ordeal of the crash. It had also managed to make it over to the outpost. Now it stood on the other side of the airlock door.

Being so tall and wearing a suit that was totally black, complete with a black helmet, Roger couldn't quite grasp what it was that now appearing before him temporarily blocking the exit. His eyes had expected to see the surrounding ice and rock formations he normally saw as the airlock door opened upwards. Now his eyes were relaying confused messages to his brain with this utterly black object in front of him.

He looked directly down. He could make out the shape of two large tall black boots. He followed up from the boots with his eyes. Slowly his eyes acclimatised, registering the shape of the humanoid just over a foot away from him. His eyes now looking straight ahead stared at the black suited chest. Finally he tilted his head back to look up to a black helmet nearly two feet above his own. The black helmet appeared to be looking down at him in return.

"Good God!" he uttered. Unfortunately it would prove to be his last utterance. He didn't see the knife that thudded into his chest moments later. It all happened so quickly his brain didn't have time to feel any pain as the razor-sharp blade sliced up through his lungs and out through his neck lifting him clear off the ground. The alien then inflicted a second slicing cut through the neck horizontally that left his head hanging backwards. Blood gushed out all over the black suited intruder. The half decapitated body seemed to bounce twice with the force of the blows in the low gravity before slowly toppling sideways towards the airlock chamber floor.

In the control room they had switched on the internal cameras just in time to witness all that had occurred to Roger in the airlock. Trevor and Leila looked at each other in disbelief.

"Bloody hell!" cried Trevor, "did you see that? What do we do now?"

"Prep the lifeboat rocket. We've got to get out of here. We should be safe unless we go outside. Whatever it is, it doesn't know the codes, look," Leila pointed at the screen.

They could see the black suited alien was crouching in the airlock pulling at the inner door. It then examined the keypad next to it. Finally it peered through the small inner airlock door porthole trying to catch sight of them. The sight spurred them into action.

Trevor was busily pulling up schematics on a glass panel display. He would tap the screen every so often. "Nearly done here," he shouted. "What's the plan once the lifeboat is ready?"

"I don't know, you're supposed to be in charge!" shouted Leila, but then realised she would have to take control of the situation. "Simple answer as I see it is this. We get into our suits, head out to the emergency lifeboat, lift off and get the hell away from here as fast as we damn well can," she suggested. "Although, I somehow get the impression it's not going to be that simple," she added as an afterthought.

"Right, emergency lifeboat rocket is now prepped and ready to launch. Let's go!" urged Trevor.

"Where's it gone?" Leila pointed at the internal web cam screen. The airlock was empty, even Roger's body was missing. All that was left was blood splattered on the walls and a smudged trail on the floor.

Inside one of the crashed spacecraft, the last remaining renegade alien removed his helmet before inspecting the now headless human body in front of him. It cut away the suit from the upper body, hands pulling open the recent chest wound. Cracking ribs out of the way it slowly removed Roger's heart. Lifting the dripping red flesh to its nose, it sniffed it over briefly before tearing out a chunk with its rows of razor incisors.

10

The Mars Facilities

Nobody dare move on the bridge of *Oceans Dawn*. A relatively small meteor was planet inbound just seconds away from passing by or possibly, right through the Mars interplanetary supply spaceship.

A still hush descended among the occupants, all except the one crew member who was calling out the meteor's progress.

James and Robert didn't really have any time to analyse the impending threat. Besides, there was nothing anybody could do about it now. There was no time to get to the spacesuits, no time to fire up the cold engines to move the vessel.

James thought to himself, to have travelled all the way from Earth, to be a relatively short hop from their destination, to be wiped out in a brief second by a direct hit on *Oceans Dawn*'s bridge, would be a very cruel twist of fate. Would they be lucky? James never really believed in luck having such a logical mind. You could manipulate situations to give yourself more favourable odds, thus giving the impression of having good luck. As for lucky charms, they were just comforters for the owners were they not? A four-leafed clover was never going to stop a two-metre-sized lump of rock no matter how furiously you waved it. Nor would it deflect a meteor's direction of travel if you happened to be standing in its flight path.

"Hold on everyone!" Captain Cooper shouted bringing everyone out of their personal thoughts, thoughts that could well be their last.

"… two, one, impact!" concluded the crewman who had been shouting out the odds. The cargo container had almost been removed from the centre of the interplanetary spaceship by the four small spacecraft that had been continuing about their business oblivious to the imminent danger.

Suddenly, there was a blur, something passed in front of every one's eyes. If you blinked at that very second, you would have missed it. Nothing would have looked any different, except, now there were only three drone spacecraft in view.

There was no discernible noise either inside or outside the vessel. The human consciousness would have expected a whooshing-like noise as the lump of rock passed by at such close proximity, but the vacuum of space does not allow for this so, the mind is somewhat deceived.

The fourth drone vessel that had been shunting the cargo container back from its mountings directly in front of them suddenly disappeared from view. One second it was there, in the next fraction of a second it vanished, just as if a magician had thrown a jet black cape over it.

The small meteor had struck it squarely with incredible velocity, causing the spacecraft to disintegrate into a million tiny fragments. A few small shards of metal and plastic debris were all that remained. This visible wreckage slowly emanated from the impact site barely twenty metres directly in front of the bridge observation windows.

"Whoa! That was close," someone muttered. People started breathing again. A metal rod a metre long, the single largest surviving piece of flotsam, bounced off the window followed by other little odds and ends, nuts, bolts and such like. They echoed round the bridge sounding like large drops of rain falling on canvas.

"Mars defences will pick it up in a second. This is quite a common occurrence for them these days," the captain explained to those unfamiliar with such occurrences. He drew an attentive audience so continued. "Most of them originate from the Asteroid Belt. I suppose you could blame the miners crashing about in there, dislodging small rocks during the course of their operations," he explained.

Below them, ground defence laser tower number four swung into action tracking the incoming object. All legitimate spacecraft sent out a simple unique identification signal that was recognised by all the defence towers, this particular fast moving object gave out no such signal.

In case a damaged vessel was struggling home with a broken transmitter, the defence tower questioned its authority to be in the space directly above the Mars facilities. If indeed there was a malfunction of the identification signal emitter, a human-voiced response was usually enough to hang fire. Only the traffic controllers could issue override counter commands if they so wished.

Having received no such response from the meteor, defence tower number four automatically fired its slim pencil sized beam of intense light. The small lump of rock glowed hot for a brief second before shattering into a million grains of sand falling harmlessly on top of the domes below it.

"Was anybody in that small spacecraft?" Robert anxiously enquired.

"No, thank goodness. They are drone vessels controlled remotely by Traffic Control VR operatives on the ground. No need for humans to be present. The VR controllers sit in a nice comfortable chair manipulating the spacecraft as if they were actually sat on board," the captain replied.

"VR?" James looked quizzical.

"Virtual Reality, a bit before our time James. It was used a lot in the twenty-first century on Earth before its almost total demise when it was proven to send you totally insane after constant use. Heavy users started questioning the difference between actual and virtual," stated Robert.

The Captain nodded in agreement. "I heard of one controller last year unfortunately, she looked out the window one day and decided she was going skinny dipping in an imaginary waterway. Stripped off completely, out through the airlock before anyone could stop her," he declared, pausing for a second while they contemplated their own visions of that scenario. "We do tend to use VR a lot in these dangerous environments as it does save lives in the long term, even with the odd controller going off the rails. Not every controller decides to try to go for a swim in one of the canals on Mars though. Most end up mumbling to themselves in a corner of a room somewhere. A totally treatable condition with certain drugs outlawed on Earth, but that's between you and me," he hastily added.

"James, welcome to the wild, turbulent, sometimes dangerous, weird, wonderful place that is the Mars Facilities! Also somewhat outside the laws of Earth," concluded Robert with a smile, putting his arms round his shoulders for reassurance.

Some time later, a passenger shuttle pulled away from *Oceans Dawn* to make its slow descent to the facilities landing fields. Captain Cooper had bidden James and Robert farewell at the airlock, thinking he would not see them for some time. Events however, were in motion that would bring them all back together much sooner than anyone had anticipated.

"Where did our mysterious third passenger get to?" asked James. "He seemed to disappear just after that little incident on the bridge."

"I expect his outfit will have made their own collection arrangements. I still think there is more to that man than meets the eye. Mark my words, our paths will cross at some point in the very near future, I'm nearly a hundred percent sure of it," Robert remarked ominously.

The twin valleys of Hebes Chasma surrounding the central mesa grew larger as the small vessel slowly spiralled down. James was awestruck by the sheer magnitude of the working complex below them surrounded by the multicoloured hues of Martian sand and rock.

"Quite something isn't it," Robert stated the obvious, as they both peered out of the shuttle's small windows.

"Your description didn't do it any justice," replied James. The beauty of this Martian natural structure now took his breath away as the vast size of the depression swallowed them up.

As the shuttle came level with the rim of the right-hand valley, James could see a defence laser tower with a large number two on the side casing, its turret hanging down at rest.

It had obviously been satisfied that their current mode of transport was a valid shuttle spacecraft.

The central mesa looked like a naked prone body lying as if it had just fallen flat on its face. It even looked like it had a spinal column running right down the middle of its back leading to two short stumpy legs. The shades and hues of the rock and sand ranged from light gold, through khaki, bronze, purple, light and dark blue to almost jet black in places.

Soon the mesa towered over them as they made their final approach to the Mars Facilities that sprawled at the base of the spine, sandwiched between the stumpy legs of the mesa.

As the landing fields to the south of the main complex grew ever larger they could see a small ground vehicle waiting for them off to one side of a large looming, white cross below them. Their vessel touched down in a cloud of sandy dust exactly in the centre of the cross. As the shuttle's thrusters slowly whined down, James and Robert undid their seat restraints. James immediately felt light.

"Remember that Mars only has thirty-eight percent of the gravitational pull of Earth," said Robert. "All your movements will be exaggerated."

James attempted to move slowly, but almost leapt out of his seat just trying to stand up.

"Huh! I see what you mean. This is going to be interesting," he said somewhat surprised.

"The trick is not to put too much effort into whatever you do. It's almost if your muscles have twice as much power here, you feel like Superman," said Robert grinning.

The shuttle pilot entered the ten-seat passenger cabin from the flight deck. He was dressed in light brown overalls with a flimsy pair of rubber soled trainers on his feet. He somehow managed to look scruffy even in standard universal clothing.

"Welcome to Mars guys. The landing crew are just attaching the umbilical walkway from the ground vehicle to us. Then we'll transfer you to the main facilities building," he said.

There came a couple of muffled clangs and bangs the other side of the airlock door. The noises reverberated round the cabin. Robert was feeling nauseous again. His pills were in his personal effects in the wash bag they had been allowed to take on board *Oceans Dawn*. That was now in the bottom of a large holdall they had been issued with to pack their spacesuits in.

The idea of opening up the two-handled holdall, diving under the carefully packed pressure suit to get to the wash bag was just too much, he felt worse so sat down again. Shutting his eyes, he tried to imagine wide open fields of grass, trees and mountains. After a few moments the feeling of dizziness had passed, only to be replaced with a feeling of nostalgia. Still, at least that didn't make him feel light headed, just homesick instead.

"Right, I think we are just about ready," said the pilot, as the curved airlock door started emitting a mechanical whirring sound. It moved slowly vertical, disappearing into the shuttle fuselage above their heads.

Gradually, the body of a large man was revealed in the doorway as the door rose up. When the door had been fully retracted they were standing face to face.

"Hello folks, I'm your welcoming committee," the big man grinned as he spoke. "Tobias Hauss at your service, in charge of security. Some jokers round here like to call me the sheriff. I'd prefer it if you just call me Toby," he added.

"Hello Toby, this is James Cleaver," Robert said, indicating towards his friend and colleague. "I'm Robert Goodyear."

They took turns to shake Toby's large right hand that had a crushing grip.

"Glad to meet you Corporation guys, if you would like to follow me please," Toby said, expertly turning round in the small enclosure only just wide enough for one person.

He walked back through the short passageway towards the ground vehicle airlock door. They followed pushing their cumbersome holdalls in front of them.

"I don't think the designers of this passageway want you to get through here in a hurry," James remarked, banging his elbow on the side wall for the second time.

Toby took their personal holdalls from them as they squeezed themselves into the vehicle. Then he ushered the three men onto a row of seats down the right hand side of the vehicle cabin whilst pushing the holdalls into a self-contained cargo area on the left.

"It's just a case of conserving air and time, the smaller the space, the quicker to pressurize and de-pressurize," Toby explained.

James looked out the window to see two figures in spacesuits working outside between the shuttle and the ground vehicle. Slowly his gaze cast further afield.

They were deep inside Hebes Chasma, the surrounding valley and mesa walls towered between five to six kilometres high all around them.

James couldn't get over the spellbinding magical colours imbedded in the valley walls. They were so different to anything he had ever seen before. He particularly liked the rich dark purple hue.

He would have to try and get a large lump of that particular coloured rock to take back with them. It would take pride of place in his apartment. He visualised it polished and mounted on a nice piece of hardwood on the mantle above his three-dimensional imitation log fire.

"Right folks, here we go," cried Toby. James had been so preoccupied with the outside world and his own thoughts he hadn't noticed what was going on in front of his nose. The two airlock doors had been closed. The two ground crew outside had unhitched the umbilical walkway which now lay to one side and were now busy performing some task on the underside of the passenger shuttle. A large grey panel had been removed that lay on the landing pad while they poked around inside an exposed landing skid. The large bright illuminated white cross had been extinguished being replaced by softer working lights.

The vehicle suddenly jerked into motion, jolting them in their seats.

"Sorry 'bout that. This ancient runabout is getting a bit stiff in its old age," apologised Toby. "It will take about five minutes to get to the main building complex. It's not that far, unfortunately we have to wind our way through the landing fields first."

James now noticed several other unlit large square and oblong landing pads around them.

"Look James," shouted Robert, pointing to a very sorry looking battered spacecraft on one of the more distant landing sites. "That's an asteroid-mining vessel I'll wager."

"You're right. That's *Crystal Star*," said the shuttle pilot. "It came back from the belt three days ago with a full load of cobalt and nickel. A very successful mining tour by all accounts."

"Tell me about it," Toby called out from the driving seat. "I had to put two of the crew in the brig only hours after they got paid! They start drinking strong Martian spirits as soon as they get their bonuses and it doesn't take long. I don't mind them letting their hair down, hell, they deserve it. After four months out in the belt we all would, but when they start fighting, start wrecking the bars, it's me and my men that have to wade in to break it up."

Robert noticed James was a little confused by all these new insights to a strange world he had only ever heard patchy rumours about.

"The place is called The Social Village," Robert started to explain. "One of the domes has been built specifically to service the personnel that live and work on Mars. That includes all the miners that work the belt and the people that refine the raw materials here. They work hard so they need a lot of unwinding. The Village has everything you could wish for, small bars, gambling, illicit hallucinogenic drugs, cinemas, there's just about everything for a price, if you get my meaning," he said, tapping the side of his nose with his forefinger in that 'know what I mean' gesture.

The shuttle pilot, who had been very quiet sat right at the back, now suddenly spoke out. "That's not all they came back with by all accounts. Apparently…" He started, about to divulge some interesting snippet, when Toby cut him short.

"That's classified!" Toby bawled out. "You should know better than to gossip, especially when you don't know all the facts. It can be dangerous in our small environment," he added more calmly.

"It's a load of old horseshit anyway, crashed alien spaceships my arse!" he blurted out.

Toby again cut the pilot short. "Until we can verify any facts it stays confidential! Now, not another word," he said, in a voice that gave the notion that it should be heeded immediately.

James and Robert looked at each other. These were interesting revelations which backed up their own preliminary speculations. Toby's commanding voice had the desired effect as not another word was uttered for the rest of the journey. Soon the vehicle approached the large central domed building.

At the front of the building an assortment of wheeled ground vehicles were reversed up to it. Toby found a gap in the line, then turned pointing the vehicle away from the building towards the landing fields, before reversing into the space.

James could now see how this worked. Toby was looking at an image from a rear-facing camera, lining up a door at the back of the vehicle he had not noticed before, to a sealed doorway leading into the complex. Toby gently nudged the building, lurching ever so slightly as it aligned itself with the doorframe. At the same time two hydraulic arms came down and located onto two lugs one on each side of them. These pulled it tight to create an immoveable airtight seal with the building. At the same time, it conveniently connected the batteries. As Toby turned off the drive power, an orange coloured symbol behind the steering wheel lit up indicating that recharging was under way. Satisfied, he stood up, turned to his occupants and indicated they should follow him.

Picking up their holdalls they followed Toby to the back of

the vehicle. He turned a handle and pushed. The rear door swung open to reveal a busy thoroughfare.

"Looks like we've arrived at rush hour," Robert said, trying to break the awkward silence that had followed the shuttle pilot's outburst and Toby's curt putdown.

"Not so much a rush hour, shift changes more like," Toby suggested.

The shuttle pilot pushed past them. He was the first through the open door leaving them without saying another word before melting into the milling throng of bodies going about their business.

"Right, I am to escort you to the Facilities Controller," he said, before setting off into the now dwindling crowd.

Robert and James followed like obedient puppies. James was still trying to get used to walking in such light gravity, striving not to jump up while moving forward. Even so, he still managed to collide into people apologising profusely for startling them. Across the foyer they turned a corner into a relatively quite corridor. James uttered a sigh of relief.

11

A Welcome Return

The moment Josie stepped out of her spacesuit, Andy grabbed hold of her giving her a big hug. Deimos and Kieron wanted to join in unable to contain their relief, they waited patiently for their turn whilst expressing their delight at seeing her alive and well. Josie willingly returned the comforting gestures to all three of them one by one as she was also delighted to be alive and well.

"What the hell happened here?" she asked, once the affectionate pleasantries had ceased. "And why is Mei-Lien on a medivac bed hooked up to a triple M?"

She had seen the hastily welded patches on the outside of the mining vessel on approach to docking. Now, inside, they were standing next to the prone body of Mei-Lien on an emergency stretcher attached to the Mobile Medical Monitoring unit.

"What the hell happened to you?" Andy asked in return, unable to contain his deep concern.

The three men had just spent the best part of two hours clearing up. They had repaired several round holes in *Lode Drifter* after being struck by a strange perfectly circular undetermined object. Once the repairs had been completed they had been standing in the control room mourning the loss of their fellow crew members. Simultaneously, all three of them had seen the one person scout spacecraft haphazardly dodging its way through the asteroid field towards them.

At first, they could hardly believe what they were seeing. A garbled sporadic message came over the communications system. They immediately recognised the voice although they could not understand a word she was saying. They soon realised the scout vessel appeared to have been damaged too. Josie was an extremely experienced pilot, even with misaligned thrusters she skilfully managed to coax the small spacecraft onto its moorings located on top of its mother ship, eventually docking with a loud satisfying metallic clang.

Climbing out, Josie slowly made her way across the top of *Lode Drifter* before floating down past the control room observation window to the main airlock where the remaining crew members had been waiting for her.

"Shall we all go and discuss our misadventures over a bite to eat, I'm starving," she suggested. The others readily agreed realising they had not eaten for several hours themselves.

"I must tell Raman I found his gold, where is he?" Josie asked smiling. She looked round the gear room for him before returning her gaze to the others. The corners of her mouth dropped as she noticed the crestfallen expressions on their faces.

"Oh no, not Raman!" Josie eventually blurted out, stopping in mid step a couple of metres from the back of the gear room exit.

"I'm afraid I've got even more bad news, Aimee… Well, it would have been quick, they wouldn't have suffered any," Andy didn't need to put any compassion in his voice, it was already there.

"Aimee, poor Aimee, she was so young," Josie couldn't hide her distress. Her eyes started to well up. She attempted to soak up the tears with the cuff of her long-sleeved overalls.

Andy took hold of her arm fearing she might misplace the use of her legs with the shock. He decided he might as well get all the bad news out the way. "And Steve, he, well he didn't make it either," he muttered.

Josie couldn't speak now, her mouth moved, but no sounds issued from it. Her chin wobbled uncontrollably. Kieron took Josie's other arm while Deimos slid open the airlock door. Supporting an arm each, they moved crablike, semi-sideways down the short passageway into the mess room. Andy guided her onto the bench seat behind the small table. She remembered the last time she was in here when she had been laughing and joking with the crew, all of whom were very much alive then.

Once they were all seated Kieron fetched Josie a hot sugary tea laced with brandy. She sipped while Deimos related the events from the moment she had left in the scout spacecraft, until her return just under fifteen minutes ago. He described the strange unknown celestial cylinder that left the perfectly round spherical hole right through the vessel. He explained the grisly demise of Raman and Josie and the mess to expect in her cabin. They had had no time to clean the walls.

Once the reality of the disaster had sunk in, had been accepted in Josie's mind, she became her more normal rational self. Inside though, she was racked with pain. She would cry, especially for Aimee at some point in the near future, not yet though, not in front of the men here, maybe later, when she was alone.

"So, tell us your sorry tale," enquired Deimos, managing somehow for once to squeeze his tall frame onto the bench seat behind the table. He put an arm round her shoulders offering some comfort. Josie sniffed which succeeded in stifling her tears, then, coughed once to clear her throat.

"Well, I contacted Andy to give him an update on my

progress or lack of it, when all of a sudden the dials on the scanners went off the scale. They had latched onto an asteroid twenty metres across by forty high. I kid you not over half of it was pure solid gold, with veins, thick as your arm, running through the rest. I couldn't believe it. It has to be the biggest gold nugget ever found, now perhaps the biggest ever to be lost too!" Josie said, shaking her head.

"Anyway, I got in close almost touching the rock. Matching its intrinsic velocity, I set two tethering lines to get some proper readings when something completely out the blue, hit the spacecraft. Whatever it was it took out half the communications dish leaving it looking just like a new crescent Moon. Then it continued to remove most of the scanner array before slicing through the starboard thrusters. Finally, just for good measure, it put a hole through the main rear thrust cowling as well. Funny thing was, that was a perfectly round hole just like you described passing through *Lode Drifter*, I've never seen anything like that before," she paused for a sip of tea and brandy mix.

Andy looked at Kieron who raised his eyebrows in unspoken acknowledgement. What a coincidence that both vessels had been hit by the same strange round object, maybe there was more than one. Cylinders that managed to cut their way through any foreign body in their flight path. While Andy pondered these thoughts, Josie picked up her story.

"The spacecraft had been torn free from the tethers. I was really struggling for control with the damage to the thrusters, in fact I was in danger of being crushed by the most expensive asteroid this side of Saturn," she paused again for another sip of tea. The warm liquid was doing a fantastic job of calming her state of mind.

"I eventually got the hang of the odd manoeuvrability of the spacecraft before plotting a course back to your last known position. That was a bit of a challenge without any navigational scanners. The navi-computer did know my last recorded position so it was more than just an educated guess as to your whereabouts. It still took a couple of passes before I eventually found you," she concluded.

There was a short pause before Kieron spoke. "We are ever so glad you did! Now then, what caused these perfectly round holes in both our spaceships?" he threw the question to the group.

"Well, we know they literally cut their way through this vessel, I suspect the same for the scout spacecraft, both being cut out symmetrically round. I bet they are exactly the same size too. There is just no way they could pass through solid objects the way they have done, if they were naturally occurring asteroids or meteors," Andy spoke his suspicions out loud.

"So that means intelligent life has created them. So, who made them, what makes them cut through metal like a red hot knife through butter, what is their purpose? The list of unanswered questions is endless. More than likely that list will get longer too," Deimos suggested.

"Well perhaps some bright spark in the Mars Scientific laboratories might have some idea," suggested Andy.

"So, what do we do now?" Josie asked shrugging her shoulders.

"We can't very well continue the tour. Not with three crew dead and one injured," she added almost answering her own questions.

"Plus, the temporary patches. This old girl has taken a few knocks, it needs to be properly repaired back at Mars," Deimos interjected.

"Also, let's not forget Mei-Lien, we have to get her back as fast as possible if we want to try and save her arm. Even though I have put regenerative proteins in her drip, the tissue will still deteriorate after a certain amount of time," said Kieron.

"Did you tag that lump of gold by any chance?" Andy asked hopefully.

"Of course, first thing I did before I tethered. Tag seven two five one, if my memory serves me correctly," replied Josie.

"Kieron, can we spare half a day? I'm thinking of Mei-Lien here," asked Andy.

"Well, I suppose if we get her into the Dormouse Torpor State straight away, it will not really make much difference one way or another," replied Kieron.

"Okay, here's what we'll do. Let's go and get it then, try to salvage something from this bloody mess. Hopefully, it shouldn't take too long to find, and judging by its size, the few of us left can chop it up quite quickly. Then we can head back home. How's that sound?" Andy said questioningly, looking for any signs of agreement. Thankfully, there were reassuring nods from the others.

"Sounds like a good plan to me," agreed Deimos.

"Right, let's have some nourishment first, build up our strength. I can't remember the last time I ate anything solid," said Andy.

"I'm not sure I'm that hungry now," Josie responded, still feeling very upset by all the revelations of the previous hour.

"Well, let's all try to eat something," suggested Kieron. "I'm going to force a chicken dinner down my throat, quickly followed by a large whiskey, to make up for the last one which was spilled," he added, glaring at Deimos. He got up heading for the mess room entrance and the galley opposite. "Can I get anyone else anything while I'm there?"

"Just do four meals the same, and make all the drinks large. I'll have ice with mine thanks," Andy stated authoritatively. Kieron uttered acknowledgement as he crossed the corridor.

Josie pushed the entire food contents on her plate round

and round thirty times before trying a small slither of reconstituted white meat. It was no good though, it would be some time before she would return to some sort of normality let alone find her appetite.

A short while later, after they had eaten or failed to eat, they all made their way up to the control room.

They picked up the unique beacon signal from tag seven two five one after a few sweeps of the scanners. It was moving quite slowly fifty-four kilometres below their current position. Andy plotted a course through the belt towards the source of the signal.

"Stations everyone, let's go hunting," he said out loud.

It took all of them in the control room to help negotiate *Lode Drifter* through the myriad of rocks large and small. Each crew member scanned a designated area around the vessel working out which rocks would cause a threat and those that did not.

Each threat was labelled as they called out potential dangers.

"A-sixty-three closing portside," shouted Deimos.

The large glass display screen in front of them showed a three dimensional mass of foreign bodies milling about. At the very centre, a black oblong shape represented *Lode Drifter*. One of the many white silhouetted shapes to the left of the black oblong shape now sprouted a red flag with the letter 'A' followed by the number sixty-three on it.

Andy, sitting in his Operations Controller's chair, could see the asteroid moving slowly to intercept their path. He made a small course adjustment to compensate. Asteroids with flagged numbers falling behind them lost their flags once they were no longer a dangerous threat.

"A-sixty-four moving in topside," Kieron touched his monitor highlighting the rock which immediately sprouted a red flag on the main viewing screen.

Every now and then they could not manoeuvre quickly enough out of the path of some smaller asteroids. A large clang echoed round the spacecraft as a small lump of rock bounced harmlessly off the hull.

"What's the distance now Josie?" Andy asked.

"Another twenty kilometres," replied Josie.

"Right, stay alert people, we've got another hour of this yet. Keep calling out those big rocks so I don't stick our nose into one," Andy ordered.

The high concentration manoeuvring cycle continued until, seventy-two minutes later, Josie shouted out. "There it is. That's Raman's nugget just there!"

"Just in time too, we're all becoming mentally fatigued with all this intense concentration," Kieron observed.

Josie pressed a button on her console then touched her screen. The three dimensional model now had a white outlined rock sprouting a blue flag with a number eleven on it. This denoted the eleventh profitable asteroid they had found on this tour.

"Right, let's get in close. Deimos, Kieron, you two suit up fast. I don't like the feel of the rock density here, it seems uncomfortably crowded."

The two men ran out the control room, the door sliding shut with an enthusiastic clang behind them, as they raced down the upper corridor.

Andy had been feeling like the whole disastrous tour had all somehow been his fault. His confidence, his self esteem had been shaken to his very core, especially losing three crew members. Now, he felt like he was in some sort of control again.

"Josie, keep a sharp eye out. I'm not going to tether just in case we need to move quickly," he ordered confidently.

Deimos led the way down to the main airlock room. Soon the two men were fighting their way into their spacesuits. They grabbed a couple of microwave frequency modulation lances, quickly placing them into the exoskeleton arm cradles. They had performed this routine a hundred times, but not with this sense of urgency.

Kieron swung the main airlock wide. Secure in their exoskeleton units, they climbed in. As soon as the door shut firmly behind them, they started decompression on maximum.

Luckily the outer airlock door opened inward, the gold meteor was only feet away from them. They set to work at once, meticulously cutting the small asteroid into manageable chunks, the bright gold veins shinning in their own luminosity. All the while they kept communications down to essential talk throughout the cutting operation.

"How long will it take now Kieron?" Andy asked the two-man team.

"Just another fifteen minutes, we're just over halfway through," Kieron replied.

"Do you want me and Josie to come and relieve you?"

"No, you're okay Andy, by the time you suit up we should be finished, hopefully."

"Okay, make it as quick as you can, these rocks seem to be closing in on us, it's as if they don't want to let go of their precious metal!" Andy exclaimed.

"There is a very large asteroid drifting our way, coming from below," Josie half muttered. A large rock on the three dimensional array displayed in front of Andy acquired a red flag with the number one hundred and five on it.

"It's moving very slowly," said Andy. "Okay you guys, we have a potential dangerous object below your position. You should easily have enough time, but just so you are aware," he added.

"Thanks Andy, Josie, keep watching our backs," replied Deimos, as he pushed another chunk of glittering metal into the ore sack.

"Damn! My lance has malfunctioned," shouted Kieron,

trying to violently shake the weapon in the weightlessness environment.

"Deimos, take over", Andy ordered. Slowly the two men transferred places. Deimos uncoupled his lance, continuing with the last cut Kieron had been working on. As soon as the chunk was free and out of the way, he immediately started a new one. Kieron grabbed the cut piece as it started to drift away. Gingerly, he pushed it towards the opening of the ore sack.

"That small delay in swopping is going to cut this job quite fine," Andy suggested, looking intently at the three dimensional display.

"We need to move out of here in about one minute. How long before the final cut?" he asked.

What was once a small asteroid twenty by forty metres in size had now been cut down to about five metres square.

Kieron looked below them where the slowly drifting asteroid was looming larger by the second, and it was a big one. Glancing above them revealed there was an equally large one hanging almost stationary ten metres above them. "We're gonna get caught between a rock and a hard place," he joked.

Deimos looked round. Kieron pointed both up and down. Deimos followed his pointing fingers before returning to the rock face with renewed vigour.

"A couple of more cuts that's all that's needed now, I'm almost back to bare rock," he said.

"Thirty seconds and I want you back on board," Andy commanded. Deimos sliced into the ever-dwindling gold asteroid, pushing his quick cutting technique to the limit.

"Just as well gold doesn't shatter, that's two mistakes I've made rushing this," Deimos said, readjusting the settings on the lance for a second time.

"Okay, that's your lot," Andy said. "Back on board now."

Outside the two men pushed the last two extracted one

metre square lumps into the mouth of the sack. Behind them was a hunk of plain rock three metres across by two metres high. That was all that was left of the gold asteroid now all the precious ore had been removed.

"We're in the airlock," Kieron announced turning the handle.

"Just in time," sighed Josie, as Andy cautiously backed *Lode Drifter* away from the converging rocks.

Through the airlock window Deimos watched as the large asteroid coming from below connected with the small worthless lump of rock they had left behind. It nudged it towards the other stationary asteroid above.

Slowly the two large asteroids came together silently crushing the small lump into dust between them. It was less than two minutes since they finished working on it.

"Can we go back to Mars now?" Kieron asked feeling totally exhausted.

"Plotting a course right now," replied Andy, firing up the main thrusters. "We will be out of the belt in two shakes, well done everyone."

Josie gazed out, into the black void, as they left the Asteroid Belt.

"We got your nugget Raman," she whispered before turning towards her cabin. Now she could mourn as the door slid shut behind her.

12

Escape from Ganymede

"This maybe our best chance to get out of here," Leila stated, staring at the empty airlock. "It, the alien thing, seems to have disappeared for the time being. I'm assuming it's taken Roger's body, probably back to the spacecraft out there," she loosely waved her hand over her shoulder towards the crashed alien vessels. "I've no idea why, but I don't think it was trying to be sociable!"

"Okay, let's go then!" Trevor shouted for the second time in as many minutes, moving towards the control room door.

"Wait, we have to unload the database first, all our research. Not to mention the logs and recordings. Our only real proof that these things exist," added Leila.

"I've already ejected the data sticks from the master computer," Trevor tapped the breast pocket of his shirt. The bulge suggested two database memory sticks were concealed within.

"What about…" Leila never finished her concerns.

"You're bloody scared aren't you? Too frightened to move eh, stalling for time by the looks of it. Well, I'm going to take my chance now, with or without you," declared Trevor, now hovering by the control room door.

Trevor punched out the code on the door security panel

that they never did change from its factory preset, along with all the other access panels in the prefabricated buildings, which included the airlocks.

"Zero bloody zero bloody zero zero! Just as well that thing isn't intelligent. It would have been worth a try, that or four nines," he said under his breath.

The door slid open allowing Trevor to step through. He paused on the other side before sticking his head back through the open doorway.

"You coming or what!" he shouted at Leila, who seemed to have lapsed into a trance-like state.

"Just what we fucking well don't need right now, hey, Leila! Get your arse into gear and shift it!" Trevor spat the words out. Leila was still looking at the airlock monitor, her gaze transfixed.

Trevor re-entered the control room marching over to her. He passed his hand back and forth in front of Leila's face.

"Hello, anyone home," he spoke directly into her ear. Finally broken from her trance, Leila jumped turning to stare at Trevor who was just millimetres away from her face. She didn't like the close proximity so backed her face away from his, very slowly.

"Eh? What," she eventually muttered.

"Sorry to interrupt your little daydream, but as you said yourself, this may be our best chance to get off this icy rock before our little friend comes back. D'you fancy your chances?" Trevor added sarcastically, one hand held palm uppermost pointing vaguely in the direction of the exit.

Leila at last found her feet, in a split second she was off running out of the control room. Trevor's mouth dropped open as if he was going to say something. As nothing verbal materialised, he just about managed to shake his head quickly in disbelief before following her out into the centre of the criss-cross corridors of the main dome.

Leila was already returning back down the short corridor that led to the emergency lifeboat spaceship hub via one of the joining corridors.

"Well, we can't go that way. It looks like the connecting corridor arm has been compromised, it has a red cross on the door which has been automatically sealed," explained Leila, who appeared to be bouncing back to being almost normal again.

"Then we'll have to suit up, then depressurise the whole central dome," suggested Trevor.

"That will take far too long. That thing will have definitely come back by then," replied Leila. Trevor just stared at her looking quizzical, waiting for the alternative solution.

Leila finally continued after a short thoughtful pause. "We'll have to suit up alright. Then we'll go out the airlock situated in the Land Crab satellite dome, the one that Roger was going to use, at the opposite end of the complex. Then we'll make our way over to the other side on foot. Using the airlock over there we can access the lifeboat rocket. When we get there, we can board the escape vessel and wham! We get off this rock for good."

"Oh that's just bloody great. If you were to ask me what would be the most dangerous route to take to get to the lifeboat rocket hub that I could think of, with a knife-wielding maniac running about outside, that would be it. I know, why not jump up and down waving our arms about as well, just to make sure we get the damn creature's attention while we are about it," sneered Trevor.

"If we confront it we will need a weapon of some kind, all it has is a knife, so far as we know," Leila said rather pathetically, trying to belittle the knife that dispatched Roger rather efficiently.

"In case it escaped your attention, this is a scientific outpost. We have microscopes, observation telescopes, and containers for rock and gas samples. We don't have guns or any other type of weapon, unless you want to count the plastic cutlery from the galley. Perhaps we could throw some experimental cultured Petri dishes at it, try to give it a virus?" Trevor said, throwing his arms into the air at the same time letting out a lengthy deflated sigh.

"I just wish you would be more helpful instead of being so negatively critical all the time. Just think of something we can make to defend ourselves, try to be positive for once. Remember, there are two of us, only one of... one of it, whatever IT is!" Leila shouted exasperated, her temper beginning to flare getting the upper hand over her rationality.

"I just don't bloody believe this, why is nothing ever simple!" Trevor shouted raising his head upwards.

The creature had indeed returned to its crashed vessel. Having satisfied its hunger by snacking on Roger's heart, the alien was now leaning over a brightly lit bench. On the bench were a myriad of small tools scattered about. It was peering into a large machine trying to repair a micro robot that lay prone like a dead beetle with its legs in the air.

Using the delicate tools under intense magnification it managed to get one set of legs working. Then the head moved slowly, rows of concentric teeth whirred into life whizzing round and round. Suddenly, there was a loud pop. The alien creature made a loud gurgling noise, a noise of total frustration as the expired micro robot emitted a small spiral of smoke.

The creature picked up a small pile of micro robot parts. They ran through its fingers like sand, they were useless now, broken and burnt out heads, legs and bodies. It threw the remaining pieces in its hand down on the bench in frustrated anger. In the low gravity the pieces bounced up flying in all directions. One small piece was headed towards its face, primarily its eyes. It made an even louder gurgling noise swatting the tiny piece out of the air like some irritating little wasp.

Trevor had been gone some time. Laboratory One had been compromised during the crash so he had headed off to Laboratory Two in search of a weapon of some description. Leila meanwhile had laid out their suits, checked the air supplies. She also ensured the batteries that powered the thermal elements were fully charged.

"Well, this is the best I could come up with," said Trevor on his return. He handed Leila a long thin screwdriver.

"Is that it?" Leila asked, turning it over in her hands. Trevor held up his hand as if to stop Leila saying any more before revealing a small cylindrical sealed unit in his other hand. It was the size of an ordinary round drinks tumbler covered in yellow and black stripes.

"A seismic charge cartridge with…" He paused for effect. "A remote control tuned to the same frequency as the detonator," he concluded.

The long thin remote control unit had been in his trouser pocket which he now whipped out triumphantly. It was the size of a small stubby pencil with a small red button like an eraser on the end.

"We can throw the charge at the creature, then, press this button and pow! Strike one alien," he finished by pretending to press the small button on the unit with his thumb.

"There's not much explosive material in one seismic cartridge," announced Leila sounding disappointed. "We only used them the once to test the density of Ganymede's iron core. If I remember correctly they were pretty feeble," she added.

"That's why I emptied the explosives from all the other remaining seismic cartridges stuffing them into this one. It should be enough to damage the alien's suit at the very least. Maybe even enough to knock it off its feet while you stab it with that," he said, pointing at the screwdriver. "Well, that's what I'm hoping. Let's just hope we don't need to use it at all," he added, followed by an exasperated sigh.

He had created a weapon, a rather good one all things considered and still she was not happy, that's just typical of women he thought to himself.

"I assume it's not armed yet?" Leila enquired, drawing herself away from the explosive device.

"No, not yet, I need to twist the bottom of the detonator to arm it. I can do that as we enter the airlock just before I put on my spacesuit gloves. I'll have to have the detonator unit inside my glove, then, if we have to use the device, a simple tap on the top of my thumb should set it off!" Trevor declared.

"As you say, let's hope we don't need it," concluded Leila as they started putting on their suits.

Outside, the alien creature had indeed returned. It had been drawn to the twinkling lights on the lifeboat spaceship. It hadn't noticed them flashing before. It wasn't as stupid as Trevor may have thought, it now suspected that the rocket was being readied, or was actually in a state of readiness, to launch.

It moved over to the airtight corridor that linked the main dome with the emergency spacecraft satellite dome. It peered through the tough plastic windows into the darkened interior.

As they had never used a real emergency lifeboat rocket, except in a simulated exercise, Trevor and Leila were unaware that their imminent departure was being announced in such a colourful way as the bright white, green and red navigation lights on the top and sides of the vessel blazed intermittently.

Eventually, after some more deliberation and heated discussions, Trevor and Leila were finally in the airlock. The walls glistened red as Roger's blood began to re-freeze, crystalizing as the temperature plummeted at the same time the air was being removed.

Trevor was careful not to bash his right gloved hand into anything as he now had the armed detonator lying alongside his right thumb. The seismic charge cartridge had been activated. Should it explode in the small confinement they now found themselves, it would probably remove Leila's hand and damage his suit. The temperature was fast approaching minus one hundred and fifty plus, they would not last long with missing hands.

Leila gripped the seismic cartridge in her gloved left hand. The screwdriver, which would be her primary weapon in close quarters, protruded from her right gloved fist.

Trevor operated the airlock controls. He turned down the lights so they would become accustomed to the outside darkness. Slowly the airlock emptied itself.

The symbol on the door finally turned red symbolising that pressure on both sides of the airlock door had equalised hitting zero. Silently, the door started to ascend. Leila dropped to her knees to look underneath through the gap. She wasn't going to end up like Roger if the alien creature was on the other side. All was clear. All she observed was the bleak distant landscape outside.

"So far so good," she spoke in a whisper, fearful the creature was only feet away hiding round the corner somewhere it could hear them. In reality, it would not have heard her if she shouted at the top of her voice.

With the door fully open, they slowly edged nearer the dark exit until they emerged out into the very thin wispy atmosphere. After several furtive looks in all directions, they could discern no obvious sign of the alien.

"What way now?" Leila asked, a distinct note of slight relief in her voice.

"Fifty-fifty, left or right," Trevor answered with a question. He also managed to shrug inside his suit, a pointless gesture as Leila didn't see him do it.

"Let's go left," Leila decided. This put Trevor in front of her which she preferred. Trevor didn't say anything if he was at all aware of her sly manoeuvre, he just turned to his left, wanting to get on with the task at hand as fast as possible.

They started a shuffling, low-gravity hopping walk, towards one of the laboratory domes they would have to circumnavigate to get to the other end of the complex just under two hundred metres away.

"Bloody hell!" Trevor exclaimed. "It's lit up like a fucking Christmas tree." It was the first time they had seen the lifeboat rocket spaceship waiting for them, its navigation guiding beacon lights flashing a myriad of whites, reds and greens.

"No chance of sneaking off this rock is there!" he shouted before adding. "I don't know why we didn't we just drive over there in the first place?"

"We were trying to be discreet remember. Now it's a bit late to turn back for the Land Crab," replied Leila. They had almost reached halfway. Looking into the windows of Laboratory One, they hoped to see out the other side, but there was too much clutter inside the room to get a clear line of sight through the building. They gave up trying.

"Here we go then," said Trevor leading the way round the dome.

They had chosen their direction of travel unwisely. The alien had inspected the smaller-domed hub at the base of the lifeboat rocket spaceship. It had determined that the remaining occupants of the main dome had yet to arrive.

It had also carefully inspected the covered walkway leading from the main dome. With no interior lighting and finding a split joint in one of the windows it concluded that it was no longer pressurised. It therefore correctly surmised that the occupants would have to exit via the far airlock where it had ambushed the first human. Logic dictated its best course of action was to return to that airlock to lay in wait for them to emerge. It chose to turn right outside the lifeboat-domed hub before heading towards one of the laboratories domes. Fortunately or unfortunately, depending if you were the hunter or the hunted, it was the same laboratory dome that Trevor and Leila were now currently circumnavigating.

Trevor saw the alien first, a fraction of a second before the alien stopped dead in its tracks just thirty metres away.

"Shit, it's seen us," sighed Trevor. "Well, it's seen me at least, maybe not you. He's one big bastard too. Right, think, think, what we could do is this. If you gently place the charge down then back off round the corner of the dome back the way we came. I'll walk straight backwards out into the open hoping it will start coming towards me. Once it gets near to the charge I'll detonate it. If for any reason something goes wrong you could rush it from behind, stab the bugger in the back," described Trevor.

"Okay, I'm putting the charge down and backing off," replied Leila. Trevor waited a few seconds before slowly stepping backwards five metres passing the charge to one side. Still he kept his eyes firmly fixed on the alien, like he was trying to outstare a cat, all the while wondering what it was thinking.

"Come on you big mother," urged Trevor, taking another couple of steps backwards. Suddenly the creature in the black suit lurched forward. It started moving towards Trevor really fast considering the low gravity. Living its entire life in this sort of environment it was not surprising it was used to it.

"Here we go. It's coming forward really fast. Boy, have I got to time this just right. Are you out of sight of the seismic charge?" he checked with Leila.

"Yes, as far as I dare without seeing what's happening," she replied, looking down at the screwdriver feeling pathetic. It now seemed slight in her small hand looking very inadequate.

"Five, four, three, this better bloody work, now!" Trevor stabbed at his gloved right thumb pressing the detonator button inside. Nothing happened. The creature ran straight past the charge. It was only a couple of metres away from reaching Trevor covering the ground between them fast.

"What's happening?" Leila shouted.

"Nothing, it's not bloody well detonated! That's what's NOT happening. Maybe the signal is being distorted by my glove. Oh my…" He never finished the sentence. Trevor had left it to the last second before diving straight at the feet of the alien.

Luckily the creature was moving too fast. It was forced to jump over him for fear of being tripped up. It still managed to lash out, its razor sharp knife missing Trevor's back by the smallest of margins.

The alien now had to stop its faster momentum before being into a position to attack again. By that time, Trevor had picked himself up. Making his way back to the explosive charge he picked it up in his left hand. Turning round, he once again faced the alien coming towards him at a more cautious pace this time. Trevor wouldn't have a second chance to dodge the nine foot plus black suited creature with a diving rugby tackle. He also felt it wouldn't be prudent to repeat that particular manoeuvre at this slower speed. Trevor now moved to put the alien between him and Leila. The creature was still not aware of her lurking in the shadows of laboratory one.

"Right, come on you, you want a fight?" Trevor growled, his adrenalin pumping. To a casual observer they appeared to be just like two cowboys in the old west sizing up for a gunfight. The creature now seemed very curious about the object in Trevor's hand. It swopped its deadly knife from one gloved hand to the other. They were now only four metres apart.

"Leila, I'm going to try this one more time. This time, I'll be much closer to the charge. If this doesn't work, you try to sneak off to the lifeboat rocket while it deals with me, takes me back to its vessel or whatever. You got that?"

He waited for an answer. Eventually there was a stifled reply as Leila was fighting for control of her pounding heart and sporadic hyperventilated breathing.

They had stopped moving. Just like the gunslingers of old, they were each waiting for the other to make the first move, to draw first. Trevor sensing the time was right launched the charge at the creature which tried to leap to one side. He stabbed the detonator switch hidden in his glove against his thigh, this time there was success. A bright intense light was immediately followed by a shockwave that knocked them both backwards to the ground. The combined seismic charges were a lot more powerful than Trevor could have ever imagined.

Leila moved quickly. She had seen the bright flash of light from her hiding place just out of sight round the corner of the dome. Realising this could be her one and only chance to do something positive, she jumped up. Rounding the dome she saw two figures lying horizontal both upwardly facing.

The black suited creature raised one arm that fell back slowly. She ran over to the still winded alien. Using all her strength, she plunged the screwdriver into its upper torso where she hoped some vital organs might be. It immediately doubled up in agony. Leila stepped back, just in time to avoid a last ditch swipe of the alien's knife. The knife wavered at the ends of its fingers for a couple of seconds before it dropped out of its twitching hand at her feet.

Finally satisfied the creature was not going anywhere, she rushed over to Trevor who had not moved since the explosion. One look confirmed her worst fears. Trevor's visor had been smashed by the blast. His face was already contorted. Instantly frozen after being exposed to the intense cold which had cracked open the freezing skin across his face in large gashes.

She made her way back to the alien. Dropping to her knees, she picked up the knife that seemed more like a short sword in her hands. Pent up anger now took hold, she screamed out loud stabbing wildly at the alien creature.

"You murdering bastard!" she repeated over and over with

each thrust until finally, becoming too tired to wield the knife any more, she started to weep uncontrollably falling slowly to the frozen ground to lie, side by side next to the dead creature.

A short while later the Ganymede emergency lifeboat rocket spaceship took off. Leila set her course to intercept the asteroid-mining vessel *Crystal Star*.

She had placed Trevor's body inside the Land Crab covering him with a tarpaulin. The ground being too hard to dig a grave to bury him, it was the best she could do.

The alien, almost cut in half out by the laboratory dome, she left with the screwdriver sticking out of its ribcage. Multiple stab wounds to the midriff glistened with frozen dark, almost black, blood.

On the flight deck Leila found an empty drawer. Inside she carefully placed the black charred computer memory sticks next to the extraterrestrial knife. Through the thick plastic windows she could just see the receding buildings of Ganymede Outpost two five three.

"Bye Roger, I'll miss you. Bye Trevor, you may have been a conceited male chauvinist pig, all the same, thanks to you for saving my life. I'll doubt I will ever forget either of you or forget this day as long as I live," she spoke out loud, before turning to get on with the tasks at hand.

13

Blake

As Robert and James descended into Hebes Chasma from *Oceans Dawn* in their shuttlecraft, a small black two man scout spacecraft made a slow lazy accent up to the interplanetary freighter. It was a sleek design of military origin, almost undetectable to the naked eye against the backdrop of space.

Not so invisible to the Mars defence towers though. Even privately owned spacecraft required a unique identity allowing them to fly anywhere over the Mars Facilities complex. The pilot complied by switching on the automatic beacon emitter that pulsed the vessel's valid identity signal code over the radio waves. The laser towers now happy, lapsed once more into their lethargic looking standby mode with turrets flaccid.

Reaching a parallel orbit, the pilot requested clearance to dock with *Oceans Dawn* to extract its third passenger from Earth. After a short pause, clearance was granted.

The third passenger to arrive from Earth was a man called Blake. Blake was a European Government undercover operative currently assuming the false identity of an experienced miner. He was patiently waiting at one of the airlocks at the rear of the vessel, at his feet was a Corporation standard issue carryall containing his spacesuit. The small scout spacecraft expertly docked with a short umbilical corridor that protruded from the larger vessel. The corridor had been activated once docking clearance had been given. It instantly created an airtight seal with the scout vessel as they touched each other using immense suction pads concealed within the corridor door frame.

Sensors immediately diagnosed safe dock allowing the inner airtight door to open automatically. There was a slight hiss as the air pressure had not quite equalized on both sides.

Without further ado, Blake moved into the short passageway. The inner door closed behind him. The lock sealed allowing the door on the scout spacecraft to open. He clambered into the small cramped vessel. After stowing his kitbag, he was soon occupying the second seat. He looked around him out of the canopy just like an early twentieth century fighter pilot would have done in his wartime spitfire.

After strapping himself into the full harness, he fished out an earpiece and microphone from a cubby hole to one side. Finding the connecting wire, he plugged himself into the secure internal communications circuit. He then placed the earpiece in his right ear and adjusted the microphone to hover just in front of his mouth. At the same time the spacecraft broke the seal ejecting the small amount of air in the temporary corridor. Then, just like a conjurer's trick, the corridor disappeared back into the hull of *Oceans Dawn* as if it had never existed.

In one fluid motion the scout spacecraft pulled away from the docking station heading back down towards the facility buildings.

"Hey, how is everything? Any new developments?" Blake asked.

"Plenty," said the pilot.

The reply that emanated from the earpiece was very muffled indicating that it wasn't working one hundred percent efficiently. Blake had to concentrate hard to hear.

"*Crystal Star* arrived back three days ago with one survivor from Ganymede outpost two five three. That one survivor hasn't been seen since. We can only assume she is still being debriefed, maybe even under house arrest. It's all rumours and hearsay, all very rife at the moment. No one seems to know what the hell went on out there. The survivor didn't even speak to the crew of *Crystal Star*, not even to the captain apparently," the pilot concluded, before cutting communications with Blake while he talked to the traffic control tower.

He had to gain clearance to proceed about their seemingly innocent business. The vessel continued to make its way to one of the smaller square buildings set behind the main complex domes.

The pilot's voice crackled once more in his ear. "We have a landing pad on top of one of the scientific buildings, that way we can avoid the main landing fields. Keep ourselves to ourselves."

The set up was quite neat. The agency operation was part of a small independent freight forwarding company working for the scientific laboratories and the Social Village businesses. The company was legitimate enough employing people totally unaware that in their midst, were a few totally unconnected with the mundane resupply trade. The supply spaceships brought in scientific equipment and provisions. Sometimes there was the need for replacement legitimate and illegitimate personnel. All this was achieved without too much fuss or bother with the authorities. Blake could have used this mode of travel to Mars, had he not been in such a hurry, but then the very nature of his job always seemed to necessitate speed.

An opening appeared in the roof on one of the buildings. A small rectangular platform rose up to meet the small black vessel. The landing and docking manoeuvre was slick. Blake was impressed. The pilot had obviously performed the procedure many times before, being totally in tune with the flying abilities of the scout spacecraft. The platform with the docked spaceship sunk back into the roof. A covering panel slid back over the opening, concealing them completely from the outside world. Inside the building the vessel was hooked up to another short airtight corridor.

Blake removed the headphones returning them to the cubby hole where he had found them. Unstrapping themselves from their harnesses, Blake and the pilot took turns to exit their seats before entering a small circular room via the short corridor. It was just big enough for two people accompanying their kit. The pilot hit the only button in the centre of a small panel on the wall.

"So, what's my brief? Err, sorry, I didn't catch your name by the way," enquired Blake, as the room started to slowly rotate.

"Hugh, the name's Hugh. The section leader wants to see you straight away. I'll take your kit to your room, don't worry about that. I must say I'm very pleased to meet our most successful agent," he grinned, genuinely pleased.

Blake shrugged an acknowledgement. He didn't like it when his reputation preceded him. He wasn't that good, just very meticulous. His own motto 'Plan for every eventuality, however inconceivable' had probably saved his live on more than one occasion in the past.

The room eventually stopped its rotation. The doorway they had used to enter the circular room was now their exit into a long brightly lit corridor.

"Thanks Hugh, nice flying," Blake extended his hand. Hugh shook it vigorously.

"Thanks. Now you want room twenty-eight down there on the right," Hugh waved his finger down the corridor. "I'll be in the canteen at the very opposite end up here," Hugh pointed in the opposite direction, indicating the way.

"When you've done with the section chief, come and find me. I'll show you to your quarters after some food, okay," he said, more as a statement than a question.

"Okay, see you soon," replied Blake, before setting off briskly down the lambent passageway.

He paused momentarily outside the room that had a large number twenty-eight on the door. He hadn't been very successful so far, this could turn out to be an embarrassing meeting. He knocked twice announcing his arrival to those on the other side.

"Come." The word came almost instantaneously on the second knock as if its owner had been waiting, almost anticipating it. Blake opened the door and entered.

"Aha, Blake! Safely here at last. Sit down, sit down," the section leader offered him the only available empty chair. "Very lucky with that small piece of rock up there. We heard all about it, very nearly didn't get to meet you after all," he joked half-heartedly. Blake eased himself into the empty chair forcing a slight chuckle at the intended witty remark.

Apart from the section leader, there were two other people in the room. They both stared straight ahead from their seats.

"Right, introductions first, probably the best way forward. Well, we all know who you are, Blake. You being sent here just proves we are in over our heads here. I'm Leon, agency section leader and co-ordinator here on Mars."

The department had a long time tradition of agents working in the field using a first name basis only. Blake had heard of Leon. He was very efficient at playing the desk jockey team leader role. His only annoying fault was a strange habit of trying to end every sentence with a comical remark if he felt it seemed appropriate. It was almost as if he believed what they were undertaking was one big jolly game. Still, it was a very convincing cover as he did appear to be a complete idiot most of the time.

"This is Jean. She works in 'Rockies' one of the bigger, and more popular bars in the Social Village," Leon paused, while Jean turned to Blake.

"Pleased to meet you," Jean smiled. She was dark skinned with very soft rounded facial features. Her ancestors must be originally from the Philippines, or maybe Sri Lanka, thought Blake.

"Jean keeps her ears open for all the gossip that goes on. It never ceases to amaze us how tongues soon start wagging when some alcohol is added to the equation. It's surprising the amount of info Jean collates. Next, we have Lee." The two men looked at each other and nodded a formal welcome.

"Lee works as a labourer in one of the furnaces. He is also one of the Union representatives, so, any gripes from the foundry work force, the news comes straight to us as well. Not that we would do much about it in any case, it would have to be an extreme emergency for us to intervene."

"Ah yes, Martian independence," interrupted Blake.

"Exactly! Mars is a sort of Free State, supposedly not under any government controls, rules or laws that apply to the poor folks down on Mother Earth. As you well know, this department is invisible. We are here to observe, monitor and analyse, reporting back every week the day-in, day-out boring stuff that goes on here inside the Mars Facilities. Secret industrial spies for the European Government," said Leon, pausing to take a sip of water out of a small paper cup. Then, he suddenly remembered he had forgotten his duties as host to this gathering. "Sorry, I should have offered you a drink, yes?" Leon enquired.

Blake nodded, realising his throat was quite parched. Leon stood up. He moved towards a plastic container housed inside an upright cabinet. Producing a small paper cup from a concealed compartment, he twisted a small toggle on the front. The cup filled with blue tinted water. Leon turned to

Blake handing him the brim full cup. Taking a swig, he swilled it round his mouth. He would never get used to the intense pure flavour of the Martian water that quenched his thirst instantly.

"Anyhow, that's our little covert family here on Mars. Oh, I missed out Hugh, you met Hugh of course. I think that's the lot. No more spies in the cupboard. That is unless you know some I don't know about," he said laughingly. They all broke out in a little stifled laugh. "Okay, now for some serious stuff," he continued.

Jean raised her hand. "Oh right Jean, you need to get to work don't you, your shift starts soon. You'd better get off then. I'll inform you of any developments, although, I'm not sure Blake has much to tell us, I think we have a lot more information for him," concluded Leon. Jean pushed her chair back. She stood up whilst making her farewells, turned and left the room.

"Now, where were we? What's your news then Blake?" Leon asked.

"I've not much to tell except I think the two Corporation employees who were on board *Oceans Dawn* suspect me of being not quite what I pretended to be, not a very auspicious start I have to say. They jammed my listening device on board the interplanetary spaceship. I could not get anything from the crew either. So, you are right, I haven't learnt anything more that I didn't already know before leaving Earth. So what's this about a survivor from Ganymede, what did they survive from?" Blake was intrigued.

"Right, let's start at the beginning. I'm not sure Lee is up to speed with all the current facts so a quick recap is in order. We know that over eight weeks ago a Dutch asteroid miner called Teunis Landry was caught out in a storm looking for some spacecraft junk, a hobby of his apparently. When they found him he had round torn ragged holes in his suit. No one can offer any rational explanation for what might have caused them or how he died, apart from obvious asphyxiation. Next we have a strange report from a mining vessel called *Crystal Star*. According to some of the crew, they say they were contacted by the scientific outpost on Ganymede with a story of two alien spacecraft fighting each other eventually crashing onto the small moon. They then waited for the lifeboat rocket ship from Ganymede to reach them before returning home. Are we all good thus far?" Leon looked for assurances. Blake and Lee both mumbled agreement to the related facts.

"Now, this is a new bit for you I think, Blake, another mining spacecraft, *Lode Drifter*, has been holed by something they determine as unnatural. By the way, they are due back in port tomorrow. It all comes down to what we have suspected for some time, we believe there must be an alien presence in our solar system," concluded Leon.

"The evidence all points to it," offered Blake. "I want to see this survivor from Ganymede. Hugh mentioned it was a she? I do hope it is. It will make my job all the easier to see her."

"Did we find out which one of the three science officers it was, Lee?" Leon directed the question at Lee who had been relatively quiet up to now.

"Indeed it was the woman, Leila Santos. The two male scientists are unaccounted for. We can only assume they perished somehow," Lee said shrugging his shoulders.

"Perhaps she just left them there, either dead, or alive?" Blake suggested.

"We can probably have an educated guess where she is being held, probably now under house arrest. I'm not sure you'll be able to walk in on her to ask a few questions," said Lee almost apologetically.

"I'll find a way, don't you worry about that. If you could find out her precise location for me that'll be a start."

Blake asserted his authority in such a subtle way that Lee agreed he would get right on it without even realising he had been given a direct order.

"This might be useful to you," said Leon, handing over a transparent electronic card full of micro circuitry he had retrieved from one of his desk drawers.

"It is a universal key card, a skeleton key as you undercover types like to call it. It will open any of the personnel apartment doors."

Blake slipped it into the top pocket of his overalls. "So, *Lode Drifter* docks tomorrow, what's the story there then?" he asked changing the subject.

"Our sketchy unconfirmed intelligence suggests that some sort of projectile passed right through the mining vessel, they sustained several casualties. The projectile left a perfectly symmetrical round hole in its wake."

"No such thing as perfectly round circle to be found in the natural universe is there?" Blake said quizzically with a grin. The other two didn't seem to recognise his obvious play on the ancient saying that there are no straight lines in nature.

Leon continued oblivious. "Not only that, but if it had been a natural small asteroid, it would have shattered. The many exit holes should have been catastrophic to the vessel. As it was, they only had the one exit hole which they patched up quite easily by all accounts. They even made time to mine an asteroid afterwards with only half the crew, that's dedication for you," he finished sarcastically.

"They're miners, it's a superstitious hang up they have. If they don't come back with a near-full load, or something very valuable, they consider it very bad luck, especially on their pockets," Lee chipped in.

"Seems they struck it rich too by all accounts, enough gold to rock the stock prices among the financial districts back home, so the story goes doing the rounds."

That caught Blake's attention. "That so," he said, showing interest in this new revelation. "Jean might be busy in the next couple of days with what's left of the crew once they cash in. They'll be hitting the Social Village bars no doubt at some point," he paused. Leon nodded in agreement.

"I'll tell her to be on the lookout for them, get chatty with the crew, she knows the drill."

"How does this all fit in with our theory then?" Blake continued, speaking his thoughts out loud.

"I'm not too sure. If they are saying it isn't natural, it has to be related to all the other odd things going on over the last couple of months." Leon replied.

Blake pondered. "Maybe," he said.

There was a long deathly pause before Leon broke the silence with his own thoughts. "So for now I suppose, we just wait and bide our time, see what happens next?"

"I see no other options. Meanwhile, I shall be doing a bit of digging on my own. Do you know this man?" Blake handed a piece of paper to Leon who unfolded the sheet and read out loud.

"Juan Carlos? Can't say I have. Perhaps Lee may have?" he said giving a little shrug.

"Yes, I've heard of him." Lee perked up. "Bit of a low life by all accounts. He does odd jobs in our little community. He gets just enough money to put him inside a beer glass for a few days, when he runs dry and out of cash, he starts the whole cycle over again. Juan is a bit of an embarrassment quite frankly, popping up in unauthorised areas, being a drunk they just push him on his way," Lee said, showed disapproval in his voice.

"Would it surprise you to know he is working under cover for one of our top rivals?" Blake waited for the impact of his statement to sink in. Lee certainly raised his eyebrows in sudden realisation that Juan's actions may not have been so innocent after all.

"Why wasn't I told about this?" Leon demanded indignantly.

"Okay, hold on. We only found out ourselves recently, besides, I'm instructing you now, okay," retorted Blake. Leon seemed to calm down almost instantly, realising it was futile to argue the point any more.

"Which rival, the CISA?" enquired Lee. Blake nodded the affirmative.

"The Central Intelligence Space Agency, a successor to the CIA," Leon spelled it out, just so everyone was absolutely sure he knew what the acronym stood for and wasn't a complete fool.

"Okay, what do you want us to do about him?"

"I want a quiet word with him too, to start with. We might need to get him to report back to his superiors, get them involved on the quiet. Put some pressure on the Corporation bosses back on Earth."

"You will have a bit of a job talking to him at the moment," said Lee all matter of fact. Finally he knew something the other two did not, he felt slightly euphoric. Blake looked to Lee for an explanation.

"He's in intensive care at the moment, managed to get into a brawl with some maintenance engineers a few days back. It was in Jean's report."

Lee paused to watch Leon go pink around the gills. Blake glanced at him, the look on his face plainly said. *"Don't you read the reports from your subordinates?"*

"Anyway, no charges have been brought so far. As far as witnesses go, they all say he made an ill-informed pass at a young blonde haired female, only to be put through a glass partition for his trouble."

"Oh well. That's that then," concluded Blake.

Leon started fishing through a pile of folders. He pulled out Jean's report from two days prior and handed it over. Blake dismissed it.

"Ah yes, just a bit behind that's all, I was just getting round to these today," muttered Leon, dropping it open on the desk. "Well, we all know what we have to do? I suggest we meet back here in twenty-four hours unless something major happens."

"Okay, but I may want to get in touch with Lee to request his help with some covert operations," requested Blake.

"We are here to help any way we can. Technically you outrank us, so, we are all at your beck and call," stated Leon.

Blake had not been at all impressed by Leon. *"Fat chance! I reckon you'll be as much use to me as a rat in a spaceman's boot,"* he thought upon leaving the room. Now, where was that canteen, he was feeling quite ravenous.

14

The Ice Tugboats of Saturn

From a distance, the rings of Saturn looked like the mice had chewed holes in them. From a distance, the diminutive Saturn ice tugboats could be mistaken for small rodents scurrying about. The tugboats were stumpy flat-faced spaceships flittering here and there as they constructed giant, roughly square-shaped ice cubes from the icy rings. In their wake, they left behind gigantic holes in the beautiful symmetrical hoops, holes approaching three hundred thousand metres wide.

The busy little spacecraft pushed, nudged and piled up the small individual ice blocks joining them with a flash of a high intensity laser melting the ice just before prodding two ice rocks together. Where they met the melted ice would then freeze immediately making an unbreakable weld. Over and over labouring tirelessly, adding more and more ice rocks until one enormous block was created. This in turn was then joined to another large block and so on until one immense ice cube had been constructed from millions and millions of small icy blocks.

The rings of Saturn, a natural wonder of the solar system, were a beauty to behold as they glistened in the dim distant sunlight through all the shades of blue. Deep ocean turquoise, clear summer sky and soft duck egg, just a few of the myriad of different fluctuating hues you could see as you traversed through the stationary frozen rocks.

It was a sad sight to see, as one more natural awesome solar creation was being systematically raped and plundered all in the name of human progress.

The Martian refineries, although very efficient at recycling, still required vast amounts of water. More than the almost depleted southern ice cap of Mars could now supply, so, an alternate water source had to be found to quench the thirsty smelting and refining factories on Mars.

The rings of Saturn were a good choice being ninety-three percent pure water. A bluish tinged water that was almost clinically pure by laboratory standards. It distilled into decent drinking spirit too.

The ice in the Asteroid Belt is spasmodic at best being quite hard to locate in amongst all the rock debris. Being in such small amounts made it unviable for the ice gatherers to even consider.

If the asteroid miners came across a small ice rock they considered it a bonus. It meant they didn't have to ration their water supply so much during mining tours. They could have more showers, which made life on board slightly more pleasant on the olfactory senses if nothing else.

The small snub-nosed Saturn ice tugboats resembled aquatic boxfish. They had stunted rectangular bodies that tapered down to a short connecting corridor section to the main engine compartment that fanned out resembling the tail of a fish.

On the front of each spacecraft was one huge ten metre square lump of hard black rubberised material. Short V-shaped side thrusters, not unlike fish fins on all four sides, enabled the adept vessel to push in every direction making it very manoeuvrable.

There were three operational ice tugboats currently

working the rings. All three were manned by aging couples who, instead of retiring, decided that life in space was their destiny for as long as possible.

Usually they were two ex asteroid miners now without the physical strength required or having sustained some debilitating injury, whereby they could not work the asteroid rock faces any more. Ex-miner couples who had hooked up with each other at some point in their hazardous careers that couldn't face settling down to the quiet life of retirement.

One such couple were Maria and Shaun Metcalf. They now owned *The Phoebe* which was the newest of the three working ice tugboats. Although relatively new, she still bore the knocks and scrapes of a hard working life in space. It certainly didn't look that new these days, with constant abusive usage, display screens, seats, doors and frames soon became to look very shabby, marked and worn.

Shaun looked just how you would expect an aging retired miner to look. His face was lined with crinkles and wrinkles making him appear ancient. His thin silver hair cut short giving the appearance he was almost bald. He was wiry too, not too thin, but nicely toned where it mattered. He could still put men half his age to shame when it came to any physical prowess using upper body strength. Unfortunately, it was his legs that let him down, strong thighs were required to work efficiently with the mining exoskeleton. Coupled with the arthritis in his worn out knees, these physical strains had forced an end to his time in the Asteroid Belt, but he wasn't going to retire from work or deep space, not just yet anyway.

Maria had managed to hold onto some of her youthful Spanish good looks although her eyes had sunk a little becoming hollow looking. Her once long jet black soft hair was now short and streaked with grey. When she laughed her cheeks became a mass of laughter lines. She was thin too, Shaun thought she could afford to put on a few pounds, fill out a little. Though, being thin helped in the small confines of an ice tugboat.

They had both stopped celebrating birthdays when they turned fifty some years before. Maria couldn't remember how many ice trips they had made. She made a mental note one day to count the holes, that way she could calculate just how many jaunts they had all completed. Then, she thought, it was all a bit irrelevant anyway, their aging process was slowed down considerably. Months would pass by whilst they were in the Dormouse Torpor State, so time became insignificant during an ice run. It took anything from five to seven months for a round trip from Mars to Saturn and back again, they would only be conscious for about four weeks of that time.

The ice cubes they amassed to take back each time were roughly three kilometres square, although hardly square shaped. A mishmash of different size ice rocks jumbled together in a haphazard fashion sometimes resembling a quarter turned Rubik cube.

"Density analysis is reading just over three billion litres. That's about our limit for this one," announced Maria, swivelling in her chair. She turned to look at her partner Shaun occupying the other tandem seat in the small, two person cockpit.

"Yeah, I reckon so. It seems like a long three long weeks putting this one together," replied Shaun. "What were those measurements again?"

Maria swivelled back to check the instrument panel. The density scanner monitor displayed a three dimensional picture of the cube they had cobbled together.

"It's three point one by two point eight three by two point nine six odd. That's just roughly you understand," answered Maria with a smirk, she had used two fingers as a guide against the monitors fixed scale ruler.

"Bit of an odd shape this one, lopsided to the right and

front. Still, we don't win any prizes for sculpture. I'll plot a course for Mars from the rally point. We can check with the others when we are all ready to depart for home. In theory we should all come up with nearly the same figures, at least to five decimals."

As he spoke, he carefully studied the love of his life and noticed she was looking very tired.

"You look like you could do with a rest, you haven't stopped once in the last couple of weeks, hardly had any sleep either as far as I know." Shaun pointed out.

"Neither have you, we could both do with a good scrub as well. As for these overalls…" Maria left the sentence unfinished as she looked over the stained and tatty plain brown overalls they wore on board.

"Yuk, what's that!" she added, flicking away some obnoxious small lump that had been stuck to the leg of her overalls. Whatever it was, it hung on the side of the console for a second before falling to the deck. It slipped like a slow moving slug through the metal grated floor to join a myriad of other detritus lurking among the cable trunking.

"That reminds me, we really must get around to giving this old boat a good clean, especially under the metal grid floor areas. Otherwise, whatever that was, will now fester under the floor for ever and a day," observed Shaun.

"Perhaps when we get back we can get someone who's down on their luck a little job of swilling out the old tub?"

"What, like that low-life piss head I gave a job to last time we were back. He was supposed to be cleaning out the food store lockers. I found him going through our log. The bloody log no less, what a nerve. I'm sure he was checking the volumes of our previous ice cube deliveries. What was his name?" Shaun asked, but suddenly remembered, so answered his own question.

"Carlos wasn't it? Little nosey drunk shit head, Jan Carlos was his name."

"Juan Carlos I think it's pronounced," corrected Maria.

"Whatever it was, I think he pretended to be intoxicated. I don't understand why he would want to do that? Anyway, I sent him away with a flea in his ear, or more precisely, a few strong words resonating inside them. No, I'd rather do it myself, besides, we have a short break when we get back if I remember rightly, before the next favourable planetary alignment will give us the shortest intercept route back out here again." Shaun looked thoughtful for a few seconds staring between his legs. What surprises were waiting below the grating under his soft soled boots he pondered?

"Wonder how the others are getting on?" Maria asked.

"Just thinking the same thing, let's find out," he said, swinging about in his chair so he was now facing the back of the small cockpit.

Shaun expertly flicked a couple of switches before pressing a button. While the button was depressed he spoke. *"The Phoebe* to *The Amelia,* come in *Amelia.* Are you there Bjorn?" he released the button. There was a short pause before the scratched monitor screen flickered into life. Somewhere a hidden speaker crackled.

"Hi Shaun. Bjorn here, how are you and Maria?" Shaun could just about make out Bjorn's face through static interference.

"We're both fine here Bjorn. This is a very bad reception. You must be quite close to the planet. We're all finished now. All that's left is to secure our load. How near are you to completion?"

"We managed to find some slightly larger ice blocks by venturing further into the rings which have helped shorten the build time for our cube. As I said the other day when we spoke, we are still a bit behind schedule. Another twelve hours should see us complete our ice block. Then we can be on our way. I spoke to Soren and Daniela on *The Lily* a few hours ago. They were already on their way to the rally point out by the Enceladus moon then, so they should have arrived by now. Looks like you will both be waiting for us, sorry about that," he said apologetically.

"Can't be helped Bjorn, shame you lost a few days when Lenka trapped her hand in the waste shute breaking two fingers, you did well to catch up and still only be twelve hours behind us now!" Shaun exclaimed.

"Well, we should still make the launch window at the rally point in…" There was a slight pause before Bjorn, reading from a small instrument, continued. "Thirteen hours and forty-four minutes twenty-one seconds, according to my calculations."

"Cutting it a bit fine there Bjorn, but sounds good to me. Give our regards and best wishes to Lenka. We'll see you at the rally point about two hours from departure. Call if there are any problems."

"Thanks, I will pass on your good wishes, see you all soon," replied Bjorn, signing off as the monitor died.

"Well, there we go. We'll go and join *The Lily* at the rally point where we will have at least eleven hours to kill before *The Amelia* joins us. Our optimum launch window can't be hurried. We'll have loads of time to wash and brush up, have a nice relaxed meal. I've got that special bottle of Fire Spirit I've been saving for a special occasion. I think now's the time to crack that open," concluded Shaun licking his lips.

"And, who knows were that may lead us," added Maria, breaking out into a wicked grin. Shaun grinned back knowingly.

"I like it when it all works out nicely. We had better get our little ice cube secure for the journey as quick as we can then. Then we can scoot over to Enceladus before settling down for a nice cosy few hours," Shaun said, now with a sense of expectant urgency in his voice.

With careful guidance from Maria, who was by far the better pilot out of the two of them, *The Phoebe* found the exact centre point of the ice block they had constructed. The spacecraft moved in to within a few millimetres before a laser melted the ice directly in front of the ten metre square blunt nose of the slowly manoeuvring vessel, making a fast bonding as the melted ice re-froze the instant they touched.

They fired harpoons attached to long straps out of all four sides of the small vessel. The long barbed points struck deep into the ice at a shallow angle. Tightening down the straps pulling all four sides of the rough cube equally, the load was finally secure for the journey back to Mars. Using the small side thrusters, they slowly made headway out to the rally point near the Enceladus moon, shunting the massive ice cube in front of them.

Visually blind, hidden behind the ice, they relied on instrumentation to put their vessel just seven kilometres away from *The Lily*. Their giant three kilometre square ice cubes separated by one kilometre of empty space.

"*The Phoebe* to *The Lily*, anyone home, Soren, Daniela?" Shaun enquired. There was a long wait before the monitor flickered into life. The picture quality here was vastly improved now they were away from the interfering planetary mass of Saturn.

"Hi Shaun, sorry to keep you, we were just having a little well-earned nap," said Daniela with a yawn, whilst pulling a loose gown tighter around her.

"Oh, so sorry Daniela, sorry to interrupt your sleep, we are planning on doing the same ourselves after a quick bite to eat. Just wanted to check in with you, let you know we are on your port side ready to go."

"Thanks for letting us know Shaun, how are Bjorn and Lenka?"

"They're nearly finished. They said they will be with us in time for our return launch which will be in just under nine hours by my quick reckoning," replied Shaun, checking his watch.

"Okay. I'm going back to bed now. I'll wake you later in five, maybe six hours," smiled Daniela before she cut the connection.

Shaun turned to Maria. "Right, I'm going to power down the console, just leave comms channels and short-range scanners operational," he said, starting to switch the console instruments off one by one.

"Okay, in that case I'm going to our quarters and start cleaning up," said Maria, unzipping her overalls while stepping out of the cockpit and into the corridor. She let them fall to the floor and stepped out of them. Now just dressed in her bra and knickers, she stooped to pick up the grubby brown work clothes.

"These are going straight into re-cycle!" she exclaimed rolling them up into a ball. Pulling on a handle opened a small receptacle drawer leading to a dark chute. Dropping the garment in the open drawer, it disappeared out of sight. She shut the receptacle with a bang, then, brushed her hands together to mimic that was well and truly the end of them.

"Don't be long," she shouted over her shoulder. Maria marched off down the very short corridor before climbing down the extremely small ladder that led to the lower floor living quarters. Everything was short or small on this vessel she muttered to herself, it'll be nice to get back to Mars where there was a bit more room to stretch out a bit.

15

The Mars Facilities Controller

Toby knocked on the door gently, waited a few moments before opening the way into a spacious office, spacious for a place where every square centimetre needed to justify its reason for not being utilised.

To James however it appeared to be quite small, especially as it was the office used by the most senior person on Mars. Perhaps it appeared small due to the overly large desk with six chairs around it he thought. Inside they were greeted by a very smartly dressed woman. She had short black hair topping a heart-shaped face. Wearing apparently no make-up, she still managed to look vibrant with bright, full lips. Her piercing grey eyes topped off a complexion that offered no hint of any age lines. James was surprised, suddenly he realised he was attracted to the older, more mature woman. He felt a little embarrassed.

"Gentlemen, how are you? A pleasant journey I trust?" she enquired, as they dropped their carryall bags on the floor away from the doorway.

"May I introduce you all," interrupted Toby before they could begin to answer. He wanted to get back to his own control room. It seemed a long time ago since he left. He also had other reasons to get out of the controller's office as quickly as was humanly possible, things had not gone well with the science officer from Ganymede.

"This is the Facilities Controller Carmen Applegate. Carmen, this is Chief Analyst Robert Goodyear and grade two Analyst James Cleaver. Now, if you would excuse me, I would like to return to my control post," said Toby, hastily turning for the door.

"Erm, Toby, I know I asked you to meet our guests which has taken up a considerable amount of your time, but can I ask you to spare just a few more moments. I know you are conscious for the safety of the people of Mars, but I have a couple of questions about your report."

She tapped a flat glass monitor screen on her desk with a long slim pencil before indicating to the chairs where they should all make themselves comfortable.

James gave a quick glance around the room as he lowered himself into a chair. Interspersed with two diminutive square windows there were several small pictures dotted around the walls. All were landscape pictures of Earth, wooded valleys, streams and mountains. He noted that throughout all of them there was not a single human in sight. The controller must be an outdoorsy type who must be extremely homesick, but didn't like other people very much he analysed. The two windows overlooked the complex. Through one he could just make out the landing fields in the distance.

Toby reluctantly flopped himself into the chair nearest the door. He looked expectantly across the desk.

"Toby, you interviewed Leila Santos for over twelve hours, I say interviewed, but it sounds more like you interrogated her. She wants to lodge a formal complaint. She says you held her in a locked room, didn't allow her to use toilet conveniences and even refused her fluids for some considerable time. Can you explain yourself?" Carmen demanded.

"Well, there was no supporting evidence to her story. The memory sticks she supposedly retrieved from her colleague were completely fried. Her explanation for the explosion that destroyed them, killing her colleague in the process, seemed a bit implausible too. How they constructed one charge out of several seismic charges to kill a nine to ten foot tall alien. Then there were the grainy, almost impossible to see pictures, they transmitted to *Crystal Star*, it all seemed a bit feeble," explained Toby. There was a short silence. Carmen was obviously still waiting for a more meaningful explanation. So Toby continued. "How do we know she didn't make the whole thing up? What's to say she wasn't responsible for a major fatal accident? Perhaps she totally flipped, contracted deep-space madness." He rotated a single finger by the side of his temple to emphasise the notion she was loopy.

"Maybe she suffered a rare psychotic state which resulted in her killing both her fellow team members in some mad fit of rage. Then she concocts this story to cover her tracks, aliens indeed!" Toby snorted, before finally adding "I didn't want some space-mad lunatic running round the Facilities, not on my watch."

Carmen opened a drawer in the desk, carefully extracted the half-metre long alien knife which she threw onto the desk with a clatter, scattering papers. All three men were suddenly startled, causing them to back up in their seats.

"How do you explain this then?" Carmen was angry now.

"She could have made it in the workshop, lost her mind and used it to kill the other two scientists, there's dried blood all over it." Toby's voice quivered slightly. It was obvious he was trying to convince himself more than anyone.

"I had the blood from the blade analysed by the Mars laboratories. Oh, there was human blood alright, but there are other fluids too, some of the fluids they couldn't explain, DNA they have never encountered before, totally non-human, certainly alien blood." She shook her head slowly. "Anyway, I've managed to placate Leila for now. I think you had better tell her you're sorry and ask her forgiveness. Pray that she doesn't press charges that you infringed her rights, also, I'd like to remind you this matter is completely top secret. " She referred to the knife that lay in the middle of the desk. After pausing for a couple of seconds in thought, she glanced at her watch. "It's getting late now, I expect our guests are hungry and tired. I presume they would also like to unwind after their ordeals of the day so I'll make this brief. Toby, tomorrow morning once you have made your peace with Leila Santos, can you ask her to join us here for nine sharp please." Carmen looked down at the desk as she dismissed Toby with a flip of her hand.

Once Toby had left the office Robert leant forward to pick up the alien knife. He was itching to examine it in closer detail.

"Gosh, it's so light and thin," he said, turning the serrated blade three hundred and sixty degrees before passing it to James. James couldn't quite believe it, according to all the facts and unfaultable logic, he was now holding a true alien artefact.

"I had the scientists analyse the metal too. According to their report, it is lighter and stronger than titanium. A compound unknown to them and certainly not any type of metal alloy found in this solar system," explained Carmen.

"Ouch!" James shouted out, as blood started oozing from a razor cut on his left thumb.

"It's also very, very sharp," stated Carmen, holding out her hands to take back the weapon.

"I shall now give you a quick tour of this dome's amenities, canteens, etcetera. We'll start at your quarters where you can dump your gear. I suggest we reconvene here tomorrow at eight. I'll bring you up to speed with the latest developments.

Then you can talk to Leila at nine. *Lode Drifter* is due in the day after tomorrow in the afternoon. We shall debrief the crew as soon as their feet touch ground. I expect you would like to be there for that too?" concluded Carmen.

Robert and James both nodded to emphasise their acknowledgement.

—

The following morning found both the analysts sitting in a small cafeteria a few corridors away from their quarters. A large digital clock hanging on the wall above their heads was showing seven minutes past seven. The minute indicator switched to eight silently. They had helped themselves to various breakfast food items from self service cabinets which they were now tucking into with hungry enthusiasm. Both had slept very soundly, their first proper full night's sleep since leaving Earth. It seemed to have given them voracious appetites. Neither spoke until every morsel had been devoured.

"Well I enjoyed that, I must say," said Robert, pushing his plate away.

"Me too, it must be something to do with the environment, maybe some after effects of the Dormouse Torpor State?" James replied questioningly.

"No. I've never been that hungry before. I've been in the Dormouse Torpor State many times and although you feel hungry soon after revival, that feeling soon passes once you can keep some food down. Perhaps it's the reduced gravity?" Robert suggested.

He smiled at some overall-clad men and women at the next table who had taken an interest in the strangers ever since they had sat down. They whispered between themselves obviously speculating. At that moment they all laughed and sniggered at a muffled comment made by a woman who appeared to have an uncontrollable mop of blonde hair. Robert dropped his smile. He figured correctly that the joke was at their expense.

"Perhaps it's something in the water?" James offered staring into his empty mug. He was oblivious that they were the butt of some tease made by the crowd at the next table. "Have you noticed the water? It's got a peculiar strange bluish tint to it. More tea?" he asked standing up.

Robert offered his empty mug over in an affirmative response, trying to ignore the grinning faces he glimpsed out the corner of his eye.

—

It hadn't taken them long to work out directions to the Facilities Controller's office. Soon they were outside her door just before eight o'clock. Robert politely knocked before entering the room. After some pleasant small talk about their breakfast they took their places round the desk.

"Right, where shall we start? Mr. Landry, I suppose, as he started the ball rolling so to speak, inadvertently of course." Carmen opened a drawer in her desk and produced a small silver metal dish. Inside were two very small objects just over half a centimetre long. She explained how they had been found the miniature metal maggot like robots during the autopsy.

Placing the dish on the desk, she handed over a small magnifying glass. "This might help," she said, offering over the visual aid. They took turns to study the legless micro robots through the glass lens.

"We are not sure what the little pins are, they were found in and around Mr. Landry's left ear. Some were even inside the ear canal."

"I can't be sure, but I would suggest they were once legs

that have now become detached. They appear to be hinged," suggested James.

"These might give a better idea." Carmen produced a set of images on paper that had been magnified several hundred times showing them at different angles.

They could now quite clearly see the rows of circular teeth. More importantly they could make out little stumps along the sides of the main body. Some of the pins resembled the hind legs of a dog being bent in the middle.

"I think you're right James, they would have needed some form of mobility to get from the holes they had made in the suit, up to his head. They were then discarded as the little metal creatures entered the body in through the ear, there's no doubt in my mind," offered Robert.

"Hmmm, definitely constructed by intelligent life forms," remarked James stating the obvious. "And these were actually removed from inside Mr. Landry?" Robert grimaced as he said the words.

"Yes, at least one of them from the base of the brain stem where it meets the spinal column to be precise. It had made a bit of a mess inside almost severing the column in the process," replied Carmen. She paused before continuing. "Only a few people know about these, we wanted to keep it quiet. There's the resident doctor and surgeon Miss Rebecca Jones, who happens to be a personal friend of mine. She carried out the autopsy and can be relied on one hundred percent. Then there was my communication back to the Corporation that prompted your mobilization and hasty departure from Earth. Obviously some of the Corporation board members will know back there."

"You didn't tell Toby? It might have saved the twelve-hour interrogation of Leila."

"Toby is very good at his job, but that's the main problem, sometimes, he is too good. He would have logged it all down, his reports are very meticulous, and, I am ashamed to say, the security on this base is just so rubbish, especially our central computer. We've tried all sorts of encryption software. It works for a short while, but then when the rumours start we know someone, somehow, has compromised our security once more. I decided to keep this very quiet until you got here. However, for the holes in his suit, we couldn't create a rational explanation. Too many of the rescue party had seen them so there are a myriad of speculative ideas about how he died being bandied about."

"I can't believe Toby is still so sceptical. The facts as far as I can see all point to a logical conclusion, that there is an alien life form present in our solar system that use these little metal things to kill people. Thing is, what are they doing here? What is there purpose? As they haven't yet made contact with us so far, I fear they do not have honourable intentions," concluded Robert.

There came a muffled knock at the door. Carmen quickly put the dish of micro robots back into her drawer as the door opened. Toby led Leila across the threshold.

"Why am I being treated like a prisoner?" Leila demanded, holding out her handcuffed wrists. Toby undid the lock and removed them. Leila rubbed her wrists scowling at him.

"I am sorry, but until we can corroborate your report, we cannot let you loose to run about the base scaring everyone with stories about aliens. Besides, it works both ways, you could say we are protecting you," Carmen said calmly.

"Protecting me! Who from exactly? Him?" she pointed a finger at Toby.

"I think that'll be all for now, Toby, if you could leave a guard outside the door…"

Toby cut in before Carmen could finish. "I'll be doing that job myself, just shout if you need my assistance," he said.

"Wait a minute, I think he should stay," blurted out Robert, before Toby made two steps towards the door. They all stopped to gaze at him.

"He is head of security after all. I think he should know everything now, I think the security of the Mars Facilities is at risk, if not immediately, at some time in the near future," stated Robert.

"Well, the Corporation sent you to advise me, I guess I should take that advice now you are here. Toby, please take a seat."

Once they were all seated, at a suggestion from Robert, Leila recounted the story of her ordeal on Ganymede, the demise of her fellow scientific colleagues, the fight with the alien on the surface, her escape via the emergency lifeboat rocket and eventual return on *Crystal Star*. She skipped the parts where they argued, fought amongst themselves, even Trevor with his ideas of making a small fortune out of the situation. That didn't seem important now.

"Well, that is some story. I can understand how Toby had trouble believing it. It does sound a bit farfetched…" Robert was interrupted by Leila.

"What was the point of this exercise then? You don't believe me either, why make me go through it all again re-living the whole shitty, sorry tale once more!" she screamed out, before burying her head in her hands.

"Oh, but that's the problem, I DO believe you," he said, sounding very genuine. Leila raised her head from her cupped hands to stare straight at Robert.

"You do?" she enquired, sounding relieved.

"Oh yes. No doubt about it. There have been other actions to substantiate your situation of events."

Even Toby took more of an interest now. Other events? Was there something he hadn't been told about? How could they keep anything from him? He was supposed to be in charge of security!

"Carmen, can we see the little bugs again, please?" Robert asked. Carmen extracted the dish from her drawer once more.

"Did you see anything like these?" Robert took the dish, thrusting it towards Leila along with the pictures. Leila leafed through them before examining the contents on the dish.

"No. No, I didn't see anything like these," she finally concluded.

"Mmmm, just as well, perhaps they had run out of working versions. Probably just as well for you if they had, these have a nasty habit of ending up at the top of your spine with an insatiable appetite for nerve endings."

Robert passed the dish to Toby who was almost falling off his chair, straining to get a closer look. Carmen related once more how they were removed from Mr. Landry for Leila and Toby's benefit.

"Plus we have the strange happenings with *Lode Drifter*," interjected James. Toby looked up from his examination of the micro robots.

"We put out a story that they had had an explosion on board," stated Carmen.

"And the real reason being?" Toby pleaded.

"They were holed by some torpedo like projectile that passed straight through the hull like, and I quote one of the crew here, it was made of butter. What's unusual is that the exit hole was a perfect circle, same size as the entry hole," explained Carmen.

"Logic suggests very strongly that if had some means of cutting its way through the vessel, that it is NOT a naturally occurring object, therefore, it was constructed by intelligent beings as yet unknown. Except that now we know they are between nine and ten foot high," added Robert, smiling at Leila.

"Any ideas what the projectiles are exactly?" Carmen looked at Robert and James for some sort of explanation.

"We have a theory, but would like to discuss the encounter with the mining crew first, before offering a plausible explanation. Did you say they return to Mars tomorrow?" James asked.

Carmen picked up her small mobile communications unit off the desk. She was soon talking to one of the traffic controllers.

"Latest we have is sixteen hundred hours twenty minutes tomorrow ma'am," was the reply to her enquiry. She thanked the operator before severing the link, and then passed on the information to those in the room.

They continued to discuss all the incidents that had happened before breaking for lunch. Carmen was worried that she wasn't going to be able to keep all the facts secret for much longer, especially now that Toby was aware of all the intricate details. What with the return of *Lode Drifter* the following day, perhaps she should start to prepare a statement to issue to the whole facility. She would get onto it after they had eaten. Lunch was now top priority.

16

Blake and Leila

Blake was concealed in a pool of semi-darkness. He was lurking in the shadow of a corridor support cross beam, waiting, deciding what to do next. It was officially night time inside the Mars Facilities.

Mars was too far away from the Sun to have a real sunrise or sunset. The occupants of the facility buildings had to settle on an artificial twenty-four hour cycle simulating a normal Earth day. At 'night' the lights would be dimmed in the corridors and halls, even the perimeter security arc lights surrounding the facility buildings were turned down. They would become increasingly dimmer as the artificial 'night' wore on, only to return to normal brightness when the 'night' was over and 'dawn' arrived.

It was the idea of an eminent sociologist at the time, who figured it would stop people working themselves into the ground. It would help define time for the Martian personnel who were constantly living in a somewhat timeless society, allowing them to structure their working day, and nightly sleeping patterns. It had also been proven to help keep everyone relatively sane into the bargain.

Just to make sure most people had some undisturbed time

preferably sleeping, everything, except the furnaces, shut down between one and four in the 'morning'. Even the Social Village bars had to close too. All night drinking was not endorsed. Mining ships returning during the shutdown hours would have to wait in orbit until the 'day' began. Residents, miners, foundry workers and even visitors were politely requested to remain in their quarters during this sabbatical three hour period.

It was just after two in the 'morning' when Blake was out running the unofficial curfew. If he were to be found lurking away from his own quarters there would be more than a few questions to be answered. Leila's apartment was just around the next corner but there was a hitch, there was a security camera between him and her door.

'Very clever,' he deliberated. She no longer appeared to be under house arrest as they had removed the twenty-four hour guard. However, the front entrance to the temporary accommodation they had given her was directly in the line of sight of a camera as it scanned the corridor. He could be sure of one thing, of the few people to be up and about at this unearthly hour, there would be several security officers checking monitors hooked up to all the security cameras.

He would have to disable it even though they would be sure to investigate. It would be too much of a coincidence for the camera to go on the blink just outside such a currently high profile person's abode. How long would he have before they came knocking? He wasn't sure what the time response would be, it was a risk he would have to take.

The corridor ceiling was low, low enough for Blake to reach up at full stretch to disconnect the wire out the back of the camera as it panned down the corridor away from him. The functioning red light indicator extinguished as he pulled out the wire. The camera continued its sweeping arc of surveillance. However, all it now relayed was blank fuzz.

Blake used the universal electronic key card given to him by Leon to gain access to the apartment where Leila Santos was sleeping peacefully. The door had made no discernible noise as he entered the main living room. Stealthily he crept across the floor to what he perceived to be the bedroom.

The door to the bedroom was ajar. Carefully, he peered inside. Leila lay on the low bed with a single silky sheet covering her curvaceous naked body. He made a slow deliberate way into the bedroom. Leila, in her sleep, decided to change the side she was sleeping on. As she turned over, the sheet slipped revealing one firm dark skinned breast. The breast nipple hardened now it was exposed to the cool room air.

Blake had stopped in his tracks between the door and the bed feeling quite exposed while Leila resettled herself. Once he was sure she would not wake up, he continued his slow slinky walk towards her.

Soon he was in striking distance allowing him to pounce. One hand clamped over her mouth while the other pinned down her body about the midriff. Leila opened her bulging eyes immediately. Blake tried to reassure her.

"Leila, don't panic, don't shout or scream out, I am a government operative," he spoke softly. Her eyes showed fear and shock, her body wanted to jump up, but was unable to move against her assailant. She wriggled trying to release herself from his clutches. Meanwhile Blake shook his head.

"Please stop struggling so you understand what I am going to say next," he whispered softly. The sheet had slipped all the way down to her waist now exposing her bare upper torso. If the sheet were off her legs she could have tried to kick him in the head, but it wouldn't work with the sheet constricting them. She stopped resisting.

"Your sleeper password is 'Amendoim ainda na casca', do you understand?" Blake whispered using her native Portuguese language. Leila stopped wriggling, she understood all right.

Never did she expect to hear those words uttered to her, especially not in a predicament like this.

"Right, I'm going to remove my hands now. You understand who I am, what I'm doing here and what's required of you?" Leila nodded under his relaxing hand. Shelled peanuts! That brought back distant memories. Her family were very poor back in Brazil when she was growing up. She was bright though, top of her class academically. She had won a scholarship to attend a mainstream university in England, but once there, she found out the real cost of her education.

"Right, now I need you to get a dressing gown on. Presently there will be a knock at the door. It will probably be a two-man security team. You will tell them everything is fine, then, when they are satisfied and go away, we can have a nice, cosy little chat," he instructed.

Whilst attending university, she played along with it at the time, what else could she do? The European Government was paying for her expensive education, and sending money back home to her family. All she had to do was sign a form and give them a secret password, that password had been shelled peanuts. She had adored them at university all those years ago, no chance of getting any here now, too much of a luxury item to ship all the way to Mars.

She could still visualise the nice man wearing a crisp dark suit as he folded up the document she had signed back then. As he slipped it into his inside jacket pocket they explained that sometime in the future, a stranger might come up to her, utter the password, then ask a small favour. It would not be dangerous. It would not involve espionage, nothing underhand like that. The stranger would just require some information, a diagram maybe, an imprint of a key, simple things along those lines. Well, that's what they said then. She had all but forgotten about it, it was such a long time ago. They had enrolled many others, she was sure, but just how many had they recruited through the years? How do they keep tabs on them all? It all seemed to be a bit of a gamble to her as they wouldn't know where the selected people were going to end up working, or how useful they could be in the future. I guess that was a risk they were willing to take.

Her thoughts were interrupted by a loud thumping on the outside door. Blake moved to conceal himself behind the bedroom door. The response was quicker than even he had expected.

"Wait for the next one," advised Blake whispering. Leila climbed out of the bed. She retrieved a previously discarded dressing gown from a dressing table chair, slowly wrapping it round her while waiting for the second thump on the door. Doing up the two ends of the waist cord she made her way to the apartment entrance, running her fingers through her hair like a comb, to flatten any wisps sticking out. Gingerly she put her eye to the glass security fish eye lens. She could plainly see two distorted security guards faces outside. At a push of a button the door opened silently.

"Sorry to wake you Miss Santos, just a routine check, are you okay?" the nearest guard asked, whilst trying to look round her into the apartment. The other went over to the camera to get a closer look. He confirmed that the rear wire was indeed unconnected and hung limp.

"Fine, just fine," stuttered Leila.

"Well, it appears the security camera has been interfered with," he jerked his thumb over his shoulder. "There may be strangers about. If there's any trouble, just press your panic button, we'll be here quicker than a Martian dust storm," he said monotonously, as if he didn't believe she was fine for one minute.

After shutting the door, she proceeded to a cabinet on one side of the living room. Extracting two glasses, she poured out large equal measures of neat Martian vodka. Offering one of the pale blue drinks to Blake, she was just about to speak when Blake put a finger to his lips, indicating she should remain quiet for the moment.

He went to the door to peer out the spy hole. He could make out the two guards meddling with the security camera. One was speaking into a communication device more than likely checking with the guard room. Finally, when they were satisfied they had botched a temporary repair they sauntered off down the corridor chatting idly. Both suddenly stopped, pausing by Leila's apartment. One put his ear to the door, he listened intently. Blake pulled back instinctively. He gave them a couple of moments before looking through the spy hole again. This time the corridor was empty.

Turning round he said, "I think they have finally gone." He took the offered drink almost downing it in one.

"So, is this how it is? Is it? You call in my favour now, then it's all over, I never hear from you again?" Leila enquired.

"Not quite. Being a sleeper is for life, unless you are exposed of course, then we might well leave you alone. Once our enemies know who you are, you then fail to continue to be reliable," explained Blake. "They, and I use the term loosely, any of our enemies could be watching you like a hawk, they may even feed you rubbish Intel to pass onto us," he continued.

"So, what do you want to know?"

"Firstly, in case we get interrupted as they may come back demanding entry with a signed warrant from the Controller, our story is we are old friends from way back. These are my details. Please remember my name at the very least." He passed over a small card. "Then, I would like you to relay your Ganymede story from the very beginning, to your eventual arrival back here, also the events leading right up to this precise point in time," he smiled.

There was a slight pause for a few seconds while Leila composed herself and gathered her thoughts.

"If you would be so kind," he added, wishing her to hurry, but still trying to be civil to this woman he had near frightened to death moments earlier.

Blake wanted to hear every last detail over and over again. He would interrupt every now and then asking Leila to repeat some incident making sure she relayed the smallest details. The death of the alien he wanted her to retell three times before she could finally move on from that painful event.

"… then, you're in my room and here we are," she concluded.

Blake was silent for a while turning the empty glass round in his hand staring at the intricate cut crystal.

He had heard how the foundry workers made these glasses as a hobby. Using fine Martian sand, the heat of the furnaces and then finishing off with a diamond laser. They had become collector's items back on Earth.

Leila got up, took the near empty glass, poured them both another generous measure before handing it back.

"Your story is absolutely fascinating. I wish I had been there. Our first real encounter with an intelligent alien life form that ends up being a blood bath," he sighed.

"Well they didn't come bearing gifts. They attacked us first remember, poor Trevor, we were just defending ourselves!" Leila exclaimed.

"Okay, okay, keep your voice down. I don't disagree with the actions you took, seems like you had no choice really. It would have been nice to try and talk with them though, find out what they wanted, what they were doing there." Blake went all thoughtful again.

"Well, I've told this story a dozen times now, no one has asked my opinion. No one has asked for my thoughts," she said.

"Well, go on then, let's hear it," replied Blake.

"Okay, here goes then." Leila, who had been lounging on

a chair in the middle of the room, now sat upright. She shuffled to the edge of her seat placing her glass on the low coffee table.

"Two alien ships fighting each other must signal some sort of internal power struggle going on in their own camp for starters. Then, there is all the secrecy as you rightly say. They must have been around for years hiding from us, why? Perhaps they are abducting humans for some purpose, a slave work force springs to mind," she paused, while Blake digested this information. She then continued with more explanations.

"Maybe they are just observing us? Perhaps the alien wanted to kill all of us on Ganymede so we couldn't spill the beans on them. It certainly looks like they don't want us to know about them, that's for sure."

"Interesting observations," muttered Blake. "So what now, I wonder," he said to himself out loud. "All this information you imparted to the Facilities Controller, yes?" she nodded in reply. "You said earlier that there were three men in the room this morning, who were they again?"

"One was the head of security, Tobias Hauss. The other two I don't know, never seen them before today," she answered.

Blake described the two Corporation analysts. "That's them," she said. "No doubt about it."

"Well, I think that's all for now, unless you can confirm the mining ship *Lode Drifter* is docking tomorrow? There are so many rumours flying about at the moment. I need positive assurance."

"Yes, she certainly is. About four o'clock tomorrow afternoon. Toby, the security guy and the two Corporation men I met yesterday are going to interview the crew immediately upon landing. That's what they agreed in front of me in the meeting yesterday."

"Good, I'll follow up that lead somehow, but for now, I think I have gleaned all I can from you, thank you very much.

If you don't mind, I shall sit here quietly until 'dawn' when it's safe to move about the base without arousing suspicion. Feel free to go back to bed whenever you want." Blake glanced at his watch which displayed it was three ten, fifty minutes to kill.

"Well, I'm up now. I'm not doing anything tomorrow so we can chat a bit more if you like?" Leila suggested.

"What do you fancy chatting about exactly," he enquired with a hint of curiosity in his voice.

"I want to know how, why I was chosen to be, what did you call it? A sleeper wasn't it. How does all that work? How many are there?"

"Whoa, too many questions all at once. Let me explain the principles behind it, then maybe you'll understand."

Blake went on to describe how young talented individuals were spotted coming up through different country's education systems. If suitable, they were given a helping hand, as it were, to realise their true potential. In return they were put into the sleeper network where they could repay the European Government at some unknown point in the future, a repayment for the financial aid for their families and schooling.

"… one good turn deserves another so they say, eh?" he concluded.

Leila was surprised to learn there were at least another three sleepers on Mars at that very moment. In what seemed like an instant, the fifty minutes had flown by. Blake rechecked the corridor through the fish eye. All was clear as far as he could see.

"Adios," he called out, opening the door. He slipped out into the now brightly-lit corridor indicating 'dawn' had arrived. Looking at the camera he noted the red light on top of the camera was visible, it was working and pointed straight at him. He smiled into the lens before turning the corner to come face to face with Toby. There were the two security guards from over an hour ago, one either side of him. Blake stopped short with a start.

"Now then, what have we got here? I don't remember seeing you about before, new to Mars are you? Hold out you hand so the chip scanner can read your personal details." Toby's voice boomed down the corridor, enough to make the most hardened person cringe. Blake held out his hand without hesitation. This surprised Toby who was of the opinion the stranger might try to run, or even put up a fight.

"Just came in yesterday on *Oceans Dawn*. I was looking up an old friend from years back, Leila Santos. She's just been telling me she's had a bit of a hard time of it these last few days." During Leila's story, she had mentioned the interrogation by Toby, now he wanted Toby to know that he knew. The chip scanner readout came up with the bone fide miner identity Blake was utilising as currently looking for work on Mars. Blake confirmed the fake identity.

Toby was now on the defensive. He knew that this miner had just been in Leila's apartment. By rights Leila should still be on her yearlong assignment. How did he know she was now on Mars? During her dramatic escape from Ganymede in the lifeboat, she would not have been able to contact anyone. He supposed she could have got a message off from *Crystal Star* before going into the Dormouse Torpor State, but that too, was highly unlikely.

"Don't mind if we check with the lady," Toby said, twirling his finger in the air indicating that Blake should turn about one hundred and eighty degrees. They called on Leila who confirmed she knew Blake by his miner's identity, Toby had no option other than let him go. Bright girl thought Blake, quick on the uptake, they were right to make her a sleeper.

Toby sensed this was all wrong, but without any proof, he could not detain this jobless miner. Blake smiled to himself as he scurried off back to his own quarters.

17

The Ice Gatherers

Shaun and Maria lay naked on their large double cradle. Maria purred softly drifting in and out of a light sleep. Shaun ran his finger from Maria's shoulder down her arm right to her waist. He traced the deep dip at her waistline then up over her hip onto her thigh where he had to stop, having reached the full extent of his arm. He then repeated the process enjoying the intimacy of the action. Sometimes he would linger in one particular place tracing circles for a few seconds before continuing down her soft skin until he could reach no further.

Sometimes his finger would deviate from the same course to slip down to Maria's breast where he would trace round her nipple a few times before returning to the outline of her body.

The Phoebe, one of three Saturn ice tugboats, was waiting to depart on the long journey back to Mars. They were in the orbit of the Enceladus moon. Next to them *The Lily* was in a similar orbit, both vessels were waiting for the third tugboat, *The Amelia*, to join them. Each of the crews had created one huge block of ice containing roughly three billion litres of water. The enormous frozen ice cube had been extracted from the vast rings of Saturn.

All they had to do now was transport them back to Mars.

They were waiting for a specific launch window that would give them the most direct route to intercept their final destination, the Mars Facilities.

Even with the most optimum route, it would still take three long months. Once they were underway, they would put themselves into the Dormouse Torpor State, a state of almost suspended animation for the duration of the voyage. Just before primary ignition they would be turning off the artificial gravity gyros to give maximum thrust to the fusion engines.

Maria opened her eyes to stare at Shaun. "That feels so nice, so relaxing," she said.

"You make me feel so nice too. That was some meal, what was it again, odds and sods you called it," he laughed.

"Just everything that was unfrozen in the fridge with some added spices, a bit of this and a bit of that, all chucked in a pan, fried up with some reconstituted freeze dried rice, easy really. Perhaps it was the Jupiter Fire Spirit that made it taste better," she giggled, still feeling light headed.

"Hmmm maybe, it is strong stuff," agreed Shaun. "Made from the very water we collect here and distilled back on Mars. Problem is, we have to purge it from our bodies before the Dormouse Torpor State, otherwise it'll pickle our livers on the long journey home," he laughed.

"Well, once we are under way we could come back here for a while, work it off in a sweat, you know how much fun it is to make love in zero gravity," suggested Maria with a grin. She edged closer so their loins touched. This provoked an instant response from Shaun whose penis started to swell once more with anticipation.

"Why wait until then," said Shaun, as his hands now started to caress her body. "Oh crap!" he suddenly exclaimed, as a light above the cradle started flashing accompanied by a low ear-penetrating single musical note.

It was not a loud noise, just irritating enough to make you have to get up to answer the communications system just to stop it. Shaun lost his erection almost immediately.

"If that's Daniela I'm gonna have a few harsh words, we've only been here a couple of hours, she said she would call us in five to start the preliminary countdown procedures," said Shaun furiously.

He jumped up as Maria pulled a pillow over her head trying to deaden the noise. "Hurry up, that damn noise is giving me a headache," she shouted, but it came out muffled from under the pillow.

It only took Shaun a few moments to drag on his underwear and make his way up the ladder to the confines of the cockpit. He answered the incoming call.

"Thanks for nothing Dan.... Oh it's you Bjorn, we were just asleep. How are things going? Problems?"

"Sorry to disturb you Shaun. No problems here, we still have a couple of hour's work left. However, we thought we ought to let you know, we've picked up something on our long-range scanners. There are several long small objects coming our way. Can we get a three-way conference going with *The Lily*?" Bjorn asked.

"Affirmative, I turned our long range off when I powered down the console," replied Shaun. He hit the internal communications link.

"Maria darling, you might want to get up here, some weird things are happening. We might need to move the spacecraft," he said quickly, agitation in his voice.

Bjorn continued. "We guessed you would power down, standard procedure and all that. That's why we had to disturb you. *The Phoebe* to *The Lily*, Soren, are you there?" Shaun's screen now split showing both images of Soren and Bjorn.

"Soren here, just caught the end of that, I'm switching our long-range scanners on now. Let's see what you've seen," he said.

The Lily's onboard scanner monitor flickered to life. Shaun had also powered up *The Phoebe's* scanners too. They all confirmed a set of objects were headed in their general direction.

"Okay, if we can triangulate our three scans, we can work out a more accurate idea of speed and direction," said Bjorn.

"Transmitting now," said Shaun, after hooking up the scanner readouts with the communications device.

"And likewise," came the voice of Soren. There was a short pause before Bjorn broke the silence.

"I've got to recalculate these figures, I can't believe they are moving that fast!" he exclaimed. There was another, longer pause, before Bjorn spoke once more. "Well, they are slowing down slightly, but still moving at an incredible speed. They will be on short-range scanners in about two minutes."

Maria walked into the cockpit room. She had found a baggy t-shirt and a clean pair of hot pant type shorts that extenuated her natural curves. Normally Shaun would have made a suggestive comment, but now was not the time. This time his mind was fully occupied with the strange objects headed towards them.

"What happens then?" asked Soren. "At that speed we don't have a lot of options. Once they hit the short-range scanners we'll have under a minute to check the exact course, if we are in their way, we've had it. Chances of one of them hitting one of the tugboats though are very, very small, but the ice blocks, they pose a bigger target," explained Bjorn.

"Perhaps we should release the cubes?" Shaun suggested.

"Sorry, I don't think we really have enough time for that. We'll just have to sit it out," he replied.

"Let's hope Enceladus helps to shield us," said Soren.

"Here they come, onto the short-range scanners... now," there was a short pause before the twelve objects appeared on all three spacecrafts scanner monitors.

"Right, I'm sorry to say it looks like the two of you we will be in the firing line for at least three of them, whatever they are. One is on course for the moon itself. Looks like they are spread out in a line about a kilometre apart," Bjorn observed. "We appear to be too far away to be affected here," he added.

"Oh crap!" Shaun shouted for the second time. "This could get very messy!"

"About thirty seconds before they hit the ice blocks. Two are definitely on course for *The Lily*, and one for *The Phoebe*. They are coming in at an angle hitting the top starboard sides of both cubes."

Shaun and Maria had not been idle while Bjorn had been performing his calculations and keeping up the running commentary on the objects telemetry. They had the main control console up and running so all the instruments were aglow in the semi-dark cabin, and currently in the process of retracting the harpoons.

"Are the thrusters online?" Maria asked.

"They will be in two shakes. Do you want to heat the nose and detach us from the ice?"

Maria considered this option for a second. "Let's be ready. I don't want to lose all our hard work just yet. It depends on the outcome of the impact, if we could just hang on to the majority of the ice somehow."

"Okay, your call Maria. Just shout the orders when you want something doing."

"Less than ten seconds. Good luck," called out Bjorn.

The twelve cylinders would have been just a quick blur to the naked eye, except no naked eye was there to see them. They had been designed to vaporize anything in their path, cutting their way through all known materials. Ice would pose no problem however thick it was, including five hundred kilometre diameter moons that were primarily solid ice. All the tugboat crew members were still anticipating the hit several seconds after the cylinders had passed through the ice blocks and the Enceladus moon. They were waiting for some sign of the impact.

"What's happening?" shouted Soren in frustration, still expecting the strike to shake *The Lily*.

"They've gone, that's what's happened," said Bjorn confused, but relieved. "It looks like they just passed completely through everything without touching the sides."

"That's impossible. They must have missed us altogether then?" Shaun suggested. All of them checked their monitors.

"No, some of them went straight through somehow, even the one that passed right through Enceladus. I'm still tracking twelve objects, now receding away from us. Each one is about fifteen centimetres in diameter and about four metres long at a rough guess."

"That can't be right? We've had rocks smaller than that hit the ice before. They do a fair amount of damage, sometimes moving us off course. I expected fractures at the very least with the speed they were travelling," said an exasperated Soren.

"Well I can only report what the instruments tell me," retaliated Bjorn.

"Okay, let's calm down here." Shaun butted in. It looked like the pointless argument was starting to spiral out of control.

"There's one way to make sure, find out exactly what happened," suggested Maria. She indicated what she was thinking by walking her two front fingers across the upturned palm of her other hand.

"Yes!" Shaun exclaimed after noticing the gesture. "That's a good idea. Okay people, I'm going for a little space walk while we wait for *The Amelia* to join us here."

"Your call Shaun, good luck. We'll be over as soon as we have finished here," said Bjorn severing the contact. Bjorn's face disappeared from the monitor leaving Soren staring at Shaun.

"Need a hand?" he asked. Shaun thought about it for a moment. "It's up to you. I guess you must be as curious as I am then?" Shaun answered with a question.

"You guessed it! See you outside!" Soren exclaimed laughing out loud, with relief more than anything now the danger had passed.

The airlock on *The Phoebe* was to the rear of the cockpit across the corridor. Shaun was inside within seconds after signing off with Soren on *The Lily*. He grabbed his suit and helmet and put it on. It wasn't long before he was breathing from his spacesuit's life support system air supply. Checking the pressure gauges and the heaters were okay, he was ready to decompress the lock.

Once outside, Shaun opened a hatch to a storage compartment. He retrieved a high pressure gas fuelled jet backpack which he carefully pulled over his head. It clipped onto two anchor points on the rear of his suit. A control unit was connected to the backpack by a long, thin cable. Putting the unit in the palm of his left hand, he grabbed the joystick in the middle of the control unit with two fingers and thumb of his right hand. He tested the direction toggles like an airline pilot would test the plane's flaps before take-off. Satisfied he finally pressed down on the joystick.

Gas jets erupted from the direction toggles. Within a split second he had corrected his forward motion flying along the side of the cube of ice, making his way to the topmost right corner. In the distance he could just make out the shape of *The Lily*. When he got to the top corner of the cube he expertly reversed his direction of flight coming to a dead stop. Then he waited. Across the kilometre void between the two three kilometre square cubes, he eventually saw a small silver suited shape heading towards him. Soren was at full throttle thought Shaun. Slowly the figure grew in size until it slowed to a stop in front of him. They faced each other helmet to helmet.

"Glad you could make it," he said. "Came as fast as I could," came the jolly reply. They set off together making their way along the starboard side of *The Phoebe's* cube.

"Bjorn said about halfway down didn't he?" Soren asked.

"Yes. Must be around here somewhere," replied Shaun.

"Ever thought this could be like looking for a diamond in a bucket of ice?" suggested Soren.

"Hmmm, I didn't think it would be this difficult, let's go back and try looking from the leading edge."

It took half a dozen passes back and forth before they found what they were looking for, a small round hole you could just about put a clenched fist into.

"Will you look at that?" Soren exclaimed adding a low whistle. "A perfectly formed round tunnel right through the ice block," added Shaun as he pulled a laser torch out of a small pocket in his suit trousers. He flipped on the pencil sized device giving out a straight green light.

"Let's get an accurate direction," he said, shining the light down through the round hole. When he was satisfied that he had an almost straight line with the laser light and the sides of the tunnel he squeezed the instrument tight in his gloved hand. Instantly the co-ordinate readings were relayed back to Maria on board *The Phoebe*.

"Looks like Bjorn was right, straight through clean as a whistle," he explained to Maria.

"We better get back now Soren. We've seen all we can see here which wasn't very much or very helpful, apart from confirming the exact direction of the objects. I'll check the bearings when I get back, maybe it can tell us where the strange objects are headed."

"Okay Shaun, I'll check in with you when I get back aboard *The Lily*," said Soren, turning to jet off in one swift movement.

Once he had returned to *The Phoebe*, Shaun was back

inside the cockpit checking the direction readings he had taken along with the rough readings taken using the scanners. Coming to a satisfactory conclusion, he made his log entry before contacting the other two vessels.

"Okay you guys listen up," he announced, once communication had been established with both the others.

"Perhaps Bjorn can confirm my calculations later. I have worked out those strange objects are headed out towards a point that will intersect the orbit of Pluto. They will take about five weeks to get there at a rough estimate," concluded Shaun.

"Pluto!" Bjorn seemed surprised, obviously confused by the readings. "Why Pluto, what in heaven's name is there?"

"Huh, who knows, I guess I'd better send a report to the authorities on Mars before we depart. I'll get on with it shortly. Just a reminder that we need to start departure procedures in one hundred and four minutes, Bjorn, you going to be here by then?"

"Yes Shaun, we will be securing the load in just a moment. We will be over to join you as quick as we can in the next hour," Bjorn replied.

"Righto, see you soon. Soren, we'll re-establish contact in one hundred minutes exactly to start the countdown procedure," said Shaun.

"It won't be a moment too soon, I can't stand this hanging around before we launch," replied Soren.

Shaun quickly wrote up a brief synopsis of the encounter with the mysterious objects, he documented his short space walk to discover the perfectly round tunnel right through the ice, and concluded with the speed and direction and his own analysis of the calculated destination. Finally he compressed the encrypted message before sending the completed package on a fairly short carrier wave.

An hour and a half later, three giant ice cubes were lined

up abreast of each other. The small ice tugboats looked very insignificant against the huge blue-tinged white expanse of frozen water in front of each one.

It was the turn of *The Amelia* to be the lead spacecraft on this return journey. Bjorn was in control of the departure launch phase. After concluding several minutes of pre-flight checks they were ready.

"Right, here we go, thirty seconds to primary ignition. Artificial gravity now offline," Bjorn commanded. The three pilots, Bjorn, Maria and Soren simultaneously pushed small buttons on their consoles. Now strapped into their cockpit seats, all six people on the three vessels heard the gravity gyros whine down. As they did so, the occupants became instantly lighter, their shoulders now strained against the full body harness straps of their seats.

"Fuel cells check at sixty percent plus, approaching launch window now in eighteen seconds. Last check that all loads are secure for launch, confirm."

This task was for the secondary crew members to carry out. Shaun, Lenka and Daniela read their instruments. Together they all gave positive affirmation that the loads were locked tight by the harpoons.

"Navigation computer course and direction authenticated." Bjorn then read a short series of numbers that corresponded with the other two spacecraft navigational readouts. All were double checked and confirmed.

"We are now all clear for launch in five… four," he counted down. All six crew members watched an automatic ignition clock relaying the same decreasing numbers.

The main fusion engines on all three vessels fired at exactly the same time as the clock tripped zero. The huge blocks of ice started to move very, very slowly at first. The engine power readouts spiked at maximum thrust. The fuel cell percentage counts clicked down at periodic intervals.

Gaining momentum with each second that elapsed, the engines automatically cut back their output having already used over ten percent of their fuel for the initial burn.

"Right on cue, right on course, wake us up in three months. Sleep well people, goodnight." Bjorn cut the transmission.

Maria and Shaun undid their harnesses, now floating in the weightless environment they made their way back to their sleeping quarters by pulling themselves along the short corridor and head first down the ladder.

"Don't forget, we've got to work out that alcohol now," said Maria, with a huge smile. Shaun smiled back pulling her close.

"I do love you," he said passionately, before planting a huge kiss on her lips.

18

Lode Drifter Returns To Mars

Carmen, Toby, Robert and James were standing behind a small control desk in the Hebes Chasma Mars Facilities space traffic control tower. They were awaiting the arrival of the damaged mining spacecraft *Lode Drifter*. It was a little after four in the afternoon. Through panoramic thick solid plastic windows they surveyed the three main, and several smaller, landing fields that stretched out before them.

They had just ascended up into the control room via a near vertical ladder that passed through a tower resembling a short, stocky twenty-first century lighthouse. The control room was perched on top of the tower where the lighthouse lamp room would have been. The dumpy cylindrical structure acted as an airlock chamber between the main building below and the room they now stood in.

There were two controllers currently on watch. Both were seated at the small desk that sported surprisingly very little in the way of equipment. Apart from the odd switch and button, the majority of the space in front of them was taken up by two large flat glass touch control display screens. Each controller wore a small earpiece incorporating a miniscule microphone that jutted out a few centimetres.

One controller was busy engaged in trying to clear a supply freighter off one of the main landing areas, whilst simultaneously talking to the VR operator of one of the small remotely-controlled drone spacecraft used for cargo haulage. A personnel carrying ground vehicle had broken down on the main landing area access ramp. It needed to be moved quickly. They could see the small bodies in shiny spacesuits like silver ants, running round the vehicle attaching lifting straps, while the drone spacecraft hovered patiently above.

The other controller twiddled her thumbs having been relieved of all duties so she could direct her full attention to *Lode Drifter*. Both controllers were dressed in fluorescent white thin emergency spacesuits. Their helmets were located on a broad shelf at the back of their chairs, ready to be slipped over their heads at a moment's notice should there be an accident compromising the atmospheric environment of the control room.

Andy Hubbins, captain of *Lode Drifter* had already made contact a short time earlier requesting permission for orbital insertion, now the mining vessel was in the process of attaining geostationary orbit directly above Hebes Chasma. In doing so, it was trying to avoid two other vessels in similar orbits, one of which was *Oceans Dawn*.

"*Lode Drifter* to Mars Control, requesting a drone to remove our ore sac before our imminent descent. Also, can we have a medical team standing by for us, we have a casualty who is stable, but in need of immediate attention, thanks."

Andy's voice came over the intercom loud and clear. His communication with the traffic controller had been put on loud speaker so they could all listen to the mining spacecraft's progress.

"Acknowledged, *Lode Drifter*, give me a few minutes to organise the pickup. Then I will inform the medical centre," the controller replied, before touching a couple of buttons on the glass display in front of her.

"Control to VR2, are you online?" she asked. There was a frustratingly long pause before she started to repeat the question a second time when the VR2 operator cut her short.

"VR2 to control, sorry for the delay, I had to answer the call of nature. I'm here now, all wired up and ready to go, what's the job?"

"Ore sac from *Lode Drifter* currently in orbit," she instructed.

"Whoa, is this the one rumoured to have all that lovely gold in it?"

"Yes, so be careful, worth a small fortune by all accounts. I also have the Facilities Controller standing beside me so even more reason to be doubly careful."

She thought to warn the VR2 operator before any sarcastic or unheralded comments issued forth, as they sometimes did, from the highly strung VR operatives. Carmen shot her a frowned look for her trouble.

"Okay, acknowledged. Patch me into *Lode Drifter's* comms so I can orchestrate operations directly with them, thanks," requested the VR2 operator, in a more refined and efficient sounding voice, obviously having taken note of the controller's hint.

Off to the right-hand side of the landing fields they observed lights flickering on. One of several small raised platforms next to the base of the cliff was now lit by a ring of interspersed yellow and bluish illuminations. Robert and James hadn't noticed the raised areas before, being quite dull and grey, almost camouflaged in semi-darkness against the cliff face. Now, however, with part of the area brightly lit up, they became quite visible. James counted ten platforms in total with seven small spacecraft currently parked on them, although one looked a bit of a mess as if it had been accidentally crashed into its landing pad. He guessed one empty space was intended for the craft that had been smashed to pieces by the asteroid that so narrowly missed *Oceans Dawn*.

James tried hard to visualise that the vessel VR2, was being controlled by a man lying on a nice comfortable couch in the same building a couple of floors below them. His eyes would be staring into a three dimensional projection of the spacecraft in flight. One hand wrapped round a joystick controlling forward and side motion, the other resting on a push button pad which controlled the small spaceship's various appendages. In his mind, he would be out there flying the drone spacecraft, as if he were actually aboard. James would have to try that experience one day. He just couldn't imagine what it would be like or the shock if something went wrong. What if the vessel malfunctioned and you were about to crash and die, when, in reality, you were safe lying down inside a building. No wonder controllers went mad occasionally.

Slowly gaining momentum, the spacecraft now headed upwards, its orange running lights flashing intermittently. As soon as it was clear of the area, the lights on its pad faded, plunging the neighbouring sister spacecraft back into near darkness. The other working space tugboat, presumably VR1, had now disappeared from view after securing the stricken ground vehicle from the main access ramp some time ago.

"Is this normal procedure for a returning mining vessel?" James asked Carmen.

"Yes, pretty much standard procedure, especially if it they have sustained substantial damage. We like to clear all the pads and surrounding area just for safety reasons. The ore sac from the vessel is removed then shipped off to one of the refineries, in this case, the precious mineral warehouse. If it's as good as they say it is it will probably be shipped back to Earth without us doing anything to it. We might retain twenty kilos for our own uses."

"What happened to the other mining spacecraft *Crystal Star*?" Robert asked.

"It departed very early this morning with a brand new crew. The vessels that work in the belt don't stay still on the ground for very long, time is money and all that. The ground crew swop the miners' personal exoskeletons, replenish supplies etc, turn around can be pretty quick unless there are repairs of course."

A few moments passed as they waited for events to happen. Finally the controller spoke. "VR2 has control of the ore sac, now descending, ETA in two minutes."

They strained to observe through the thick plastic roof, but the spaceships were too distant to see anything other than little dots of light intermixed with the stars above. Robert turned to face Carmen, he felt a little bit uneasy about being in the tower, although the feeling of openness and exposure had done his claustrophobia the world of good.

"I noticed that most windows throughout the facility buildings are quite small, like rectangular portholes, except the ones in here that is. Is it dangerous being here? Is that why the controllers are dressed in case of an emergency?" he asked.

"Yes, you're quite correct. The windows in the main complex are kept small, like those in my office. They offer greater protection from dangers such as micro meteorites. This isolated elevated tower however is quite vulnerable with these windows being so large, the operators like to keep a visual eye on the landing fields at all times. It can get very busy. We have the airlock," she said, turning to indicate the entranceway. "And emergency procedures if the tower is breached, that airlock door will close instantly with its air tight seals protecting the lower floors. If the tower is somehow dislodged entirely, the lower airlock door is strong enough on its own to seal the building underneath," she answered calmly.

Robert looked at James who was obviously quite alarmed as they were not wearing any emergency attire.

Carmen seemed to sense their unease. "Don't worry. We are quite safe for the moment. Once *Lode Drifter* is in descent we will be leaving here."

As soon as Carmen had finished her explanation, as if on cue, the very clear, but obviously tired voice of Andy Hubbins could be heard once more.

"*Lode Drifter* to control. Starting our descent now, where would you like us to park this poor old wreck?" Andy studied the worn, battered and scratched console with sad affection.

"Traffic control to *Lode Drifter*, I'm lighting up lower landing area three for you, remember it will be the sunken landing pad inside the repair hangar. Once you have landed inside the hangar, it will be sealed from above and then pressurised. There will be no need for you to don suits once I give you the green light to exit." She pushed a green button on her screen with a numerical three underneath it.

They couldn't see the large bright white cross on the landing pad had become illuminated as it was below the level of the ground, but they did notice a luminescence appear above a small area within the landing fields. As they watched and waited the first thing to appear was the returning drone spacecraft. It had the ore sac slung below it attached by three long extending arms that had sprouted out from under the small vessel. Approximately thirty metres from the ground it came to a complete stop, hovered for a second, before travelling off to the left towards some distant buildings. James wasn't sure but he thought he could see a golden glow radiate from the within the mesh.

"Those are the ore sheds, it all starts there. Mined ore gets graded then sorted before conveyers take it over to one of the refinery buildings over there." Carmen pointed out. They could see several over ground V-shaped conveyer belts exit the sorting sheds on a series of little towers that carried it across the Martian surface. Currently they carried the spoils from *Crystal Star* before disappearing into the first round massive refinery building.

As they watched the small spacecraft, it flew to the very

end of the block of buildings before slowly lowering its cargo out of sight into a small enclosure.

"The sorters will ascertain the weight and value from scanning the raw material. We should get a valuation within a few hours depending on the work load over there," she rambled on, having had the feeling she should explain everything to the visitors before they started asking more questions of their own volition.

"How long now before she lands?" Robert asked. Carmen looked down at the controller for the answer.

"No more than five minutes," the controller responded.

"Perhaps we should make our way over to the underground repair hangar," suggested Toby, who had remained very quiet up until this point. An annoying habit of his, sometimes you almost forgot he was there. Only his large bulk stopped him from becoming totally invisible. Toby had also noticed that their guests had become quite uneasy, all the time keeping at least one eye on the only exit.

"It will take us about five minutes to walk to the tunnels that lead under the complex, then another couple to the hangar airlocks. By the time we get there they should be in the process of pressurizing the repair hangar."

"I could do with some refreshment on the way if we have time, a nice cup of tea wouldn't go amiss," suggested James, thinking it might have a calming influence on his unsettled nerves too.

"Okay, sounds good to me, let's go now then," suggested Carmen. "Let me know if there are any problems via my personal communicator," she added waving the small telephone-like device in front of the controller.

"Sure, will do, ma'am," came the reassuring reply. They made their way down the ladder that led down to the floor below. One by one they descended. Toby, now bringing up the rear, closed the upper airlock door with a slight thwump.

Robert sighed with relief as it shut, however, it wasn't long before that nauseous feeling that the walls were closing in returned once more. He fumbled for his pills that would allay his annoying condition.

The small party continued to make its way down the three-storey building to the ground floor opening out to the main passageways and concourses that accessed all the other buildings. They managed to pick up some hot drinks from a small cafeteria as they followed Toby leading the way. Robert judged he could probably do it blindfolded if asked. It didn't take long before they arrived at the large hall James remembered as his first sight inside the Mars Facilities buildings after disembarking from the ground vehicle only a few days previously. There were a few people milling about, nothing like the mob they fought their way through on that first day on Mars.

From this main hall they descended via a small elevator to a large brightly-lit circular chamber. Leading off the chamber were two long subterranean passageways that allowed people to move between the refineries and the main facility buildings, or the main facility buildings and the ore sheds. People would travel on small buggies, a line of which were parked against the rear semi-circular wall, plugged in keeping their batteries charged up.

Toby strode across the middle of the chamber to a couple of small doors on the right of both main corridors. As they walked past Robert and James couldn't resist a look down both of them. They could just make out the other end of each in the distance as they were also brightly lit. In between it was pitch black, the lighting only coming on if someone or something was traversing down them.

"These tunnels are relatively new," said Toby. "They save us a lot of time, no more ferrying to and fro on the surface in ground vehicles. The older tunnels under the landing fields are off through here."

He opened one of the doors to reveal a much smaller rough hewn tunnel only wide enough for two people. Several minutes later the tunnel opened out into a large workshop with a large semi-buried boulder in the middle. Around the outside were lockers for suits. Two large workbenches supporting various sized vices were pushed up against the left-hand wall. They were scattered with odd tools. Bits of pipe were laid on the floor against stacked sheet metal panels.

There were two small observation windows that looked into the underground hangar at the very end of the room, Carmen marched to the nearest and peered through.

"They've touched down, you can see the temporary repair patch on this side," announced Carmen. "The overhead shutter is just closing. I expect the controller will start compression shortly."

Carmen was just about to check when there were sounds behind them in the tunnel. Suddenly, the room had become crowded as the medical team arrived carrying a stretcher. Dr. Jones was with them.

"Carmen," shouted Rebecca. Carmen looked up from her communicator to greet her friend and confidant.

"Rebecca, come to supervise?"

"Heard the call from the control tower to the medical station, decided I might tag along as I have nothing on at the moment. Your workers seem to be behaving themselves lately, not losing any fingers, breaking any legs, that sort of thing," she said jokingly.

"Glad to hear it!" Carmen responded with a smile. "I'm just finding out the current situation, hang on a sec," she held up a hand, palm facing out whilst putting the communicator near her right ear.

"Traffic control, status of *Lode Drifter* please," she asked.

"Compression now in progress, automatic airlock controls

are in effect. They will let you know when it is safe to enter the hangar," the controller responded.

"Okay thanks, you can resume your normal duties now."

The airlock entrance was in the very far right, bottom corner of the room, both the inner and outer doors showed red crosses glowing dimly barring access. As they waited Carmen related the tale of *Lode Drifter's* current casualty to her friend, information that had previously been withheld for security reasons. The paramedics also took note. No doubt the story would be common knowledge before too long.

"Aha!" Toby exclaimed as at long last, the airlock doors' green triangles replaced the red crosses. The inner door swung wide, it was big enough to accommodate the medical team plus one, Carmen took the remaining place leaving Robert and James with Toby in the workshop. In theory, as both areas were now equally pressurised, they could have opened both sets of doors were it not for certain safety protocols, measures that forbid both inner and outer airlock doors being opened simultaneously.

Robert and James observed through the small windows as *Lode Drifter* opened its huge forward facing airlock. A sloping ramp appeared, up which disappeared all those that had already passed into the hangar.

"Shall we?" Toby suggested behind the two engrossed observers. Passing through the lock they were soon standing at the bottom of the ramp with Carmen and Rebecca. The paramedics emerged carrying the prone body of Mei-Lien between them. They paused at the bottom of the ramp as Kieron ran down after them. Rebecca lifted the sheet to examine the damaged forearm, Kieron giving a brief rundown of the medication he had administered, Rebecca nodded approvingly.

"Okay, let's get her to the infirmary, no time to lose. I'll catch up with you later Carmen."

The surgeon led the way for the stretcher-carrying paramedics who left an odd silence behind them before the rest of the crew, looking very rough and tired, emerged from the spacecraft at last.

"Good to see you back Andy." Carmen held out her hand which Andy shook instinctively.

"Glad to be back alive and in one piece," he sighed. She introduced Robert and James to the weary party. Andy reciprocated introducing Josie, Deimos and Kieron to the Corporation analysts.

"I was hoping to debrief you now, but you all look totally washed out. I suspect you'd all like a rest, wash, brush up and a decent meal. Shall we say we all convene in my office at about twenty hundred hours? Meanwhile, if you don't mind, can we take a look inside," she indicated up the ramp. Carmen wanted to see the circular holes that crossed the spacecraft.

"Be my guest. See you later," replied Andy, as he and the tired looking crew trudged off. Carmen led the way up the ramp quickly followed by Toby, James and Robert.

19

Open Harvest

The ten-wheeled ground vehicle bobbled along quite happily. Its self-levelling suspension system coping adequately, keeping the vehicle cabin stable as it ran over the rough Martian terrain. The small drive engine purred. The output power dashboard indicator showing all was normal.

Inside the cabin the three-person maintenance crew joked and laughed about the previous evening. They had trawled the Social Village bars, drinking and relaxing for the most part. Here and there they had had the odd flutter at the gaming tables until they closed heralding the start of the unofficial curfew. The trio, Diego, Zelda and Trinidad had been a team since arriving on Mars some years previously. They were a very close knit group often working and playing hard together.

All three of them had slight builds, Diego probably more so than the other two. Diego had thick jet black hair, light brown eyes with sharp distinctive jaw and cheek features. Trinidad, in contrast, had thin curly wispy hair that was receding at an alarming rate, so he thought every time he looked into a mirror. His eyes were also brown, maybe a slightly darker shade, complementing his facial features that were soft and rounded. Zelda had a mop of blonde hair that had a mind of its own. She let it get on with whatever it fancied doing all by itself. She had pale soft skin with blue eyes that shone like polished sapphires. Out of all of them she was the most outgoing, having an outrageous attitude. She had a fearsome reputation often the cause of many brawls with the tough miners. She craved working in the harsh dangerous Martian environment. It fuelled her almost insatiable appetite for destruction. A psychiatrist might have been able to work out why she was like she was, for the most part people just tended to keep out of her way.

Overnight, one of the south polar water supply pipes had registered a pressure drop. The system had automatically closed down the entire pipeline isolating each section by initiating cut off valves installed at each service hatch. The distance between each access service hatch was roughly five thousand metres. The pipes originally ran from the South Polar Region where ice water was once plentiful in the early days of Martian colonisation. Now, all of the water used by the Mars Facilities derived from the ice deliveries from Saturn.

Just over ten kilometres to the south of Hebes Chasma, alongside the existing pipes, was a large natural depression that had provided the ideal location for the ice dump. With each delivery there grew a small ice mountain that shone with a faint blue iridescence against the faint pink backdrop of sky. Every day, a small team of people flew in to carry out the important task of bulldozing ice into underground melting reservoirs before pumping the water onto the Mars Facilities storage tanks using the existing specially heated pipes. Now one of these pipes had sprung a leak.

The Mars Facilities Works Supervisor had dispatched a maintenance team to deal with the breach. It should be a simple routine patch-up job once the team located it, but locating it was a little more complicated than one could possibly imagine. Firstly, they had to make their way out of the protection of Hebes Chasma valleys. The vehicle had to drive up the gentle sloping high valley walls out to the East. Upon reaching the top plateau above Hebes Chasma, they then turned south to follow the rim round before going due west. Then there came the long haul across the top of the southern valley wall before they eventually approached the pipes that made the steep drop down into the valley below. Finally, they had the arduous task of actually testing for the leak.

They checked each section by releasing a relatively small amount of compressed air in between service hatches and measured pressure retention. Luckily, maybe it was by design, there was a hatch at the very top, before the long drop down into the southern valley, with the next one at the very bottom on the valley floor. That had tested negative for a pressure drop. As it happened, the top hatch also turned out to have a perfect seal which was a godsend thought Diego. The last thing he desired was scrambling down the steep valley wall, tramping over rocks, boulders and shifting sand for six kilometres, carrying his thermal welding lance and equipment, seeking out a small frozen patch of dusty water that would be the tell tale sign of the leak.

It was now well into the middle of the working day. They had stopped and tested several sections, now the vehicle was trundling along the pipeline to the next access service cover, all the while narrowing down the search area. The laughing had stopped awhile back as time seemed to drag into tedious monotony.

"How much further 'til the next testing hatch?" moaned Diego.

"Patience my dear boy, patience, it's not too far now. Certainly closer since the last time you asked," replied Trinidad grinning, his voice sounded just like a refined Shakespearian actor in its delivery.

"Another thousand metres give or take a few, according to our satellite navigation coupled with the chart I have here." Zelda shouted out from her position at the navigation desk in the back of the cabin. Diego picked up his coffee to take a sip when then there was bump and a crash as they went over a largish rock.

"Damn you! Steady with the driving Trinidad," groaned Diego, brushing the contents of his mug off the front of his overalls, "that's just what I don't need, a bath in bloody coffee! I swear you did that on purpose."

"Just quit your whinging for once will ya, or I'll come and give you something to really moan about," cried Zelda, holding up a clenched fist, but smiling at the same time to indicate she was only teasing. After a short pause she broke the uneasy silence that had descended. "We should be nearing that next service hatch. Can you see it yet?"

Trinidad turned back to the job at hand. "Yeah! I can see it coming up now. I'm slowing to a crawl for the last few metres." He down changed the gearing with a crunch causing the motor to whine in agony.

"Useless gearbox," he muttered under his breath. Slowly the vehicle came to a halt besides the hatch cover.

Diego was already pulling on his spacesuit over his thermal overalls happy to be doing something at last. Inside the small airlock he picked up a canister of compressed air with its nozzle attachment waving about. Outside, he set to work brushing the fine sand off the half-covered hatch before turning the small wheel to release the locking mechanism. He swung the hatch open to reveal a small cavity. Attaching the floppy tube on the canister to a socket in the cavity he released compressed air into the pipe. Intently, he monitored the needle on the pressure dial that remained stationary for at least a minute.

"Bugger it, no loss here. It looks like we'll have to move onto the next one."

—

The bridge on board *Oceans Dawn* was incredibly quiet. Captain Edmund Cooper was almost dozing off in his command chair. There was nothing to do but wait until their shipment was ready to be transported back to Earth. He called for some music to soothe his mood, but that just made him feel even more relaxed and drowsy. He was seriously contemplating returning to his cabin for a couple of hours' catnap when his second officer, Francisco Garcia, brought him out of his dreamy thoughts.

"Uh! Captain, there appears to be an unknown vessel travelling very fast just over the Martian surface," after a pause, he called out the co-ordinates.

"Put it up on the big display please," the captain ordered politely.

The huge flat glass display screen that hung in front of the main observation windows flickered into life. A set of various diagnostic maps instantly came into sharp focus showing tracked speed, density, overall dimensions etcetera. Another panel showed the unidentified flying object in relation to the Martian surface by three dimensional mapping.

"It looks like it's following the old polar pipeline north. Where has it come from? I don't recognise it as a Corporation spacecraft from the stats readouts. I think it might be wise to contact traffic control, let them know what's happening," suggested Francisco.

The captain turned to his Chief Officer, Adriana Rodriguez. "If you would please, Adriana, and pass on the technical data at the same time."

"Aye Captain, I'm right on it," she said, calling the control tower in her next breath.

"It looks like it's started slowing down," called out Francisco.

"Can we zoom in on the area? See what it looks like close up," Captain Cooper suggested.

A live external feed popped up on the display that started homing in on the unknown spaceship. Watching the alien vessel, its distinctive rugby-ball-shaped image become larger in the centre of the display, all those on the bridge suddenly became aware of the stationary small ground vehicle on the edge of the view.

"What's that? Someone out for a surface jaunt by the looks of it, pass this info onto traffic control as well," he said commandingly, but still managing to deliver his words in a pleasant enough manner. Adriana complied with a running commentary to the ground controllers.

"Sir, should we not put the rest of the crew on alert or something?" Francisco suggested.

"I can't see much point. We are assuming the vessel is hostile. We have no weapons to defend us, nor have the Mars Facilities for that matter. We cannot do very much other than observe and report. If they have weapons and attack us we would be powerless to do much about that either," Captain Cooper declared.

—

Carmen was with James and Robert when she received the call from the traffic controller on her mobile communications device. Now, all three were quickly making their way to the control tower building. They met Toby with a couple of his henchmen at the entrance.

"What's happening ma'am?" Toby asked, very officially. Robert guessed he was trying to impress his subordinates.

"It looks like one of our maintenance crews is going to have first contact with our recently discovered alien friends. I fear the encounter will not last very long, nor will it be entirely friendly," she replied. She turned to Robert and James. "Don't worry, we won't be going up in the tower, we can co-ordinate operations from the third-floor control room," she hastily added, just in time to see their surprised looks subdue having read their alarmed thoughts concerning the control tower's vulnerability.

—

Blake knocked once before entering Leon's office. Leon turned towards him putting his index finger to his lips whilst issuing a low shushing noise. Hugh nodded towards Blake from his position sitting in one of the visitor's chairs. Blake half smiled an acknowledgement coupled with a slight nod in return. There was a small display console on the desk to which they turned their attention while they could hear the commentary between the control tower and the orbiting spacecraft.

"*Oceans Dawn* just gave a description of the vessel. It looks like the aliens have broken cover." Leon whispered.

"Wow! This is going to stir things up a bit!" Blake exclaimed. "I wonder what they intend to do?"

"They are slowing down headed towards a three-person maintenance crew who were out trying to repair a leak in one of the water pipes," replied Hugh.

"They must be getting very desperate to be so bold. They must also know we can see them from the vessels in orbit." Blake said frowning, trying to fathom their intentions.

"Perhaps they know, apart from the immobile defence tower lasers, we don't have any weapons, armed spacecraft or in fact, any real means whatsoever of defending ourselves," said Leon, with a deflated sigh.

"Well that's not strictly true," interjected Hugh. The other two turned to look at him in a quizzical way. He decided not to keep them in suspense for too long.

"Our scout spacecraft is ex-military stealth. It still has a four chemical rocket payload coupled with a small cutting laser. I doubt the laser would be much good, but the rockets could be effective in close proximity," he explained.

"What are you suggesting? You go out there to assist the maintenance crew? There would be an awful lot of questions to answer afterward. That's assuming you were successful, and managed to return in one piece," shrugged Leon.

"But if we don't do anything, those three personnel are as good as dead!" Blake blasted out. "Anyway, I think it is about time I put my cards on the table. We are all in this together. This has become a much bigger issue than a bit of government spying. We are talking about our first alien contact or rather, being attacked by an alien force during our first contact. Just how good a pilot are you Hugh?"

Hugh's grin from ear to ear answered that question. "I'm game if you are? I've been itching to fire those rockets for so long. If I were gonna go down, might as well be in a blaze of glory!"

"Okay, but from now on you two are on your own. I'm still going to remain covert here. Just how you are going to explain yourselves I don't know? I, being pessimistic, think you might not have to. Sorry, I should be wishing you all the best of luck. However, I can't help fearing the worst." Leon looked very sad and dejected.

"I don't plan on dying just yet, but if it does start to go horribly wrong, then we will have proved your pessimistic doubts right. Come on Hugh, we'll be heroes one way or another, either dead, or alive," he winked.

Hugh jumped up. "I'm sure it won't come to that. Let's go kick some alien arse!"

—

Diego was just about to climb into the airlock. He had one foot on the threshold when he saw it out the corner of his eye. He put his boot back down in the dust before turning to face the alien spacecraft looming larger with each second. His mouth gaped open in surprise before it caught up with his rushing thoughts.

"I just don't bloody believe it! Hey you guys, have you seen this?" he shouted. Trinidad turned in his driving seat. His immediate reaction was of a similar vein to Diego's initial thoughts. He couldn't believe what he was seeing either. Zelda rushed from the back of the cabin.

"What the f…" She never finished the expletive.

The alien probes containing the destructive micro robots had already been launched earlier, they were on their way before Diego had finished reading the pressure gauge. All the dashboard dials suddenly slumped dead while Zelda was in mid sentence. Instinctively Trinidad tapped the power dial with his knuckle.

"Looks like we just went offline," he stated.

"Fuck it," was all that Zelda could reply.

The micro robots had performed their efficient destructive task disabling the main drive unit. The ground vehicle was going nowhere fast. Diego vaguely felt the thuds as two probes hit him square in the chest. The casings split open on impact. He stared down puzzled, momentarily stunned, as the little micro robots clamping tight to the outside of his suit using the vice like pincers on the ends of their tiny legs, their rows of round circular teeth immediately started chewing at the outside of his suit.

"What's all this? Get off! Get the fuck off!" he screamed, trying to brush them off with his gloved hands. Then panic set in as within seconds, one had bitten clean through the outer fabric membrane disappearing into the inner insulation layer. He dived into the airlock pushing the button to shut the door. All four of the bug like robots had now vanished leaving behind four round ragged entry holes. Even before the pressurization started he was disrobing his boots and gloves. Now his freezing hand rested on the zip of his suit watching the airlock pressure and heat gauges rapidly climb. Sweating through fear, he could now feel them inside his thermal vest pinching his skin beneath as they climbed up his body. He took a chance fearing time was running out fast.

Taking a deep breath, his helmet clattered to the floor closely followed by a dislodged micro robot. It seemed to squirm on its back for a few moments like some Earthly insect before righting itself. Diego then unzipped his suit. Pulling out of the arms, it fell round his knees. The dislodged micro robot scurried over to his foot before getting lost under the tumbling folds of his crumpled suit.

He managed to fend off two of the little metallic cockroach like robots darting about his body, one hitting the wall with a satisfying pop and wisp of smoke. However, the one remaining managed to reach its target. Diego screamed in agony holding his head in both hands as it chewed its way inside before he finally slumped to the floor, with eyes wide open.

Inside their cabin, Zelda and Trinidad were unaware of Diego's painful demise. They were staring in shock as a tall humanoid clad in a black spacesuit and black helmet emerged from the spaceship before them. It stood staring for a second before diving back inside just as a ball of flame erupted between the alien vessel and the maintenance ground vehicle. The shock wave rocked them causing Zelda to fall to the floor in a heap, her mad hair falling in front of her face. She puffed the hair away from her eyes.

"What the hell was that!" she demanded as another eruption occurred, this time much nearer the alien vessel, which retaliated with a slim beam of light that flashed upwards. This second explosion made a considerable dent in the side of the copper-coloured spacecraft, which now fired indiscriminate small bursts of laser in random directions. It majestically turned on its axis before rapidly moving off, obviously not damaged to any great extent.

Blake slapped Hugh on the shoulder. "Looks like we got them on the run, the stealth mode works just fine, they hadn't got a clue where we came from. I'm not sure they even know where we are now," he joked.

"We certainly took them by surprise, should we follow, give them another rocket?" Hugh asked enthusiastically.

"No, we've done what we set out to do. We took them completely off guard, they certainly weren't expecting us. Let's keep them guessing. Besides, if they knew we only have two rockets left they might be inclined to take a risk and come back. Best not push our luck. Now I suppose we had better introduce ourselves," said Blake, switching on the external communications. They were met with a very irate Facilities Controller in mid sentence.

"… and just who the hell do you think you are anyway? I want you to land immediately surrendering to our security officers while we impound your vessel!"

"Okay, okay. You might want to start thanking us for saving your crew out here first before you start demanding anything," replied Blake calmly.

Carmen was on the very edge of hysteria. Suddenly, she realised most of the occupants in the third floor control room were staring at her. Composing herself, she re-addressed the unknown occupants of the military spacecraft with a more controlled, civilised voice.

"Just consider yourselves now under arrest. I want to see you in my office in half an hour for a full debriefing whoever you are!" Carmen severed the communications link. "Toby, would you please meet and escort our wannabe space cowboys to my office as soon as they land. Thank you."

20

War Council

Two days after the attempted, very public, Martian abduction, the Mars Facilities Controller called a meeting. It was held in the main cafeteria, the biggest single room available. Toby had been instructed on whom to summon. Mostly department heads and supervisors who could pass on the conclusions of the meeting to their subordinates. Regarding Hugh and Blake, he personally escorted them from the brig to join the busy congregation.

There was a general hubbub in the assembled crowd until Carmen called for order. The majority of the main ensemble were seated in a crescent-moon-shaped semicircle of chairs. The remainder had to stand up at the back of the room. They all faced a couple of tables behind which sat Carmen Applegate presiding, Rebecca Jones and Tobias Hauss. The room descended into hushed silence.

"Right then, where to start?" Carmen said, opening proceedings. She had been dreading this moment, not really knowing where to even begin to explain all events that had occurred or how to clarify what had befallen certain members of the Martian community. Over the previous two days there had been seemingly endless discussions with the European

Government. There had been lengthy debates with the bosses of the Corporation. They had thrashed out many options on possible scenarios. Now, she was feeling emotionally and physically drained from it all.

"I think some of you know some of the people here, but I'm almost sure that not everybody knows everybody. So I will perform general introductions throughout the meeting while asking certain questions about the main points of discussion. Hopefully this will make for a clearer picture for all concerned as to the extent of our current situation. Hopefully, by the end of the meeting everyone should know all the facts, and by due process, know who everyone else is." Carmen paused for a second, to allow that somewhat confusing opening sentence to sink in. "I will attempt to approach matters using the timeline of events that have happened so far. I will get around to all of you that have input, this may take some time so please be patient. Please leave all questions to the end, as I said, I will be asking for certain points to be clarified along the way so hopefully, there will be no stone unturned and therefore, no questions forthcoming." Carmen took a sip of water. This meeting was going to take a long time. Also, she fully expected a lot of questions at the end of it, as well as a few during.

"Firstly, it all started with an asteroid miner called Teunis Landry. Unfortunately he cannot be here with us as he was killed, as it turns out, by some miniature alien metal robots, for want of a better description. These little metal things chewed into his head making a mess of his spinal column at the base of the brain stem. The damned things, similar in design, with small variations in detail, were used to kill Diego, one of our maintenance crew members, two days ago. Miss Jones," she paused whilst pointing out the resident physician at her right hand side. "Miss Jones performed both autopsies. Details of the autopsies can be found on the medical database in the common folders. However, the main point to observe is once they are inside your suit, they then gain entry into your body via the ear canal. Using their drill like teeth they carve a pathway to the spinal column to wreak havoc paralyzing their victims. They have a very limited power source and are remotely controlled by the aliens using some sort of low-frequency radio waves not too dissimilar to our own VR operators, but on a much smaller scale. We are assuming this procedure is performed to disable their victims, this would make abduction very straightforward. Why Teunis wasn't taken, but left for us to find, is still a bit of a mystery. Maybe they were interrupted before they could get to him physically, very like Diego? Now, moving on to the next incident. *Lode Drifter*, an asteroid-mining vessel sustained damage by what appeared to be a round cylinder object that cut or burned a pathway right though the spaceship. If I could call upon Andy Hubbins, the mining tour co-ordinator and captain on that last fateful tour, to come forward and give a brief account of the events for the benefit of those that do not know all the facts, please," she said, looking towards Andy.

Andy stood up, walked to the front of the desks where he turned to face the stunned crowd. Briefly he related the fatal events of their last mining tour. It was a shorter, less detailed debriefing than he had already performed for Carmen, Robert, James and Toby. Again he deliberately missed out the intimate details regarding Aimee and Ramon's untimely end. He saw no point in relaying that part of the story. Once he had finished he returned to his seat, flopping down quite dejected. Relaying the tale yet again was doing nothing to ease the pain he felt about his dead crew members. Some of the people in the room who knew the deceased offered their condolences. He thanked them, blinking back tears. Carmen then asked for an impromptu moment of silence to honour those deceased. Eventually, after what seemed an appropriate passage of time, Carmen spoke once more.

"One question I would like to raise here and maybe get some sort of clarification is what the cylindrical objects might be? We know they must be manufactured, and I think we can assume they are part of the alien culture. I would like to ask Robert Goodyear, an analyst from the European Space Exploration Travel Corporation to come forward. He has a theory that might explain, I understand."

Robert stood up remaining by his seat. This wouldn't take long or so he thought. The room adjusted themselves to look at him. For most, it was the first time they had laid eyes on the Corporation Chief Analyst.

"We, that is my colleague James Cleaver and I, believe that the objects are resupply vessels," he said, beginning to sit down. Carmen stopped him with his legs slightly bent.

"Can you elaborate your theory please?" she asked.

Robert stood upright once more. "Well, the way we see it is this. The deadly robot bugs used by the aliens are ostensibly very disposable. Given time, their supplies must eventually run out. Other electrical components on their spaceships would ultimately be superceded by newer technology. We have no idea how long the aliens have been amongst us, we can assume a good number of years, maybe even hundreds. Technology, as you know, moves at an alarming pace. Also, as we know only too well, it is a harsh environment out here in space. Vessels are easily damaged, constantly needing repairs. We make do, adapt, repair and patch up. They use an alloy that we have not seen the like of before so they might well require fresh supplies from time to time. There are no DIY universal hardware stores out here." Robert waited for these new revelations to be absorbed, before continuing, with what he assumed everyone else was now thinking.

"This means of course either the aliens have a home planet out there or another, maybe larger base in another solar system. Somewhere they can send the objects from. Without alien life on board they could achieve immense speeds. Trekking vast distances, we have no idea how far they have travelled or in which direction they have come from initially." Finally he sat down.

"I think we may have some new information to help on that front." It was now Carmen's turn to seek a reaction, especially from Robert and James. Both now looked intensely at her like well trained dogs looking at their masters for a treat after performing an obedience trick.

"We have just received a long distance communiqué from the Saturn ice tugboats who are currently in transit returning with new ice supplies. The transmission is a couple of days old now. In it they have reported an encounter with twelve cylindrical objects roughly one kilometre apart, some of which passed clean through the ice blocks they had constructed. We are almost sure that one, possibly two, of these twelve caused the damage to *Lode Drifter* and its scout spacecraft. Within the message were details of course and speed. These two sets of co-ordinates, those that Andy took, and these new ones, will allow us to calculate a rough trajectory of origin. I'm sure our Analysts from the Corporation would like to get started straight away with this new information. However, they will have to be patient. We have a lot more information to discuss and digest yet."

Robert turned to James who smiled back at him. This was something they could really get their teeth into. A tentative hand from Josie Carter lifted into the air. Carmen stared at her sternly, but didn't say anything. She waited patiently for the interruption.

"I know you said no questions until the end, but I was thinking about the ice-tugboat personnel, do they know about the aliens? Are they in danger now as it seems to be open season on all humans?"

Carmen dropped her frown. "Toby, what is the state of play with the ice tugboats at the moment, do we know?"

Toby shrugged. "We can only guess all the crews will now be in the Dormouse Torpor State for the duration of the return journey. They have no weapons, they would be at the mercy of any aliens should they decide to attack them. There's really not much we can do, they are still way out beyond the Asteroid Belt. Even if we invoked emergency override procedures to wake them up, they still wouldn't be able to stop them, not with the miniature robots they control that seem to be able to enter all manner of spacecraft and ground vehicles," he said, feeling somewhat helpless.

"And the other small vessels?" prompted Carmen.

"We have been in contact with the two mining spacecraft, *Astral Gem* and *Mother Lode*, currently on tours out in the belt. We've recalled *Crystal Star* which only left the other day so they are on their way back already. The thing is, at the moment, we are at the complete mercy of these aliens whatever way you cut it," he added.

"Well, Josie," said Carmen. "There you have it I'm afraid. Not much we can do at the moment. Perhaps we can get back to the vessels we have out in space later. There are facts still to come that might have a bearing on what we decide to do next. Now we come to Leila Santos. Her incident happened shortly after the murder of Teunis Landry. I would now like Leila to stand up and give a brief account of her involvement on Ganymede."

Leila made her way to the front just as Andy had previously. She told her tale raising a few eyebrows as she did so. When she got to the point of frantically stabbing the alien creature, a shout came from the back of the room.

"Good for you girl! I'll do the same if ever I get the chance. I'd like to get a piece of one of 'em for Diego's sake!" Zelda shouted. A few raised cheers of agreement followed. Carmen called for order, allowing Leila to finish her story after the sudden outburst.

"Now, just for those who might have doubted Leila's events, I have had the blood on the knife analysed. It does appear to be non-human. In light of more recent events, I think I can say now there can be no doubts about the authenticity of her story." Carmen looked sideways at Toby. Toby took the opportunity to make a public apology to Leila. She half smiled for the benefit of the others in the room. She would never forgive him for not believing her from the start though.

"Now a point I'd like to raise and discuss here is this. Why were there two alien spaceships fighting each other in the first place?"

It was Blake who spoke out this time. "Leila has a theory about that. Perhaps you ought to let her explain her suspicions."

"Leila, would you like to elaborate?" Carmen looked genuinely surprised by this revelation. Leila revealed her ideas about the possible clannish infighting that might be occurring. James was inclined to agree that there could be some sort of political inter-tribal war transpiring. He spoke out giving his views before others offered their opinions. Soon, the room degenerated once again into a general verbal melee. Carmen again called for order. She needed to bang on the table with her water tumbler to achieve silence this time.

"Right, I think we can surmise that we have exhausted that line of enquiry sufficiently to conclude that there might be some unrest within the alien camp. Now, moving on to more recent events two days ago, right before our eyes, we had an alien vessel come here to try and abduct three of our personnel. Luckily for us, our two heroes here, who just happen to be government agents, turn up out of the blue with an armed ex-military stealth spacecraft. With it they managed to beat off the attack, saving two of the maintenance crew personnel in the process. We all thank you for that, that doesn't exclude you from breaking Martian law on two major counts. I have, as you know been in touch with both the Corporation who own this installation and the European Government, who have denied sending you here at all. The government don't deny you are both employed by them, but as far as they were aware, you are on vacation." There was a general outburst of laughter intermixed with some jocular remarks from around the room.

"Yes, quite. Okay enough, enough." Carmen held up her hand to restore quiet. "The fact is that we may need these two individuals again so, there will be no charges brought against them. I have been instructed to say no more on the matter in light of the fact that we are now technically at war with an unknown alien species." She waited while this comment sunk in. An air of greater seriousness seemed to descend on the occupants of the room.

"So, now I ask the question. Why are the aliens paralysing and then abducting humans in the first place?" she shrugged, looking to Robert for an answer. He stood up slowly. Once again, all eyes in the room moved as one coming to rest staring straight at him.

"They only logical conclusion I can come up with is they are using us as fodder much like we use cows and sheep. It makes sense when you look at the facts. We believe they have been around in our solar system for many years. What do they eat day to day? Assuming they could, if they wanted, grow vegetable crops like we do using hydroponics, perhaps they require animal protein far more so than humans. We have all our meat products shipped freeze dried from Earth. They have to get their animal matter from somewhere. Maybe they obtained what they required from Earth too or possibly did so in the past. Now, perhaps, it is harder for them to obtain human bodies and they are getting desperate, any human source available will do."

"Are you suggesting they will come here in greater numbers next time?" Carmen asked.

"Who knows what could happen next? We can only make logical deductions from the given facts. What we must do is make some sort of provisions for such an attack. It would be nice to know where they are operating from. The alien vessels we have seen so far I guess are ones they use for the abduction and collection of human bodies. They must have a large base, perhaps a mother ship somewhere in the solar system, hiding near one of the outer planets," Robert finished, once again leaving more questions than answers. He sat down once more.

"Right, that concludes all events leading up to the present. Now, just to let you know what is happening right now. The British Government have offered some of their elite army personnel to come here to protect us. An interplanetary spaceship, a sister spacecraft to *Oceans Dawn, Stellar Dusk,* is being prepared as we speak. I have been informed the soldiers will be equipped with full body-armoured exoskeletons with a veritable arsenal of highly destructive weapons at their disposal. This small army of fighting men will primarily be for our protection once they arrive here. Unfortunately we are now in an unfavourable window for resupply vessels so they might not get here for at least fifteen days after a week of groundwork." She paused looking round the room for any reactions, thankfully, none were forthcoming. So far so good she thought.

"What happens here in the meantime is down to us. This facility and the vessels we have out in space are at the mercy of the aliens. So what can we do? Now, as I have said, I have spoken at length to the powers that be. They have given me complete authority to use any means I see fit to protect this base and the people in it. I can commandeer any vessel here owned by either party." She stared at Blake and Hugh specifically. Hugh signalled thumbs up. Carmen continued, hiding a slight smile.

"As I understand it, *Oceans Dawn* once had weapons, a weapons array system albeit now decommissioned. Apparently, all early interplanetary spaceships carried weapons. I have spoken to Captain Cooper who has informed me that when its weapons were dismantled the spaceship was here on Mars. The weapons, two high power cutting lasers, two microwave beam weapons and several ancient solid fuel guided missiles were disassembled here. The chemical rockets were destroyed. The other weapon systems were dumped in some of the old supply sheds here in Hebes Chasma. Those old sheds are some kilometres up the valley away from the facility buildings. We intend to find them and restore *Oceans Dawn* to become a gunship once more." There were general shouts of approval from around the room with an accompanying ripple of applause.

"Further more, the captain requested volunteers from his crew to operate the vessel once it is reacquainted with its lost weaponry, suffice to say not one of them refused. I have also authorised immediate repairs for *Lode Drifter*, I want this to be a backup, a sort of lifeboat, for *Oceans Dawn*. More importantly, its magnetic shields will provide some protection for *Oceans Dawn* as well. They will be coupled together where the supply vessel normally carries its cargo containers. If any of the miners want to man that spacecraft we will be looking for volunteers for that task. Our engineers have come up with a plan to attach the fusion power drive unit, it will be in very close proximity to the main vessel unfortunately, but we can't really help that. In a few days we hope to have this mishmash of vessels capable of going out to find and escort all our vessels home safely."

Andy Hubbins stood up. "I think I can speak for what's left of my team, we will crew *Lode Drifter*. We have some very dear friends to avenge if we get the chance or die trying. Besides, our exoskeleton units are already on board."

"Right then Andy, I will accept your offer to captain *Lode Drifter*. We have a few days to take names of all those others who wish to volunteer to help out in any way they can. The two captains will work out who they would like for crew, ideally I would like those who have some sort of encounter with the aliens to be at the top of the list. Their experiences might just prove useful as another encounter is more than likely," she concluded, hoping to escape soon. This meeting, as well as becoming tiresome, was now hindering progress in setting important plans in motion.

"Okay, I hope I covered everything, dare I ask if there are any questions?" She was surprised only one hand went up. That was Toby.

"When *Oceans Dawn* and *Lode Drifter* depart to rendezvous with our mining spaceships and ice tugboats, what's left to defend the Mars Facilities until the army soldiers arrive?" he enquired.

Carmen took a deep breath. "We have the defence towers of course. We also have the ex-military scout spacecraft although with only two rockets left, I believe. We are hoping to use the drone spacecraft somehow, pack them with some explosives to ram invaders if it comes to it. However, our Corporation analysts here think they will try for the remote vessels first, especially after our little incident the other day that took them by surprise. Those vessels out in the belt and beyond will be easier targets for the aliens to capitalise on. Once there are no more spaceships with humans out beyond Mars, then we will become undoubtedly the main focus of their attention. Meanwhile, we will be concentrating all our effort on the combined rescue spaceships." Toby nodded and seemed to accept Carmen's explanation.

"Right, I'm going to adjourn this meeting now. I ask all heads of department and supervisors to pass on the information you have heard and we have discussed here today to all those that couldn't be present. All volunteers can leave your names with Toby. Not you Blake or Hugh. We need both of you to fly the scout. I will call another meeting when our plans are nearly finalised, until then keep your fingers crossed for a peaceful few days. There is a lot to do, so just ask how you can help out if you find yourself at a loose end. Robert, James, with me please. I need you to head up my War Council, help me with my master plan to co-ordinate all we have discussed here today."

"Of course, we would love to co-operate in any way we can," replied Robert. Carmen picked up a sheaf of papers before heading for the door. She was in dire need of a large shot of spirit of any description. It had been a long few days and things were not going to get any easier.

21

Camp Sandhurst

Alexander Manso stood by his office window. His fair skin, short wavy mouse-coloured hair, and well-defined chiselled facial features, were semi-reflected in the double-glazed glass panel as he surveyed the scene below. The window overlooked Camp Sandhurst parade ground in the leafy countryside of Surrey, England.

A group of recruits were being put through their paces by a rather loud and abusive non-commissioned officer. The window was slightly ajar letting in the warmth of midsummer, along with the noises of birds chattering and insects buzzing about their daily business. Every now and then he heard the raised voice of the drill sergeant. "Left... left... get in step. You there! Bloody well get in step... left..." wafting in on the breeze. In the distance he could hear the unmistakable, if faint, whap, whap, whap noise a Tesla MKII Pulse Rifle makes emitting highly accelerated groups of anion particles, not dissimilar in action to a twentieth century machine gun spitting out bullets. After each rifle discharge, he could also make out the almost instantaneous dull thud as the ionised particle, travelling near the speed of light, slammed into, sometimes right through, the thick metal human silhouette targets situated in the rifle range butts. Each particle discharge, bursting with gigajoules of dissipating kinetic energy, crackled, giving off miniature forks of white flashes, like lightening on a stormy night. The ranges were the other side of a small hillock just out of view, but there was no confusing the sound of the powerful infantry weapons. He pulled the window shut, cutting out the assorted different noises altogether. A pleasing silence descended on the room allowing his inner thoughts to wander until there was a gentle knock on his open office door.

"Enter," he said positively. He turned from the window as a uniformed sergeant marched in through the open doorway. The sergeant came to an abrupt stop, heels clicking together. She stood silently at attention in front of his desk unflinching eyes staring straight ahead. The sergeant didn't salute as Alex was not wearing a uniform. The main reason for this, as being a non-combatant Military Analyst he didn't possess one. The Military Analyst had replaced the old rank of lieutenant, a rank that now no longer existed in the modern army. Answerable to the platoon Captain, the Military Analyst was purely an advisor to the squad sergeants in the overall scheme of things. He had been trained in most aspects of military strategy encompassing the Roman Empire, the Zulus, the Two World Wars, the Gulf and South American conflicts and finally the World War for Antarctica. His job involved designing and planning defensive shields and giving advice on attacking options for the fire teams. He could study and absorb a five-square kilometre topographical map in three dimensions. Later, visualising that map in his mind, he could advise how to utilise the terrain or make use of any natural resources helping create any advantages possible. The Military Analyst was also trained in statistical analysis, making calculated snap decisions based on mathematical odds. He couldn't give direct orders except in exceptional circumstances. Ultimately, it was down to the squad sergeants to give the final commands to subordinate corporals and the privates. Most of the time the squads acted on the advice given by the Military Analyst however, they didn't always heed his advice. Utilising his advice or not, they still performed as an efficient close-knit fighting team, a team that generally worked very well.

"Can you shut the door and sit down Paula," he said, pulling his own chair out from under the desk to sit down.

"Sir!" the sergeant barked back. Standing easy before turning to gently close the door, she then swivelled back, sliding onto the visitor's chair all in one seemingly fluid motion. Alex had given up trying to stop Paula being so formal in his presence. She was a disciplined soldier, trained to obey or be obeyed. She was good with both, but it had to be regimented, there were no two ways about it.

Squad Sergeant Paula Alvarez looked tanned, some of her father's Argentinean ancestry showing through Alex thought. She had dark alert eyes under very short dark hair that was not much more than jet black stubble, the soft complexion of her face belaying the hard, rugged trained killer underneath.

"Well, we have some new orders. I'm not sure what to make of them to be quite honest. It's a bit of a rush job. We have four days to get our crap together, equipment, personnel complete with their fighting exoskeletons, the whole kit and caboodle in fact."

"The whole platoon Sir? That's a lot of organising for a lot of bodies in such a short time. By the way, where is the Captain?"

"No. Not the whole platoon. There will only be enough room for two, four-man fire teams, along with the two of us on this mission, ten souls in total. The Orbital Space Elevator scheduled lift is eighteen hundred hours on Friday, we have to be ready to depart from Borealis Station without fail by sixteen hundred," he said, waiting for the expected reaction. A reaction that was almost instantaneous.

"The Orbital Space Elevator?" she looked quizzical. There it was, just as he expected. She picked up on it like a kestrel spotting a field vole while hovering, and just like the hawk now diving, continued to swoop.

"Where exactly are we going on this rushed mission without the Captain?"

"Mars," Alex said, almost as a whisper.

"Mars!" Paula shouted in return, somewhat taken aback.

"Shhhhh! For the love of Pete, keep your voice down. This is supposed to be a top secret mission."

"Excuse my language, Sir, but what the fuck do they want with two army fire teams out on Mars?" she asked sardonically.

"Ah! Now we come to the good bit. We are at war evidently…" He nodded to emphasise the point. "And, it gets better. We are not only at war, but at war with an alien race of creatures three metres tall who happen to be flying around the solar system apparently abducting people at will." He raised his eyebrows, not quite believing what he just said himself.

"Excuse me for asking Sir, but have you been drinking?"

Paula had known Alexander, or Alex as he preferred to be addressed, for many years now. In all that time she couldn't recall seeing him being drunk once. She thought she had to ask though, there was always a first time for everything. She leaned forward to smell his breath the next time he spoke. He leaned forward in response, huffing in her face realising what she was trying to achieve. She blinked in reaction to the warm breath on her eyes, a breath that was distinctly alcohol free.

Alex resumed his lazy seating posture. "Look Sergeant, I don't know if this is some sort of wind up or we are going to be made a laughing stock at the expense of some slightly-mad Field Marshal, whose sick joke has just back fired. All I know is this, last night I was summoned to the Major General's office where I was introduced to a senior political figure, and believe me, they don't get much senior. Also, the Managing

Director of the European Space Exploration Travel Corporation, who as everyone knows, is inclined to be somewhat of a recluse under normal circumstances. I don't know who was more surprised out of the two of us. He didn't look at all comfortable, just as I didn't feel that comfortable being in amongst that lot of high-ranking hobnobs. Anyway, between them, they convinced me, and believe me, I did take a lot of convincing, that what I just told you is the truth," he said, pausing briefly while Paula absorbed this revelation.

"I personally have decided to look on it as some sort of training exercise. In fact, that's exactly what it is going to look like, until we are well under way on the Corporation interplanetary supply vessel *Stellar Dusk*. Even our two fire teams will be none the wiser. They are not even going to enlighten the Captain until we are well on our way and have left Gateway. Until then, this is just between you, me and those three individuals I met last night, understood?"

"Sir!" she barked. "Just a training exercise, I fully understand."

Alex continued where he had left off. "They picked our company, obviously as some form of retribution for our past sins no doubt, mainly because we have had the only real experience of any major incident in outer space. They have assumed, rightly or wrongly, that we might be able to handle ourselves better as a result."

"If you're referring to that little skirmish involving the Chinese, I'd hardly call that a proper fight? A bunch of Chinese terrorists, or should I say teenage student extremists. I don't recall anyone of them being over twenty years old, who tricked their way up to Satellite Two. Calling themselves 'The Saviours of Mankind', they successfully hijacked a shuttle using imitation small arms before somehow managing to fly it to, and take over, a defunct military rocket platform in low Earth orbit. Not long after, they are holding the Chinese government to ransom, threatening to launch rockets at Beijing parliament buildings demanding the government increase ordinary people's daily food rations. We had a bit of a tussle with them, but they were easily overpowered as their weapons were non-functional, also, they didn't have any fighting exoskeletons. It was a shame they had no prior knowledge that all the warheads had been removed years ago so the missiles were totally harmless apart from the possibility of making some large impact craters. They should have listened more intently in their history lessons about the global strategic arms disarmament treaty drawn up in two thousand and fifty-five, than plotting to take over a space platform. All turned out to be a bit of a waste of time for them in the end. Although, in hindsight, it was fairly well organised and planned out. You've got to give the youngsters some credit for that." She allowed herself a rare smirk.

"Yes, very well remembered. Thanks to that rare tactical experience in zero G by our boys and girls, they think that our Company are now experts in space combat. I suppose to some extent they have a point looking at the facts. It has been the only real live fire experience in the outer atmosphere to my knowledge. Certainly more than any other company or platoon in the history of the British army," he said, before standing up.

"Coffee?" he asked, moving over to a large antique sideboard on top of which stood an ancient coffee percolator.

"Yes please," Paula answered.

"One sugar isn't it?" he enquired, while pouring two cups from a half full glass jug sitting on the heating plate.

"No Sir, I gave up taking sugar the tour before last, that little stint in the Med."

He brought the two brim full cups back to the desk placing one down in front of the sergeant. A little spilt over one side that left a ring on the desk as she picked it up to take a sip. It was hot.

"Perhaps you should have had a sugar in it, it might well

have helped with the shock of what I have just divulged," he mocked, feigning a smile at the same time.

"Not so much shock Sir, more disbelief," she replied, while blowing over the top of the steaming liquid.

"Right, forget all that alien bullshit for a second, let's get back to business. Now I've been looking through the personnel files trying to pick out our most experienced corporals and privates, especially those that were involved in the China crisis. I've created a shortlist of about fourteen from the platoon," he said, retrieving a number of folders from his left-hand bottom drawer.

"If you got Smith or Patel in there, they're out. Smith is in the infirmary doubled up with suspected food poisoning. Patel requested leave for a sick parent, at death's door by all accounts. He left the camp two days ago on a week's compassionate leave."

"Damn! Smith was one of my first choices. He has more hours using the fighting exoskeleton units out in space than anyone else. He practically designed all the latest main adaptations to the mining exo for military use as a direct result from that Chinese fracas. We could have done with him. I'm not so bothered about Patel. He was way down my list." Alex leafed through the piles of folders carefully extracting two. He dropped them back in the bottom drawer with a dull thump.

"Right then, let's start at the top with you and me. Alex Manso, male, aged thirty-four. Military Analyst and Advisor to Squad Sergeant Paula Alvarez, female, aged thirty-one. Now then, who have I dug up for the first fire team?" he muttered, opening up the top folder.

"Fire Team One led by Corporal Frank Lloyd, male, aged twenty-eight." He read out the rest of the Corporal's personal details then looked across the desk.

"Okay, a good corporal who can be relied on in a tight spot. I'll go along with that," agreed Paula.

"His team consists of Privates Mercedes Brett, female,

aged twenty-seven, veteran Aban Hossini, male, aged forty-one and Sergio Laurant, male, aged twenty-five." He looked up with questioning eyes. Paula stared back blankly at him, so he continued.

"Team Two led by Corporal Ross Perez, male, aged twenty-six." For a second time he paused after announcing the Corporal's name. Paula nodded, again he returned to the folders in front of him, happy that his choices had not been overturned so far.

"His team will consist of Ricardo Irvine, male, aged thirty, Jacqueline Reilly, female, aged twenty-seven and finally the baby of the bunch, Nasrine Ben Ali, female, aged twenty-three."

Whilst reading out the names he had placed the folders on the desk in a hierarchical overlapping pattern of the two teams.

"I'd swop Ricardo Irvine with Aban Hossini. The teams will work better together that way round in my opinion. Don't ask me why, it's a long story."

"Okay, Paula, it's your call on that front," he said, exchanging two of the folders from one pile to the other.

"Any other thoughts on my choice of team members, what do you think about Hossini? Is he up to the task? He's getting on a bit now, even though according to his dossier, he's just breezed through his last medical and fitness analysis with flying colours." His hand hovered over his selections, ready to make any changes at Paula's suggestion.

"Hossini is a good soldier. He's probably fitter than some of the younger ones, a lot of experience too, a good choice in my opinion," she concurred. The remaining folders then joined the others in the bottom drawer which Alex pushed shut with his foot.

"So, we have our squad. We have our two fire teams. Now, we just need to get them organised. If you can round up the lads and lasses, get them to sort out their kit, check out their

Tesla Rifles, flash grenades, sonic shells, you know the general list. Get them to walk their exoskeletons over to hangar five, we are using temporarily as the disembarkation area to store our gear. It also holds the cargo carrier jet already requisitioned that will take us up to Borealis Station on Friday."

"What shall I tell them about the mission, Sir?"

"Right, well you can tell them that we have an exercise to perform, at very short notice. Just to test our readiness for…" Alex was lost for words. "For…" He stammered, looking for some inspiration from Paula.

"Why not say a possible alien invasion, that should make them laugh if nothing else," she offered politely.

"We need them to take it seriously. I want this mission to be treated professionally, even if someone is trying to jerk us off!"

"Don't worry. I will make them take it seriously just after I let them have their first, and last laugh."

Alex believed her. "Once we get up to Satellite Two we'll tell them there has been a change of plans. We'll tell them they need to don their exoskeletons for an impromptu space walk, just for the experience you understand. The Corporation have a singular interplanetary container, designed especially for the military. It holds ten fully-armed and equipped soldiers with their fighting exoskeletons along with all their personal paraphernalia and weaponry. We have to test it out for size and functionality, yes, that's a good story, I like that, I like that a lot. They won't need to bunk down in there as there will be ample room inside the main spaceship. Once we trick them on board it's a simple case of a shuttle dragging the container up to Gateway where *Stellar Dusk* will be waiting for us. The Corporation has promised every resource they have will be at our disposal. Well, I suppose they would do, especially as they have a rather large vested interest in the Mars Facilities." He lingered for a moment before continuing.

"So, how will they react, will they buy it?" Alex grimaced, expecting the worst response from Paula.

"Well, I don't think they will like it, but they will have to lump it. On the job training I shall tell them. Are we really going all the way to Mars? It will be an elaborate, not to say expensive, waste of everyone's time and money if we are. I still can't quite believe it. It has to be some sort of hoax. Three metre tall alien creatures indeed," she muttered shaking her head in disbelief.

"Well, believe it or not, you'd better get started. I've got to sort out all the intelligence and tactics, pull up some maps, inside and out of the Mars Facilities, plus the surrounding Martian valley where the refining complex is set up, any other questions?"

"No, Sir. Permission to be excused, get the troops motivated," she replied.

"Permission granted. You can leave the door open on the way out thanks."

Alex Manso turned his attention to his clear glass desk monitor as the sergeant opened the door and marched out. Already he was studying the maps of Hebes Chasma and the surrounding topographical area, building up a three-dimensional picture in his mind. There was a lot of swotting up to do so this better not be a waste of time he thought to himself. Trips to Mars don't come along every day though, so it might be fun, certainly an experience if nothing else.

He smiled to himself at that notion. What he didn't realise then, in the coming weeks, he would be doing a lot more frowning than smiling, if he managed to smile ever again.

22

Weapons Operational

The Mars Facilities were a veritable hive of busy bees following the emergency mass meeting, or the first council of war as Carmen Applegate, the Facilities Controller liked to describe it. Three days had elapsed since then. All refining crews had ceased operations, even the furnaces had been powered down. Now they were dark, cold, silent, ghostly and deserted. Most of the facility personnel were now assisting in a number of different projects. Each project designed to help protect the Martian complex in some way or other against the threat of alien attack.

Oceans Dawn had undertaken the risk of landing on the Martian surface where it was at its most vulnerable. At least in space it might have a slim chance of avoiding any pursuing alien vessels. However, stationary on the Martian surface it was more akin to a turtle turned on its back in the baking desert sun, it had no protection whatsoever. The sole reason for landing was to permanently alter that vulnerability.

"So, you've never landed on Mars before?" James Cleaver quizzed Captain Edmund Cooper. He had been witness to the skilfully conducted descent a few hours previously, whilst strapped securely into the spare navigator's chair on the bridge.

The spacecraft had ceased its centripetal rotation leaving them temporarily weightless for the duration of the landing.

The bridge had been locked at the lowest-most position in the circular-drum construction of the spacecraft. This at least now allowed them the weak Martian gravity which, over the last few days, James had slowly become accustomed too.

The interplanetary vessel had not been designed to land except in extreme circumstances. It was primarily designed to operate in either a weightless environment or rotating during flight, giving all its floors an artificial gravity. Trying to traverse the vessel in its current state was like living in a strange sort of nightmare. At least the bridge was the right way up. Above them you could find yourself walking on the walls or ceilings whilst moving from room to room. Luckily, all hazardous loose items had been stowed away whilst the current rearmament modifications were taking place.

The Captain turned to look down at James, who was slightly shorter in stature than the Captain. "Never needed to land before. The spaceship is normally always loaded or unloaded in orbit. We've only landed now to save ourselves some time, which we have very little of. We could have taken the equipment required up into orbit to reattach the weapons hardware, but that would have required much more manpower. What with the drone spacecraft having to take up tools and cutting gear as well, well, you get the picture. Here, we are directly in front of the old storage sheds where we managed to locate the carefully-stored weapon systems. Even as we speak some of my crew members are helping the facility personnel outside weld the support struts back in place that were removed along with all the weapons hardware. Hopefully, we shouldn't be down here more than twelve hours. Had we tried to do what we plan to do here, up there in orbit, it would have taken us at least two extra days," he remarked, jerking his thumb upwards indicating exactly where 'up there' was.

Both James and the Captain stared out the bridge observation windows towards the west, right down the left-hand valley of Hebes Chasma. The left hand southern valley floor had a dark colouring, almost black, signifying hard base rock. Unlike the right-hand northern valley, that was a much lighter colour, consisting of golden shifting sand. Behind them, some kilometres to the east, the Facility buildings were tucked out of sight round the base of the central mesa.

"There's one question that has been bugging me. Why were the old weapons left here in the first place?" James enquired.

"Ah, that's a good question. Like I recently explained to Miss Applegate, back in the old days, all space vessels were fitted with weapons as a matter of course during construction. During the last fifty years or so, they were deemed unnecessary as they were hardly, if ever used, certainly not in anger. So at some point, someone in authority decided they were to be removed probably due to some global space peace treaty. Most likely they were decommissioned during one of the many refits. Probably an early Corporation analyst, one of your predecessors no doubt, decided that leaving them here was a good idea at the time. I'm not sure why. I'm glad that the Corporation listened though. It could have been something to do with preservation, with next to no atmosphere on Mars they would not corrode. Also, it was about the time of some pretty intense international terrorism with the overcrowding problems on Earth, they didn't want any powerful weapons somehow getting into revolutionists hands. Here on Mars they would be quite safe, tucked out of the way. Once we extract them from the storage sheds, they should be unmarked and in full, perfect, working order," he concluded, holding up his crossed fingers. James seemed satisfied with the explanation.

He grinned at the captain's show of optimism, then

crossing his own digits and holding them up in a show of positive solidarity.

"I'll keep mine crossed as well. Right, I feel like a spare wheel here, what can I do to help?" James had been assigned to *Oceans Dawn* after Carmen, Robert and he, had discussed their various options. One thing that they had all agreed on was having both Corporation analysts in one place would be a waste of resources. Robert opted to stay inside the Mars Facilities to assist Carmen with operations there, while James had been assigned to the interplanetary spaceship to support the captain and crew in any way possible.

"What can you do?" the captain replied to James question with a question.

"Well, I'm not much good with tools. I'm not sure I'd know where to start with a thermal welding lance. As for working outside in a spacesuit, in a low gravity environment, I've not had any training at that either," he stated with a shrug.

"I know!" the captain exclaimed. James almost saw the light bulb ignite above his head. "Follow me," he said, leading the way across the bridge.

James had an overwhelming feeling of déjà vu as the captain prompted him to sit in the same chair offered to him on his first visit to the bridge, during Mars orbital insertion when they first arrived from Earth.

"The weapons console," he announced grandly, as if it was suddenly going to perform a song and dance routine whilst he held his outstretched arms towards it.

James looked unimpressed at the dull lifeless hardware in front of him. Several dials and level indicators stared back at him blankly, showing absolutely no signs of activity.

"Now, we haven't switched this on in quite a while. There should be a manual here somewhere."

The captain rummaged through a shallow drawer he pulled out from under the desk. "Aha! Here we are," he said, as he plonked a grubby-looking scratched electronic media device in front of James. James switched it on, the operations manual cover page appeared.

"If you would like to acquaint yourself with the operational procedures, you can become a weapons array controller if you like? I have to say at this point you don't actually get to fire the weapons, that directive remains fully within my remit. What you have to do is make sure the weapons are ready to be fired with my requested fire power output. Don't worry about direction or distance too much. Although we can program those figures in, we usually let the targeting computer sort that out. It's just nice having a human overseeing the whole system that never was very reliable," he joked, trying to comfort James.

James began to tab through the manual's pages. It explained what each of the dials represented, how to read each one, what the individual meter readings meant and how to adjust their power levels.

"Okay, it looks easy enough," he finally said, nodding to himself.

"Good," Captain Cooper said with satisfaction. "We might be able to test the weapons some time later today with a bit of luck."

He left James pushing pages on and off the small screen with his fingers while he went to chase up the weapons installation teams outside the vessel.

—

Robert sat across from Carmen sitting behind her desk. Her office was becoming very familiar to him, it seemed like he had spent more elapsed time in here than anywhere else, even more time than in his sleeping quarters. This fact also showed on his face. He was tired, the last few days had taken its toll.

"Well, everything seems to be working according to our plans," announced Carmen, looking up from several pages of printout, intermixed with handwritten notes and the interactive electronic media devices on her desk.

"So far touch wood," Robert said. He taped his head referring to the ancient superstition. "James reported back to me a short while ago, they plan to test the weapons on *Oceans Dawn* within the hour. They are going to test them while grounded in the valley first, just to make sure the set up is correct. They can fine tune later once they are back in orbit."

Carmen smiled, at last some good news that was long overdue. "That's good, the quicker they are back in orbit the better I will feel. At least then we will have some mobile weapons for our defence," she said.

Robert nodded his agreement.

"All the other projects are progressing, albeit slowly, as predicted. Two of the four drone vessels assigned for remote kamikaze bombs have been completed. The scientific technicians mixed some explosive concoction very much like the obsolete nitro-glycerine in composition, but a lot more stable thankfully. The only unknown factor will be the VR controllers. I'm worried about the physiological effects? You know how twitchy they are normally! The drone spacecraft packed to the cross beams with the synthetic explosive, will make a substantial hole in whatever they happen to smash into!" Carmen finished in a crescendo, smacking one fist into the palm of her other hand.

"Let's hope it's an enemy vessel they crash into and not one of the facility buildings…" Robert retorted cynically, unfazed by Carmen's enthusiasm. "And the VR controllers, being at one mind with the vessels, don't go mad as they hypothetically commit suicide blowing themselves up! How are the scientific people getting on with the new scanner?" he asked, changing the subject.

"The lab techno guys are progressing well. Now they have tested the type of alloy employed by the aliens. With it, they have managed to adapt a long-range scanner to sweep specifically for its particular resonant molecular frequency. So far, they have managed to penetrate space just past the Asteroid Belt, but unfortunately, no further. Thankfully, after performing a thorough search of the entire belt, there are no signs of any alien spaceships at the moment. I relayed that information to Captain Cooper who was very relieved as he considers himself to be a 'sitting duck' at the moment," replied Carmen.

"That's good news, it gives us some warning if, or perhaps I should say when, they come," he said sombrely. The two of them continued to leaf through the accumulated plans scattered on the desk.

"What about the two mining spaceships out in the belt at the moment?" Robert liked to recap, turning all the information over in his mind, checking he hadn't forgotten anything.

"The same message has also been sent to both of them several times. *Astral Gem* has confirmed they are headed back albeit with only half a mined load. The other vessel, *Mother Lode* has not even acknowledged receipt. Still maintaining a stationary position, it would appear they are ignoring our warnings for the time being, continuing to mine for as long as possible."

"Can you send another urgent message, it is imperative they start back as soon as possible."

"We can but try," she said, picking up her personal communicator. "However, they are stubborn miners who are practically a law unto themselves."

"The longer they stay there, the more chance they will end up DEAD stubborn miners!" Robert exclaimed.

—

"Right, let's try that one more time please," Captain Cooper called out. "Testing microwave beam weapon number one, power output level five, range one thousand two hundred twenty-two metres, direction two hundred fifteen." He looked across at James who checked the instruments in front of him.

The weapons console was split into four sections. Two sections on the left were for the microwave beam operations. Two sections on the right were for the cutting lasers. Each section contained identical instruments pertinent to one of the four weapons that now adorned the outside of the vessel. Looking straight on at the circular drum shape, the four weapons had been installed at each main compass point. The two lasers were positioned north and south, with the two microwave weapons positioned east and west. On the weapons console, each individual weapon control section had three touch buttons. One recessed on/off glowed green when the weapon was operational. A second, if touched gently, would recharge the weapon when fully discharged, while a third would reset the weapon in case of a malfunction or computer glitch. A round concave dish-shaped glass screen illustrated a fish-eye three-dimensional display of the outside world directly in front of the vessel. It showed where the weapon was pointed using a bright red dot of laser light. Next to this was a power level readout with a simple touch slide control facility.

The slide control was currently set in the middle on level five. The south west wall of the Hebes Chasma valley over a thousand metres away showed clearly in the display dish with the readings showing the exact direction and range. The small laser dot, visible on the indented screen highlighted the outcrop of rocks the weapon was currently trained on.

"All readings correct, microwave beam weapon one is ready to fire Captain," replied James, just as the electronic manual had instructed him to respond.

"Firing now," the captain called out, touching the image of a switch on the glass control console in front of him. The only discernible sign that anything was happening was the slowly decreasing power output level for the microwave beam being fired. Once it was completely drained, James noticed the second touch button in front of him turn red. He gently tapped it to start the recharge process for the weapon. It would remain red until enough charge had been stored for a level five discharge. Unseen and undetected, a burst of micro radio waves hit the targeted cliff face at the speed of light. A small area of rock was instantly agitated causing small boulders to erupt from their surroundings. As the beam continued it began to melt the rock face creating small rivulets of molten lava. Those on the bridge witnessed a small dust cloud followed by some very slow falling pieces of rock face debris. James wondered if there was any way he could get out there to retrieve a lump or two. He remembered the very first time he laid eyes on the dark rock formations and thought it was almost magical looking. The Captain brought him out of his daydream.

"Mr. Cleaver, microwave one appears to be functional. Can we move onto microwave two please, set the same power level at five, range one thousand three hundred fifty-one metres, direction two hundred twenty-five," he announced.

James had noticed the Captain had this wonderful way of issuing an order, making it sound like he was asking you nicely if you would like to join him for a cup of tea. He set the instruments as he had been instructed. "All readings correct, microwave beam weapon two is ready to fire Captain."

Once again the captain touched the button to fire the weapon. Instead of the usual silence, there was a low audible whooping noise. The display also flashed a hypnotic sickly orange colour.

"Mr. Cleaver, cancel please."

James touched the reset button. The flashing light and noise ceased immediately.

"Okay, looks like we have a malfunction on microwave two. Please power down Mr. Cleaver," he ordered James politely, before talking to the outside crews. James sat back in the chair after cutting the power for the microwave weapon.

"Crossed wiring, or something similar I would imagine. They are looking into it," Captain Cooper announced to all those on the bridge.

Most of the crew had returned once the weapons installation had been completed. Now, it was just the facility personnel outside attempting to remedy the problem.

After a short while they were informed the fault had been rectified. James was instructed to power up the weapon once more. Again the Captain tentatively touched the firing square button on his glass console.

This time the weapon fired successfully. They then moved onto testing the cutting lasers one by one. Each test also resulted in satisfactory success. The valley wall now had several scars emblazoned on it as testimony. James was still a little worried and confused. He addressed the Captain for some answers.

"Captain, this process of alignment seems painfully slow to me. Even the targeting computer, seems to take forever, by the time we line up with an alien spacecraft and be ready to fire, they could have flown right past us," he said, sounding very concerned.

"These weapons are not designed for close quarters combat, far from it. It's definitely not like those fast action computer games of old. Out here, in real space, you have to think in a different context, the vast dimensions of space. Vessels covering huge distances in space are pitifully slow, more than you can possibly imagine. We will have plenty of time to set up, align and fire our weapons accurately. Remember, our weapons have almost unlimited range in the vacuum of space. Laser power does degenerate over distance eventually, but the microwave's power is constant, it will travel at the speed of light continuing to do so until eventually hitting something. If a hostile vessel ever got so close, close enough we couldn't line up on the target, we probably wouldn't be in a position to fight by then anyway. We would more than likely have been destroyed long before that point."

The temperature of the room must have dipped otherwise James couldn't understand why a little shiver passed down his spine. He sensed the other crewmembers on the bridge had had a similar reaction. The overall mood had become very sombre all of a sudden. This whole exercise was leading up to the point where they were going to have to do battle with alien spacecraft. The realisation, when it hit them, was like they had all simultaneously received a sobering slap in the face. Captain Cooper eventually broke the deathly silence, realising the seeds of fear he had just planted in everyone's head.

"Right then, lets continue with our testing. We need to make sure that both sets of weapons, when fired concurrently, work together. We require both lasers as well as both microwave beams to fire as one on any target subject thereby doubling the overall power impact. Mr. Cleaver, if you wouldn't mind. We will start again, this time with the cutting lasers."

The Captain continued to call out range, power and directions until he was satisfied that all the weapons were tuned correctly. James quickly picked up the speed at which he set the controls. Finally, after more combination testing, Captain Edmund Cooper addressed the entire crew via the intercom. He proudly declared they were fully armed and operational. There was a celebratory cheer from those facility workers outside, accompanying the clapping of hands by those on the bridge.

—

Carmen closed the connection on her personal communicator before turning to Robert. "Well. Do you want the good news or the bad news first?" she asked him.

"Good news, always good news first," he replied.

"*Oceans Dawn* is now weapons hot. The vessel just took off to return to orbit five minutes ago…" She paused, keeping Robert in suspense, not really knowing how to soften the blow of the bad news.

"And…" He pleaded.

"And the bad news is the new long-range scanner has picked up two alien spaceships entering the asteroid belt, it looks like they are headed directly for *Mother Lode*! The controllers have sent yet another alert message, but we fear it may already be too late."

"God help the crew," replied Robert who, whilst not being remotely religious, could not think of anything else to say on the spur of the moment.

23

Mother Lode

The asteroid-mining vessel *Mother Lode,* received the third alert message from Mars at about the same time its own scanners picked up the alien spacecraft traversing the asteroid belt on an intercept course.

The vessel's medical officer Krisztina Rizzo, who had been on watch on the bridge and received the latest priority one message from Mars, immediately woke up Sebastian Morris, the *Mother Lode* captain and mining operations controller in his quarters. As soon as he had emerged onto the bridge from his cabin, she replayed the message word for word just for his benefit.

Krisztina had a small stature and build, actually quite petite and delicate, which was unusual for an asteroid miner. Her plain facial features were marred by a diagonal scar running from the bridge of her nose, continuing under her right eye down the right cheek, the result of a microwave frequency modulation lance malfunction in the gear room a few tours back. The raw looking scar and neck-length auburn hair cut unevenly giving a ragged saw-edge appearance, made her look rather intimidating.

At first Sebastian listened uninterested whilst yawning and

scratching various personal parts of his anatomy until the seriousness of the message, and the scanner readouts finally sunk in. Now, he deeply regretted ignoring the two previous warnings about possible hostile aliens. His thinking up until that point had been one of his rival mining captains was playing a very complicated joke on him, trying to make him leave behind half of the as yet un-mined ore. Perhaps, between them over the years, the various mining captains had played one practical joke too many on each other, he contemplated as an afterthought. Now the whole crew would suffer the consequences.

Sebastian Morris shouted into his personal communications transmitter that was so close to his mouth he almost swallowed half of it in the process. "JJ, Tarek! Get your arses back on board now, we've got company," he growled, before dropping the device onto the console table top in front of him.

Outside, Jerome Jackson, the first officer of *Mother Lode*, along with crew member Tarek Miah, had been making the last few cuts to a manganese-rich iron asteroid. They had virtually finished raping the asteroid of its precious metal when Sebastian called the abrupt end to their gruelling endeavours.

Sebastian had a habit of never shaving for the duration of a mining tour, now his six-week silver-streaked facial growth was long enough to run his fingertips through, which he did so quite often. He liked to think it helped him focus his mind. He certainly needed a huge amount of deep mental concentration now.

"Looks like we might have to have to make a run for it," he muttered under his breath. After several quick mental calculations regarding the alien vessels' speed bearing down on them, he soon realised that was no longer an option. The velocity of the alien spacecraft was far superior to the maximum thrust of *Mother Lode,* even if it dumped the three-quarter-full mined-ore cargo sac.

"Open all channels and frequencies. I have an announcement to make."

Krisztina complied with the abrupt order. They were all used to his overbearing bossiness. Nodding in Sebastian's direction once, she indicated that all channels were now open for him. Every member of the crew could speak to everyone else. It also ensured anything said would eventually be relayed back to the Mars Facilities Communications unit.

"Attention all crew members, this is your mining ops controller, Sebastian," he announced, just in case they hadn't already recognised his voice. "We have a situation developing. It would appear that what we originally perceived as hoax messages about aliens coming to kidnap us, may actually have some bearing on reality after all. We have two unidentified vessels coming straight towards us. According to our statistical readouts they are four times the size of *Mother Lode* and even larger than the Corporation interplanetary vessels, also, they are not responding to any of our hails for identification. They will arrive in our space in approximately twenty minutes. I have calculated that it's too late to outrun them, we have very little option but to await their arrival. I'll highlight the contents of the previous messages, just so we know what we are up against."

He then replayed the main contents of the previous Martian warning messages that described in detail the aliens, the alien micro robots as well as a brief synopsis of deadly human encounters with them so far.

"… so we have been warned they are very hostile and have specifically targeted us. Apart from the microwave cutting lances, we have no weapons to speak of, so I'm open to suggestions to what we might do to protect ourselves," he paused, hoping for some positive response.

Viktoria Larsen and Pierre Lefebvie, who had been asleep in their cabins, were now sitting up in their bed cradles. Viktoria was rubbing her eyes, Pierre was yawning uncontrollably while they both listened intently.

Isaac Jacobs and Nicky Palmer were midway through eating supper having finished their shift a couple of hours previously. They held spoons of spicy food poised in front of open mouths. Both, acting like a pair of identical twins, instantly lost their appetites dropping the two spoons simultaneously back into their bowls. A few specks of curry sauce splashed the plastic-covered table top as a result.

Viktoria struggled to brush her long blonde hair away from her face that clung there with the help of static electricity. She swore in her native Norwegian before letting loose an uncontrolled outburst.

"You bloody fool, I told you to take those messages seriously! They were from the Facilities Controller for Christ's sake!"

Sebastian felt hurt, the words stabbed at his soft insides. Although he looked mean and acted serious most of the time, he actually had quite a sensitive soul.

"Look, I'm really sorry okay. We all discussed it. Hell, we even had a vote either to return, or stay and finish mining the asteroid. I'm not taking the entire blame for this situation now," he replied indignantly.

"Well I didn't want to stay. Just make sure there is an entry in the log saying I voted to get back to Mars, as soon as we received the first of the official warning communiqués," she said in a huff, arms now folded tightly across her large ample chest.

Isaac and Nicky, leaving their bowls of steaming tikka masala on the mess table, without saying a word, had arrived at a similar conclusion. They entered the gear room making their way towards the spacesuit lockers.

"Nicky and I are going to get suited up," Isaac said out loud, just as the inner airlock door opened. JJ and Tarek stepped into the gear room and immediately set about removing their spacesuits and exoskeletons.

Nicky waved at them before ripping open her locker door. She dragged her suit out sending boots flying. One was accidentally aimed at Isaac. Instinctively, he dodged out the way as it sailed past him.

"Hey! Slow down will you!" Isaac shouted.

"Just in a hurry that's all," Nicky shrugged in reply.

"What about the one-person scout spaceship? Couldn't one of us get away in that?" Pierre suggested, now out of his bed cradle pulling on some clothes.

"How do we decide who?" Sebastian queried.

"You're the boss, you decide," Pierre replied impatiently, placing the decision fairly on the shoulders of the controller. Sebastian thought about it for at least one second. The most experienced pilot for the scout would be the asteroid surveyor. The one person who was used to flying inside the belt would be the best choice he decided.

"Okay, Nicky. Once you're suited up, grab the emergency survival pack, get up to the scout and disappear fast!"

No one questioned his decision. They would have all come to the same conclusion it was that obvious. Besides, the main thought on everyone's minds at that moment was probably the same. They were all going to be killed and abducted by the alien creatures. It was a question of when, how and where. Escaping in the scout spacecraft would probably just prolong the when.

"Okay, I'll try to get away as best I can, but I don't reckon my chances much," she said, accepting the proposal.

"Well, we'll be putting up a bit of a fight one way or another. It might give you some time to put some distance between you, and us and them. Maybe you'll be so far away once they finished with us they may not bother chasing after you. Now then, we have eight minutes before they arrive. So, I'll ask again, does anybody have any constructive suggestions?"

JJ and Tarek swung back the exoskeleton head protection bars and removed their helmets.

"Well, if we are going to stay and meet them head on, I'm going back outside with full air tanks and a fully-charged microwave lance. If one of the bastards comes anywhere near me I'll slice the fucker in two."

"Okay JJ, your choice."

"I think I'll join him, we might stand more chance outside in our protective exoskeletons, especially if they are the giants they are reputed to be. It might give us the edge we need," added Tarek, turning towards Jerome. "Okay with you JJ?"

"Fine by me," replied JJ with a half smile. Although he didn't feel too happy about the prospect of hand to hand combat with alien adversaries, the thought 'the more the merrier' popped into his mind.

Tarek and JJ proceeded to replenish their suits with full air supply cylinders swopping out half empty ones.

"That'll be three of us then. And you, you better get going," said Isaac, giving Nicky a big hug before pushing her towards the airlock inner door.

She blew him a kiss. "Take care. All of you," she shouted, pulling the airlock door closed behind her.

Isaac spun on his heels and bounded over to his own exoskeleton unit. "Grab a fully-charged lance for me while you're there Tarek," he said, stepping back onto the foot plates of his mechanical machine.

They now had less than five minutes before the aliens would be upon them as Nicky launched the scout from its dock on top of *Mother Lode*. From the cockpit she looked out in the general direction of the approaching alien vessels, but couldn't see anything through the myriad of rocks and boulders as far as the eye could see on the horizontal plain. Above her current position, she could see the distinctive boundary at the very edge of the Asteroid Belt.

Being the asteroid surveyor on this tour, she had located the manganese-rich lump of rock even before they reached the beginnings of the Asteroid Belt. She remembered thinking at the time, how lucky they were, not to have to go hunting deep inside the Belt for something valuable and worthwhile.

Reading her current situation, Nicky thought she might have a slim chance of getting a fair distance when she reached open space that was so close. So close in fact, she felt she could reach out to touch it. However, she had only just lifted off when an ear shattering, mind-piercing noise, cut through everybody's head.

A hollow cylinder, similar in design to the alien resupply cylinders only much larger, four metres larger in fact, sliced right through *Mother Lode* amidships. Everything along its leading edge was vaporised leaving a four metre diameter cylindrical void in its wake. The core cross section of the spacecraft, cut out by the cylinder, trailed after the alien device as it exited the opposite side of *Mother Lode*. Parts of cabins and corridors were now visible from outside the vessel through the swirling mess that was evacuated air and debris from within. Eventually the noise subsided as the cylinder receded away from them, slicing semi-circle sided chunks, even complete cylindrical tubes of rock, out of any asteroid that happened to be in its path. Where it would end up was anybody's guess.

On the bridge, the screeching noise was replaced by decompression klaxons, along with various other audible and visual alarms, informing the crew in operations control that all was not quite as it should be elsewhere on the vessel.

"What the hell was that?" Krisztina shouted, after regaining some composure. Her jaw ached from grinding her teeth as a result of the painful noise.

"Whatever it was, it has successfully managed to sever helm control. The fusion drive just went offline. Now, we're like a sitting duck in a bucket of water!" Sebastian shouted angrily in reply.

Having regained control of her spacecraft after the excruciating noise subsided, Nicky just managed to avoid crashing into a small boulder-sized asteroid.

"Bloody hell, whatever that noise was went right through my head! Okay people, I am outta here. Bag a few bad guys for me," she said, manoeuvring between the last two large asteroids allowing her clear access to the vacuum of space beyond.

"That's just bloody great! Now I'm stuck in my cabin," called out Pierre, as he noticed the red cross on the inside of his airtight cabin door.

"Whatever that was just put a hole right through the spacecraft, including the corridor outside."

"You not alone Pierre, we now cut off in operations control. How are you others coping?" Sebastian asked no one in particular, hoping everyone would respond. There was quite a pause before Tarek broke the silence.

"The three of us are outside the airlock now."

Sebastian leant forward to look down out of the panoramic window of the control room. He could now see the three figures in spacesuits below him inside their protective exoskeleton units, their backs to each other. Each one brandished a microwave cutting lance.

"What about Viktoria?" Tarek asked.

"Gone I'm afraid, along with whatever it was that passed right through the vessel. She was in the next cabin to me. I am almost sure that room has been compromised. No points for guessing what happened to her if that was the case," replied Pierre.

No one wanted to contemplate what happened to Viktoria once her body was exposed to outer space without a suit.

"Will you look at that?" JJ exclaimed, pointing out into the mass of asteroids with his free hand, all thoughts of Viktoria suddenly forgotten.

Isaac and Tarek swung round to look in the direction he pointed out using the barrel of his cutting lance. Two copper-coloured oval objects were moving fast. They dodged and dived, twisted, rolled and turned expertly to avoid the mass of different sized rocks and boulders as they flew past them. They resembled two fish swimming fast upstream avoiding all manner of rocks, tree branches and snags along a river bed. Tarek thought they looked quite majestic in a way. It was a shame he silently considered, that whatever creatures lurked inside these amazing looking vessels, were so intent on killing them all. He snapped out of the trance-like spell under which they had all somehow become engrossed.

"What'll we do now?" he asked the others, as they maintained their position in front of the main airlock.

"There was talk about little tiny robot devices. They look like little insects and try to get into your suit by chewing holes in it, watch out for those and watch each other's back," advised Sebastian.

The pair of slick, two-hundred-metre long spaceships slowed, as they made their final approach towards the stricken mining vessel.

"Exactly how small ARE these little robots?" Isaac asked, sounding quite terrified.

Tarek visualised him being as white as a clean new bed sheet behind his visor.

"I mean, can we see them at all?"

"Well, according to the original warning messages, just one of the many reasons I didn't believe them, they are supposed to be just over half a centimetre long. They attack in small groups travelling together in spherical probes. The probes themselves are only about two centimetres in diameter," explained Sebastian.

"Well, we might be able to see those coming towards us providing they are not travelling too fast," Tarek insisted. "Keep your eyes peeled," he added, as they prepared as best they could for the impending attack.

—

On board the scout Nicky checked the instruments one more time. She sent a mayday distress signal followed by her current co-ordinates, her planned flight path, trajectory, estimated speed and expected final co-ordinates. Once programmed, it was just a simple case of handing control to the auto-pilot. She touched the small glass display panel that allowed the onboard computer to assume automatic control.

The fusion drive immediately kicked in, pushing the little vessel faster and faster. Behind, the Asteroid Belt grew steadily smaller with each passing second. She had no idea what fate she had left her fellow crew members to, but for now, she had to look out for herself.

Reclining the seat into an almost horizontal position she readied herself for the injection of drugs that would put her into the Dormouse Torpor State. It was a little more complicated, wearing a spacesuit inside the cramped single person spacecraft, rather than being on a fully crewed mining vessel. In those situations, without being so confined, other crew members could perform the necessary tasks required, especially the medical necessities. Here, on her own, she had to insert the multiple intravenous lines into her arm, through the spacesuit special airtight medical access panel situated in the crook of her left elbow. The several tubes clicked into a small containment rack strapped to her lower arm. She had to rely on the life support machine to inject the correct concoction of drugs for her specific metabolism. Then the machine would continually monitor her bodily readouts, especially after the spacesuit heating elements plunged her body to near zero temperatures.

She didn't trust machines. What if something went wrong? She didn't like the idea of giving the control of her life over to a bunch of wires, micro transistors and computer chips, but she had no choice. She wasn't sure if she would ever wake up, especially if the aliens caught up with the scout. What if there were more alien spacecraft out here waiting to intercept her vessel? What if her suit elements failed to heat up to defrost her? Too many what ifs! At least being drugged in the Dormouse Torpor State she wouldn't feel any pain, or suffer should anything go wrong, one way or another.

She set about carefully programming her current personal details, height and weight, along with the fluid volumes of each of the separate drugs that she normally required. There were six separate fluids to put her into suspended animation, and then five that would bring her out of it. The amounts would also need to be adjusted slightly for the simple fact she had eaten a small amount of food recently and, even more importantly, not evacuated her bowels, there had been no time. That problem in itself could lead to serious complications. However, that was the least of her worries at the present time. At last, she was instructed to touch the button that would inject her to start the whole process. Within seconds she was unconscious, now at the full mercy of an analytical medical technological device.

The small scout spaceship plunged on, faster and faster into the dark void that lay between The Asteroid Belt and Mars.

24

A Simple Army Exercise

Sergeant Paula Alvarez tapped the table in front of her with the blunt edge of a rifle laser sight. The eight soldiers that sat in front of her abruptly stopped their speculative mutterings. The two chewing gum, suddenly realising they could be heard, stopped abruptly. Ricardo Irvine sat on a chair that was facing backwards, his legs spread either side of the backrest upon which his elbows now leaned. All those whose bodies were not facing forward, turned in their chairs to face the front of what could loosely be called a classroom. It was in fact the briefing/debriefing room at the rear of hangar five. Paula stood on the raised stage area giving a clear line of sight to the back of the room. She was definitely high enough to see that all of them had recently been to have their hair cut very short for the upcoming exercise, a normal practice.

"Right, let's have a final run down of the equipment check list. Are all combat exoskeletons now stowed securely?" she asked. All nodded as one person.

"Including mine?" she looked sternly at no one individual in particular, just at the group as a whole.

"Saw to it personally myself Sarge," instructed Corporal Frank Lloyd. They had been hard at work since 06:00 hours that Friday morning, loading the cavernous cargo jet with their essential equipment. Stopping once for breakfast at 08:30, the half hour respite was but a brief pause before the seemingly never-ending insertion of military gear on board the jet continued unabated. They used their exoskeleton units to fetch and carry as the units could lift five times the weight a normal human being could, with the added bonus that they never tired out.

"Tesla rifles?" she quizzed. They all grumbled affirmatives as every time Paula, using the rifle laser sights thin bean of pinpoint light, ran down the check list projected on the rear wall. Spacesuits, stun grenades, sonic and flash grenades, these were the new ones she pointed out, capable of temporary blinding for at least thirty seconds. Spare weapons crate, rifle refill hydrogen gas cylinders, uniforms, spare boots, spacesuits etc, the list went on and on. She then moved onto the larger items, the heavy ground-based weapons, dual-seat ground vehicles, even down to the two-person stealth scout spacecraft that was nicely packed away in its transportation crate. Paula was going to have fun assembling that piece of hardware she thought to herself, as she finally came to the end of the long itemised list, a list that appeared to have gone on forever.

"Okay, now the rest of today's itinerary. Lunch is 13:30 hours, make it brief. If you suffer from travel sickness I would advise that you make it very light unless you want to see your menu choices again later this afternoon..." Corporal Ross Perez interrupted by sticking his hand in the air.

"Perez, can it not wait until I have finished the briefing?"

"Well, I was just curious why we need the outer atmosphere exoskeleton propulsion attachments? Also, our two vehicles have been fitted with extra-wide off-road soft-tread tyres normally used on the moon. I was just wondering what this exercise is all about. Can you cut out the crap and tell us where we are going exactly?" he enquired.

"Corporal Perez, you've always been an impatient, inquisitive and impetuous sod. You'll just have to wait like all the rest, now shut it. I'll get to the exciting details this afternoon. It's just the boring stuff for now. Okay, where was I? Ah yes lunch, after lunch we assemble back here for the final briefing where I will THEN inform you of our destination," she smiled sweetly, a smile directed specifically at Ross Perez. He felt like giving her the finger, but decided it wasn't worth getting put on a charge, missing the mysterious exercise and having his pay docked just for one lousy insult.

"Until then you'll have to carry on speculating. You see, I just can't trust you to keep your traps shut for one minute, especially in the canteen. After the final briefing, we take our places on the jet for departure, everybody happy with the plans so far? Are there any other questions?"

"Yeah. What crap have we got for lunch today?" joked Aban Hossini. Some of them chuckled. Paula did not.

"Okay, be back here at 14:00 hours on the dot. Dismissed," she said, just before the noisy shuffling of hastily vacated chairs began as they rushed to exit the room. Alex Manso wanted to enter just as they got to the door to leave. He held it open for the rush of departing squaddies narrowly avoiding being bowled over. Some of them looked hard into his eyes as they passed him by, he half-heartedly smiled, not quite sure what they were thinking. He always considered himself a good military strategist only having their best interests at heart. He considered what they really thought about him? His considerations were short lived as Paula appeared in the doorway.

"Ah, Paula, can I join you for lunch? I have a few points to go over, last-minute details, that sort of thing."

"Yes, of course Sir. I'm just on my way to the Sergeants' mess," she said, placing the laser site in her small official-looking briefcase.

"We can talk on the way there if you like," she added, while switching on the electromagnetic buckles.

"Shall we then," he said, offering her the chance to lead the way. He considered it was the gentlemanly thing to do. She hated male chivalry, sighing heavily to show her distaste, before taking the lead and heading for the hangar exit in disgust.

After lunch, with the squad now fully nourished, they re-assembled in the briefing room at the rear of hangar five. This time they were eager, thirsty for more information regarding the whereabouts of their secret mission and eventual destination. There would be no more speculation, now was the time. They were attentive, quiet as mice.

"Right ladies and gentlemen," Paula addressed the silent group. She paused momentarily before continuing. "I shall now pass you over to our Military Analyst for a brief outline of our plans for the next few days."

Alex took Paula's place at the front of the room. "Afternoon," he started. There was a mumbled jumble of replies from the group. "I understand that Paula, sorry, Sergeant Alvarez, has hinted to you that we are in the process of testing how much time we need to ready ourselves for a possible invasion at Borealis Station by a hostile force, potentially extra terrestrial."

There was a ripple of light malevolent laughter round the room that quickly abated.

"You may think this exercise is amusing, but I would like you to take it seriously from now on. This will be a precision military operation that I want to run like clockwork. Wherever we go, wherever we get posted around the globe, we are respected as the most efficient professional fighting force in the world today. Let's try to give the impression that's still very much the case, on what you may deem a meaningless and amusing venture."

He waited a second or two to let that definitive sentence sink in. "So, as you already know, we are scheduled to fly out of here in about twenty minutes, our destination is Borealis Station. Once there, the next stage of the exercise will begin. We are going to deploy all our equipment onto the Elevator to make sure there is sufficient space."

There were sighs, grunts and general moans from the small fighting force. All they could see was more humping of gear off the carefully packed cargo carrier into the elevator, more work and effort for no valid reasons. Alex held up his hands to calm the mumblings.

"Okay, listen up. I know you're thinking it's a lot of physical effort for not much in the way of return. However, once fully loaded, we are going to ascend with all our equipment, right up to satellite two." Now there was silence. "Once at the top we are going to perform a few tasks in our skeletal units, I'll give you more on that once we are underway and are safely in the Elevator. All I will say at this point is this, the Corporation have a piece of hardware they want us to test out, give it the once over, a full military hands-on opinion."

It was so quiet if someone dropped a pin you would have heard it. They hadn't actually considered they would be ascending in the Elevator.

"Right then, any questions?" Alex concluded.

Two hands went up, those of Private Sergio Laurant and Private Ricardo Irvine. Alex pointed to Ricardo as he thought his hand was slightly faster punching the air above his head.

"Sir, there have been some pretty strange rumours coming back from Gateway about civil unrest out on Mars, unexplained deaths, industrial espionage, is there any truth to those? Is that what this exercise is really about? Are we perhaps going a bit further than Satellite Two?" he quizzed.

Alex sighed. He'd been expecting this sort of question and was only too aware of the idle gossip that had recently sprung up around the base. He decided to dodge round the issue for now. They would get the full picture soon enough.

"I too have heard some of the scaremonger stories. At the moment all you need to know is that we are going up to Satellite Two to test a piece of Corporation hardware. That's what the press, news agencies and even the Company Captain, has been briefed is about to happen. That's it as far as us, this base and the media are concerned!" He noticed a few glances take place between some of the soldiers. They were beginning to suspect all was not what it seemed. He pointed to Sergio.

"Yes Private Laurant. You had a question."

"I was going to ask much the same sort of thing as Private Irvine. However, what I will like to add is this. You've got a good team here, some of the best from the platoon as far as I can see." He glanced round the room. There were some agreeing gestures and mutterings from some of the others. "Also, we respect you Sir. You are one of, if not the finest Military Analyst on the base. What I will ask is you are totally honest with us up front. We suspect something's going on, there's some sort of hidden agenda here. You don't have to feed us this bullshit…" He was cut short mid-sentence.

"That's enough soldier!" shouted Alvarez. "Right, this briefing is over. Squad Shun! Now fall out into the main hangar," she barked out the order.

The squaddies jumped up to attention before filing out through the door without another word muttered.

"That could have gone down better," Alex half whispered to Paula, feeling a bit dejected as the last soldier shuffled through the doorway.

"Smart bunch Sir, hard to fool," she replied with a wink.

"Yes, I'm sure they will keep me on my toes."

—

The flight to Borealis Station was fairly non-eventful, as was the near perfect touchdown on the ice runway. The cargo jet parked itself directly under the main Elevator platform. Lifting cranes started hoisting the crates of equipment up onto trains of flat bed trailers. The trailers were headed by small, squat, powerful tractors with soft rubberised tracked wheels. With full payloads, looking like giant caterpillars, they trundled across the foyer into the main hangar.

Fire team one helped unload the jet and load the flat bed trains while fire team two helped load the Elevator. There were very few Corporation personnel working. It was as if the majority of employees had been given the day off.

The Elevator was nearly full to bursting by the time they had finished loading all the equipment including, the last bulky items they had to stow, their fighting exoskeleton units, many of which were almost drained of power. The squaddies plugged them into portable recharging units. Without further ado, they all donned spacesuits. With air supplies and heating elements checked for functionality, they climbed into the Orbital Space Elevator personnel cabin. Alex spoke briefly with an elevator technician who initiated the slow accent to begin.

"What's the Elevator maximum payload? Have we exceeded it do you think?" Paula asked Alex, as she clipped on her belt seat restraints. They were now speaking using the spacesuit intercom units.

"No, not quite. Very close to it, but we're still within tolerable limits. It's the storage area that's turned out to be the main bugbear. We've had to leave some of our heavy equipment spares behind. Even then, it might take a little bit longer to reach Satellite Two than a normal lift, but we'll get there eventually," he replied.

"Attention everyone, you'd best try to get some sleep while we have the luxury of some spare time," Paula suggested, addressing all the soldiers under her command.

The accent was slow, arduously so. Some of the soldiers managed a snooze, most just welcomed the rest. It had been a busy day so far. It was far from finished.

A slight muffled clunk woke Alex. He sat up with a jolt, the waist of his suit pulling at his restraints. He hated sleeping in a spacesuit. The inside of the helmet was no soft pillow. Slowly climbing into the weightless environment of space, it does become easier to sleep without squashing your ears against the inside of your helmet. He wanted to rub his eyes, but had to settle with blinking rapidly to rid them of the small amount of built-up crusty mucus residue.

"We've arrived Sir," said Paula, floating weightless beside him. He undid the restraining clips from his belt trying to stretch as best he could in the restricted cabin. This was not a good idea as he started to drift backwards with the reaction. He grabbed an upright handrail to steady himself.

"Okay Sergeant, you know the drill. Don't forget, they need to attach propulsion devices to their exoskeletons before doing anything else."

Alex hung onto a cross beam support as if his life depended on it. He had just about forgotten how it all became very different up here. You had to start thinking in three dimensions and being weightless, that took some getting used to. One small push in one direction and you carry on forever in the opposite direction, unless you hit something first, even then you don't stop, but rebound off in a new direction.

Sergeant Paula Alvarez set her subordinates to work. In this environment, it was a lot easier to move the now weightless crates and boxes from the Elevator cargo bays into the container. This container had been purposely modified to contain military equipment. Special recessed areas matched the array of sizes that made up the standard army cargo crates. They were secured by thick cross straps to keep them drifting around during flight. Along one side of the container were alcoves designed specifically for ten fighting exoskeletons. As Alex didn't possess a fighting unit, only nine of the alcoves would be used on this trip. Once loading had finished, the power units now discarded by the soldiers, were also secured by straps into the skeletal unit moulds. In securing, they automatically plugged in to recharge from the solar power panels situated on the outside of the container. The ninth unit had just finished being tied off when the orbital cargo shunting spacecraft arrived.

At the opposite end of the specialist container could be found the main living quarters. They were all instructed to make their way there now, taking turns via the main airlock that could only manage two human bodies at one time. As the last two soldiers took off their helmets, all ten of them were now assembled in the main reception room. Several short corridors led off this main room leading to sleeping quarters. Alex addressed the last of the soldiers to arrive.

"It's alright. Just remove helmets. We're not stopping long so keep the rest of your suits on. This area is automatically shielded so we can speak freely. Now then, the real reason we are here," he paused as they shuffled closer together. There were a few 'I told you so' elbows dug into the ribs of the less sceptical types among them.

"I didn't say a great deal before, and you'll understand why in a moment, mainly because Paula and I still can't quite believe the real reason we are here ourselves, anyway, here goes. I know some of you suspected an ulterior motive regarding this exercise…"

"I knew it!" Laurant shouted, unable to contain himself before apologising for the interruption.

"Okay, as I was saying, some, if not all of you, suspected

there was more to this exercise than I was letting on earlier. I'm sorry, but it was necessary for the reasons I hope you will come to understand."

Alex went on to describe the situation on Mars in great detail during the time they were hauled up to Gateway. There were some open mouths, some disbelieving stares, even one crooked smile. All remained silent until he finished.

Paula realised she needed to pull her troops back from the brink of insanity to the real world. "So, now you know the full story. It's hard to fathom and I still don't believe in these aliens myself. I don't think I will either, not until I'm face to face with one! However, they are determined to send us to Mars, so there must be substance to the mission. Meanwhile, we have to be professional about this. Remember our motto, 'Assume the worse, fear the unexpected. Adapt and overcome'. We should be getting some intelligence from the Mars Facilities once we have hooked up with *Stellar Dusk*. That Intel will be invaluable in understanding our potential new enemy," she finished.

At first they just stared amongst themselves, still undecided about what they had just heard. Then, one by one they started talking, then asking questions that couldn't be answered by Alex or Paula. The noise levels increased, becoming louder, as questions spawned yet more questions.

"Okay, hold on everyone, quiet down," pleaded Alex, trying to restore order.

"SHUT IT!" Paula shouted, the words cutting through the air like a samurai sword. Instantly, quiet descended. Alex smiled at her as a way of saying thank you.

"Right, well, there's not much more to add to be honest. You know as much as I do now. I can't answer any more of your questions even if I wanted to. We'll just have to wait to see what information has been sent from the Facilities."

There was still a general air of uneasiness within the ranks, but they remained quiet and thoughtful.

Suddenly, out of the hush, Nesrine Ben Ali spoke up. "Hey Sergio, didn't you once mention your little sister had gone to Mars?"

"Yes, that's right, last time I spoke to her she said she was going out into the Asteroid Belt on a mining vessel, all part of her training to be an asteroid surveyor. I wonder if we'll get the chance to meet up. I hope she's alright," he said thoughtfully.

"She's a bit of a looker by all accounts," Ross Perez chipped in.

"Don't even think about it!" Sergio sneered, and then added. "Looks like I'm gonna have to keep a real close eye on you."

His eyes narrowed becoming slits as he stared back at Ross. Ross gazed hard in return, until both cracked up laughing, grinning broadly and hugging one another as only good friends and comrades can when sharing a deep meaningful tease.

25

All Quiet Before...

The Saturn ice tugboats were making good progress on their voyage back to Mars. Three small spacecraft were now currently flying an inline formation traversing the void between Saturn and Jupiter. Apart from their unique names blazoned in large capital letters down the sides of each vessel, they looked like peas from the same pod. *The Amelia* was leading the way, followed by *The Phoebe* in the middle, with *The Lily* bringing up the rear. They were precisely on course having almost attained maximum top speed.

The small spaceships, resembling tropical box fish, were dwarfed by the enormous roughly square lump of bluish ice they were transporting. The massive blocks, three kilometres by three kilometres in size, were effortlessly pushed before them through the vacuum of space.

On board, within each ice-tugboat bridge control room there could be found a very similar scenario. All were bathed in almost complete darkness, the distant feeble sunlight refracted through the ice casting a lighter shade of grey on the rear walls behind the observation window.

The usually noisy artificial gravity gyros were silent, switched off for the duration of the flight home. The fusion engines were maintaining a faint throbbing constant output, waiting for the halfway point just after Jupiter gravity assist, where they could switch off altogether. They would fire up again to turn the cubes and initiate reverse thrust once they were between the Asteroid Belt and Mars. This would eventually slow the spacecraft to a safe speed as they approached their final destination, the Mars Facilities, or more precisely, the ice dumping grounds to the south of Hebes Chasma.

All six crew members were securely strapped into their double bed cradles while hooked up to the medical units that had put them into the Dormouse Torpor State for the duration of the journey. Every so often the cradle would vibrate the comatose bodies to agitate their muscles. Even with the liquid chemical thinners in their blood streams, their haemoglobin also required stimulation, helping its immensely slow progress round the body, pushed by a heart performing only three to four beats every minute.

The spaceships' auto pilots were in complete control now, ready to correct any course deviation that may occur to the pre-set flight plan. Indeed, this automatic action had been already been required by *The Phoebe* during this flight, shortly after they had left the rally point. The enormous ice cube had been peppered by a flash of micro meteorites knocking it slightly off course. A concise, controlled burst by one of the side thrusters, nudged the spacecraft back into line with the other two vessels on their exact calculated trajectory.

Suddenly, simultaneously, the onboard long-range scanners for all three vessels reacted as one. Image display screens sprung to life, lighting up to cast eerie shadows round the ghostly control rooms, then dimmed automatically in contrast with the surrounding darkness. The view exhibited was identical on all three spacecraft display screens. Two unidentified objects appeared on the bottom edge at the furthest limit of the scanner's range.

Dimensions for both identical objects popped up inside small boxes set to one side. Thin black lines joined the information boxes to each displayed item. These readouts were also repeated on all three spacecraft displays. The alien vessels were two hundred kilometres long by one hundred kilometres broad travelling at one point four million kilometres per hour. The only information the scanners couldn't relate, was the fact that they looked distinctly like enormous copper-coloured rugby balls in outside appearance.

At the moment they were so distant, they were no immediate threat to the Saturn ice-tugboats' progress. If they came within half a million kilometres, triggering the short-range scanners, then the auto pilot on each vessel would have no choice other than to start the lengthy task of reviving the crews. They would issue the override command to the medical units to bring the crews out from the Dormouse Torpor State, back to full consciousness to investigate the close proximity danger.

As the two alien vessels slowly progressed further onto the long-range display from the bottom edge, a large circular object started to descend from the top of the screen to join them. It was in front of the vessels offset to the left slightly. A small box appeared next to it with a thin line joining the box with the emerging circle. The box had one short word inside it. That word was Jupiter.

Miss Rebecca Jones fired the gas injector syringe into the patient's good arm where the administered drug hit the bloodstream immediately. The physician then shook the patient by the same arm trying to awake her from a previously drug-induced coma.

"Mei-Lien, Mei-Lien," she called softly. There was a low

groan, a disgruntled mumble issued forth as Mei-Lien finally stirred. Her distinctive oriental eyes flickered briefly before opening slightly, but not without putting up quite a struggle.

"Watch out, watch out," Mei-Lien muttered, trying to put her arms up to protect her face. Rebecca held onto the undamaged arm to stop her poking herself in the eye, the other injured arm, now severely restricted from the elbow down, lifted an inch off the bed before falling back. That was a good sign, Rebecca deduced.

Mei-Lien's lower arm was encased in a tube twenty centimetres in diameter. Extending from the wrist to the elbow, it was packed with a glutinous gel protecting the surgically repaired forearm. The thick sterile goo would also ensure there was no scarring once healed. The whole contraption was quite heavy.

Her eyes shut tight once more as Mei-Lien lapsed back into unconsciousness. Rebecca called her name again, slightly louder this time. For a second time the patient stirred, but this time it seemed more controlled. Finally, her eyes opened fully, staring blankly at Rebecca sitting on the side of her bed until slowly, looking around, she focused on her surroundings. The ward held six beds, three each side. It was bright, with walls painted white, reflecting bright strip lighting from the ceiling. The floor looked like it was covered in a shiny light yellow plastic material. The white light intensity suddenly made her squint and blink.

"Whoa, this looks distinctly like a hospital to me," she mumbled eventually. She was the only patient. The other five beds were neatly made up with their clean white sheets folded down.

"Can you turn the lights down please? They're hurting my eyes," she asked, bringing up her free hand to shield her face.

"Reduce lighting, twenty-five percent," Rebecca called

out. On the wall next to the entrance to the room, a slide control display automatically moved from one hundred to seventy-five percent. This action met approval from Mei-lien who smiled in appreciation.

"Sorry about that. Now, can you remember the very last thing that happened to you?" Rebecca asked.

"I recall I was cleaning, no, I'd finished cleaning, I was checking the hydraulic oil levels on my exoskeleton ready for the next shift. That's the last thing I can… wait though. Something must have hit the spacecraft. I felt a jolt and remember being knocked over. I fell to the floor. That's all I can recall I'm afraid. I must have cracked my head or something, there's nothing after that."

"That sounds about right. The crew found you on the floor in the gear room after the spaceship was hit and holed by a celestial object, you did have slight discoloured bruising on your head," Rebecca explained.

"So what's all this?" Mei-Lien pointed out the large heavy cylinder attached to her lower arm.

"Well, I don't know if I should say you were lucky or not? Apparently, your exoskeleton unit toppled over and fell on your arm. Unfortunately the artificial gravity was at ninety-five percent of one Earth G. It smashed the two bones in your forearm to splinters. You were lucky it was only your arm, and not your body it fell on, which would have been less repairable. Kieron McCabe, your medical officer, and I, managed to culture grow new bones from some of the broken splinters in the lab. You need to thank Kieron when you see him again. I don't know what he did on Earth before he came here, but he certainly knows his stuff in that department. It's a form of primitive cloning, very specific. It works extremely well with bones, not so good with human organs so he informed me, very hit and miss apparently," she added, as an afterthought.

"Anyway, I digress. I successfully operated to repair your

mangled arm by fitting the new bones, reattaching the muscles and so forth. Once the liquid protective bandage is off in two weeks' time, you should recover full use of the arm with very little physiotherapy," concluded Rebecca.

"Well, in that case I thank you now, and I shall thank Kieron as soon as I can. Can you ask him to come and visit so I can thank him personally?"

"Ah! That could be a bit difficult at the moment. I think I need to explain all that's happened while we've had you sedated in an induced coma. I think we could do with some refreshments first though as this catch up could take some time, tea or coffee?"

Rebecca disappeared for a few moments before returning with some tea for herself and coffee for Mei-Lien. Sitting on the bed once more, she explained all that had transpired since the accident, right up to the present time.

"Phew! That's some story," Mei-Lien stated, after what seemed like hours that was in fact just forty-five minutes. "And I'm going to be stuck in here for the next week or two. What if we are attacked by the aliens while I'm in here?"

"Hopefully, the army, with the help of the facility defences, will stop them, but if it comes down to it, I'll make sure to get some weapons for both of us. We can make our last stand here. I don't intend to go without a fight. This ward will be our very own Alamo. Now, I've talked for far too long keeping you awake, you need to get some more rest. I'll check on you later."

"Thanks again," said Mei-Lien, as Rebecca turned to leave.

"You're welcome, besides it's my job. I'm just glad we managed to put your arm back together in working order."

—

The music was pleasant, not too loud. It gave you the option to listen or talk over it. The piped recording, a four-piece group, had a reasonable singer too. The bar, in the heart of the Social Village was busy. Luckily, they had managed to find a secluded booth to themselves. Blake ordered another round from the passing robot waiter, two large gin and vodka martinis. The simple metal contraption, utilizing dull metallic voice recordings, informed them it wouldn't take long. It trundled off to perform the menial task. Blake returned to look at his companion.

Leila smiled at him. This was their third date in as many days. She felt herself falling for him head over heels, even though she had tried hard to resist. She kept reminding herself it had been a very long lonely stint on Ganymede, and she was only human after all, with human needs and desires.

"So Blake, I think it's time you told me some more about yourself. Is Blake your first, last, or indeed your real name?" Leila enquired.

"Well, actually, Blake is just a code name the government issued to me a long while ago. Traditionally, our department all use single names, none of which are associated with our real names," he explained.

"Well that's a typical government-type reply. I ask a straightforward question and you manage to answer without answering!" she joked. He laughed too.

"Michael Bennett. That's my real name. Thing is, using the name Blake for so long now, I've just got so used to it. If someone were to shout out 'Hey Mick' or 'Mike' I wouldn't bat an eyelid, it just wouldn't register."

The mechanical waiter returned with two drinks they had ordered on a tray. It transferred them from the tray onto the table. Blake offered his hand which allowed the robot to scan his implant between thumb and forefinger. The cost of the drinks would be debited from the bank account of a nonexistent out-of-work miner. The account was funded, via a third party, by the European Government.

Satisfied, the machine told them it hoped they would enjoy their alcoholic beverages, before trundling off once more to seek more trade.

"Thanks Michael, sorry, Blake," she said taking a sip. "So, do all spies drink vodka martini, is it part of their training?"

Blake looked at her quizzically, head tilted to one side.

"Don't tell me you have never accessed any of the old classic novels in the world's archive databases. James Bond was one of my all time favourite heroes when I was growing up. Twentieth century all action spy created by writer Ian Fleming," she offered.

"Sorry, can't say I have come across him, he sounds interesting though. I shall look him up next time I'm near an access terminal."

"Well, I think you should, after all, you're in the same profession, he, well the author of course, selected this very drink. 'Vodka martini, shaken and not stirred'," she croaked, trying to imitate a deep male voice, but managing to fail miserably. They both sniggered at the attempt.

"This gin and vodka cocktail certainly has a bit of a kick. It has a real bluish tint to it, even the ice looks blue," Blake remarked, examining the drink after taking another sip.

"They distil the alcohol here don't you know? They use the waste vegetable matter from the hydroponics greenhouses, usually the high starchy stalks to make the mash. Reconstituted synthetic sugar and pure blue water from the rings of Saturn, that's what gives its distinctive bluish colour. Most bars have their own private stills," Leila explained.

"Well I didn't know, thanks to you, now I do. It is certainly a nice drink, not too heavy, crisp and refreshing. I have to be careful otherwise alcohol goes straight to my head. I'm not really a heavy drinker. In my business I have had to stay pretty focused, keep my wits about me most of the time. Hey, we better get off soon, curfew is fast approaching," Blake said, quickly glancing at his watch. "I've got to escort you home before getting back to my own apartment."

"You don't want to stop at mine for a nightcap then?" Leila teased with a big grin on her face. She had had just the right amount of alcohol to set the mood. She was feeling quite randy, besides, these were stressful days. Worst case scenario, they could all be dead within a week. What the heck she thought to herself as they left the bar with their arms round each other. They were headed for Leila's apartment content that nothing, not even tall, marauding, knife-wielding alien creatures, were going to spoil the magic of the next couple of hours.

Robert had requested a meeting with Carmen Applegate, the Facilities Controller. He had discovered a couple of interesting facts whilst digging through the Corporation databases and archives. Although not exactly relevant to their current predicament, he wanted to share the findings with someone. He felt excited, like an innocent schoolboy who had just read the first half of the John Fowles novel *Mantissa*, he had stumbled across miscataloged in the children's section of an antique bookshop. He knocked on the door with a vibrant rap.

"Enter," Carmen's voice floated faintly through the door. Robert entered the controller's office, a room he had grown very tired of lately. He had almost lived in here, day in, day out for about a week, whilst they had discussed the ongoing personnel reorganisation and construction of the limited Mars defences.

"Hi Carmen," he said, sitting down with a flourish. He waited while she finished reading a report from her glass monitor screen. Absent minded, he tapped his fingers on a chair leg until he received a stern glance from Miss Applegate, who was obviously trying to concentrate on the words in front of her. He stopped immediately.

"It says here they have had a malfunction with the new long-range scanner. At the moment, we are temporarily blind to the whereabouts of any alien vessels. What went wrong?" she enquired.

"Someone thought they would be smart and boost the signal, run a bit more power through the control box. It sort of shorted out. They are currently sorting out new replacement parts. It should be fixed within the hour."

"Who was this irresponsible idiot?" Carmen demanded to know.

"Well, there's no denying it, it was me, sorry."

"What did you think you were playing at?" her voice softened slightly. She realised Robert would not do something so rash, not without good reason. There would be some sort of worthy explanation. Well there better be, she thought to herself while waiting on Robert's response.

"I just wanted the signal to reach Jupiter before our rescue spacecraft set off for Ganymede. Just so we could keep an eye on them once they passed out beyond the Asteroid Belt. Like I say, it should be repaired soon," he winced, hating to have to own up to a mistake. He had miscalculated and hadn't factored the age of some of the components into his equation. Some parts couldn't take the extra power surge like they should have been able too. Now, if they had been brand new, it would have been a different matter.

"I'd be obliged if you'd square it with me next time you start experimenting with our defence equipment, and it better be fixed soon. Now, let's change the subject. What did you want to see me about?"

"Well, I discovered that early in the twenty-first century, N.A.S.A. the space agency of that era sent out a probe. The probe was called '*New Horizons*'. The mission was to fly by Pluto, taking pictures of the planet including its three main moons, Charon, Nix and Hydra. The '*New Frontiers*' mission took off early in the year two thousand and six. All was proceeding according to plan, even the gravity assist from Jupiter the following year went very smoothly. The pictures of the Jovian moons were some of the best ever taken at the time. After Jupiter, the probe is on course to intercept Pluto in the year two thousand and fifteen, however, some months before that, just as it was starting to get some faint long-range images of its intended target, it just died. Everything went down. Earth never managed to re-establish contact or receive any images after that point. It was a major upset at the time. N.A.S.A. never managed to work out what went amiss."

"You think it might have had something to do with the aliens then?" Carmen asked. Robert nodded.

"It seems more than a coincidence that the supply cylinders are headed that way. I think it more than confirms my suspicions that Pluto is home to the alien creatures, one way or another," he suggested.

"That would also imply they have been with us for at least one hundred and thirty years! Wow, that is amazing. I'll get onto the Corporation. See if we can't get one of the Earth orbital telescopes dedicated to studying Pluto. They can let us know if anything is anyway out of place there. Now, you mentioned a couple of interesting things, what was the other?"

Robert paused for a moment. "I'm still investigating my other interesting finding, but there is not a lot of information about them. In fact, it is almost as if they were hushed up. I discussed it with James and we are keeping an open mind about it. All I will say now is that it concerns mysterious metal cylinders being found on Earth back in the late nineteen sixties, in a quarry in France buried deep in chalk rock formations millions of years old."

"Are you suggesting they are alien cylinders?" Carmen asked.

"Mmmm, that's what I'm trying to ascertain, like I said, there seems to be very little information that I can dig up presently. I have set up a couple of data mining programs on the Corporation historical data storage devices. Hopefully, they will unearth something interesting. Meanwhile, I suppose we ought to get back to our current day to day problems."

"Yes, and for your sake, let us hope the scanner has now been fixed," she said indignantly, picking up her personal communicator to enquire about it.

26

Tarek's Last Stand

The asteroid-mining spaceship *Mother Lode* was dead in the water. One of the two attacking alien spacecraft had launched a four metre diameter hollow projectile that had effortlessly carved a cylindrical cavity crossway through the middle of the mining vessel. The magnetic shield defences, normally used to help deflect the majority of iron-based asteroids within the Asteroid Belt, had been totally ineffectual stopping it.

The simplistic idea behind using this strange weapon was twofold. One, to remove a section of the spaceship making entry to the interior as easy as possible for the attacking alien force, and secondly, to disable the helm-control lasers that ran through from operations control room at the front, to the engine room at the rear. This effectively killed the vessel. How the alien attack force knew about the human technology was a mystery to the doomed mining vessel crew, maybe it was just an educated guess on their part, they would never know.

Before the two alien vessels came to a complete stop approximately two thousand metres distance from the mining spacecraft, several small probes containing the deadly devastating micro robots had been launched. Three of the miniature spheres had been aimed directly towards the three asteroid miners outside the main airlock. The first spherical probe they encountered they were totally unprepared for. It connected with Isaac Jacobs squarely in the chest before splitting open. The four micro robots inside quickly scurried out to set about their deadly business.

It happened so fast they were all taken somewhat by surprise, most of all Isaac. There was a split second stunned silence before all hell let loose. Isaac started screaming out obscenities while frantically brushing down the front of his exoskeleton frame. The rib-like protection bars worked in favour of the attacking robots. It gave them little crevasses into which they could lodge themselves providing a safety zone where they carried out their fatally-industrious work. All four began to bore into his suit material immediately they emerged from the probe.

Tarek looked on helpless, unable to assist Isaac. JJ was shouting too, trying to grab the disappearing back end of one micro robot between two gloved digits, he may as well have been trying to pick out marbles from a jar of grease. Sebastian's voice could also be heard in the melee demanding to know what the hell was going on. Tarek couldn't understand a single word that was being said between the three of them, while they continued shouting out at the top of their voices. All the time, precious air was now seeping out of Isaac's damaged suit.

Deciding that he needed to do something constructive, Tarek set the twin modulation frequencies on his microwave cutting lance to the maximum opposed settings. This would give the cutting device a wider and deeper range, albeit with weakened power, to the microwave cutting beams. It was all he could think in the heat of the moment. If he were to slice into an asteroid right now with these settings so wayward, they would shatter the rock face into a million pieces.

He pulled the trigger of his makeshift weapon which, as it

turned out, was only just in the nick of time. A second probe was less than a few metres away hurtling towards them. He still didn't see it until it started sparking as the spasmodic microwaves emitted from his lance cooked the alien electronics contained in the small round sphere. Tarek had just enough time to push JJ out the way as the fragments of the disintegrating probe flew between them. He was worried the jagged pieces could have punctured their suits. JJ looked annoyed thought Tarek, as much as you can tell from looking at the partially shaded facial features of someone inside their space helmet. All the shouting had now ceased as the body of Isaac suddenly went limp.

"Set your lance on max split-range frequency with full power and quick about it, it's those probe things we were warned about and we can't bloody well see them until they're on us." Tarek spoke loudly and coherently so JJ understood, he didn't want to repeat himself.

Although Jerome was technically senior in officer grade, he obeyed the given instructions from his junior ranking without question.

"Fire all around especially behind just in case they worked out what happened to that last thing, whatever it was."

Jerome turned his back to Tarek to comply. So shocked at what had just happened to Isaac he was quite happy taking orders from his subordinate, too upset to cause any fuss. Glad too that someone else was taking the lead, while he got his head and thoughts together.

No sooner had JJ pulled the trigger whilst waving the lance about when the third probe that had been stationary five metres away, glowed briefly before sparking twice. It burst into tiny pieces. JJ finally found his voice.

"That's another one gone. I wonder how many more of these little murdering bastards are out here. That one appeared to be standing station, just waiting for something to happen."

"Maybe they were testing the range of our lances?" Tarek suggested before continuing.

"Right, I suggest we keep sweeping the area in front, behind, up and down, until we know they have stopped sending those, those bloody things."

The two of them waved their lances in all directions indiscriminately with the trigger fully depressed and repeated this action every few seconds.

"What's happening out there?" Sebastian demanded, now all the shouting and commotion had ceased jamming up the communications link.

"We've just lost Isaac to those metallic robot insect like things. They chewed into his suit before we knew what was happening. We've managed to stop another couple of what we assume to be the robot carriers with our lances. Now we're making sure no more get anywhere near us."

"Okay, looks like we got some of those things inside here now, I can hear faint buzzing sounds outside. They are probably trying to bore holes through the airtight door and the walls."

"Yep, the same thing is happening here with me," Pierre interjected, hearing the sound made inside a wasp nest outside his door.

"There's no way we can get to the lances either, looks like we're stuck inside with no defence at all," confirmed a dejected Sebastian.

"No, but what I have got, is a micro meteorite repair gun somewhere!" Pierre exclaimed jumping up off his bed cradle top bunk. He ripped open his locker before rummaging through the contents. Odd bits and pieces of his personal possessions fell out before he found what he was looking for. He grabbed the small device that resembled a child's brightly coloured toy water pistol with a large cavernous bulb on top. He turned to the door just as a small whistling noise started.

One of the micro robots had cut though the plating just enough to allow air to pass out into the vacuum of the corridor. He squirted the hole that sealed instantly with a resin that was advertised as being harder than steel.

"That's stopped it in its tracks," he laughed. Just then another small hole appeared, the beaming smile instantly dropped from his face. He squirted the second hole, then the third, fourth and so on. Finally, one more irregular small hole was plugged with the last squirt of the instant hardening gel. As he squeezed out the last drops from the end of the nozzle he shook the small handheld device. It was empty. The door was one mass of patched up holes. He stared at it hoping against hope that he might have stopped them. Suddenly, the hissing noise started once more, then another, and another. Pierre backed away from the door to the very back of his cabin to grab onto some racking. Air was leaking out quite rapidly and there was no way of stopping it. The attacking creatures didn't need to do any more. They would collect his body later from the airless room, some more fresh meat for their larder.

"Pierre! Pierre!" JJ shouted in panic.

"It's no good, he's gone!" Tarek exclaimed.

"How you coping Sebastian?" JJ asked.

"He's a bit pre-occupied at the moment," replied Kitsztina. She watched distraught as Sebastian was performing Pierre's trick with the gel gun, except his was larger, much larger. A more industrial operations control room two-handed sized one, rather bigger than the standard cabin equivalent.

"It's only delaying the inevitable I fear," panted Sebastian. "I can't stop them forever. As soon as I plug one hole, they bloody bore through in another place," he moaned, sounding almost breathless.

"Is there nothing else you can use?" JJ asked feeling helpless.

"There's just nothing in here except the sealant gun, which

is now about half full," he answered, as he struggled to keep pace with the alien micro robot intrusions.

"I'll be there as fast as I can, just hang on. I can get through to you via the hole the aliens cut with that cylinder weapon," stated JJ, before turning towards Tarek. They stared at each other through their helmet faceplates.

"Are you coming to help, Tarek?" JJ pleaded after a long pause. He was scared and it showed.

"No. To be totally honest I think we're all dead anyway. Personally I think we stand more chance by staying out in the open. Besides, you'll have to lose your exoskeleton unit going inside the spaceship. It might be the only real advantage we have increasing our human strengths and, giving us more protection against them," suggested Tarek.

"I disagree. It didn't help poor Isaac here," JJ spluttered. He secured his lance on the arm of his exoskeleton before grabbing the lifeless body of Isaac floating nearby.

"They are not going to get you without a fight either!" he exclaimed.

"Wait!" Tarek shouted. JJ paused while Tarek extracted the lance from Isaac's dead grasp.

"Okay, go help Sebastian if you want to!" he shouted, sounding disappointed as JJ turned to head back to the spaceship with Isaac in tow. Tarek set the second lance on a similar broad cut to his own cutting tool. Now he held a lance in each hand allowing him to cover his immediate surroundings up and down and both sides simultaneously.

JJ made his way down the outside of the mining vessel until he came to the four-metre circular hole that had been cut through the middle of it. He peered into the opening. Two opposing cabins, the main corridor and the ceiling of the gear room had been removed quite spectacularly. There was also a section of the middle airlock wall missing. It looked just like a technical cut-out drawing he thought while tethering Isaac's exoskeleton and deceased body onto a now exposed metal cross beam.

Switching his own skeletal protection unit status to unload, the titanium and tungsten protection bars swung open allowing him to step out. Having also removed his external means of propulsion, he clung onto the exposed insides of the spaceship whilst tethering his now powerless exo unit next to Isaac's. He unclipped his cutting lance from the right forearm mountings before heading inside.

"Hang on Sebastian, Kitsztina. I'm coming," he shouted desperately. There was an eyrie silence in reply.

Making his way to the upper central corridor opening, he pulled himself into the passageway. Through the hole in the floor, a misaligned communication laser hit his eyes temporarily blinding him. He swore loudly while trying to blink away the black ghostly lines burned into his retinas. The artificial gravity gyros were still maintaining a field in the front third of the crippled vessel causing him to slump to the floor. The operations control room was quite close. Picking himself up, he cautiously made his way forwards until, through his blurred vision, he saw a myriad of round holes in the lower half of the air tight door. There were yet more holes in the walls either side as well. Still there was no reply from either occupant inside, he feared the worst. Peering through the thick clear plastic window in the upper half of the door, the room was bathed in emergency lighting making it difficult to pick out objects clearly. Becoming accustomed to the half light, he could just make out the figure of Krisztina slumped over the control desk. Off to one side on the floor lay Sebastian, the empty gel gun still gripped in his hand. The aliens using their little robot controlled devices had won. The air had escaped from the ops control room. It was too late to save his friends.

"I was too late Tarek, too late to be any help here," he said dejectedly, before turning round in the corridor to retrace his steps. He had decided to make his way back outside to rejoin Tarek, help him anyway he could.

"I'm coming back out…" But he didn't get the chance to complete his sentence. A black suited alien, towering in front of him, shocked him into silence. The alien was forced to stoop within the low confines of the corridor ceiling so it was looking down on the top of JJ's head. JJ jumped in surprise looking back up at the creature. He tried to bring up the lance that was dangling loose in his hand parallel to his right leg. It never reached higher than his knees. The alien thrust his serrated-edged knife upwards into his chest cavity with such force that it continued up under his ribs piercing one of his lungs. The force also lifted him half a metre off the deck. A couple of seconds passed as he hung suspended on the knife edge with his mouth wide open incapable of making any noise. Blood amassed in his throat causing him to gag. Finally, with his last dying breath he coughed once, covering the insides of his helmet face plate with a splattering of dark red blood.

As life was slowing ebbing away, he mustered all his strength, all his will, to move just one small part of his dying body. With his last physical effort, he pulled the trigger of his lance which, still slightly raised, was pointing at the alien's left shin. JJ never got to see the alien topple sideways as the concentrated microwaves shattered its shin bone into tiny fragments. It was small retribution. Now it was the alien's turn to scream, or rather let out a blood-curdling gargle in agony, before passing out. The alien toppled forward, and then sideways, onto the now crumpled body of JJ, crushing his body in the process.

Outside Tarek mumbled through the list of his crewmates' names, hoping for at least one response.

"Sebastian? JJ? Pierre? Krisztina?" There were no replies

forthcoming. He realised now he was all alone, the last man standing.

One more probe had been destroyed by swinging the two cutting lance microwave beams in all directions. It had sneakily approached him from directly below his position. That was some time ago. He guessed they had stopped sending them out now for being ineffective, but he couldn't be sure. So he kept waving his arms about like some demented loony just in case, although his arms were now beginning to tire.

Suddenly, he felt a rush of adrenalin surge through him as he observed two distant figures approaching from the direction of the two alien spacecraft. They were dressed completely in black he noted, top to toe, extremely hard to spot against the black backdrop of space. He doubted he would have noticed them at all, had they not been silhouetted by their own lighter coloured spaceships. He changed one of the two lance beam frequency settings to the more usual one metre short-range precise cut.

The two aliens approached cautiously, advancing each side of him. They both had their half-metre-long knives held in their hands. Both also adorned backpack propulsion devices. They were very adept at using them as well, dodging his sweeping cutting strokes with some skill. Finally, one of the alien creatures came within the bounds of the five metre set lance that had worked so well destroying the spherical probes. This time the power output was not enough to affect the creatures. It probably just gave them something like an electric shock thought Tarek. He quickly set that lance on the more precise, more powerful short cut as well, now if only they would just get close enough, within one metre. Again and again they teased him, keeping just out of his reach. Tarek was really frustrated now. They must somehow know the range and power extent of the lances, could they somehow read minds he thought?

"C'mon, which one first?" he shouted out, desperately trying to give himself some courage while inside his suit, he was shaking like the last leaf on an autumn tree in a stiff cold breeze. His mind was racing, trying to remember his early army days. What was the best form of defence, attack? That was it, attack! It was now or never, he decided, getting very tired of this cat and mouse game. Also, he was getting really physically tired and doubted he could last much longer.

Setting one lance trigger to the locked-on continuous mode they use for prolonged asteroid cutting, he thrust it forward towards one of the alien beings. Firing his forward propulsion jets he launched himself straight at the other alien while pushing his second lance out as far as he could. This tactic forced the second alien backwards fast to avoid the cutting beam. He would show them that he was just as adept as the aliens using the space propulsion units. Tarek then feigned, swinging back round at full power to confront the first alien that had dodged out the way of the propelled lance. Luckily Tarek had guessed correctly the alien would dodge to the left intercepting it perfectly, just as he had planned and hoped for. With a swinging wide sweep across its chest, a huge gash appeared in the tight black spacesuit, just like it had been unzipped. The alien grabbed at the torn suit that was venting some form of gas, jettisoning its deadly knife in the process. There was also fluid gushing out, a lot of fluid that froze in lumps. Maybe it was blood Tarek thought, he hoped so.

"One down, one to go!" he shouted euphorically, turning to find the second startled alien had regained composure faster than he had expected. Swinging the lance back round he hoped to perform the same operation as before. However, this time it was checked by the long gangly arm of the alien that had moved in close now. The parried lance bounced out the way allowing the creature to use its knife in such close quarters. It clipped a protection bar on the exoskeleton before slipping through his suit like it was cutting tin foil, through his suit and penetrating his rib cage. He stared into the black, reflective face plate, now only centimetres away, trying to see his assailant's eyes as his life ebbed away. All he could see in the black abyss was his own startled reflection behind his visor.

"You... you... fuck... bas..." Tarek stuttered with his last dying breath.

—

With two casualties, one fatal, the aliens decided pursuing the escaped scout spacecraft would be futile. They needed to get medical help for their fallen comrade with a shattered leg. Nicky would wake up when she neared the Mars Facilities. She would be the only survivor of *Mother Lode*.

Later it would transpire that Tarek Miah would be credited as the second human to take the life of one of the alien creatures. However, that credit came at a deadly personal price.

27

Ganymede Revisited

The interplanetary supply spaceship *Oceans Dawn,* with the mining vessel *Lode Drifter* as salient cargo, slipped silently through the inky blackness of space. They passed through the solar system as quiet as mice searching a farmhouse kitchen for scraps in the dead of night. Their scanners, seeking signs of hostile alien spacecraft, were finding nothing, much to everybody's relief.

"*If they could accomplish their mission without any alien contact, so much the better,*" thought James. "How long since we left the Mars Facilities? Thirteen days? It seems like forever," he moaned, whilst sipping his morning tea. "Perhaps we should have put ourselves into the Dormouse Torpor State for a few days," he added as an afterthought.

"It's fifteen days to be precise. Anyway, you would have missed observing the Asteroid Belt yesterday if you had been in suspended animation now," Able Crewman Ian Watson stated.

Since they had set out, it had become somewhat of a morning ritual for both of them to have their breakfast together. Now they looked forward to the morning discussions.

"Besides, you know we need to be fully alert and ready, just in case."

"Yes, I know, I was being somewhat flippant. There's just not much to see in the Asteroid Belt except a jumble of old rocks and boulders. Admittedly fairly spectacular visually, stretching as far as the eye can see in both directions on one apparent orbital plane, the significant curvature of that plane which can be seen with the naked eye. Okay, I concede, it was worth seeing up close," James smiled.

Before they had left Mars, the asteroid-mining spacecraft and the interplanetary vessel had been successfully integrated together. *Lode Drifter* was now secured within a stationary framework structure at the very centre of the rotating drum that made up the three decks of *Oceans Dawn*. The hastily constructed framework was situated where a static cargo container would normally be carried. The framework was indeed part of the carcass of an old ruptured container, with the outer skin removed. Various padded buffers, locking clamps coupled with a short sliding ramp, allowed the mining vessel to dock and undock within the frame structure. This would permit the two vessels to separate when necessary. The skeletal framework continued aft of the two vessels for a couple of hundred metres. At the end of the snapped-off frame, an interplanetary fusion propulsion unit had been welded. This was now quite happily pushing the mishmash of spacecraft and metal girders towards Jupiter or more precisely, Jupiter's moon, Ganymede.

Since the demise of *Mother Lode*, and the return of the other asteroid-mining vessels, the only spacecraft now in any immediate danger were the ice tugboats. Planning to intercept them near Jupiter before escorting them back home, they had seized upon the opportunity to visit the Jovian moon on the way. Their hope was to find some answers from the crashed alien spacecraft, as well as anything that could help them to understand the alien way of life and culture.

"There has been no sign of the two vessels that attacked *Mother Lode*. They must have scampered back to their little hidey hole wherever that is. Speaking of which, did you manage to discover where the mysterious resupply cylinders came from or where they were going to?" Ian asked.

"We, Robert and I that is, had a close look at the readings of both Andy Hubbins and those taken by the ice tugboats. They appeared to be very similar trajectories with very minor course changes. Those differences could have been influenced by the collision with *Lode Drifter* and their passage through the Asteroid Belt. As far as we could tell, they originated from a planetary system in the Helix Nebula over four hundred and fifty light years away," James explained.

Ian whistled in amazement. "So, where are they headed?" he asked.

"As far as we could ascertain, based on course and speed, they were on an intercept course for Pluto, which, incidentally, concurred with the last transmission from *The Amelia*. We think the alien base headquarters, or hidey hole as you so aptly called it, is on Pluto. Either that, or one of its three moons."

"Just a teeny bit far for us to go chasing after them then," stated Ian.

"One thing it does prove is their human collector spaceships can travel at a speed far greater than our vessels can. Even *Oceans Dawn*, that is twice as fast as the mining vessels, faster even than the ice tugboats, is still relatively slow compared to them," declared James.

"*Oceans Dawn* at full thrust can attain just over seven hundred thousand kilometres per hour. Assuming the planets were in perfect alignment, it would currently take us nearly a year to get to Pluto. How much faster do you think they can travel?" Ian enquired.

James hypothesized that Ian, knowing so many technical facts about *Oceans Dawn,* could make a nice living giving guided tours of the vessel.

"We're not exactly sure. We estimate at least four, maybe five, times faster. We are looking at maybe two months for them to go from the Asteroid Belt to Pluto. We are hoping we can get to Ganymede, and then back to Mars before they return."

"What about the ice gatherers? Do you think the same aliens that struck *Mother Lode* will have a go at them on the way back to Pluto?" Ian asked, genuinely concerned.

"Luckily, the current alignment of the planets, primarily Saturn and Pluto, are right angles to the Sun. They would have to go a long way out of their way to intercept the ice tugboats. Remember also, they have just abducted the entire crew of *Mother Lode*. It's a sad, but probable true fact, the loss of *Mother Lode* with all hands may have ultimately saved the ice-tugboat crew members," he speculated shaking his head.

"You are of course assuming they are the only the two alien vessels in existence. Maybe, some more of these, what I shall now baptize 'The Human Harvester' spacecraft, may have already set out from their base, even worse, they may now be on course to us intercept us!" Ian exclaimed, raising his voice. A couple of crew members seated nearby, concentrating on studying their screens minding their own business, gave a glance indicating their annoyance.

"I like that, it's about time we gave these alien creatures some sort of title, The Human Harvesters. Mmm, maybe, just The Harvesters?" James raised his eyebrows at the suggestion to shorten the new title he had bestowed on the alien creatures.

Ian shrugged. "Call them what you damn well like, what about them being on our tail right now!"

"Well, that may indeed be the case. Who knows? We will

have to hope The Harvester spacecraft are not currently hunting us down. Our scanners have not picked up anything yet, that includes not locating the ice tugboats either. They must be well and truly blindsided by Jupiter at the moment," replied James in a hushed voice, so as not to upset those sitting nearby.

—

Observed from the bridge, Ganymede loomed large before them. Its surface colour consisted mainly of greys and dark browns, a slight hint of orange here and there. It was covered in numerous impact craters, some of them looked fairly recent.

James was conscious that there were a lot of people on the bridge at this particular moment in time. It looked, and was, very crowded. In fact, apart from a couple of particularly singular individuals he could identify, it was playing host to the entire crews from both vessels. From the original compliment of *Oceans Dawn's* twelve crew, four had been left behind. These included the third engineer, two ordinary crewmen and the steward. Although they had volunteered, along with the rest of the crew, Captain Cooper decided the vessel could function adequately without them for this particular mission. Those four crew members were left behind in the relative safety of the Mars Facilities. James had joined the crew primarily as an advisor, now also as a recently-trained weapons console operator.

The surviving able-bodied crew members from *Lode Drifter,* Andy, Kieron, Deimos and Josie, had been joined by Zelda. She was keen to obtain some vengeance for the loss of her close friend and colleague Diego. Zelda had been very withdrawn on the outward journey, hardly venturing out of her cabin except to eat. Some of the backhand mutterings and idle gossip had resulted in a visit from Kieron, just to discover if she was okay and not going cabin stir crazy. She passed her examination from the Doctor. However, James still worried. Zelda was missing this awe-inspiring spectacle, as Captain Edmund Cooper expertly piloted both spacecraft into a low-orbit trajectory around Jupiter's moon Ganymede, placing them directly over the outpost buildings. There was a general melee of approving mutterings once the main thrusters powered down.

"So, what are the plans now?" Josie asked Captain Cooper.

"*Lode Drifter*, under the command of Mr. Hubbins, will land near Outpost two five seven and investigate. I'd like Mr. James Cleaver to go with them, put his sharp analytical brain to work. Let us hope that the alien Leila Santos dispatched, is still around. I'm sure Doctor McCabe, along with our second engineer Mr. Jean-Marc Lesueur, who is also our medical officer, would like to have a poke about inside that creature. See what makes it tick. We have located the two crashed alien vessels just as they were reported, about one kilometre thereabouts, off to one side of the scientific outpost. I'm sure James would like to investigate those. Meanwhile, we are currently scanning for the ice tugboats, which we should be picking up on our long-range scanners, but have failed to make contact with as yet. I suspect it's to do with the interference from the gas giant that is between us, currently blocking our scanners. We will have to wait for the orbit of Ganymede to take us into a more direct line of sight as we pass round Jupiter."

"Captain, how long do you think, before you can locate them?" Josie asked, obviously worried for their well being.

"It takes Ganymede seven days to orbit Jupiter so every day takes us a bit further round to a more favourable alignment, two, maybe three days at most, before our scans detect them."

"Well, keep trying. Let us know how you get on. Now, we had better go and prepare ourselves. By the way, nice flying captain," said Andy smiling.

Captain Cooper grinned in return. "Good luck Andy.

Keep in constant communications please, that goes for all of you. If you find anything that's relevant, relay back to us as soon as you can. We will store all your conversations, recordings and observations about your findings, then send the information back to Mars periodically."

—

A little while later, Andy was running down the short flight check list on board *Lode Drifter*. "Fusion engines online, both steady, ticking over at idle?"

"Check," called out Deimos.

"Magneto gyros operational, artificial gravity at point nine seven nine."

"Check," replied Kieron.

"Magnetic shielding is level at one hundred per cent. Okay, let's see just how good the engineers on Mars have been. Prepare to release from dock on my mark... mark."

He touched a small illuminated square on his monitor screen. The switch relayed a signal to release several clamps holding *Lode Drifter* within the cage like framework that sat in the centre of the slowly rotating *Oceans Dawn*. Now free from restraints, the tick over pulse output from two drive units was enough to edge the mining vessel down the ramp and slowly away from its makeshift moorings.

Andy increased the downwards thrust a fraction. He had to be careful not to damage any of the structure behind them from the engine's output, they needed to come back at some point in the near future.

"Josie, let me know when we are clear behind and above so I can manoeuvre fully."

"Will do Andy," she replied.

"I shall try and put us down as close as I can next to the ground-vehicle airlock."

"All clear aft Andy," Josie stated, after a minute or two. Andy increased thrust and eased *Lode Drifter* down and away from *Oceans Dawn* before heading towards Jupiter's moon. Ganymede had gravity slightly less than the Earth's Moon. He had landed similar-sized vessels there so he followed almost identical procedures. Using the gentlest of touches on the thrusters, it was easy to float the vessel down nudging it this way and that, towards the outpost satellite dome that housed the ground vehicle. Soon, the surface below was fast approaching. He applied more downwards thrust to compensate.

"Extending landing struts," Andy continued calling out operations. Four panels became detached from the underside of each corner of *Lode Drifter*. They grew downwards on long hydraulic rams, the concealment panels becoming the broad foot of each extended leg.

There was a gentle bump as the vessel settled on three feet, one foot managing to find itself inside the hollow of a small crater. The dangling leg extended further down while the other three contracted to compensate for the tilt until the fourth pad touched the frozen crater bottom. The spacecraft rose up slightly as it automatically levelled itself out, before finally coming to a complete rest.

"Okay, where do we start? Do we have any sort of plan?" Andy asked James.

"Well, I suggest we break out the ground vehicle, get that working first. Then, perhaps I can be dropped off at the alien vessels. I can't wait to have a poke about inside one of them. Then you can have a look for the alien that Leila encountered. Hopefully, it will still be out by the laboratory dome. Once retrieved, we can then bring it back inside the vehicle hangar. Even though it will be frozen solid, Kieron can still perform a preliminary external examination."

Andy nodded. "Sounds like a good starting point. Josie has

agreed to stay on board, co-ordinate and oversee events from here. Okay, the rest of us, let's get suited up and outside. I don't think we will need our exoskeletons, just spacesuits for now."

They continued chatting while heading for the door.

"What are we going to do with the body? Trevor's body I mean, according to Leila, it's in the cabin of... What did they call it, the Land Crab?" Deimos asked.

"Well, the poor bugger would have been frozen stiff like concrete all this time in the hangar. We can't bury him, not in the solid rock and ice on the surface. I shall properly enshroud it in part of the tarpaulin Leila mentioned she had covered him with. When we leave here we can place him in the airlock once we rejoin *Oceans Dawn*. Perhaps then, we could say a few words before giving him a gentle shove towards Jupiter," suggested Kieron.

"Sounds like a good send off to me," agreed Zelda, who had been quiet up until now. She had sat patiently on the bridge, unable to assist with the disembarkation or the recent landing, not really knowing the intricacies of the instruments. She was however a quick learner and having watched Andy carefully, if push come to shove, she could at a pinch, probably fly the mining vessel in an emergency. For now though, she was quite happy to sit back and observe, let the others do the work.

The landing party traversed the upper corridor, down through the crossway bulkhead, past the mess and galley doorways, before finally proceeding through the airlock door entrance to the gear room. They sealed it behind them. It wasn't long before the five of them were standing in their suits taking turns to exit the main airlock. Without exoskeletons, they might have just about all managed to squeeze in together, but they would not been able to open the outer door. The outer door on mining vessels always opened inwards, the complete opposite to all other spacecraft. This was to stop them getting damaged, even ripped off by passing lumps of rock, during operations within the Asteroid Belt.

James and Andy were the first to get outside. They carefully monitored their suit readings during decompression, a standard procedure. Josie, using the internal control panel, extended a previously hidden ramp down to the moon's uneven surface.

Andy pushed open the airlock door, allowing the two of them to proceed down the ramp. The other three were soon following after their airlock decompression process. The entrance to the ground-vehicle hangar was ajar. Inside the five of them found it just as they expected, as Leila had described it in minute detail. Trevor's body was lying across the front seat, the tarpaulin draped over his rigid remains.

Kieron, Zelda and James manhandled the body out of the cabin, down the short ladder and onto the hangar floor. Kieron then set to the task of mummifying Trevor in a large section of the canvas tarpaulin. He finished the job tying off with sections of long canvas strips that Zelda ripped off the main sheet. The end result was reminiscent of the contents of an Egyptian Pharaoh's sarcophagus.

Andy then checked the battery power levels on the eight-wheeled ground vehicle. They were all full bar one which must have been malfunctioning. It would still perform at ninety per cent efficiency with one fuel cell depleted. Luckily for them, the recharging unit had been still operational, running a trickle charge from the outpost's small fusion power plant, keeping them topped up. James climbed back into the cabin to take up position in the co-driver seat. Behind them, the second row contained three seats, behind that was an open receptacle. The middle pair of wheels on each side of the vehicle protruding further than the other four at the corners giving it an oval shape when looked at from above.

"Land Crab, I see what they mean now, what with the rounded shape and, especially with those two front pincer like robotic soil-collection arms. Zelda, can you give me a hand with the hangar doors please," asked Deimos, as he struggled to push one side open, the cold having frozen the hinges fast. Between the two of them and a large volume of de-icer, they managed to force open both hangar doors. Andy drove the vehicle straight out, then swung it round. The short ladder to the cabin now exposed to the other three standing in front of the open hangar.

"All aboard," he called out light heartedly, as if they were going on a trip to the seaside. Just before they were about to climb up to the cabin, Josie grabbed their attention.

"Andy! Urgent message coming through from Captain Cooper, he wants to address all of us at once. I've patched him into our general comms circuits. Go ahead captain," she boomed.

"Sorry to interrupt all of you, we got a situation developing. The long-range scanners have at last managed to pick up the ice tugboats. We have moved round Jupiter sufficiently enough to pick up their faint trace. Each second the picture becomes clearer. There are three very large lumps of ice travelling along quite steadily on course. However, we've also picked up two smaller objects that seem to be shadowing them. We can only assume the worst," the captain explained.

"Do you want us to come back, so we can all go after them?" Andy suggested. He looked up through the open roof of the vehicle for the low geostationary orbiting spacecraft overhead. He could make out a small dark shape, could that be *Oceans Dawn* he wondered.

"Well, I think time is of the utmost essence. Can I suggest you stay there while we attempt to be the cavalry, go to their rescue, if it's not too late that is? I'm just a little concerned about leaving you here unprotected though. We have all the weapons remember," Captain Cooper replied.

"We'll be okay, just make sure you come back for us. Good luck and good hunting, keep in touch with progress periodically," Andy said, not showing his real concerns and fears.

James shouted out. "Tell Able Crewman Ian Watson he was right. We should have anticipated they have more of what he and I refer to as the Harvester spacecraft. Gods speed captain."

"Thank you James. I will pass on your message. I just pray there are not more of the Harvester spaceships about waiting to attack you once we've gone."

As *Oceans Dawn* broke orbit, Captain Edmund Cooper swore under his breath.

"Damn, damn, damn it. I've just realised we've left our new weapons console operator down on Ganymede!"

28

Mission Mars

All ten military personnel on board the military container somehow located a somewhat tentative vantage point to peer out, scrutinising the initial soft dock with *Stellar Dusk*. With only a few small round portholes through which to observe, some of them only managed to get one eye to the thick clear plastic windows. Even Alex and Paula crammed their heads together to observe the precise container choreography currently being performed outside.

The vessel that had hauled them and the container up from Satellite Two to Gateway space station was now joined by another. Between them, they gingerly manoeuvred the military container back towards *Stellar Dusk*. The small spaceships, adept at shunting cargo containers, were covered with rubberised flat protrusions, perfect for shoving and pushing around anything including stricken spacecraft, immobile satellites and interplanetary cargo units. With the container lined up precisely, it was slotted into the very middle of the round drum-shaped interplanetary vessel. Slowly, metre by metre, one of the shunting spacecraft nudged the unit back until, inside they felt, and heard a series of muffled, almost simultaneous clunking noises, announcing it was now locked into its docked position.

Another container five hundred metres long, guided by another cargo shunting space tugboat, was attached to the smaller military one that now stuck out fifty metres aft of *Stellar Dusk*. The container cajolement was achieved using several tongue and grove type slots in the ends of both square metal boxes that fitted together flush, like a very well made piece of antique furniture. At the end of the second extensive supply container sat the fusion drive engines. Fully fuelled, ready to transport the spacecraft complete with its cargo of soldiers, food, clothing and medical supplies to Mars.

"Sir, can I enquire what's in the other supply container if we have all our equipment in this one?" Private Jacqueline Reilly enquired.

"It's full of replenishment stores and equipment, especially extra medical items, according to the shipping manifest," replied Alex.

"Extra medical supplies eh, what exactly are they are expecting on Mars, a bloodbath?" Paula stated sardonically.

As soon as both containers and drive unit were all secure, the shunting vessels quickly vacated the area. Soon they got word that it was now safe for the soldiers to transfer to the mother ship. They donned their helmets once more to make their way outside using the small container airlock. For some inexplicable design reason, it only allowed occupancy for two people at a time. Alex made a mental note to inform the Corporation that this was a bad oversight. In a real emergency they all needed to get out quickly, at least five minimum would be his recommendation. As each two exited, using their small suit thrusters, they joined those already outside, positioning themselves into a military line at attention. Eventually, all the army personnel were outside the container and in front of *Oceans Dawn*.

"Right, when I give the word, fire team one, make your way to the portside airlock. Fire team two, to the starboard," Sergeant Paula Alvarez instructed.

She turned using her thrusters to face Alex. "Sir, would you mind accompanying team two, while I accompany team one?"

"Okay, will do. By the way Paula, I've been in touch with Captain Amanda Treadhouse. As soon as we are in the airlocks they will begin rotation to attain artificial gravity. It'll be nice to feel some weight beneath my feet again, see you on the inside," replied Alex. Paula turned back to face the relatively straight line of squaddies.

"Squad… Fall OUT!" Paula shouted. At the command, two groups of five broke away in opposite directions towards the second level airlocks positioned on either side of the round interplanetary vessel. Opening the outer doors with the tell tale illuminated red crosses on both sides, there was plenty of room inside the two cavernous chambers.

"Right, park your arses on one of the benches. Use the straps and carabiner clips on the seats, clip them to the hoops on your suit belts until we have obtained full gravity," ordered Paula, still in full communication with both separated groups.

Once Alex and Paula confirmed all were secure, they informed the captain. Instantly they all felt a jolt as the spaceship began its artificial gravity rotation cycle. It didn't take long before they had attained downwards forces equal to standing on the surface of the Earth. Soon after, a breathable atmosphere was also acquired, indicated by the inner airlock door display, switching from a red cross to green triangle. They disrobed their suits stowing them neatly in the airlock's square lockers. They didn't need to be instructed to remember which numbered small alcove was theirs.

Once the inner airlock doors were open, both parties were met by able crewmen who escorted them to cabins on deck three. They paired off as they had been instructed during the trip up to Gateway.

The cabin-allocation business was a fairly rushed affair, as it always seemed to happen when vessels left Gateway, eager to be on their way. So, it was no surprise when before too long the captain informed them the countdown had begun and they should all be strapped in their cradles in the upright seating position.

Ignition went without a hitch. The soldiers had been trained for the accelerated G forces, none of them passed out. Once underway, hurtling through the void with Earth receding rapidly by the second, the designated able crewmen appeared once more, to escort them to the canteen galley for an audience with the captain of *Stellar Dusk*. Once they were all comfortable, she began.

"Hello everyone," she beamed, and then waited patiently for some of the group to return similar greetings before continuing. "I'm Captain Amanda Treadhouse. I would like to take this opportunity to welcome you all aboard our hastily arranged voyage to the Mars Facilities, but before we put you into the Dormouse Torpor State for the duration, I have a little update on current events," she paused for a deep breath.

"I would have liked this voyage to have been a little more enjoyable and pleasant for you all. Unfortunately, there were valid reasons behind our rushed launch window. Those reasons, up until now have only been confined to the pages of horror sci-fi novels, or so I would have said a couple of weeks ago, had I not been in touch with my friend and colleague on *Oceans Dawn*, Captain Edmund Cooper. His crew have witnessed firsthand, an attempted abduction by the alien creatures at the Mars Facilities. The crew of *Oceans Dawn*, with the help of the facility personnel, have also been involved in changing his vessel back into a warship, by reinstating its original armaments. Even now they are en-route to intercept the Saturn ice tugboats, hopefully to escort them safely back to Mars. Now, the next bit of news is extremely unpleasant. It is my sad duty to inform you that we have lost an asteroid-mining spacecraft with all hands bar one. *Mother Lode* was warned of the pending dangers. The crew decided they knew better and chose to ignore them, continuing to mine deep within the belt. That has ultimately cost them their lives. They did however leave communications links open whilst being attacked. We have transcripts of the actual voice recordings during that horrendous period, along with some very graphic visual clips. You may wish to listen and watch them as contained within are numerous items of interest that may help your defence of the Mars Facilities inhabitants and the buildings."

Everyone was hanging on every word. A few days ago they were under the impression this mission was a joke, then an ordinary, if expensive simple army exercise. Now, the realisation this was for real, was hitting home big time.

"Captain, you said bar one. Did someone survive then?" Alex enquired.

"Yes, it is understood that one of the crew members escaped in the asteroid surveillance scout spacecraft, currently en route back to Mars. It's not confirmed though and we have not been informed of its latest progress. I will get an update on that, as well as other situations when we near the Mars Facilities," she answered.

"Sweet mother of Satan!" Ricardo exclaimed. "And we all thought this was going to be a nice little jolly trip…" He tailed off as Alex got to his feet, rubbing his hands together. They knew this sign, a prelude to an outspoken thought. They watched him expectantly.

"Thank you captain, I think I speak for all of us here, this has come as quite a shock. I mean, we were informed about the aliens, but we assumed, even now, it was just some sort of elaborate hoax. May I suggest our squad be put into the Dormouse Torpor State as soon as humanly possible? Then, can you wake us up five days before Mars orbital insertion?

That way we can catch up with the latest intelligence, plus, bone up on all the events that have been logged, recorded and relayed to you so far. I need to get some sort of plan worked out before we even set foot on Martian soil."

"Sounds like a good idea, Sir," agreed Paula. "I'll help co-ordinate any way I can," she added, before giving one last order. "Squad, Shun! At ease. All back to your cabins. Let's all go for nice long nap, but let's not forget what we all have to do first though," she said, handing out the suppositories from the small box she was carrying to each squad member as they passed her.

When they awoke three weeks later they had that awful hungry feeling. Some were also feeling a lot groggier than others. Aban had previous experience of a spell in the Dormouse Torpor State, so knew what to expect. Although feeling rough himself, he managed to help some of the others through this first hour of dreadful nauseous awakening.

They had reconvened once more in the canteen area, most taking small sips of water whilst nibbling the customary very dry hard biscuits. Eventually, they all eased through the painful transition back to some sort of normality. They were a tough bunch though, tough as old boots, and soon most were fighting fit once more. Some even started simple exercises, push ups and arm wrestling one another, until Paula called them to order so Alex could address them.

"Right, now we are back to some sort of normality, we have a great task ahead. I want everyone to go through all the information that has been pooled regarding the alien race, twice, if you have the time. Note down anything you might think is relevant and bring it to my attention. I'm going to catch up with the latest transmissions, see if there are any new developments. Any questions?" Alex looked across the tables.

Some of the soldiers still had a little greenish complexion. They had no questions at that time.

"Okay then, we'll meet up here tomorrow morning at eight hundred hours. We'll have a working breakfast, discuss facts, figures, and as I said, anything that you think could be relevant. I want no stone unturned, no communication missed, even dig up the numbers of missing persons over the years. I want a mountain of information, so, until tomorrow ladies and gents," Alex declared, before leaving in haste to meet up with the captain on the bridge.

After had had left, those closest took up stations with the three canteen consoles, the rest scuttled down the corridor to find the two recreational rooms, where they could find more of the database access terminals.

Using the at-a-glance markings, Alex negotiated his way through the corridors and ladders to the bridge control room. His standard-issue overalls were patted down by the first officer, standard procedure for any non-crew member entering the bridge. Having found nothing concealed about his person, he was finally admitted. Glancing out of the forward-facing windows, he could make out Mars as a small reddish ball to the left, off mid centre from their current course. Mars would have five more days of orbital travel before *Stellar Dusk* reached the exact rendezvous point. He supposed it was just like a clay pigeon shooter giving the clay lead when firing, allowing for the target and shot to intercept at the correct point. They were right on course and on schedule to intercept each other in exactly five days' time.

"Hello Captain," he said, approaching Amanda Treadhouse who was sat in the Captain's chair in the very centre of the control room.

"Hello Mr. Manso. Welcome to my bridge. I assume you're here for the latest intelligence?" He nodded in answer to her question.

"Well, there is very little to report since your extended snooze. I guess that's not so bad in the overall scheme of things, no news is good news as the old saying goes," she looked blankly at him, waiting for a reaction.

He was still feeling queasy and couldn't make out what she was implying. He shrugged so she continued. "What I'm trying to say is this. There have been no more incidents so far. Which is far better than me telling you the Mars Facilities lay in ruins and we are surrounded by a hundred alien vessels waiting to attack," she explained jokingly.

"Ah! I see, yes, much better for all concerned that there is nothing to report," he replied, still slightly confused.

He thought to explain himself. "You'll have to excuse me. I'm not up to speed yet, still a bit heady after coming out of the Dormouse Torpor State."

"Yes. Well quite," Amanda said, happy they had cleared the matter up. "What I can tell you is *Oceans Dawn* is nearing Ganymede. They should have made contact with the ice tugboats on their scanners too. They have a plan to drop off the asteroid-mining spacecraft *Lode Drifter* for a look round the moon, maybe gather some more information about our unfriendly invaders. That's all to report I'm glad to say."

"Okay, if that's all there is, I'll like to get back to my cabin. Sergeant Alvarez and I have plans to discuss. Please let me know if there are any new developments," he said, before turning to leave the room.

"As soon as I receive any relevant information, you'll be the very next person to know. Catch up with you later," Amanda shouted after the retreating Military Analyst.

For the next five days it would appear to outsiders that the squaddies were revising for exams by the number of reports they each read over and over again. Although, the information they were swotting up might give them a pass rate with distinction, it also might just save their lives. They studied the events from very first incident, the demise of Teunis Landry, to the most recent, the loss of *Mother Lode* and its crew. Two days out from Mars they convened for the daily morning brainstorming session.

"These probes," Alex began. "The ones that contain the robots that resemble small insects responsible for all the grisly deaths, we have to find a way of detecting them. We need a handheld device, a low frequency scanner that can detect them at close quarters. Paula, who are our two best people with electronic gizmos, circuitry, that sort of thing?"

"Corporal Perez and Private Ben Ali Sir," she replied.

"Okay, you two, do you think you can make a couple of compact, much smaller versions of the long-range scanner the Mars Scientific Laboratories came up with? They tested for the specific resonance frequency of the alien alloy. Their design information is stored away in a file somewhere, it shouldn't be too hard to find."

"We'll have a go Sir. It should be fairly straightforward. Do we have permission to raid the stores?" Ross Perez asked.

"I've cleared it with the Chief Engineer and Captain Treadhouse. The entire spaceships onboard amenities are at our disposal, an order direct from the Corporation Director apparently," Alex explained, raising his eyebrows.

"Wow!" the corporal exclaimed in response.

"You also have full use of the small lab on level one."

He gave them the at-a-glance address of both the store room and laboratory. They almost ran out of the canteen, leaving their half-finished breakfasts on the table, thankful to do something constructive for a change.

—

Five days later, two Martian drone spacecraft, VR2 and VR4 were extracting and disassembling the two containers from

Stellar Dusk while high in Mars orbit. Alex was approaching the bridge. He should have been on board the small military container advising the squads. However, he had been summoned by Captain Treadhouse. She addressed him as soon as he entered the bridge control room after the usual security pat down.

"Aha! Mr. Manso. I'm so sorry to drag you away from your duties, however this is very important. We have been informed by Mars Space Traffic Control that they have been tracking the scout spacecraft from *Mother Lode* for some time now, the whole of last week in fact. It would appear to have escaped the clutches from the aliens that attacked the mining vessel. Our scanners have confirmed by its size and speed that, it is indeed a one person asteroid scout, and one person is aboard."

Alex looked bewildered. "How can I be of assistance?"

"They're getting zero response from hailing the vessel. Do you know much about the medical technicalities involved with Dormouse Torpor State?" she asked.

"Sorry, no," he said, shaking his head in response.

"The problem is the system is quite delicate. Usually there are conscious people about, to help monitor and evaluate those coming round from the drug-induced hibernation state. The asteroid surveillance scout spacecraft is designed for only one soul. It would have been a hasty departure when the person escaped from *Mother Lode* in the scout vessel. They may have not allowed for the exact concoction of drugs to wake them up. It is possible they will remain in the Dormouse Torpor State until they reach the intended programmed destination. This looks very much like the case here."

"So, what's the problem? The spacecraft will enter Mars orbit under the guidance of the auto pilot. A shuttle containing a medical team could match orbit, extract the occupant and correct the dosages," suggested Alex.

"It's not that simple I'm afraid to say. The auto pilot hasn't factored in the Martian satellite moons, unless we do something very quickly, the scout spacecraft will intercept and crash into the surface of the inner moon Phobos. Can you think of how we might go about saving the occupant before that happens?"

"Have they consulted the Chief Analyst, what is his name, Robert something or other… Robert Goodyear? Did he have any ideas?"

"He, like you, is somewhat naïve about the process of the Dormouse Torpor State. He also has limited knowledge of the way the scout spacecraft works. They have consulted an asteroid miner, who informed them that the canopy can be opened using an emergency release gizmo on the outside of the cockpit. It's not a pressurised cabin. The occupant must wear a spacesuit at all times. The real problem is the logistics of getting a person on the outside and into the position of activating the gizmo. The vessel is slowing, unfortunately it needs a slight course adjustment to avoid the moon and achieve safe Mars orbital insertion. That really needs to be performed by the pilot, who, as I already said, is currently unresponsive. Otherwise, it will crash for certain," she punched one fist into the other, just to emphasize the point.

"How do the crew members of the ice tugboats get round the same problem? As I understand it, the entire crew are all out for the count for the duration of any long-range flight," Alex declared.

"Three reasons how they surmount the same problem. One, the chances of all six of them remaining in the Dormouse Torpor State is just so remote as to be unthinkable. Two, they have been doing it for so long now, they just know the precise quantity, down to the micro millilitre of each drug that is required to revive them. Three, departures are usually very clinical with precise calculations. It's normally never rushed like this one was in probably what I would consider to have been panic mode. It's a good guess that the escapee in the scout, Miss Nicky Palmer, has underestimated the correct mixtures, probably one of the two heart stimulants. There is also the distinct possibility that the portable medical unit, which is hardly ever used except in extreme emergencies, could have malfunctioned administering the wrong dosage," she added.

"Hmmm," pondered Alex. "How long do we have?"

"Two hours tops, beyond that will be too late," she replied.

"Speed in one hour's time?"

"Roughly fifty thousand kilometres an hour, I can calculate the exact figure for you if you give me a couple of minutes."

"No, roughly fifty kph is okay. I think we should be able to help. Can you talk to traffic control please? We need to get one of the grounded mining spaceship scout spacecraft up here and over to our container as soon as possible. Now I need to discuss a rescue plan with my squads. We will do what we can, if you would excuse me," he said, turning on his heels.

"Okay, good luck. Keep me abreast of developments please," Amanda shouted after Alex, as he left the bridge with some urgency.

29

The Harvester Spaceship

For the first time since leaving Earth James felt isolated. A feeling of vulnerability washed over him soon after *Oceans Dawn* had departed, leaving the scant crew of *Lode Drifter* down on the surface of Ganymede. Being a very long way from home, stranded on a gas giant moon far out in the solar system, he fought to remain calm as he watched the ground vehicle aptly nicknamed the Land Crab drive away, leaving him even more marooned. It was bleak and desolate here, apart from two massive copper-coloured crashed alien spaceships now towering behind him and a woman he was becoming more convinced was totally deranged.

An hour previously, they had been discussing their plan of action in relative safety, inside the asteroid-mining vessel soon after landing. It had appeared to be a reasonable strategy at the time.

"James, I don't think you should be on your own when we drop you off by the crashed alien wrecks. I think Zelda should keep you company, if she doesn't mind," suggested Andy, looking in her direction for confirmation. Zelda replied silently giving him double thumbs up.

"You two can have a good old nose about on board while

the rest of us, except Josie that is, search for the alien body the other side of the complex. What with *Oceans Dawn* dashing off in a hurry, our time on the ground here may be limited now, so we may have to cut some corners along the way. I wouldn't worry about being too thorough," urged Andy.

"Okay. That sounds good to me," agreed James at the time. Sixty minutes later watching the Land Crab drive back towards the outpost buildings these awful, desolate feelings, descended on him. Although Zelda was standing right beside him, she was a total stranger as far as he was concerned. They had hardly spoken two words to each other on the entire trip from Mars. She also appeared to possess a wanton lack of self preservation which worried him immensely.

Standing outside the strange alien spacecraft, with these mixed emotions coursing through his bodily fibres, he decided to analyse himself, he had to find a solution to regain control of his inner mind. After a short while he concluded that, if he was being totally honest with himself, it was more than simple isolation or feeling totally vulnerable, it boiled down to being just plain scared shitless. Once he had isolated and identified the problem, he felt better immediately.

Zelda, on the other hand, didn't seem to know the meaning of the word scared. Her mad hair was squashed into a weird looking, gravity defying pony tail inside her spacesuit helmet. With eyes wide open, looking untroubled and alert, she looked like she wanted confrontation. Studying James's face through his helmet visor, Zelda recognised his sudden nervousness and apprehension from the prolonged silence and strained facial expressions.

"James, JAMES!" The eccentric maintenance worker shouted out loudly, now they had switched to a private one-to-one intercom channel.

"What, eh? Right, let's get on with it shall we," he

spluttered, turning towards the stricken alien spacecraft. He took several deep breaths to compose himself.

"We need to find that opening we saw on the way over here, it was nearer the other end I think," he said positively, setting off alongside the outer ovoid copper-coloured hull. The very nature of the oval shape did not allow them to see beyond a few metres until they reached the very centre of the vessel.

Behind them, they could see the two crashed vessels had left shallow gouges in their wake cutting into the concrete like hard rock and ice of the moon's surface, such was their final impact. The one they now skirted actually rested against the second vessel, which, had come off decidedly worse out of the two. One side of it had been totally caved inwards suggesting a vast hollow interior about the midsection.

"Aha, here we are!" James exclaimed, coming across the dark foreboding opening. It was an upright rectangular hole almost twice their height. They switched on their helmet lights before venturing inside. James paused on the threshold turning to his companion.

"Keep your wits about you Zelda. Logic dictates we should be safe, but you never know. One of them could have been unconscious, only to come round after Leila departed in the lifeboat rocket spaceship. Actually, it might be better to check it out with the others before we proceed any further. "

He opened a new intercom channel. "Andy, James here, how are you progressing?" he enquired. His logical analysis dictated that if the body of the alien was still on the moon's surface, the chances of anyone else still being about would be almost negative.

"Okay James. We've just arrived by the laboratory building. It looks like there is a bodily shape lying out there. We're just swinging the Land Crab round to shine the spot lights on it. Oh, yes, it looks like we have found it alright. How are you getting on?"

"We've finally located the entrance to the alien vessel. We are just about to cross the threshold. Curiously, there is no sign of an airlock, just a single thick door panel that's actually been dismantled from its mountings. Perhaps the opening mechanism jammed when they crashed. We're moving inside now. I'll report back later once we have done a bit more exploring."

"Okay James. Shout if you need any help."

James felt a lot happier now. With them having found Leila's dead alien, there was a very good chance there were no more alive on Ganymede. He switched back to the close-proximity intercom channel.

"Zelda, you okay to proceed?" he asked.

"I'm fine James, especially as I have my new friend at the ready," she held up the microwave frequency modulation lance, to show him what she was referring to. Josie had given her a crash course on how to use the asteroid cutting tool.

Although it had a very limited range, it was the only weapon they could utilize at their disposal. One of the outside cameras on *Mother Lode* had caught the moment Tarek had been attacked. The footage had been relayed back to Mars which, in turn, was distributed for all to scrutinise. They saw how he managed to cut, and presumably, kill one of his attackers before falling victim himself. It gave them something to work with. It also gave them a belief that they were not totally at the mercy of these creatures. Tarek had unwittingly become a hero and martyr to the Martian cause, a cause centred round Martian human survival.

"Okay, do we head off to the left or head off right?"

The opening led up some steep steps to a broad tall curving corridor James assumed ran the entire length of the vessel in both directions.

"Well, you're the bloody analyst! What way do you deduce will be the more constructive?"

He noted the blunt sarcasm in her voice. Well, he could retaliate to that. "Well, I assume we will explore the entire spaceship eventually, so I propose we head towards what I DEDUCE is the front first. That's where I would expect to find some sort of control room."

He turned to his right and walked off briskly, before she had the chance to reply. He really didn't want to fall out with this woman. However, she did have a way of rubbing him up the wrong way. Perhaps, he thought afterwards, she rubbed everybody up the wrong way, not just him. Luckily, she now remained silent following him at a short distance, hoping the space between would allow them both to calm down. Zelda, who knew a thing or two about temperament, recognised when someone was close to the edge.

The upwards sloping corridor followed the curve of the outer hull for a short way before coming to a left-hand turn, taking them in towards the centre. Midway across, there were doors both sides of the corridor. The right hand one was a simple affair that had a large clear viewing window. James could not tell if it was similar to glass or some sort of synthetic clear polymer, all he did know was he could just about see over the bottom edge. He felt like he was in a pantomime giant's house with four-metre-high corridor ceilings coupled with three-and-a-half-metre-high doors. He fumbled round the door frame on both sides as far as he could reach up the wall. Ultimately he found what he was looking for, a small movable square panel which gave way at his touch. The door shot upwards at an astonishing rate. Taken by surprise he stepped backwards bumping into Zelda in the process.

"Hey, watch it!" she yelled, pushing him off her back towards the now open doorway. Cautiously, they edged inside. The walls were fronted with bank upon bank of black-cased boxes, like stacked coffins, floor to ceiling. In the centre of the room were two long padded benches set at an angle, the top ends pointing inwards like an arrow head.

"What's that?" Zelda pointed to something sticking up from one of the benches. As they moved closer the shape became clearer.

"Looks like the outline of a large foot, or more precisely, a boot," offered James. They moved round the side of the bench to see that it was indeed a boot, a long black boot about size sixteen by James's reckoning. The boot was attached to a leg. The leg in turn, belonged to a sprawled body of an alien lying on its back. Thankfully, it was a very dead alien.

"Will you take a look at this!" he exclaimed. They were now standing over the body that had evidently slid off the bench, apart from one foot that was now hanging by the boot heel. The black faceplate had been smashed open to reveal the alien's facial features. Its mouth was wide open, caught in the final moment of death when it had tried to breathe nothing but space. They could see the rows of pointed shark like teeth.

"Pretty damning evidence of a carnivore if ever I saw one." James looked up at Zelda who agreed with his deduction.

"Yep, I can't see it looking at the menu opting for the nut bake," she couldn't resist making a joke. James chose to ignore it, now was not the time to crack funny remarks, not in his world anyway.

"I wonder what it breathes, air like ours or some other type of gaseous substance?" So many questions were flooding James's brain, like a salmon river in full spate.

"This must be the control room. There are no obvious instruments as such, I mean, instruments we would recognise." He spoke his observations out loud while turning his head slowly round the room. Spacesuit helmet cams logging images of the room, its contents including the dead creature, were being constantly relayed back to Josie, who was busy collating the footage along with that of the search party outside.

"Right, time to move on." James said firmly.

The door opposite the control room looked far more elaborate. It had all the classic designs of being an airlock, even down to having a faint orangey light glowing from a small inset panel. What did that mean James wondered?

"It looks like the majority of the spaceship is unpressurised. This looks different though, like the entrance to a pressurised area, possibly the creatures' living quarters." Try as they might, they could not find a way to open the thick plated door. There were no hidden panels, handles or levers. This door was also solid with no window so they couldn't see beyond it.

"I think we are going to have to come back to this one if we ever have time. It very much looks like we might need to cut it open. Let's proceed down the other side towards what must be the stern of the spaceship." James said, leading the way.

Zelda slung the cutting lance over her shoulder so it hung down her back with the cutting nozzle pointing at the ground out of the way. She couldn't see a need for it here now. You could almost see her vexed disappointment that there would not be an opportunity to use the makeshift weapon after all.

On the far side of the vessel, the corridor turned left. It sloped downwards curving round the not so smooth hull. This side showed signs of battle with large dents protruding into the corridor that ran parallel to the one they had entered. Once they had just about enough room to squeeze past a huge inward bulge. Sixty metres from the end, the corridor turned left once more.

"It looks like this corridor runs round the entire vessel, I bet if we continue we will eventually come back to the entrance with the dislocated door," James said, feeling much more relaxed now they had found absolutely no sign of alien life forms alive.

In this corridor that ran across the bottom third of the

vessel for eighty metres, they found three high doors. Two doors on the right were situated almost at the junctions of both corridors that ran down the sides of the vessel where they met the crossways one. The door on the left-hand side was in the middle, exactly half way across.

The first opening on their right had double doors joined by a short corridor. It didn't take much working out that the inner sanctum could be pressurised allowing the room on the inside to be given an atmosphere for some reason. Luckily for the two would be explorers, both the outer and inner doors had been left wide open, jammed somehow as James tried, but could not shift them away from the walls in an attempt to close them.

"The door operating mechanisms must be linked to some sort of hydraulic and pressurization controls, probably somewhere inside," James stated, for the benefit of the continuous video and vocal recordings.

The short airlock corridor opened into a triangular-shaped room, with the outer wall continuing the curvature of the hull. It was roughly twenty metres on each of the three sides. There was a huge viewing window in the middle of the internal wall.

"Well, I guess we found the engine room," declared Zelda. A workbench, under the viewing window, ran almost the entire length of the room. Scattered along the bench were a few small glass fronted display ports that now showed nothing more than an inky blackness.

"I bet these used to show power levels when the propulsion unit was active or maybe life-support readouts for the living quarters, that sort of thing. These switches probably control the level of the power output. It all looks pretty dead at the moment. Ha! There's no prize for guessing what that door sign says even without understanding the alien language."

James pointed to a door in the very corner with a sign on

the front. It consisted of a picture and some sharp high lettering underneath. The drawing, an alien outline with crossed lines through the middle, was an obvious warning not to enter the engine bay or do so at your peril. As there was not much else to see, they decided to move on.

The door opposite the rear engine room, in the very middle of the spacecraft, opened in a similar way to the control room door once they found the flush fitting panels. There was a shock waiting for them inside.

"Oh my God!" Zelda exclaimed.

"I really hate to say it, but it looks like Robert and I were right all along," James said, feeling sick to his stomach.

The room resembled a poorly-stocked butcher's shop. Almost directly in front of them was a naked male human body hanging by two hooks, one through each ankle. There were several smaller joints of meat, suspended a short way from the door. The room itself was vast, at least forty by fifty metres square. Row upon row of sharp S-shaped hooks hung empty on metal rods that ran from the back of the room to the front. Several steps led down onto dark criss-crossed metal grating, the room itself was thirty metres high with a secondary set of cross bars and hooks above the ones in front of them.

"This looks like the cold store then. That must be the body of Robert Taplow, one of the three outpost personnel. Poor sod looks to be intact apart from that large hole in his chest, oh, and his missing head of course," remarked Zelda.

"Just how many bodies could they hold in here? It's beyond belief!" James was truly shocked.

"And, by the looks of it, they were definitely running short of fresh supplies," added Zelda. James had to agree.

"Let's get out of here. I can feel it even through my spacesuit, this room feels morbid, desperate, grotesque, it's… it's like the place is full of a million ghosts all clamouring for some relief, some respite," howled Zelda, not really explaining her true feelings adequately. Feelings that made the hairs on the back of her neck stand out. James shut the door behind them. This really was a sick nightmare he thought as they carried on in silence.

"Right, last door before we come full circle on ourselves I reckon," declared James, trying desperately to shut out of his mind the visions he had just witnessed.

The last entrance on the right led again through two sets of permanently open doors, into a similar triangular sized room to the one on the opposite side which accessed the engine control room. This room however, contained an impressive array of machinery along the outer wall. A similar full-length bench ran the extent of the internal wall, but this one lacked an observation window. In place were a number of mounted spotlights on stalks that could be moved to shine onto any work surface on the bench.

"Aha, some sort of workshop! I've seen these before," said James, picking up a handful of broken micro robot parts from a pile on the bench. There were hand tools, scopes and other, larger instruments that James could not comprehend the tasks they might perform. Most had old fashioned switches, dials and turning handles, unlike the control room that was devoid of any type of mechanical switch or button.

"I am assuming this room, and the engine control room on the other side, can be pressurised so the aliens can perform tasks like repairing the micro robots while outside their suits and helmets, I wonder…" James drifted off down a river of thought. "That might explain the distinct lack of physical control switches everywhere on this spaceship except for these machines," he concluded out loud.

"I'm guessing you're talking about some sort of mind control or telepathy," suggested Zelda, quick to pick up on his meanderings. James had almost forgotten she was there he had been so carried away in his own little world.

"Maybe, let's go back to the control room. I need to test out a theory. I require an alien's head, or more precisely its helmet."

They tested James's reasoning logic that the corridors were in fact all joined up which turned out to be true. Soon, they were back in the helm control room after passing the entrance they had used to gain access from the surface of Ganymede.

"Right, let's try to get the damn thing off," he said, after examining the join round the neck between the black suit and the huge black shiny helmet. Try as they might, they could not work out the unlocking mechanism.

"Hang on, I've got an idea," said Zelda, patting down the alien body. It only took a few seconds for her to find what she wanted. A concealed flap lifted up to reveal the haft of the alien's knife. She extracted it from its hidden sheath that ran down the back of its thigh.

"He we go. Move back a bit, I don't want to cut your suit by accident." The blade cut the suit material with ease.

"Wow! Are these bloody sharp!" she exclaimed.

Carefully easing the point of the blade under the joint with the helmet, she worked her way round until the cut material joined up with the initial incision. The huge helmet came off the alien head easily once it was fully detached. She handed it to James to hold before returning her attention to where the knife had been concealed.

"I wouldn't worry about putting it back," said James, reading the situation wrongly.

"I'm not. I want the protective sheath," she replied, cutting away the suit just below what they assumed was the alien's waist, then down its thigh. She extracted a protective hard scabbard and slipped the knife back inside, an invisible force pulled the blade in tight for the last few centimetres.

"Hmmm, some sort of magnetic type of lock to hold it in

place," she said, examining the sheathed weapon. It pulled out just as easily as she tested the release mechanism would work once it had been extracted from the alien spacesuit. "Clever, very smart," she muttered.

"We have an awful lot to learn yet. I can't wait to get this helmet back and take it apart, the more I think about it, the more convinced I am it really is important," James said enthusiastically. He opened a communication frequency channel to the others.

"Andy, I think we have learned all we can for the time being. Can you come and pick us up please?"

"Hi James, no problems, see you in fifteen minutes," responded Andy.

"Zelda, what do you intend to do with the knife?" James asked.

"Oh, this…" She said, holding up the half-metre-long blade with its wicked looking gleaming serrated edge. "I fully intend to return it to a living alien one day very soon, one of this one's relatives with any luck!" she said, kicking the body on the floor with her boot. Carefully, she eased the blade back in its protective cover once more. James got the distinct impression Zelda was imagining she was effortlessly sliding it into an alien stomach. He wasn't far wrong.

30

Deep Space Combat

Captain Edmund Cooper studied his monitor screen with intense interest. The two pursuing alien spacecraft had not deviated one iota from their course shadowing the ice tugboats. They were roughly seventeen million kilometres astern, but the gap was closing. Once free from intense disruption from the giant planet Jupiter, they were able to track, and log, all the spaceships' tract and speed. The Chief Officer, Adriana Rodriguez, calculated that for every hundred kilometres the tugboats put behind them, the pursuers covered a fraction over four hundred.

The calculations were about right, Captain Cooper considered to himself. A distance-closing ratio of roughly four to one, almost precisely what the Corporation Analyst predictions had been regarding the alien vessels' possible top speed, compared to the slower ice-tugboat maximum thrust.

It also meant, as he ran the easy computations through his brain, according to the same predicted estimations, the alien vessels had the potential to be twice as fast as *Oceans Dawn*. His vessel would not be able to outrun them should developments turn nasty. The upcoming confrontation could only have one of two possible outcomes.

"Ms Rodriguez, can you give me an update of approximate bearings regarding all spacecraft positions relative to ours, please," the captain requested. He shifted uneasily in his command chair as he carefully regarded his previous thoughts.

"According to triangulation calculus, the alien vessels are just over twelve hours from hunting down the ice tugboats. Our intercept course to the alien spaceships is just under an hour. In less than fifteen minutes they will start to enter Jupiter gravity assist, starting to pull away from us even faster, albeit slightly. Sir, may I suggest, that whatever we intend to do, we do it fairly soon," concluded the Chief Officer.

"Ms Rodriguez, your comments are duly noted, thank you."

He paused for reflection for a few seconds, a little unsure what the next course of action should be. He mused that perhaps the best option might be to sit tight for a few minutes, see how things pan out.

"They must have seen us by now, picked us up on their scanners. What are they thinking?" he muttered out loud. They had taken three and a half hours to reach the far side of Jupiter after leaving Ganymede. Now, they were just half a million kilometres, less than an hour from the pursuing alien vessels.

"Suggestions welcome anyone?"

The captain threw open a general request to those present on the bridge. He respected his highly intelligent crew, especially his officers.

"Perhaps they don't currently regard us as any kind of threat," Raymond Doucet, the Chief Engineer declared. "I mean, they are unaware we are armed now. Historically, they have not seen weapons on any human spacecraft for a long, long time."

"That is a good observation Mr. Doucet. Is it safe to deduce then, until we open fire for the very first time, they will carry on assuming that fact? If that is indeed the case, it just might work in our favour," speculated Captain Cooper. "Also, the closer we are, the more accurate and damaging our weapons could be against them. It's going to be a difficult call though. I've got to judge this just right as we've no idea of the range of their weapons. The real problem we face is we don't even know if our microwave beam or cutting laser weapons will actually have any effect on them…"

Adriana cut in, stopping him mid sentence. "Sorry to interrupt, Sir. There are two small cylindrical objects coming straight for us. The projectiles conform to the same dimensions from previous documented encounters with these objects."

"Well, that decides it, how long to impact?"

"Four minutes ten seconds Sir," she replied instantly.

"We'll have to open fire now. We have no choice. I'll use the microwave beam weapon on the alien vessels and the lasers on the cylinder projectiles. The power of our lasers on those two spaceships at this range would be seriously diminished. Mr. Garcia, as we are currently missing our weapons array controller, would you kindly take control of the console. Push and twist every dial and every slide control to its maximum setting for me please. If anything turns red, initiate the reset. When I call out for the power levels, please relay them back to me, is that clear?"

"Yes Sir!" the Second Officer, Francisco Garcia, shouted out the affirmative. The weapons console had been powered up as soon as they had left Ganymede low orbit. All four weapons had been charging since then. Francisco checked all the instruments as he had been instructed.

Captain Cooper opened up a brand new view on his monitor screen. The targeting computer displayed comprehensive detailed magnified visions of both the near and distant threats. It used a high resolution optical particle electron telescope, the vacuum of space being the perfect medium for the powerful image enhancing beam.

He had four separate targets to mark. There was the immediate threat of the two incoming, presumably empty, resupply cylinders, as well as the two alien spacecraft. He decided to split the lasers, one for each of the cylinders, doubling up the two microwave beams to hit the lead alien spacecraft. He instructed the crew on the bridge of his intentions, just so everyone was kept up to speed. He confirmed with his second officer that all power levels were at maximum, before being totally satisfied he was ready to commence combat.

"Okay, here we go. Firing all weapons in three... two... one," he declared, touching the firing control on the monitor in front of him.

Just after the captain had initiated the firing of the four weapons simultaneously, several events occurred concurrently. Firstly, the crew observed from the bridge two prolonged bursts of visible pencil sized beams of light emanating from opposite sides of *Oceans Dawn*. The laser beams ended several thousand metres distance at a point in space directly before them. They couldn't actually see the small, torpedo like cylinders hurtling towards them until they were illuminated by the intense power of the laser cutting beams. The long circular objects seemed to glow brightly for a second, as the concentrated energy of the laser was absorbed, before disintegrating into two separate showers of quickly fading sparks. Cheers went up around the bridge, even the captain smiled with relief when Adriana confirmed the potentially lethal projectiles were now ancient history.

Secondly, the concentrated microwaves from both weapons, even at this extreme range, started to melt a hole in the side of the lead alien vessel. That was really quite impressive, considering the alien vessels were just no more than mere pinhead specks to the naked eye across the void. An area, approximately two metres across in the middle of the copper-coloured hull, turned to viscous fluid like melting wax, under the molecular agitation. Very soon there was a breach in the hull as the frequency modulation continued to wreck havoc. Unbeknown to the crew on *Oceans Dawn,* the alien spacecraft was almost totally unpressurised. Therefore, only specific areas would be vulnerable to attack from the microwave-beam weapons. The most obvious target would be the alien bridge with all its enclosed instrumentation flat boxes or perhaps the aft engine room. Any hit in the majority of the middle of the alien vessel, would not achieve any serious damage or impede its dangerous potential.

The power to the cannons faded. The weapons would need to be recharged. Francisco activated all the right switches, but the recharging process seemed awfully slow. It was just like watching a kettle that seems to take forever to come to the boil.

The third, and final action that followed all the weapons being activated, was the eventual course deviation of the two alien vessels. Both turned as one to head straight towards *Oceans Dawn*. The euphoric atmosphere on the bridge rapidly dissipated, changing to despair, as the failure at the first attempt to stop the vessel became apparent.

"Captain Cooper to James Cleaver. Come in James," the captain suddenly blurted out, after selecting an emergency communications channel. He needed constructive input from James on the surface of Ganymede and he needed it urgently. The emergency channel would override all spacesuit communication units, automatically disregarding any personal settings. James and Zelda were just leaving the crashed alien spacecraft after a pretty thorough tour of inspection. James physically jumped at the unexpected verbal intrusion.

"James Cleaver to Captain Cooper. Go ahead," he responded.

"James. Have you been inside the alien vessel yet? Can

you give us any help in our attack on the two very hostile spaceships we have bearing down on us?" He asked two questions at once, a perceptible urgency in his voice.

James described the layout inside the alien vessel in swift accurate detail. "We are of course, assuming that all the enemy vessels are similar in internal design," James rounded off.

"There're no reasons to assume otherwise," the captain suggested. "If I target the first or last twenty metres of the hull, we should do some serious damage, do you agree?"

"Theoretically yes," agreed James. "If we logically assume that these vessels have all been constructed to the same design," he added, trying to make the point that they could not really assume anything.

"That's good enough for me James. Stand by Mr. Garcia, how are my power levels?" He decided to leave all channels open, so those down on Ganymede could listen to the ensuing battle, and its eventual outcome.

"Currently ninety percent and climbing, full power in about twenty seconds Sir."

"Right! Time to give one of these two a bloody nose," the captain muttered, while setting up the targeting computer.

"Captain, aim off dead centre, try five to ten metres either way. That should insure you hit some of the coffin like instrumentation down either side of the bridge. What damage you may inflict is anybody's guess though," James called out. His aim was to give them as much help as he possibly could.

"At this extreme range it's not going to be easy to target so specifically. I will try to fire just a fraction off the exact middle of the target. Okay, just about set here, Mr. Garcia, call out when the power levels hit one hundred percent. I want to give this next shot everything."

"Approaching maximum power now, ninety-eight… ninety-nine… okay, that's it, microwave beam power levels at one hundred percent," the Second Officer called out.

The captain had already pressed the fire button before Francisco had finished his sentence. Once again the concentrated microwave beams, travelling at the speed of light, smashed into their intended target. They cooked the outer metal skin to a liquid, before penetrating inside the hull. The crew of *Oceans Dawn* observed the microwave power levels dropping quite rapidly. It looked like they would be exhausted before long with yet again, no apparent effect. However, Captain Cooper had been very fortunate in his choice of aim. The instrumentation that the microwaves, in the very last throws of power were now turning to mush, just happen to be one of the main processor units for the alien onboard artificial intelligence.

The two alien beings lying on their control room cribs, hooked into the spacecraft controls via the telepathic links concealed inside their spacesuit helmets, suddenly found they were losing various vital functions. One main function that failed dramatically was the forward lateral control. Their spaceship started to peel away from its sister vessel, before heading straight towards the nearby gas giant. Once trapped in the immense gravitational field, there would be no escape.

There was a rush of telepathic chatter between the two doomed alien crew members. They also conversed with the pair in the other spacecraft. The damaged vessel, in its final moments managed to fire its weapon, which resembled a short burst of thick laser light. It was a couple of wild parting shots aimed roughly in the direction of *Oceans Dawn*. Without proper targeting though, the shots missed wide of the mark.

The undamaged alien spaceship still had all its faculties in full working order. They now realised they were under a very effective, and dangerous attack from the human-controlled spaceship. The second alien vessel fired its laser type weapon with a lot more accuracy.

"Mr. Lesueur, damage report if you please!" the captain

demanded, as they watched with dismay the burst of light from the alien vessel hit *Oceans Dawn*.

"The alien weapons' discharge appears to have entered through the front of our spacecraft on level one, before exiting the port side. Luckily, it passed through two empty storage rooms, one of which was in a decompressed state. It avoided the bridge thankfully by about twenty metres," Jean-Marc Lesueur, the second engineer replied.

"So all we've lost is some air from one empty storage room. Good, now for some retribution. Mr. Garcia, how are my microwave power levels?"

"Eighty-seven percent. Sir," answered Francisco.

Jean-Marc interrupted. "They've fired again Sir, this time they have hit one of our laser weapons. It has been sliced clean off its mountings on the outside of the spaceship. It's a good bet that's what they were aiming at the first time they fired, but didn't realise we are in rotation."

The far right-hand laser control panel started flashing orange accompanied by the low whoop, whoop noise of malfunction.

"Shut down that racket please. We'll have to speculate later how they know where our reinstated weapons are situated. Whatever the power levels of the microwave beam weapons are at present, they will have to suffice. I'm targeting now and will fire as soon as I have the second vessel's nose lined similar to the one before. Keep me informed…" The captain was cut off in mid-sentence.

"They have fired once more Sir, that one just missed one of the microwave weapon mountings."

"Damn! It looks like they are trying to disable our weapons one by one. I'm firing our weapons now, before they get a second chance."

The alien spacecraft started to turn into the invisible microwave beam, its two crew members had quickly determined exactly how the microwave weapon emanating from *Oceans Dawn* worked. In response, they turned their vessel to protect the vulnerable instrumentation on the inside of a two-metre wide gaping hole that now adorned the port side of their bridge. The microwave beams continued to cut a dripping copper-coloured melted smile across the front of the vessel hull. Realising they could not sustain a second bout of the microwave device, with one last feeble parting shot that missed *Oceans Dawn* completely, the alien vessel turned tail to run. If it had a physical tail, it would have definitely been tight between its legs.

"Ms Rodriguez, can you tell me the status of the first alien vessel?" Captain Cooper asked, wondering if it was still a threat.

"It has disappeared, drawn down into Jupiter's cloud by the powerful gravity field. We won't be seeing them again," she informed him.

The captain addressed his crew, a beaming smile on his face. "Well Ladies and Gentlemen, it looks like we have created history here today. We have successfully come through the first ever battle with the alien spaceships, defeating one of the hostile vessels in the process. Well done everybody."

The communication airwaves erupted with congratulations from those on Ganymede, along with all ecstatic men and women both on the bridge of *Oceans Dawn* and elsewhere on board.

"Well done to you too," the captain whispered, fondly patting the console table top in front of him.

"Now, we need to contact the ice-tugboat crew members before they begin the slingshot manoeuvre round Jupiter. Mr. Watson, what is the status of the ice gatherers' vessels?" the captain asked, bringing the brief celebrations to an abrupt halt.

"We have successfully interfaced with the onboard controls including the medical units and issued the override codes.

The three pairs of crew members are now being resuscitated out of the Dormouse Torpor State as we speak," replied the able crewman and acting helmsman.

"Can we re-program the tugboats' guidance control system altering the gravity assist to put them in orbit round Jupiter instead?"

"No problem Sir. I'll get onto that right away. If I could ask for Chief Officer Rodriguez to help confirm my telemetry re-calculations, it shouldn't take more than a couple of minutes."

The captain instructed Adriana to assist accordingly. The two crew members between them recalibrated the ice-tugboats' flight status, putting all three vessels in orbit about one point one million kilometres around Jupiter, just outside the orbit of Ganymede.

Without further interaction, the vessels would eventually catch up with, and overtake the moon. The crews however, should be wide awake well before then. It was going to take a certain amount of explaining, when they eventually rubbed the sleep out of their eyes, why they were seeing Jupiter, and not Mars, outside the viewing windows.

31

Phobos

Military analytical strategist Alexander Manso removed his scuffed silver spacesuit helmet upon exiting the airlock. Stepping into the weightless interior of the military transport container, he was immediately confronted by an agitated, somewhat angry, Squad Sergeant Paula Alvarez. The two attentive army fire team members standing behind her were in a similar state of emotional unrest.

"Why in hell are we still here, Sir?" she politely demanded to know, before adding. "We should be down on Mars, inside Hebes Chasma at the Facilities, setting up our defences."

Alex held out his hands, pushing his palms in a downwards gesture signalling that Paula and the others should calm down, before there was any chance of him offering any explanations.

"Yes, I know, I know. Believe me, no one is more eager than I to get cracking setting up the defence shield, especially as I have designed most of it, however, there's been a development. Right now I need two volunteers. Two reckless individuals for a highly hazardous mission," he enquired, looking round the room at the assembled throng.

One rule all army personnel learn very quickly is never, ever, volunteer for anything. No one raised so much as a finger nail.

"Perhaps I should ask Paula to just pick two of you at random?" he suggested after a short silent pause.

"Okay, if I give you some intimate details of the mission, then maybe, depending on your sexual persuasion, some of you may be inclined to want to help rescue a young damsel in distress."

Aban Hossini raised his right hand. "Okay, on that one fact alone, I'll break one of my personal golden rules and volunteer, seeing as it is a young lady that needs rescuing. She'll be forever grateful, wanting to marry me instantly and have my babies! At my age, it's 'bout time I started to look for someone to settle down with," the veteran soldier chipped in, with an accompanying broad grin across his sharp-chiselled dark facial features, features that were darkening daily with his periphery of ever growing stubble.

"You settle down? That'll be the day," smirked Corporal Lloyd. Some of the others laughed at the witty comment.

"Okay, maybe we'll just skip to the babies bit," replied Aban, still grinning.

"Thank you private. One down and one to go. Right, here are the brief details. The sole survivor of *Mother Lode,* who managed to escape in the mining scout spacecraft, is planet inbound, ninety plus minutes out from Mars. The problems are twofold. One, she is not responding to hails from Mars Traffic Control. They are assuming she has failed to resuscitate from the drug induced Dormouse Torpor State. Onboard life-support readings suggest she is very much alive, it will require a doctor's intervention to correct the mix of drugs to bring her round. Problem two, the spaceship needs a course adjustment to stop it crashing into the Phobos moon. Something the auto pilot, and navigation control system, had not factored into the carefully plotted guidance flight path after it hastily vacated the Asteroid Belt."

"I'll go, Sir. It might just be my sister?" Private Laurant

butted in. "What's the plan?" he added enthusiastically. Sergio's short crop of wispy blond hair sat on top of very light, almost pure white scalp above a soft rounded face. His two piercing sapphire blue eyes shone bright in the twilight of the container interior.

"Any minute now, the scout spacecraft from *Astral Gem* will be delivered to us by one of the facility ground crew. The controls are very similar to our own stealth scout so, flying it will be relatively straightforward for any one of us. One of you…" He indicated to the two volunteers in an either or gesture. "You will be required to hang on to the outside of the vessel, while the other flies to intercept the scout from *Mother Lode*. Once both vessels have matched intrinsic velocities, whichever one of you has chosen to be on the outside, crosses over to access the canopy. They will then interface with the flight-control panel to instigate the course correction. The new direction programmed so the spacecraft misses the moon to find safe orbital insertion round Mars. Once safely in orbit our job is done. The unconscious occupant will then be the responsibility of the facility medical personnel. Are we all okay with this fairly simple plan so far?" He took a deep breath and looked directly at Aban and Sergio, waiting for an affirmative response.

"Okay with me, but I hate it when a plan sounds simple. In my experience nothing is ever simple," stated Aban, before adding. "I'll fly the mining scout spaceship. Sergio can go rescue his Sis."

"Sorry to disappoint, the lady in imminent danger is not Laurant's younger sibling. She is however, an asteroid surveyor called Nicky Palmer, just so we are all aware of the precise facts," said Alex, with his usual air of authority, like a teacher presiding over a class of unruly children.

"Sergio, are you still okay with this now?" he asked, just to clarify his volunteer status after watching Sergio's face drop at the sudden understanding he wasn't going to dramatically pluck his sister safely from the jaws of death.

"Still okay with me, Sir," he replied, pulling himself together after a couple of seconds of tumultuous thought. It would be impertinent to back out now, not after volunteering so enthusiastically. He would lose all respect from the others.

"Okay you two, suit up quickly, time is a major factor here. Make sure your oxygen levels are sufficient for at least three hours," he said, glancing at the time and motion displacement function on his wrist-mounted miniature control panel.

He had input and set the distressed vessel's co-ordinates, its current rate of speed reduction and exact course after being informed of the predicament earlier.

"She's now an hour and twenty-five minutes out, slowing down all the while, but still travelling at just under fifty thousand kilometres per hour. By rights, you should have ample time to perform the set rescue manoeuvre. Just remember to take your time and avoid taking any unnecessary risks."

Alex rambled on as the two have a go heroes wriggled into their spacesuits helped out by some of the other soldiers. They checked air levels and the suit heater elements before stepping into the lock.

Alex leaned close to Paula's right ear. "Poor Sergio. I managed to make some discreet enquiries. When he gets back, I've got to inform him his sister was killed aboard the mining spaceship *Lode Drifter*. As it turns out, by one of the alien resupply cylinders," he whispered.

Paula was visibly shocked. "Sir, can you make sure that all of us are there when you tell him. I'm not sure how badly he will react. After Aimee, we are the closest thing to family he has, maybe we can help him come to terms with what will be devastating news," she mumbled back under her breath. Alex agreed thankful for the support. He was not looking forward to the prospect informing the tough soldier the sad news.

—

Private Aban Hossini turned out to be the right person for the job in hand. He was an excellent pilot, having logged many flying hours in the military-stealth scout. They were now forty-five minutes out from Mars as he skilfully edged, ever closer, to the out-of-control scout spacecraft carrying the comatose unresponsive body of Nicky Palmer on board. There were less than two metres separating both vessels hurtling towards Mars at a more sedate twenty-two thousand, one hundred and eighty-two kilometres per hour towards the slowing growing rustic coloured disc, between them, the small moon of Phobos had become an unwelcome obstacle.

"Any time you like Laurant!" Aban shouted from inside the cockpit. With both spacecraft precisely matched intrinsic velocities, he locked down the pursuit vessel's exact speed and course.

"Okay Hossini, here I go," replied Sergio, as he gave the slightest tweak to both suit forward and sideways manoeuvring thrusters. As he was also intrinsically matched to the same speed as the two spacecraft, theoretically, he needed the tiniest use of his suit thrusters to hop from one spacecraft to the other. Skilfully, he gently floated across the two metre gap, like a theatre actor drifting across a stage, attached to invisible wires. Luckily, without the requirement to be streamline traversing the vacuum of space, there were all manner of appendages protruding from the hull of the scout he could attach himself to. He grabbed hold of a sample collection arm and proceeded to haul himself over to the cockpit emergency release handle utilizing other bits of the vessel's external knobbly hardware.

"Aha! I can see our sleeping beauty through the canopy. Well, I can see the outline of a woman's body in a spacesuit. I'm now releasing the canopy and sliding back the cover. How long have we got before the course change deadline?" he asked Aban casually.

"Loads of time, eight minutes at least," Aban replied.

"Okay, I've pulled myself as far as I can inside the cockpit. I'm making an interface with the onboard control system now."

Sergio continued his running commentary whilst detaching a small plug-in unit from his spacesuit control panel. The panel was about the size of a small book, situated on his left forearm. Using a small pointer, the size and shape of a pencil extracted from the same control unit, enabled him to quickly key in the override access passwords on the very small display screen. Having gained security clearance to the guidance controls, he set about the task of altering the flight course settings calculated to avoid the small, but increasingly dangerous moon. Try as hard as he might though, it would not accept the new coded co-ordinates and alter course.

"It looks like we have a serious problem! The flight unit will not accept 'engage' after typing in the new settings. There must be something wrong with the interface, perhaps it's damaged. How close are we to our deadline now Hossini?"

"Four minutes twenty-one seconds until impact Laurant. What do you want to do?"

"I don't have the power in my suit unit to run a ship-wide diagnostic sweep on the scout control system. So, without being able to fix it quickly, I'm gonna have to go for an extraction," he decided almost immediately.

The securing straps holding the body of Nicky clicked open easily at his touch. However, the medical unit was proving to be a right pain in the arse, that's precisely how he described it to Aban Hossini.

"Shit! These damn securing snap bolts appear to be corroded together with the housing! They are designed to snap in half with the slightest bit of force," Sergio grunted, trying to lever himself against the cockpit surround all the while pushing and pulling the stubborn, unyielding medical unit.

"We have just passed by the point of safe course correction. Now we have about three minutes before impact. Would you please get a move on Laurant?"

"You had better not leave me here!" Sergio replied indignantly.

"Of course not, well, not until the last possible moment, I promise," replied Aban, a slight agitation appearing in his voice.

It took Sergio twenty seconds to locate and open the small cockpit toolbox. Keeping as calm as he could, he extracted a large adjustable spanner, probably the biggest tool in the box. He swiped at the first mount hitting the head of the snap bolt. It was a good shot. He was convinced he actually saw the bolt crack with a satisfying cascade of small particles. With one corner now free, it allowed more leverage to break the other three securing bolts at their desired weak points more easily.

Slowly he extracted Nicky, and the unattached medical unit, from the cockpit. Turning her body sideways on to him, he joined their two suits together using the large waist hoops and clips. Carefully sandwiching the medical box between their joined bodies, he took valuable time to check none of the feeder tubes were kinked or in any danger of being pulled out of the suit-arm airtight-junction plate. No point in going through this intense rescue only to find out he'd killed her during the extraction process.

"Thirty seconds. Look lively! After that I'm gonna split, with or without you!" Aban shouted. Time appeared to stop during the transfer back for the tangle of arms and legs joined together like a four-pointed star. Before they set out on the rescue mission, they had taken the time to weld a short elevated protruding bar onto the outside hull of the rescue scout ship for Sergio to hang onto. His first attempt to grab this bar failed, his gloved fingers slipped off the end. He cursed profusely.

"One last chance!" Aban shouted in Sergio's ears, as he watched Sergio's failed attempt to catch the bar, and the moon looming larger before them. This time the tweak of thrust from Sergio's manoeuvring thrusters was almost too much, but somehow, he managed to grab the rail, before it disappeared out of sight beneath Nicky's waist. The counter lurch on his arm that stopped both of them shooting off into space hurt, probably dislocated at the shoulder he guessed. He hooked his other arm under the short bar and, in the process, wedged himself tightly secure by the crook of his elbow.

"Go... Go... Go!" was all he could shout wincing through the throb of pain from his disjointed bones.

Aban turned just as the moon was almost upon them. They whistled past the right-hand side with just a few metres to spare. Skimming the moon's surface, the rescue vessel created a dust vortex looking like a small tornado in its wake. The now empty stricken scout vessel from *Mother Lode*, that stubbornly refused to change course, plunged headfirst into the surface of Phobos, burying itself almost up to its tail fins beneath the soft surface crust.

"Phew, that was close," Aban whistled through clenched teeth. "Let's get you two to the Facilities as fast as this old heap will let us. Hang on Laurant. By the way, well done," he added, with a higher level of respect for his daredevil comrade in arms.

"Thanks for the thanks, but hurry please, I'm in agony here," sighed a weary, but relieved Sergio.

"*Astral Gem* auxiliary scout spacecraft calling Mars Space

Traffic Control, come in please," Aban called out, as they headed down towards the landing fields.

"Mars control to scout, status please."

"Mission accomplished, however, it did not proceed according to the simple plan. We require an emergency landing with a medical crew standing by.'

He related a brief description of the events up to current period in time. The medical crew, headed up by Rebecca Jones, had been waiting to ascend in a personnel shuttle to help Nicky. Now they hurriedly transferred to the underground hangar three observation room. The pad had been cleared for the emergency landing with the roof of the hangar still in the process of being retracted. Luckily, by the time Aban arrived, the gap was now big enough to squeeze the small spacecraft through and carefully set it down inside the hangar, as directed by the traffic controller.

"Sergio, Sergio!" Aban shouted. He had been talking to him right up to the final descent, before needing most of his concentration to steer in through the half-open hangar door. He expertly landed the scout directly on top of the illuminated white cross inside, but now there was no verbal response from his fellow rescuer.

"You had better have only passed out," he said, sliding back the cockpit canopy with a flourish. He leant over to check the bio readouts on the outside of Sergio's suit before laughing out loud with relief.

"You little git! You had me going there for a while," he managed to blurt out at long last. Once the overhead hangar roof had shut, the room began to pressurize. While waiting for the room atmosphere to stabilize, Aban separated the two suited figures, laying the unconscious Sergio on the hangar floor. As he stood up, several medics rushed in through the airlock, followed closely by some of the army soldiers led by Squad Sergeant Paula Alvarez.

Rebecca, assisted by two medics examined Nicky's seemingly lifeless body. Eventually satisfied she could be moved without danger, they carefully passed her inert body down to some of the hangar technicians before swiftly carrying her off to the infirmary.

"What's wrong with him?" Paula queried, looking at Sergio sitting propped up with the top half of his suit round his waist, helmet cast to one side. Two medics, one each side of him were positioning themselves, one holding his torso, the other holding out his arm. They moved in unison and there was an audible crunch. Sergio gave out a short agonised snort as his shoulder and arm were relocated.

"Nothing now," said a smiling medic, getting to his feet. The other medic helped Sergio to stand upright before wandering off to the airlock.

"Outstanding work Laurant. I'll put in a recommendation in my report. If we ever get back to Earth, who knows, could be a medal in it. Meanwhile, we have a lot of work to do and we are behind schedule. Hossini, Laurant, and the rest of you, we have about a hundred crates of ordnance to unload and unpack."

32

Interesting Discoveries

Inside Ganymede outpost two five seven, the crew of *Lode Drifter*, acting as an impromptu exploratory force, assembled themselves in the main hub canteen area. The six of them were discussing the amazing news that *Oceans Dawn* had successfully fought, and won, the first ever space battle with two of the alien Harvester spaceships.

"Here's to the crew of *Oceans Dawn,* very well done!" Andy raised his glass, the others followed suit. It wasn't long before they finished off their celebratory assorted refreshments toasting the interplanetary supply vessel's victory, a victory that also assured the freedom of the ice-tugboat crews and their vessels.

Andy Hubbins, the captain of *Lode Drifter* currently in charge of this motley bunch, finally called for calm. He had no wish to end the joyous festivities, but there were important issues to discuss, they had to move on. The temporary meeting room eventually descended into silence.

"Now then, back to our own situation. Kieron, has the alien body thawed enough for an internal examination?"

"Just enough for a quick look before you dragged me away. I have to admit I was grateful in a way, the smell, it was just awful," he declared, waving a hand under his nose. "I'll need to go on oxygen next time I take a look at that body," he said jokingly.

The others laughed even though the comment wasn't that funny. However, the euphoria of the recent victory mixed with alcohol coursing through their veins, their spirits were high. Indeed, events were going well for them at that precise moment. Finding the remains of what was becoming known as 'Leila's alien', they had transported and isolated the alien body in the now empty hub used for the lifeboat rocket. Meanwhile, James was learning new discoveries about the alien foe all the time. The ice gatherers had been rescued. All things considered, events were definitely proceeding in the right direction for the rescue team.

Kieron continued with his snapshot diagnosis. "As we all know, they are humanoid in bodily shape, they also resemble us in almost every other aspect as well. They have what appear to be two lungs, one heart, small intestines, all similar to human organs, some larger in size by comparison. I'm assuming they have a brain similar to ours inside their skull, I haven't checked that yet. It's almost as if they progressed down a different branch to our own evolutionary path. I hadn't located the liver or kidneys by the time you called me to this meeting. I suspect they will have very similar organs in there somewhere. Though, it is all a bit of a mess around the alien body's midsection thanks to Leila. She really went to town with that knife."

"You mean to say they are related to humans in the dim distant past?" queried Deimos.

"It certainly looks like it, although, we don't have the same desire for fresh raw meat like they do, or the insatiable shark-like thirst for blood. I can't quite believe they are so technologically advanced and yet, have the most basic dietary habits of say, a captive lion or the now long-extinct tiger. That doesn't make logical sense to me, do you agree James?" he said, passing over the conversational baton.

"It doesn't make logical sense to us. That's not to say it makes perfect sense for this particular cosmic nomadic parasitic species to evolve the way they have," he said, confusing the issue somewhat.

"What I'm trying to say is this, who are we to say what is right or wrong for their metabolism? A meat-only diet would eventually kill us. However, they seem to thrive on it. Contrary to what we originally contrived, I have found no evidence of them growing any organic matter whatsoever. Mind you, we have yet to explore the alien living quarters. We may find some other types of organic vitamin or nutrient supplements there? I checked the Corporation databases, even carnivores like the long-extinct tiger, used to eat fruit occasionally to supplement their diets."

"Have you discovered anything else interesting?" Kieron asked James, now he appeared to be the centre of attention.

"I dismantled the inside of the alien helmet. There are some very interesting micro electronics inside the casing, some circuitry I couldn't begin to comprehend. I suspect they control an interface of some sort between their consciousness and the spacecraft, and ultimately, other alien minds." He concluded.

"Can we confirm they are telepathic, and communicate that way with each other?" Andy interjected.

"I don't think they are naturally telepathic, maybe their minds are enhanced by the advanced electronics. It's hard to say at the moment. We need to do so much more investigation. I don't think we can even begin to comprehend the enormity of what we can learn from these beings. We've barely scratched the surface," replied James.

"What's happening with the ice tugboats now Andy?" asked Zelda, instantly changing the subject. She was getting irritated by what was rapidly turning into an alien biology and sociology lesson.

"They are now in an orbit round Jupiter, an orbit similar to this moon, just slightly moving faster which means they will be catching up with us soon apparently. Captain Cooper and the officers of *Oceans Dawn* are monitoring the crews as they are being resuscitated from their Dormouse Torpor States. We should be hearing from them any time soon," he explained.

It was Josie's turn to speak. "So, according to our remit, we have accomplished our mission. We have secured the alien body, which, if we want to transport back to Mars may pose a problem with the decaying stench. James has explored and mapped the alien vessel. We have discovered some interesting facts about our foes into the bargain, that's all there is, isn't it? May I suggest we get off this rock just as fast as we can, dock with *Oceans Dawn* and get back to Mars with the ice tugboats before our luck runs out," she said.

"Sounds like a good idea to me," agreed Kieron.

"Yep, let's go home," said Deimos, at about the same time.

"What do you think James?" Andy asked.

"Well, ahem…" He spluttered, trying to find the right words. "I realise you all want to leave this moon as quickly as possible, but I have a theory I need to try out that might be potentially dangerous…" He then added swiftly. "To me that is, dangerous to me. I desire to go back to the alien vessel, into the control room to be precise, and somehow it will necessitate my head being inside one of the alien helmets."

He watched the look of bewilderment and confusion appearing on some of the faces staring at him.

"Kieron, have you removed the helmet from your new smelly biological specimen?" he asked the doctor, before anyone could make a comment.

"No, Andy stopped me before I really got started on any serious dissection. I guess you want me to separate the alien from its helmet with the head gear still intact? How will you modify it to fit our suits? Have you seen the size of theirs, it's almost twice that of our helmets," said Kieron somewhat exasperated.

"I will need the alien helmet to be connected to the top half of the black spacesuit as well. I'm sure somehow we can attach it to one of our suits. We have repair resin, cutting tools in the laboratory and above all, human ingenuity. I'm sure between us we can come up with something. I just need to lie on one of the couches inside the Harvester spaceship bridge. I have a hunch and I need to see, or rather experience, what happens," James said, smiling weakly, hoping for a sympathetic ally.

"What could happen is you could end up with your brain being turned to mush!" Andy responded angrily.

"What would we say to Robert if something bad happened to you?" Josie added, showing genuine concern. "He specifically asked Andy and me to take good care of you."

James felt embarrassed. Josie had hit his conscience right in the testicles. What would his mentor, who was just like a father to him, say to his suggestion? Having thought about it though, in the interests of possibly saving the human race, he would probably arrive at the same logical conclusion by attempting the same action. His pangs of guilty conscience dissolved in an instant as his mind was now well and truly made up.

"Well, I think if the telepath link works I can handle it. I have to at least try. I'm sure Robert would do exactly the same thing in this situation. Besides, Kieron can monitor my vital signs, if the experiment looks like it's going sour, I'm sure Deimos will have me out of there in a flash."

"You bet I would!" Deimos growled, but at the same time he winked at James, hinting his silent approval. Here was the ally James was looking for. "Go on Andy, let's give James a shot at it," added Deimos.

"Okay, but as soon as we get James hooked up to do whatever he needs to, then we can clear off this lump of ice-covered rock once and for all. Let's get to it people!" Andy ordered, getting up from his chair.

—

The entourage of four men made their way from the Land Crab towards the crashed spacecraft entrance doorway. Josie, acting second in command, remained behind once more on the bridge of *Lode Drifter* overseeing operations. She was joined by Zelda, who seemed to have lost interest in almost everything, ever since she realised there were no live aliens to be found that she could dispatch.

James looked very strange, the oversized top heavy black helmet, sat broadly on his shoulders. Deimos had to help support the awkward size of it whilst walking close behind him. Luckily, being that much taller, it wasn't too much of a challenge for him.

They had removed the top two thirds of a human spacesuit helmet leaving the communications microphone in the chin piece so James could still communicate with the others. The alien helmet slipped over what was left. The top metre of the alien spacesuit plastic type fabric had been glued and sealed over the top of a human suit. The circulating air inside the mishmash of two suits appeared to be stable.

"No leaks James," stated Andy, who was monitoring the concocted suits pressure level.

"So far so good then," James replied.

As they drew closer to the alien spaceship hull, strange three dimensional images started appearing in his line of vision. They appeared inside the helmet, between him and the visor.

"Whoa! It's started sooner than I expected," he announced.

"I'm getting visual images, I can't quite make out what they are, but they are definitely there, like two hundred year old celluloid movies, flickering away. This is not what I was expecting so soon."

They had now reached the open doorway down the side of the spacecraft. Stepping inside the entrance, James felt the full force of the mental telepathic link from the control room instruments. Streams of data flooded in trying to dissect his brain, overwhelming him. He physically staggered back under the impact. Luckily Deimos and Kieron were there to steady him.

"Wow," he declared. "It's like being hit with a million data streams of facts and figures all at once. It's all jumbled up, I can't unscramble it... I can't..." He was in danger of being totally overcome, swamped by the huge deluge of information, and then drowned in a sea of overwhelming knowledge. They quickly extracted him a few metres back outside the portal where the data torrents subsided to a few tumbling streams of information. James slowly recovered.

"You may be right Andy. There's so much going on. Perhaps our minds cannot cope with the enormity of the input. I was in danger of being swamped completely there."

"What the hell do we do now then?" Andy asked, feeling at a loss.

"Let me see if I can't get to grips with it, try to get a hang of it all by reducing the volume. I just have to find some sort of dimmer switch to the data deluge," James said, now being supported on all three sides by the others.

He carefully selected and concentrated on one information stream, then another, and a third and so on. Slowly, he found that if he concentrated on the main streams, others around them seemed to melt into the background. They were still there lurking, seemingly under control as small branches to the main stream. Eventually, he whittled all the data threads down to just one main strand of information, the rest falling in behind with various levels of degrees of importance.

"Okay, there seems to be one main thread of data now. If I focus on that, then I can branch to other, lesser data streams. There must be a knack to this. Can we try to enter the vessel again, this time millimetre by millimetre?"

The four of them edged forward a fraction at a time until they stood on the threshold once more.

"Okay, steady as we go now. I'm slowly getting to grips with the workings of this."

"You just keep talking so we know you're alright!" Kieron insisted, before checking the monitor readings once again. "Your breathing and heart rate are way too high for my liking," the doctor added. They shuffled their way forward again, a fraction at a time into the doorway.

"Okay, hold it there for a moment, the data input is increasing now, I just need to keep control of this main flow. Right, there's a stream that seems to be dealing with spacecraft functions, engines, they are currently offline, life support, weapons, all branch off the strand of that thread. Here's another regarding navigation, there's even a three-dimensional map of the solar system, planets, asteroids, moons. If I go off down a sub branch for a particular moon or planet, it gives me all sorts of information, thing is, I can't understand any of the symbols. There are possibly words in grammatical sentences. It's all complete gibberish at the moment. As we know what the planets and moons are in our solar system, I expect with a bit of careful study, these symbols could be deciphered."

"Sorry to bring you back to reality James, we can't stand here indefinitely while you learn what, is in reality, a new foreign language," declared Deimos.

"Yes, I realise that, but I seem to be getting better at sorting out the different data streams now, can we move a little further inside please? Let's see what else I can discover."

With James chatting inanely to verify he was still in touch with his faculties, they made their way down the curving corridor to the control room. James was inundated with information, but he now had it under better control, the facts and figures were not rushing by any more. Now more sedate, it was like driving down a small town main road, with side streets every few yards, each street signposted for a different purpose. He could perform a U-turn to go back to a specific side street data thread, explore it, before returning to the main road once more. The hardest part was pushing past the rush of symbols that came with every twist, turn and fork of the main road. He had to keep his thoughts narrow, limit the field of vision of this new strange world that could easily run rampant swamping his mind.

"What's happening now?" Deimos enquired, as they stood motionless just inside the tall entrance to the alien spaceship control room.

"I'm trying to trace where all this information is coming from. If we can secure the units responsible, maybe we can take them with us, just think how invaluable all that stored knowledge will be to us. Now let me work my way through this maze," he said falling silent.

His mind now followed the paths, some leading eventually to dead ends. He was looking for the particular data stream he stumbled across at the very start of this mental journey, the spaceships readouts. Then, he saw a side street signpost that was depicted with a picture of the Harvester spacecraft, the distinctive copper-coloured rugby-ball shape. Having previously mapped the spaceship, he could now follow the sections springing up before his eyes. All the different rooms came into his mental vision one by one. The engine room, the workshops, the collector room that made him shudder. Finally, he came to the bridge. The coffin like boxes correlated to performing most of the vessels functions and he needed to locate the main data storage unit. He took a step backwards in his mind, looked at the way things were laid out in the room. Then it all fell into place.

"We need the right hand cradle. It's specifically linked to relaying information data streams to this particular helmet. Then, we need these three coffin-like boxes," he said, pointing to three specific black oblong-shaped units that had invisible communication links to and from the cradle. There were two on the left hand side, one on the right. Kieron took out a small can of spray paint to mark the black oblong boxes along with the right hand cradle.

"Let's hope they'll work once it's all detached, away from the alien vessel," said Andy, intently studying James's suit controls.

"Uh oh! Looks like our botched suit has sprung a leak! There is a definite pressure drop. Let's get back to the outpost, we can come back for the storage devices coffins and cradle later," he commanded.

—

Near one corner at the far end of the gear room on board *Lode Drifter*, there were empty alcoves for three mining exoskeletons. Here they stacked up the three recently acquired rectangular black boxes containing the alien technology. They extracted the units from the alien vessel, rather easily as it turned out. There were no connecting wires or power leads, each unit being standalone and evidently with its own self contained power source. Somehow they communicated with each other via the pivotal cradle using some sort of technologically advanced low-wave communication transmission.

The control room cradle, not dissimilar to an oversized psychiatrist's couch, stood at waist height in front of them.

James lay back on the slightly contoured yielding surface, looking much like a small child lying on its parent's bed. He slipped the massive alien helmet over his head. The black coloured faceplate had been completely removed so he closed his eyes to shut out the light and help focus his mind. Instantly, his head was filled with the data streams once more, not as prolific as they had been aboard the alien spacecraft.

He had not yet identified all of the information sources. Perhaps, in hindsight he thought, maybe all the black boxes were data storage? This time, with the limited amount of information, he was in complete control, almost mastering the use of the alien telepathic technology. He recognised some of the data streams that were missing now as there were not so many side streets off the main information highway. Even with the limited data, he could still set about the task of trying to decipher, and learn, their strange language. Before he could get his teeth into the task, he was quietly interrupted.

"James, we are just about to lift off to rendezvous with *Oceans Dawn*. Are you okay down there?" Andy asked.

James had the foresight to fit an ear microphone before putting his head inside the oversized alien helmet.

"I'm fine here thanks Andy. This alien technology is fascinating. I was just about to lose myself inside their world for a while," he replied.

"Right oh, I'll give you a shout in a while when we are docked back with *Oceans Dawn*, maybe by then the ice-tugboat crew members will be up and about."

"Thanks Andy, speak to you soon." James signed off, eager to begin the mental exploration of the complex alien technological world.

33

Defence Shield

Hebes Chasma is a remarkably unique valley on Mars, mainly due to its central mesa. Mesa, the Portuguese word for 'table', or in this case, referring to the elevated five kilometre flat plateau that runs, west to east, through the middle of the six-kilometre-deep valley.

The eastern end of the mesa splits at right angles into two distinct downwards sloping ridges. Tight against the steep cliffs, in the crutch of the split, protected from wild dust storms, the Mars Facilities had built up over many years. Now, it was a sprawling mass of dome-shaped offices and recreational constructions, square-shaped laboratory buildings, accommodation blocks, hydroponic greenhouses, spacecraft landing fields, huge chimney-topped refineries, large smelting works, ore sheds and all manner of smaller buildings scattered in between. Most were joined by pressurised covered walkways and sealed underground tunnels.

Alex considered it to be possibly the worst complex he had ever come across to try to defend. He had to remind himself, it was never intended to be defended from an attacking force. The only existing danger, until quite recently, were small stray meteors and asteroid fragments falling on them. The four existing laser defence towers were more than adequate to cope with those risks.

"I'm happy to place our five static ground Tesla pulse cannons around the facility buildings, here, here and here," said Alex, pointing out positions on a three-dimensional topographical diagram of the installation.

"The three main large facility domes are the most likely to be targeted, especially the central one on top of which perched the Space Traffic Control tower. I propose to place two cannons where the mesa ridges met the valley floor, setting up an effective cross fire across the front of the facility buildings to protect this main area in the middle, particularly the landing fields."

Alex was addressing Carmen Applegate, the Facilities Controller, Robert Goodyear, a Corporation Chief Analyst, Tobias Hauss, Head of Mars Security and Blake, formally an undercover operative, now a bona fide representative of the European government that employed him as a industrial spy. They were all crowded round Carmen's desk in her small office. There was one spare chair, although it didn't feel like you could physically get any more people into the room without it feeling uncomfortably crowded.

Alex continued his briefing. "These two will stop anything flying in down either valley from the west."

The other three he pointed out would be interspersed with the existing laser towers on top of the mesa, one pointing directly west away from the Facilities, the other two looking out east high above the tops of all the buildings.

"These three Tesla cannon will defend space directly above the complex, both to the east and west. I predict we can expect to lose fifty percent of these defences in the first onslaught of an attack. That will leave certain areas of the Facilities wide open and vulnerable I'm afraid."

"How are the Tesla cannon ordnance operated?" Robert

asked with noticeable apprehensive signs of anguish in his voice. He was currently having a nightmare with his claustrophobia, especially in this stifling room. He had run out of his anti-anxiety medication a few days previously, it was beginning to show.

"We can switch them to automatically seek, lock onto, and destroy anything that is not physically touching the ground. We can also take manual control when we have friendly vessels flying about in between any attacking forces," he answered professionally.

"Toby, are you still able to isolate individual buildings?" Alex asked the head of security, switching the subject of conversation once more. Alex had studied the Mars Facilities building plans back on Earth, but they appeared to be very out of date. He needed current specifications to see if the old primitive atmospheric breach precautions were still operative, or had been improved at all.

"At each main corridor junction we have the old airtight shutters. They can be activated in case of emergency, but they effectively isolate and seal most, if not all individual sections of the buildings. If any of those areas are compromised, the occupants could be cut off with nowhere to escape to."

"Could we use individual ones as makeshift barriers?"

"Only if they are operated manually, it's normally a case of all or nothing." Toby answered.

"Are there any airtight rooms within any of the singular buildings that could be utilised as a safe haven?" enquired Robert.

"There are experimental chambers within the scientific labs that could be modified to accommodate refugees, for a short period of time at least. We have airtight locker rooms over in the refineries and smelting works that could be used for temporary shelters," said Toby thoughtfully. "I think you can rule those out though, my main concern is that they could turn into potential coffins," he added sombrely, staring at a blank spot on the wall.

"I have to agree with Toby there, each defensive position must have at least one escape route, somehow. For the most part, it looks like all of the personnel that remain, will have to wear spacesuits when the inevitable attack comes." Alex declared, before quizzing Carmen once more. "Have you started evacuating all non-essential personnel onto *Stellar Dusk* to return to Earth?"

Robert had suggested it might be an idea to remove as many people from the danger area. If they could place as many non-essential personnel on the interplanetary spaceship that was tangibly possible, then they could start on a course back towards Earth. If the ultimate confrontation went well for the human inhabitants, they could be recalled. If not, they would have a head start on any pursuing alien vessels. That was assuming there would be some left intact to give chase.

"Already underway," replied Carmen. "The Social Village is being shut down even as we speak, all the bars, gaming rooms etcetera. Most of the junior admin employees, basically all those that don't need to be here now there is no refining production ongoing, are being shuttled up. Those that have decided to stay have all volunteered, especially those with any sort of past military background. I understand the army brought some surplus weapons just in case this very situation should arise."

"Yes, another one of my many ideas," muttered Alex. "Some of the soldiers are currently training those that have volunteered in using the latest MKII Tesla Pulse rifles. The fire teams will obviously be in the front line, there's no harm in having some militia reserves at the rear, just so long as they don't shoot any of my soldiers in the back!" Alex paused for a moment before proceeding.

"Moving on then, we come to our ground vehicles. We have a couple of two-person buggies that have been built for use on hostile terrain. These vehicles will be used to ferry the army personnel to and from the ground-based weapons. That takes care of four of the squad team members, two on top of the mesa and two at the bottom. The other four squaddies at my disposal will be inside specific buildings. Two of those will be with us in the control tower dome. The last two will be split, one each to the two other main domes either side of the control tower. I'm hoping to have some trained facility personnel for them to boss about," Alex said light heartedly, but no one laughed.

The prospect of being in a fire fight with the alien race, possibly to the death, was no joking matter to those sat around the table that day. He realised his mistake and moved on quickly.

"Good, that's agreed then. Now, I understand you have a military-stealth scout spacecraft that has already seen some action," he smiled at Blake. "And you are the gallant pilot, yes?"

"No, not me. Hugh, my colleague, is someone far better at flying than me. I was just a spare part sitting in the passenger seat giving moral support," said Blake humbly.

"Well, we have one as well, maybe a newer, slightly upgraded model, very much the same design with a decompresurised combat mode feature which allows the pilot to pop the hatch and escape fully suited if required. Something the older models couldn't do. I understand the aliens were a little perplexed when you attacked them," he said, recalling from memory Blake's report regarding the incident.

"They may appear to be technologically advanced in some ways, I suspect however, that they are not very military orientated. Have you noticed they don't seem to have developed any personal long-range weapons for a start, they only have those knives which, could be likened to a late nineteenth century fur trapper's Bowie knife," suggested Robert.

"Well, we can't rule out the possibility they have other weapons we are currently unaware of, or have not seen yet!" Toby interjected.

"Other weapons or not, they would appear to be good at sneaking, hiding and creeping about. Let's hope the aliens are rubbish at full on confrontation," stated Carmen.

Alex was quick to offer his opinions. "I hope they don't have any military orientation or any unseen weaponry for all our sakes. I'd be happy for any advantage that may save anyone from getting killed, especially my squad. Now, that just leaves these drone spaceship bombs of yours."

"That's right. We have made up four VR-operated drone spacecraft that have been filled with a concoction of high yield explosive. They have been designed to detonate on impact. The VR operators can remotely fly them into the alien vessels. That's the theory anyway," Carmen explained.

"Can I ask that we keep those in reserve for the time being? I'm fairly sure our ground-based Tesla cannons will be far more effective against the alien spacecraft. If we need to use them, then I will give the command, is that okay with you?" Alex asked Carmen.

It was more of a direct statement, establishing exactly who was in charge of the Mars Facilities defences. Carmen had no choice but to reluctantly agree. The drone spacecraft bombs had been her idea. She felt a little peeved that they were being dismissed so easily and placed into reserve status.

"Who will be flying your stealth spacecraft?" Blake asked.

"Our squad sergeant, Sergeant Alvarez, she is a very accomplished pilot with a hell of a lot of hours' experience. Obviously, we'd like the two stealth vessels to make a wing." Alex answered.

Blake considered who would be the lead, and who would be the wingman? Sensing an internal clash fast approaching, he would have to deal with it first when talking to Hugh later.

While he was thinking how to broach the delicate subject there was a gentle knock on the door. Carmen looked at her watch letting out a brief exclamation of surprise. A young woman entered at her bidding.

The newcomer was slender, with drawn cheeks and a petite nose. Above steel-grey eyes, her head supported a weighty mop of mousey coloured short hair that just about covered her ears.

"There's one new aspect we have to consider that was highlighted during the demise of *Mother Lode*. May I introduce Miss Nicky Palmer, the only surviving crew member from that ill-fated vessel," Carmen announced, indicating the empty chair which was the only space available for the newcomer to accommodate. Carmen went round the table introducing Nicky to all the other occupants of the room.

"We observed what transpired to your vessel from some of the relayed outside cameras. I wanted us all to hear first-hand about the large cylinder the aliens used on the mining spaceship."

The room fell silent as they waited patiently. Carmen was impatient though.

"If you would be so kind, Nicky, a description when you are ready please, I do realise you have had a traumatic time of it lately, but it's important that we know the facts, they could help," she said, smiling politely.

Nicky took a deep breath. Then explained how she was just about to leave in the scout spacecraft when the excruciating noise began, followed by the cylinder striking the mining spaceship.

"It was quite awful. It created a huge hole right through the middle of the vessel. I doubt I'll ever forget it. As the cylinder emerged, it dragged out a round core of cabins, corridors and all manner of debris it had sliced through. The last thing I saw, something that will probably haunt me for the rest of my life, was half a human torso, spinning about with other loose objects. It had been neatly cut in half, cauterised by the cylinder's cutting edge."

"I'm truly sorry Nicky, if I had known about that I would not have asked you to relate your experiences. We didn't see that on the monitors. Are you okay?" Carmen now sounded deeply concerned and felt guilty about hounding the girl earlier.

"I'm okay, really, if reliving the horror helps us in the fight to beat them, then, I don't mind," she said, putting on a brave face while wiping away a stray tear.

"Thanks Nicky. That'll be all for now. Oh, I understand you have opted to stay behind. Thanks for that, I also heard you once trained to be a nurse before becoming an asteroid surveyor. We might well need some of those very soon," Carmen said, with raised eyebrows in a 'god help us' expression. "If you would like to report to Miss Rebecca Jones in the infirmary, she will take you under her wing. I've told her to expect you."

After Nicky had left the room, they discussed the use of the large cylinders. Alex had not been able to come up with any plausible explanation for them.

"I can understand them re-using the small resupply cylinders as weapons. We know firsthand how devastating they can be," said Robert.

"So, what's with the big cylinder then?" Toby asked.

"Maybe it was once used to carry larger objects. I can see the logic in using it on *Mother Lode* the way they did, in one foul swoop they gained instant access to the interior, disabled the vessel and stopped all crew movement within. Quite clever really," remarked Robert.

"Clever or not, they pose possibly the most dangerous threat to the facility buildings. We have to take them out first chance we get," sighed Alex, whose job seemed to be getting harder by the minute.

—

"No, No, NO!" Paula shouted at the top of her voice. "That doesn't go there. Here, give it to me."

She shoved Private Jacqueline Reilly out of the way while, at the same time, grabbing the metal rod out of her hand.

"Like this. In here, y'see Reilly," she said, demanding a certain level of basic engineering acknowledgement.

"Okay, I gotcha now, they tighten up there and there, right. The other side the same, yes?"

"Yes! Remember I have to fly this bucket of nuts and bolts. It's my arse in the pilot seat. If it falls to bits out there in the height of a dog fight, I'll come looking for you, even if I am dead!" Paula screamed, almost at the end of her tether.

They had commandeered a corner of hangar three to assemble the stealth scout spacecraft. The large wooden crate sides rested against the far wall. Various sized labelled bits and pieces were strewn about the floor and across the workbenches. The main fuselage sat upright on four landing struts. They still had a long way to go. Paula had hoped to get some help from the facility mechanics, but apart from old George, who looked to be a hundred and was riddled with arthritis, the rest had all been evacuated. George was next to helpless when it came to manual work, his hands having no real dexterity or strength, so he was resigned to making refreshments whilst giving advice, usually sarcastic in content. He shuffled over with a steaming mug in both hands barely able to hold them upright, spilling some of the contents.

"Here you are ladies, a nice strong coffee for each of you. Well, it doesn't look like you've got much further since I was last here," he commented, after surveying the pieces strewn about.

Paula bit her tongue. Jacqueline turned her grin away from Paula's gaze. It was all she could do to stop herself laughing out loud. She had instantly liked George. It turned out he certainly had plenty of character, and, a seemingly endless supply of witty stories.

"Thanks George." Jacqueline said, accepting one of the pre-offered mugs. Paula indicated that her hands were full. He understood the gesture by putting the other steaming mug on the nearest bench.

"So why are you still here George? Didn't you fancy being repatriated with the other mechanics?" Private Reilly asked. Paula gave her a stern look that said, stop chatting and get on with the work in hand. Jacqueline ignored the look.

"I live here now, Mars is my home. I came here a young man many, many years ago. So long ago now, I can't really remember when. I have nowhere else to go to tell you the truth. I don't even know where my family are living on Earth."

There was an awkward pause, no one knowing quite what to say next.

George sensed the embarrassing silence. "Anyway, did I tell you about the time one of the workshop guys lost his eyebrows? Well it all started…" He lapsed into relating another one of his funny stories, while the two women soldiers continued the arduous flat-pack assembly of the military-stealth scout spaceship.

—

"She has assumed command of the lead, and for me to be the wingman!" Hugh sounded indignant.

"I know it doesn't sound fair. We have no idea how adequate or inadequate a pilot she may be, but it does sound like she has loads of experience if it's any consolation. I do know you are very good, one of the best I've had the pleasure to fly with."

Blake tried to reassure and calm Hugh down at the same time. It seemed to work as Hugh took the edge off his voice.

"Well, she had no right to make those assumptions. We were here first and, have had first-hand action with an alien vessel."

"I know that, but to be fair, the army have given us the chance to join them, it's not the other way round. Sergeant Alvarez would be flying out there by herself in normal circumstances. Plus, they have the replacement chemical rockets, without which, our spacecraft is just a harmless, nearly invisible, piece of ingenious space junk," explained Blake.

Hugh remained silent, his feelings still simmering inside.

"C'mon, let's go have a drink. I hear there's one bar in the Social Village still open, the owners opting to stay behind. Seems only right we show them our gratitude. We'll stop for Leila on the way," Blake suggested, grabbing Hugh round the shoulders giving him a manly hug.

"Okay, we might just as well, while we still have the chance," agreed Hugh, accepting the offer. "It doesn't mean I like the idea of having to be the wingman though!" he moaned through gritted teeth.

34

First Wave

Robert rushed headlong into the third floor Mars Space Traffic control room somewhat out of breath. "What's happening?" he blurted out before gasping, trying to regain his posture and catch some air.

He had been having what he considered was a well-deserved afternoon nap in his quarters, the first real sleep he had had in a long while, when the internal communications device emitted its low irritating shrill waking him from his slumber. Carmen had been very curt in her summons to the control room.

"They're attacking. Five of the Harvester vessels, came up over the northern horizon ten minutes ago. They have taken us by surprise, somehow avoiding the long-range scanner. They must have spent days, if not weeks, coming in on the planet's blind side. The attackers will be here in less than two minutes," replied Carmen, remaining very calm under the circumstances.

"Your soldiers?" Robert directed his concise blunt question towards Alex, ignorant to the fact that there were two armed soldiers standing in the room directly behind him. He noticed Alex was wearing a small earpiece with attached microphone, in his hand was a small control box with a number of indicators on it. He assumed it allowed him to advise one, or a combination of any number of the foot soldiers.

"Sergeant Alvarez, Hugh and Blake have been scrambled in the two stealth vessels. They should be up and operational in five minutes. I have Irvine and Brett on top of the mesa taking manual control of two of the three Tesla pulse cannons installed up there. Our two ground cannons on the valley floor, are being manned by Corporal Perez and Private Reilly. There are two privates currently on patrol over at the refinery buildings, I've recalled them. The other two..." He finished pointing out the two army personnel in the control room to account for the full complement of both army squads. Robert noticed the heavily armoured duo with a raised eyebrow. They had not registered in his mind when he entered the busy room moments previously.

"When did *Stellar Dusk* depart?" he fired out another quick question, this time aimed at Carmen.

"About ten hours ago, they should be at a relatively safe distance by now," she replied anxiously.

A slim figure of a woman suddenly appeared climbing down from the open plan control room above them. She sealed the airtight hatch at the base of the lighthouse-like tower behind her as she descended. Carmen gave a nod towards the controller. She placed the emergency spacesuit helmet on the floor at the back of the room before jogging over to occupy the second controller seat at the console directly in front of them.

"Here they come," said the first controller.

The small wave of alien spaceships flew at least seven kilometres above the valley floor. The stationary automatic defence laser towers appeared to stir, but soon resumed their non-committal positions, as the pending dangers flew past very fast.

"They're banking to port, looks like they are going to swing round to come straight in at us from the east," the controller announced, relating the readouts from the display screen before her. Robert recognised her immediately. She was the same controller that had been on duty when *Lode Drifter* had returned almost seven weeks previously.

"Straight down our throats!" Alex declared, before relaying the information to the squad corporals.

"I doubt the two stealth vessels will be up and ready by the time they return," commented Robert.

"They are slowing down considerably during their banking."

The controller continued reading out the flight changes in course and speed for the benefit of Alex, who in turn, passed on the information, along with any worthwhile recommendations.

"Wait until they are ten kilometres out, concentrate on one, preferably the lead vessel, fire simultaneously…"

At the suggested distance, as one, the four manned ground cannons fired on the foremost alien spaceship. The anion particles riddled the fuselage mostly without effect. The five vessels broke formation, two splitting each side of the lead spaceship that was still being peppered relentlessly by the ground weapons. The static defence towers also joined in after waiting for flight acceptance codes that never came. They managed just a couple of bursts of feeble laser fire that scored harmless lines down the flanks of the nearest attacking spacecraft. The effort was totally non-effective.

"We might be better of throwing rocks! Paula, what's happening? Where are you?" Alex demanded.

"Just making final preparations here, Sir. We should be on our way any second. Where are the attacking spacecraft now?" she asked in return.

"The lead vessel must have been hit by at least one

thousand particle rounds, and it's still flying!" he said dejectedly.

"They have just passed over the facility buildings east to west, before reforming in their V-shaped attack formation. Now banking to the port again to come in from the south," he added.

"We'll be able to give chase after the next pass. We are just lifting off now, Sir," declared Paula.

Robert whispered quickly to Alex who nodded in approval.

"All ground crews, same procedure as before. I have just been reminded about the communication we received from *Oceans Dawn* two days ago, they are most vulnerable in the first or last twenty metres of the vessel. Aim straight at the nose, or backside, if you can. Okay, here they come once more. Remember, ten kilometres out. Concentrated firepower on the lead vessel," he advised.

This time, one of the ground weapons scored a direct hit on the lead alien vessel's bridge. The two alien pilots were riddled with particle rounds that killed them instantly. The vessel, now pilotless and totally out of control, plunged into the northern valley wall. It smashed into a mangled mess in the process, possibly due to the vast number of holes in its fuselage that compromised its structure.

The remaining four following vessels now opened fire with their laser beam type weapons. They targeted two of the static defence towers, as well as the two manned Tesla pulse cannons on top of the mesa.

There was a brief ball of fire as Private Ricardo Irvine, and the cannon hydrogen fuel cell, were both hit simultaneously by the alien weapon. The cell's hydrogen contents, mixed with the ruptured oxygen cylinder contained within the weapon controller's spacesuit, ignited quite spectacularly. The Tesla pulse cannon and the unfortunate operative were now nothing more than a small crater. Small parts from the exploding cannon flew off in all directions, some unfortunately in the direction of Mercedes Brett manning the other nearby ground weapon with equally disastrous results.

"Come in, Private Irvine, come in," pleaded Alex, flicking through the settings on his little control box.

"It's no good Sir. There are no replies from either Irvine or Brett," declared Corporal Frank Lloyd after trying his own personal communications link. Alex sighed heavily, that was far too easy for the aliens to knock out the ground weapons he thought.

Paula pulled back hard on the controls. Her movements mirrored identically by Hugh in the second stealth spacecraft. The two small, almost undetectable vessels, started to climb up out of the valley.

"Okay Hugh, keep tight on my starboard side. Alex, can you warn the ground crews we are now up and in flight."

"Will do sergeant, although be aware, we have lost communication with Irvine and Brett from the top of the mesa."

Alex then went to inform Perez and Reilly to be aware that their colleagues were now in the space above the Mars Facilities. He also told them about the worryingly easy demise of the other two cannons.

The ever-alert traffic controller sensed the pause in the conversation. She spoke up, before anyone else could cut in.

"The four alien spaceships have split into two pairs. They are now approaching from the east, one pair five kilometres in front of the second."

Alex related this new information word for word to the remaining two cannon operatives, as well as Paula and Hugh, a split second after the information was called out by the traffic controller. It was like there was a quiet echo in the room.

Outside, Paula surveyed the scene, deciding on a course of

action. "Right Hugh, we'll climb above them, then latch onto the second pair once they have flown by us."

"Whatever you say, you're calling the shots." Hugh replied, still not that happy about being the subordinate in this current set-up.

"Don't worry Hugh, once I've fired all my missiles, you can take the lead and I'll watch your back," she said, sensing his downhearted mood. It had the desired effect as Hugh perked up immediately.

"Thanks Paula, I'd appreciate that," he replied, more enthusiastically.

Blake slapped Hugh on the top of his shoulder. "What goes around comes around as my old Mum used to say. You'll get your chance, don't worry about that."

"Right then you two, let's get focused. Once we make our presence known, there's going to be some sort of retribution, I can sense it," said Paula.

Steadily they climbed out of the six-kilometre-deep valley. Passing by the top of the high mesa, they instinctively looked towards the three ground-based weapons that had been sited on the very top. They could make out a few small objects, but they were just too far away to see anything in detail. They continued climbing higher, another two kilometres higher, then, started circling each other faster and faster to gain some individual momentum.

"Paula, they will be below you in ten seconds, can you see them yet?" Alex asked, just as the two remaining ground weapons fired once more.

"I can see the trace of our cannon fire from the valley floor, yes, I can see the alien vessels now. Wow, they just opened fire too. Get ready Hugh, we going to give chase in five… four…"

Robert felt the floor move beneath his feet. Two short bursts of alien weapons fire ripped into the control room luckily missing all the occupants. Decompression klaxons sounded, voices were raised to compensate. Air was leaking out of the two very small tubular holes in the wall, not enough to cause disruption, only concern. One of Toby's security officers had been ready, a sealant gun in his steady hands. He sprayed a cloud of opaque vapour towards the front wall with its small viewing ports. The vapour was instantly sucked towards the outlets conferring their location. The officer moved in to plug them. They were permanently sealed within seconds from the initial attack. The upper control room and connecting tower above them had come off a lot worse. It almost disintegrated under the main deluge during the attack. Large pieces of what was once the huge clear thick plastic windows were slowly raining down past the small viewing windows in the lower control room.

"What the hell!" exclaimed the controller, emerging from the shock of the attack.

"Well done Steve," said Carmen, acknowledging the security officer's quick handy work in preventing the situation worsening.

"Well, it would appear they seem to know a little bit about your facility buildings, the layout and, where the traffic control tower placement once stood," declared Alex.

"Mmmm, they must have taken long-range observations at some point in the past, recognising the tower was an important building overseeing the landing fields. They obviously didn't know about this room below it, otherwise, we would have also been targeted in my professional opinion," stated Robert.

"Where are they now?" Carmen demanded.

The main controller answered almost immediately. "The alien vessels are banking round again, still in pairs. They are going a long way out this time around. I can't quite work out where our spacecraft are. There is a strange sort of glitch on the monitor following the second pair of alien vessels. Our scanners are certainly being deceived by the stealth mode. It is quite remarkable that even our scanners cannot see them."

"These actions from the alien spacecraft, they look planned, clinically co-ordinated. It's almost as if they are testing how we going to react to each pass," said Robert thoughtfully.

"You mean they are testing our defences to the limit…" suggested Alex. Robert nodded his agreement. "Even to the point of sacrificing themselves?"

"For what possible purpose?" Carmen asked.

"That remains to be seen. I fear a bigger schedule is going on here," declared Robert.

Outside, Paula, Hugh and Blake witnessed the concentrated weapons fire from the first two alien spaceships hitting the control tower. Paula missed out the number two while counting down as a result.

"Three… wow! … one, here we go Hugh, stay close."

The two stealth spacecraft swooped down after the second pair of attacking spaceships.

"Alex, I've just reached maximum throttle and we're only just keeping up with them," explained Paula after a few minutes.

"And that's after they have slowed down considerably," he added.

"Well, I'm going to let them have two salvos of two rockets, seconds apart, see what that achieves. How's our rear Blake?"

Blake had been very quiet, letting the pilots and ground personnel get on with the important babble. He quickly glanced around them.

"Paula, all clear behind. You're free to engage."

She switched her in-built helmet monitor to targeting control, zooming in on the selected alien target.

"Okay, weapons locked. Attack plan programmed. Here we go, firing now!" she shouted, touching the cockpit control to launch the stealth spaceships complete complement of four rockets.

The alien spaceship design had very little in the way of protective shielding, especially round the engine room, a small oversight on their part really. Paula's plan worked spectacularly. The first two rockets blew a large hole in the rear of the alien vessel. The second pair of chemical rockets disappeared into the breach resulting in a direct hit to the alien propulsion unit. The detonation caused the entire back third of the spacecraft to disappear, erupting into a million small fragments. The two scout spaceships could not avoid the debris trail. All sorts of odd-shaped bits and pieces of metal, plastic and rubberised type particles pinged off the cockpit canopies of the human-controlled vessels. Blake instinctively raised his arms across his face. Hugh did not, desperately trying not to take his eyes off Paula's vessel. He was forced to blink and wince a few times, as some larger particles bounced off the tough canopy plastic directly in his line of vision.

"Nice shooting Paula!" Hugh exclaimed, once they had come through the cloud of remains unscathed. The damaged spaceship, having lost all operational direction, tumbled out of control away from the planet.

"Thanks," she replied. "Now, what's happening with the last three attackers?" she muttered to herself. "Alex, I can only see two on my small cockpit scope, where's the third alien spaceship? It seems to have disappeared."

Alex checked with the controller. "It's peeled off from the other two, possibly trying to understand how they cannot detect you. It has gone vertical so it will be high above you somewhere. One thing's for damn sure, they now know you are out there somewhere," he replied.

"Looks like the first two are changing course, away from the Facilities. They have gone after the remains of the damaged spacecraft, maybe on a rescue mission?" Robert suggested.

"So, what do we do now?" Hugh sounded deflated.

"Well, you take the lead like we agreed," said Paula, slowing her spacecraft slightly so Hugh edged in front. Paula was now Hugh's wingman on his port side. They spiralled round in large circles gaining height for a short while waiting for the remaining Harvester vessel to reappear.

"I don't like this, where is that third bastard? Update please Alex." Paula sounded agitated, voicing her concerns.

"Paula, according to our scanners here, it seems to have vanished completely. The lead two vessels are pulling away now, heading away from the planet. No, wait, it's there!" Alex shouted pointing. A shape suddenly appeared on the outer edge of the controller's monitor that was scanning in the short range. It was moving very fast.

"Paula, Hugh, you got to get out of there now! The alien spaceship, it's travelling at an astonishingly fast speed, directly down to your position. I'm not sure if it can see you, but it's headed your way. Move it!" Alex shouted.

"Hugh, you break high starboard, I'll go low to port. If they have managed to find a way to see us, it can't go after both of us at the same time. If it follows me, try to get behind it, get off a couple of rockets after it," she ordered.

The small military-stealth spacecraft broke formation as Paula suggested. The alien vessel continued to hurtle downwards.

Blake scanned the heavens above until he saw it, a copper coloured meteor, streaming through space towards them. "There, there it is. It hasn't changed course by the look of it. It's just coming straight down to where Paula knocked out its companion," he said.

The alien vessel started firing its laser type weapon in a sweeping sort of pattern.

"Look, its firing blind, hoping to hit us. So, we're still invisible to them. Why not pull round and give it a couple of explosive surprises Hugh?" suggested Blake, a wild grin on his face.

Paula was quick to interject. "No, wait. Once you launch, you will give away your position, the rockets will be visible to them. The aliens will fire at the source!" she shouted, but it was too late.

Hugh had positioned his spacecraft to intercept the fast-moving alien vessel. He set his targeting control to track it, while programming the firing sequence for two rockets. Gently touching the cockpit control, the rockets launched on a preset course.

The alien vessel immediately altered direction, concentrating its weapons on the two chemical rockets headed for it. They were destroyed in an instant. Hugh had already put the stealth spaceship into a steep dive towards the planet's surface, but it was far too late. With a now more precise firing pattern covering a smaller area to aim at, a random shot from the alien spacecraft laser weapon hit the stealth spacecraft in retreat.

"Oh crap!" Hugh exclaimed, as he struggled desperately with the flight controls, trying to pull the non-responsive vessel out of a shallow dive as it headed towards the Martian surface. They hit hard, sending up a shower of sand and dust. Blake felt a shooting pain in his legs before blacking out.

35

The Victor's Return

Shaun realised something was amiss as soon as he came round from the drug-induced state of suspended animation. It just didn't feel right. He didn't feel right. The numbered image in the top right hand corner on the large bedroom monitor screen confirmed his suspicions when it finally came into readable focus. The countdown for Mars arrival had stopped at forty-one days, thirteen hours and eleven minutes. Also, there was that continuous infuriating noise from the communications speaker, someone wanted to talk to them. He shook Maria forcefully who groaned in response.

"We've stopped, somewhere near Jupiter I'd guess," said Shaun, hopping out of bed. He disconnected the redundant tubes from his arm, grabbed his shorts and pulled them on.

"Whoa," moaned Maria, semi-conscious and still feeling nauseous.

With his head pounding, Shaun dashed out the sleeping quarters, up the short flight of stairs and headed for the bridge control room. Sitting down in his chair, the eerie orangey-yellow light cast by Jupiter flooded the cockpit. He turned at once to the communications console stabbing the open communiqué button.

"What the hell!" he spouted, expecting to see one of the other ice-tugboat crew members staring back at him. He was somewhat taken aback when a stranger, Captain Edmund Cooper, appeared on the monitor screen.

"Aha! *The Phoebe*, at last, and you must be Shaun Metcalf. You're the first one to respond. Let me introduce myself…"

Captain Cooper then proceeded to acquaint himself and his officers currently on the bridge, before giving a short explanation why they had been stopped and woken up. By now, Maria had joined Shaun, both sat open-mouthed as the captain described the short fight with the two alien spaceships. By the end of his detailed ramblings, the other two ice-tugboat crews, Bjorn, Lenka, Soren and Daniela had also patched in to listen to the hard-to-believe catalogue of events. Captain Cooper had to recap several times for the benefit of the later arrivals. When he had finally finished, there was a stunned silence.

Finally Bjorn spoke. "Well, I think I speak for all of us, in thanking you, and your crew, for saving our souls, Captain. I can't imagine what it must have been like to take on the assailants with untried weapons. I shall convey our immense gratitude and appreciation to the Corporation on our return. I do hope they reward you all accordingly."

These sentiments were echoed by the other ice-tugboat crew members much to the embarrassment of those on the bridge of *Oceans Dawn,* who desperately tried to play down the episode.

"So, when do we start back?" Daniela asked, once the hubbub had died down somewhat.

"We've just had confirmation that *Lode Drifter* has just lifted off from Ganymede. Once they have docked, Chief Officer Rodriguez will calculate and plot a course for all of us. Hopefully, we can get back to Mars unmolested. What happens to us all then is anybody's guess."

"We'll need some food supplies if we are going to stay awake for the rest of the way back to Mars," chipped in Lenka.

"That's okay. We have to empty out a cold storage room we require for another purpose. We'll begin shipping over supplies to you once you have co-ordinated with my Chief Engineer, Mr. Doucet."

"Okay Captain, please inform us when we can expect the food transfers," replied Soren.

"Now, I have to see about *Lode Drifter* successfully docking back with us. Miss Rodriguez will be in touch shortly with new flight details for all of us," the captain concluded.

Five minutes later, Andy Hubbins's rugged face replaced the ice-tugboat crew member peering out of the communications console monitor on the bridge of *Oceans Dawn*.

"Mr Hubbins, how long before your re-docking procedure starts?" Captain Cooper asked him.

"We're coming up beneath you at present. You should be able to see us in your downwards viewing screens."

They waited patiently in silence as *Lode Drifter* majestically rose up finally to appear in front of *Oceans Dawn*. Turning to face away from the larger vessel, it showed its two rear fusion drive exhaust ports.

"We're just lining ourselves up now captain, reversing slowly onto the makeshift ramp any second now," Andy explained.

There was a slight scraping grumble as the alignment wasn't quite true, the slight error being rectified through sheer force, taking some paintwork off the outside hull of *Lode Drifter* in the process.

"Sorry captain, we seemed to have misjudged that manoeuvre slightly," Andy confessed with a grimace.

"Just so long as you haven't damaged the ramp?"

"We're still reversing very slowly so it looks like we managed to get away with it."

There was a satisfying series of loud clunks as the improvised ramp-securing clamps located onto the recently welded anchor points on the hull of the asteroid-mining spacecraft.

"That's it, all secure now captain, now we can transfer over to you once I've powered down the fusion drive. Have you found somewhere nice and remote to store the alien body? It needs to be put on ice somewhere. It seems to be deteriorating at an alarming rate and the smell…" He held his nose between two fingers screwing up his face in gesture. "Also, we have James's new toy that needs a home. I'm sure he would like to play with it ALL the way back to Mars," joked Andy.

"Everything's well in hand, don't worry. We will soon have an empty cold-storage room for the alien, and we have created space in one of our two recreational rooms for James's contraption. According to the specifications you transmitted to us, it should be big enough. If not, we'll just have to take out some more recreational recliner chairs and the crew will just have to sit on the floor," he said smiling. Andy reciprocated with a short exhale of laughter, enjoying the light-hearted banter.

A few hours later the various and numerous transfers between all the spaceships had been accomplished. The vessels were then ready for the long haul back to Mars. Chief Officer Adriana Rodriguez calculated, with help and input from Bjorn, the quickest route back using a velocity-enhancing sling shot round Jupiter as a starting point.

There was a short ten second count down by Adriana before they bid a final farewell to Ganymede that orbited the gas giant planet whose revolving red spot, like a giant eye, watched them leave.

—

"Mars Traffic Control, interplanetary supply vessel *Oceans Dawn* and asteroid-mining vessel *Lode Drifter* accompanying *The Phoebe*, *The Amelia* and *The Lily* requesting Mars orbital insertion co-ordinates, please respond?" Captain Edmund Cooper requested a second time. James looked at him from the weapons console chair catching the eye of the captain who just shrugged. James raised his eyebrows, both slightly confused, what was taking so long for them to answer?

"*Oceans Dawn*, sorry for the delay in responding captain. I wanted to welcome you back personally," said Carmen Applegate, the Facilities Controller, whose recognisable heart-shaped face suddenly appeared on the monitor screen.

"Phew! You had us worried there for a second or two, glad to see you once again Miss Applegate. I trust all is well?" Captain Cooper enquired, still slightly worried by the delay.

"Well, we have both been in the thick of it, although, you came off a lot better than us I hear."

"Yes, it would appear so, but..." The captain was cut short.

"Can I just say on behalf of all the facility personnel what a truly brave and magnificent task you and your crew have performed? Saying 'well done' doesn't reflect your selfless act or do any sort of justice I know, but from everyone here, I bid you and your crew a very hearty well done." The traffic control room must have been full of people who all started cheering as soon as Carmen finished.

Luckily, saving Captain Cooper from any further embarrassment, another female face, ice-tugboat crew member Maria Metcalf, appeared next to Carmen's on the captain's monitor. Her face also appeared simultaneously next to the face of the captain on Carmen's monitor.

"Hello Miss Applegate. Captain Cooper, hello there, once again many thanks from all of the ice-tugboat crew members. Sorry to interrupt the welcome home committee Carmen, we will be taking our leave now, we have some ice to dump," interrupted Maria. Carmen recognised the ice-tugboat pilot immediately.

"Sure thing Ms Metcalf, once you have made your deliveries, we would like to ask all six of you to stay at the ice-processing plant for the time being. We are not sure how the next, almost-certain forthcoming alien confrontation will proceed. We are hoping that all of you will be willing to help defend the ice-facility buildings. The army personnel have installed a ground-based Tesla pulse cannon outside the main building. I think they left some other military supplies there as well. Once you dump your cargo and get settled, contact Military Analyst Alexander Manso, he'll brief you on all the equipment. Meanwhile, it's great to see you all back in one piece. Oh, and another thing, I have arranged a small gathering for the day after tomorrow, alien non-presence permitting that is. I will arrange a transport vessel for all of you nearer the time."

"Thanks Carmen, the reason we are all safe is totally down to the fearless Captain Cooper and his valiant crew. We look forward to seeing them all and having a drink to toast our victorious rescuers in person, have no doubt about that. See you all soon," she ended, cutting the connection. Her face instantly disappeared from both monitor screens.

"Miss Applegate, there is no need for celebrations for my crew and I. Not yet anyway, we still have so much to do…"

"And if I say we will have a party to relieve the tension and let our hair down because I think we need it, we will bloody well have a party. I will feel very upset if you and your, as Maria so elegantly put it, valiant and victorious crew do not attend. I agree we still have a lot to do, but we have a lot of knowledge to impart amongst one another as well. Also, I want you to meet the military personnel who have now seen some horrific action. When the crunch comes, you will be fighting alongside each other."

The captain felt he had no choice but to concede. "Okay, okay, but only if there is no immediate danger to the Facilities. How can we be sure they won't spring a surprise attack again by sneaking up on the blind side of the planet?" he asked.

"We have sorted out a medium-range scanner on the far side of the planet that is relaying scans via a satellite link, they cannot sneak up on us again, not without giving us ample warning," she replied smugly.

"Alright then, you win. I'll be there with the officers and crew I can spare, but I want a shuttle ready on the pad, just in case we need to move fast. I insist!" he concluded. He tilted his head while offering the compromise. Carmen, displaying a wry smile on her face in response, nodded approvingly. *"Touché"* she thought to herself.

—

The Lily had its tail sticking out into space, its retro rockets keeping the space tugboat motionless facing the planet's surface, whilst maintaining Mars low orbit. In front of the vessel the cargo, the huge three-kilometre-square block of ice hewn from the Rings of Saturn, was still connected via the cable harpoons. It was now hanging between the spacecraft and the Martian surface. Soren had expertly piloted the space tugboat to be directly lined up above the ice dumping ground. The cables were slowly unwinding allowing the cube to descend metre by metre. The fin-like thrusters on the ice tugboat started to strain as they produced more and more reverse thrust to compensate for the increasing weight of the cube the further it progressed towards its final destination on the planet's surface below.

This was the easiest way to deposit the ice. The containment walls surrounding the natural dumping ground depression had been activated. The ice cube would be released to free fall into the enclosure once it had reached the end of the cables. Upon impact, it would smash into its smaller component parts, just like dropping a three dimensional jigsaw puzzle into a large pudding bowl.

"Releasing now," Soren called out, as the powerful little tugboat fusion engine was at its almost absolute limit, now shaking the spacecraft with the strain of maximum reverse thrust. He touched the display that retracted the barbs of the harpoons, cutting the thrust at the same time, causing a slight jolt for those on board. The intricately-constructed cube, pulled down now by Mars gravity at just over three and a half metres per second, started its descent to oblivion.

It was then the turn of *The Phoebe* and *The Amelia* to follow a similar procedure. The sight of nine square kilometres of light-blue-coloured ice crashing into the planet's surface, as well as into each other, was quite a spectacle. Luckily, the containment walls were curved, much like sea-wall defences surrounding a Cornish fishing harbour on Earth, throwing the smaller lumps that slid down the stack back towards the centre of the immense pile.

"Well, that's another successful delivery," announced Bjorn, as they watched the final cascade of ice subside.

"Let's go and see what our temporary accommodation is like. I don't think any of us have ever landed here before? Who knows how long we are going to be spending here now. We'd best try to make it comfortable," said Maria pulling a grimace.

"You never know, it might be okay. Anything bigger than the inside of an ice tugboat will be pure heaven for us," teased Shaun.

"That's true," agreed Maria laughing.

"Okay, follow my lead," shouted Bjorn, as the three small vessels lined up behind each other to make the descent down to the ice-processing plant buildings. One behind the other they flew down to a small landing field, its illuminated white cross lay between the currently receding containment walls, and the main building. Several bulldozers, along with other tracked vehicles, were neatly parked up outside the main building entrance.

The ice-tugboats' fusion engines pitched whining noises faded right through the musical scale as they finally powered down. It almost sounded like they were sighing, thankful for a rest, after the immense workload they had just undertaken.

There were two airlocks to the main building, one large enough for the tracked vehicles to pass inside, and a smaller one, big enough for half a dozen people. Inside the smaller airlock they disrobed once compression had taken place. After storing their suits, they turned to greet each other like long-lost friends. Although they worked together day after day for months, the three separate crews rarely met each other in the flesh. Now they hugged one another and gossiped, just like old friends meeting up once a year at Christmas. It was certainly easier to chatter face to face outside of their spacesuits and spaceships. Exiting the inner airlock door they were greeted by a small pile of plain grey crates. They had stencilled writing on the tops and sides. The chatting came to an abrupt halt as they surveyed the scene.

"Tesla pulse rifle MK II times ten, hydrogen refills, sonic grenades, body armour," Lenka read out loud, running her eyes across the dull boxes.

"Bloody hell!" Daniela interrupted. "They weren't kidding, looks like we are going to be fighting for our very lives. Maybe even to the death..." The words trailed off as they looked at each other in horror.

—

The Mars Facilities main canteen was quite crowded. Carmen had arranged a small soiree in order to honour and thank the captains and crews of both *Oceans Dawn* and *Lode Drifter*. Almost all the facility employees that had volunteered to stay behind, as well as the remaining eight army personnel were in attendance. Captain Edmund Cooper had left his Chief Engineer and Second Officer behind to man his spaceship in Mars orbit. The ice-tugboat crew members had been ferried over earlier in the day. All were now mingling, chatting, debating and discussing a whole host of facts all based about the aliens and their threat to the Mars Facilities or more precisely, the people therein.

"You need to ask James," said Andy, who was discussing the battle with Captain Cooper.

"Here he is. James, the captain has a question for you," he said, pulling James away from another small crowd. Robert appeared from yet another group to listen in.

"Hi James, something is really bugging me. Apparently, you may have the answer. How is it the alien creatures knew exactly where the recently-installed weaponry was located on my vessel?"

"That's easy. Since I've been scrolling through the alien artificial intelligence data-storage devices, I have discovered some amazing things. One of which supports Robert's theory that they have been among us for a very long time. There is a section that contains pictures of us or rather, our evolution into space from our humble beginnings. There are pictures of World War Two German V2 rockets, the Saturn Five Apollo launch vehicle, the space shuttle, the creation of the original International Space Station launched in 1998, the building of the Orbital Space Elevator, the early Martian settlers arriving in the Neptune interplanetary carriers, even I daresay, a very detailed picture of your interplanetary spaceship. It is my deduction that they have a high resolution image enhancer which they used during your fight. Comparing their historical pictures, it would be relatively easy to spot any new additions and alterations to the vessel's exterior."

Captain Cooper smiled. "Easy when you know how. Thanks for the explanation."

Robert stood open mouthed. He was desperate to quiz James on the alien equipment that was slowly being shipped down to the Martian surface, when Carmen called for order.

"Good evening everybody. I hope there is enough food and drink to satisfy everyone. After tonight, I'm going to have to introduce some severe rationing, just in case we are in for a long siege."

There were a few greetings in return as Carmen paused. There were also a number of mumblings about the use of the word siege.

She picked up where she left off. "Yes, I chose that word as it sums up nicely the news I have just received via a communiqué from the Corporation back on Earth."

Again she paused. All eyes were fixed, not a sound could be heard now. "The Earth orbital telescope that was assigned to monitor the region around Pluto noticed something they would like to share with us. The moon commonly known as Nix isn't a moon of Pluto any more. It, well how can I put it plainly, it's moving. The whole fifty-kilometre-diameter moon started on a journey towards the centre of the solar system some three weeks ago. The consensus of general opinion is it is their intention to pay us a visit…" She trailed off.

The silence continued for a few nanoseconds, before raised voices started asking a new series of totally unanswerable questions. One question however was repeated, higher than any other. Again and again it boomed out, until the room went quite, its occupants confused. As the question echoed out one more time, people across the room strained to see who was calling out. Those that knew the owner of the voice smiled to themselves. It was Zelda, and she wouldn't stop until she received some sort of an answer, they knew how persistent she could be.

"How long?" she repeated once more, her voice quieter now there was no one to talk over. "How long do we have before they arrive?" she asked one last time.

Everyone could hear the question clearly now, the room as one turned back to face Carmen.

"At the rate it's travelling, and the distance it has already covered, I have been informed we have just less than five weeks' grace, before it arrives on our doorstep!" she declared.

36

Nix

Blake was in a coma. He was slipping into the underworld, his physical body already halfway across the river Styx. His conscious mind however was working overtime, trying to delay the arrival on the far bank. Stabbing thoughts and bright lights were burning holes in his cerebellum. His body flatly refused to respond to any of his commands. He willed his muscles to move, concentrating intensely trying to force open his eyelids. It all seemed totally hopeless. Was he incapacitated? Perhaps he was totally paralysed, destined to be a human cabbage for the rest of his life, one very active mind inside a useless, dead body. There were so many questions and no answers. *"Damn, damn and damn it,"* he repeated, over and over in his thoughts. Finally, just when he had found someone he really cared about, someone who meant something to him, a kind and caring person, who had lavished those very same feelings on him. It wasn't fair, but then, life had never seemed fair to him. His thoughts and visions descended once more into the delirious abyss with the vision of a beautiful, sensuous woman, the love of his life, before his eyes. He was caving in. Leila's image was slowly fading, becoming misty. *"No, no, NO!"* he blurted out loudly inside his head, his imaginary fists hitting out, punching the jet-black darkness before him. Now he fought, fought back against internal demons that had suddenly appeared grabbing hold of his legs, trying to drag him down into the eternal raging fires. The fire licked and singed his feet, but he was not going to give up, not now. Leila was worth fighting for, Leila was hope, and she was his only salvation. The outline of her face started to grow stronger, more refined. The hideous demons wailed as, one by one, he kicked them off, to fall back into the flames of internal damnation. The fires dimmed and it grew cold and dark once more. Now he was alone again, lost, wandering around, stumbling and tripping over. Once he went sprawling and couldn't get up. He lay there sobbing to himself, frightened, an intense coldness eating into his bones, he shivered uncontrollably. Then, when he thought all hope was lost, he saw a small pinhole of bright light in the distance. Slowly, the virtual body inside his head stood up as the light grew larger, brighter and warmer. He moved towards it, where it became so intense he had to shield his eyes with the back of his hand. Through his parted fingers he saw her face again. Something grabbed at his wrists, wrestling with him, he fought back. The more he fought, the stronger he became. The light grew brighter still, almost blinding, until it was obscured by her soft features. He saw her lips moving, he could hear faintly at first, becoming louder, she was calling his name. Now aware of his surroundings, he blinked Leila into focus, tears welled in his eyes.

"Hello," she said, as reality finally took control. "I thought I'd lost you forever," she added.

"Hello my darling," he replied.

They hugged as best they could with Blake in a hospital bed, both legs in bulging bone repair tubes, while Leila was squeezed into the only small free space at his side, next to the life-support monitoring unit.

"I dreamt I was going to hell, you saved my life. Thinking of you brought me back. Thank you," he whispered in her ear, hugging her even tighter.

She smiled whilst being embraced in the awkward cuddle. Eventually, they let each other go, albeit reluctantly.

"You were in a coma, we thought you were never going to snap out of it," she explained, as a single tear ran down her cheek.

"I came back because of you," he purred, then gently wiped the tear away with his finger.

"That's just as well, cause I was coming after you if you hadn't!" she joked. They both laughed, Blake winced. Laughing pulled something painful inside his chest.

"What happened here then?" he asked, as he started to assess his body and what the many tubes and wires stuck in here and there might actually be for. Both his legs were encased in clear thick plastic healing tubes, the glutinous opaque gel inside concealing the damaged skin. He guessed his legs were broken. A tight bandage around his chest would indicate cracked, or maybe broken ribs, hence the pain when laughing.

"The scout spacecraft Hugh was flying was hit. Luckily you had a soft landing when you crashed. They rescued you in ground vehicles, brought you here to the infirmary. You were pretty broken up, Rebecca Jones operated on you for hours, but it wasn't the physical side of you she was concerned about. You'd slipped into a comatose state. They have no immediate cure, no operation for that sort of thing. Then, these last few hours you have been mumbling, tossing and flaying arms, fighting against yourself. Once you shouted out 'NO' at the top of your voice, I tried talking to you, holding you, but it didn't seem to be helping."

"You have no idea how much it did help." Blake said, shaking his head slowly just as the Mars Facilities resident physician, Miss Rebecca Jones, then appeared at the end of the bed.

"Aha. Blake, back from the dead at last," she smiled.

"Do not jest, you have no idea how close I came. If it wasn't for Leila here, I, well… I don't know what would have happened, she came to my rescue in here," he replied, tapping his head with his right forefinger.

"She has been here every day, and most nights, while you have been fighting your inner demons. Time and time again I have ordered her back to her quarters for some much needed rest."

Blake looked closely at Leila. "How long exactly?" he quizzed, deep furrows crossed his forehead.

"Six weeks, give or take a day," replied Leila.

"SIX WEEKS!" Blake exclaimed, wincing once more forgetting about his damaged ribs. "Bloody hell…"

He was cut short by another arrival at the end of the bed. Hugh appeared looking downcast. He was sporting a sling on his left arm. "Oh my god, you are out of the coma! I'm so glad, so glad you're back. I'm sorry Blake, so sorry for all this." He gestured towards the bed with right hand semi-outstretched.

"Sorry for what? We, no you especially should not be sorry. We can both be very proud of ourselves! Well, I am anyway. We took them on, showed them that we will not lie down and roll over. Showed them we are prepared to stand up and fight. Don't be sorry for me Hugh, please. If I knew I was going to end up here like this, I would still do it all over again."

Hugh seemed to perk up a little as Blake, continuing to play down any remorseful feelings he might have, heaped and lavished yet more praise on him.

"Between you, me and Paula, we got one didn't we? So, let's forget all this nonsense about being sorry once and for all.

Now, what's been happening while I was away with the fairies? I've got six weeks of catching up to do!" Blake exclaimed out loud.

"Well, after you crashed, the three remaining Harvester spaceships retreated, we presume to make their way back to Nix, the alien mother ship..." Leila started to explain.

"Nix? Mother ship," queried Blake.

"Yes Nix, the third moon of Pluto, it would appear is the alien mother ship. It has now left Pluto's orbit and is only three and a half weeks from reaching Mars. The good news is *Oceans Dawn* safely escorted the ice tugboats back just over a week ago."

"That is great news. So... hang on a minute, Nix is coming here? Presumably to attack us and I'm going to be stuck in this hospital bed when they arrive in force next time. That's just bloody great," sighed Blake.

"The scout spacecraft is totalled anyway. Luckily, it stayed in one piece when it hit the deck. Its atmosphere was contained thankfully for us, but the internal structures twisted off their mountings. Your seat collapsed and mine, well mine, sort of fell into your lap. All the hangar technicians and engineers have been evacuated, apart from some doddery old guy who cannot even hold a spanner these days. So the stealth spacecraft cannot be repaired. Anyway, that's irrelevant, we couldn't fly it now, not with our injuries," concluded Hugh, holding out his arm in the sling as if to emphasize the point.

"What happened to you?" Blake asked. Rebecca jumped in before Hugh could answer for himself.

"Hugh managed to trap his wrist which got a bit mangled, a few bones mashed and dislocated, torn ligaments, severed tendons, quite messy, but all repaired nicely now. You are performing your daily physiotherapy," she said sternly, looking at Hugh.

"Yes doc, I promise, morning and night, twisting my wrist

and wiggling fingers so that the repaired tendons don't stop moving and heal rigid."

"Good." Rebecca nodded approval before turning back to Blake.

"Right Blake, as you appear to be in no immediate discomfort, I'll leave you with your friends for a short while. I have another recovering patient to see right now. I'll come back later to give you a thorough check up."

She spun round before striding off towards the examination room located opposite the ward. She almost bumped straight into Mei-Lien stepping into the corridor at the same time as her patient arrived. They greeted each other before disappearing into the small examination room.

"Now then, tell me everything else that's happened," said Blake, addressing Leila and Hugh after Rebecca had left. He had miraculously recovered back to his old self in remarkable time they both thought.

"You sure you don't want to rest a bit more?" Hugh asked the question that was on both their minds.

"Not likely, I've been out of it, resting for six bloody weeks. Now I want to hear everything mind, don't miss out any detail however small," he insisted, settling down to catch up on current events, his hand gripped tightly with Leila's to reassure her of his devoted affection.

—

Carmen Applegate's office was full to bursting which seemed to be the norm these days. Not surprising as it was the centre of operational planning. To say her desk was in a bit of a mess was an understatement. It was covered with printed plans, drawings and list upon list of statistical figures. It looked just like several filing cabinets had exploded. Sitting round her table were Robert Goodyear, James Cleaver, Tobias Hauss,

Alex Manso, Andy Hubbins and Edmund Cooper. Nix was two weeks away from Mars and the unknown danger was closing fast.

After the usual general welcoming pleasantries they all made themselves comfortable. Carmen then opened the official proceedings.

"How do we stand with the ground defences now?" she decided to start the questioning with Alex.

"Out of the three ground-based Tesla cannons on top of the mesa, we have substituted the part-vaporised one with our last spare replacement. We managed to repair one of the others to operational status. The third is just a total mess. The alien laser beam weapon is very destructive. I'm going to leave those two operational cannons on top of the mesa unmanned on automatic. I don't suppose they will last long before being put out of commission once more and I do not want to lose any more of my people. The two cannon situated on the valley floor have been dug in and we've upped the defensive shielding as best we can. I can only ask for volunteers to operate those two weapons considering it almost guarantees suicide in doing so. We have trained everyone left at the Mars Facilities in the use of the MKII Tesla pulse rifles. My squads will be armed with grenades as well of course. The installed ground-based Tesla cannon over by the ice-storage sheds hasn't fired in anger yet. The ice-tugboat crews have enough rifles and ammo to supply a small army. Sergeant Alvarez has been over to instruct them in how to utilize all the weapons they now have at their disposal. And, whilst talking about Squad Sergeant Alvarez, she will be flying the remaining stealth spacecraft. We are hoping she can disable one, if not two, of any attacking alien vessels before running out of missiles, after that, well, let's just hope. You'll be pleased to know we have salvaged the rocket-firing mechanism from the crashed stealth vessel and jury-rigged it up to the front of one of our ground vehicles. There are no guiding mechanisms so it will fire blind to whatever it happens to be pointing at, it was the best we could do. That's about it for the ground forces. Apart from Paula in the stealth, our main aerial weapons platform is of course *Oceans Dawn*. I'll now pass over to Captain Cooper to explain his battle readiness," concluded Alex.

"My spaceship is safe for the moment on the other side of Mars. We're not sure what weapons the alien mother ship has, so Mr Manso and I have decided to play it safe for the time being. I mean we could fire long-range on Nix now, but with it being such a large target we probably wouldn't even scratch the surface, let alone inflict any damage. We also run the risk of burning out, or damaging our weapons by maintaining such a constant barrage. So we are going to hide, staying out of sight hoping the alien attack force think we have abandoned those here. We will only come into the affray once the automatic ground-based weapons have been disabled. How much damage we can inflict once we arrive within the combat arena is anybody's guess. How long we can survive is also an unknown factor, the weapons we have recently re-installed were not designed for short-range combat. We will be a fair distance away at the start of the battle, although, I fear, not far enough. Once the Harvester spacecraft close in on us we will be outnumbered, outgunned, and entirely at their mercy."

Sensing that was the termination of the report by Captain Cooper, Carmen turned her attention to Toby. Without saying a word, Toby recognised her inquisitive look that said, louder than any verbal words ever could, it was time for him to speak.

"I have ensured that all current personnel have a correctly fitting spacesuit with additional air supplies in readiness. These have been strategically placed near their work stations or defensive positions. Speaking at length to Mr. Manso regarding his battle plans, he expects multiple breaches once the main attack is under way. May I suggest I might co-ordinate the mass de-pressurisation of the main facility domes once we are sure they are about to launch any attack. That way, with no internal pressurisation there will be no sudden expulsions causing severe damage to the structures."

"That is an excellent idea," said Carmen, nodding her approval. Robert bit his tongue. He was going to suggest that it might be beneficial to get the remaining personnel to suit up, and the total depressurisation of the facilities before the imminent attack. However, he was pleased Toby had mentioned it first. Toby was slowly obliterating the numerous black marks in Carmen's naughty book, albeit slowly.

Toby continued, having taken the rare compliment as a sign of confidence in his abilities. "I have issued instructions to shut down and seal the refinery buildings, the ore sheds and the landing fields. The underground tunnels have been barricaded so they shouldn't be able to get in underneath us…"

"I wouldn't take that for granted," interrupted Robert. "James and I have been analysing the attack on *Mother Lode*."

All turned towards Robert in anticipation for a detailed explanation.

"Perhaps I should let James explain as primarily, it was his discovery."

Attention now moved focus on James, who felt his face flush with the sudden interest.

"Well, not as much as a discovery, more a revelation. Robert and I had some concerns as to the use of the large cylinder used in the attack on *Mother Lode*. As you know, we worked out that the small cylinders were in fact resupply modules. So, what could they possibly use a cylinder four metres in diameter for? Well, it was used initially as a mining tool, a device for gaining entry to the inside of any object to hollow it out. At this point I have to say I cheated somewhat by accessing data from the alien artificial intelligence. Locating the right data thread I found out they were used primarily as boring machines to carve out the interior of Nix. They have since been modified to carry a sled on which a complement of six aliens can stand on, three each side. On approaching an object they wish to gain access, the sled is jettisoned out the back allowing the cylinder to continue forward, making a four metre round hole into whatever is in front of it. It can cut, even vaporise the contents of the hole during the cutting process. The cutting process itself can be limited from a couple of seconds to an indefinite period. Setting the vaporisation to a very short period will allow penetration of the building wall and then leave the cylinder as a readymade entrance tunnel. The alien invaders carried on the sled, can now enter into the target object, through the entrance, ready to carry out whatever task they intend pursuing."

There was a short pause while this rather startling information was absorbed. Toby looked pensive. At last he spoke.

"So, using this device they could gain access to any part of the facility buildings or our underground access tunnels," he said thoughtfully.

"In theory, yes," agreed James.

"How about putting two barricades in the access tunnels, one at each end? That way, if they use the cutting device it will be wasted and the alien force will be stuck in a tunnel that goes nowhere," suggested Alex.

Toby was first to agree. "A great idea, I'll get my lads onto that task right away," he said excitedly.

"Andy, I understand you have some input to this meeting at this point?" queried Carmen.

"Indeed I have. Also resulting from the attack on *Mother Lode* where Tarek modified his cutting lance to destroy the robot carrying spheres, my crew have offered to protect any group with our modified mining microwave frequency modulation lances. I heard the army guys have developed some sort of scanning device that can detect the alien spheres. If my crew could have one of those to complement our lances, I can't see any of the spheres getting in close to anybody," he suggested, hoping his plan would be accepted.

"That sounds great. How many of the scanners have you got available Alex?" Carmen asked.

"How many do you need? I can get the squaddies to knock up some more, no problem."

"We'll need four in total, one for me, Kieron, Josie and Deimos. If Robert, Carmen and Alex would like to assign each one of us to whatever defensive groups you think is appropriate, we'll split up accordingly." Andy finished.

"Good, we'll let you know and thank your crew. Well, I think that's all we can do for the moment…" Carmen was interrupted by Robert as she tried to conclude the meeting. His interruptions were becoming more irritating she thought. Perhaps it was sign of the amount of stress building up within all of them.

Robert's analytical mind was stuffed full of concerns about the forthcoming engagement with the alien forces. "Who are the volunteer VR drone spacecraft controllers left?" Robert asked.

Carmen redirected the enquiry. "Toby, anyone left qualified to operate the VR drones?"

"Actually there is thankfully for us and it was more by accident than anything else. It's quite an amusing story as it happens. A chap called Duncan Seafare was in his quarters hooked up to his music station. Having taken a mild hypnotic drug, he was quite happily tripping to some ancient psychedelic music and completely missed the departure of *Stellar Dusk*. So, he is still about somewhere."

"Good, can you introduce him to James please?"

"What's on your mind Robert?" Carmen asked out of curiosity.

"I was thinking about your drone spacecraft packed with explosives. They might be useful against the moon Nix itself? They may have similar laser type weapons to us, we are assuming they have superior numbers on the ground and in the air, and maybe they do, but if we could surprise them, maybe if we could do something to shorten the odds at the outset, we might stand a better chance?"

Alex nodded his agreement. "Anything that gives us an edge is okay by me," he said before adding. "I also don't believe for one moment they would expect an attack on the mother ship. How about we stick a couple of the kamikaze drone spacecraft out on Phobos? It wouldn't hurt."

"Even better!" Robert exclaimed. "James, you said you wanted to experience flying one of the drone vessels, now's your chance to learn."

"Great, it will be a crash course if nothing else!" James said wistfully. Some groaned while others let out a snigger, thankful of the slight relief it brought to an otherwise tense meeting.

37

Second Wave

"How close do you think the alien mother ship, the small moon Nix, will actually venture towards the Mars Facilities?" Carmen Applegate asked the experienced Military Analyst Alex Manso.

"That depends," he paused to gather his thoughts, leaving the people in the Mars Traffic Control Room hanging on his every word, waiting for his theoretical explanation. What would he do if the situation was reversed? If he were in charge of the attacking force inside the small moon, how would he begin his offensive campaign? He could only hazard a guess at the actual alien headcount available. He suspected, along with Robert's earlier input on the matter, it was now a rather depleted alien presence at the present time. He cleared his throat prior to delivering his thoughts. "If I were the attacking force, I personally wouldn't get too close to begin with, possibly using one of the small Martian moons as cover. I'd then deploy at least half of the available foot soldiers, keeping maybe the other half in reserve. Carefully monitoring how the first attack progressed, before committing the remaining troops or the main mother ship to any danger. So, it would be logical to probably stop somewhere in the region of the small moon Deimos. Maintain a similar orbit, say, between twenty-three and twenty-four thousand kilometres out, hold station there while my most experienced troops attacked." He concluded what he considered to be a reasonable battle plan, would he have been the alien attack co-ordinator.

No one needed to ask the controller for any confirmation exactly how far Nix was away from the precise position Alex had just detailed. They could plainly see on the projected viewing screen before them inside the third-floor traffic control room, precisely how far the alien mother ship was closing in relation to Mars and its two moons.

"So, give or take a few minutes either way, we are talking about three hours from now, that's according to your calculations…" interjected Robert, after performing some quick mental arithmetic. He continued. "However, could it be a lot sooner? Perhaps we should start the decompression of the domes now, get everyone ready in spacesuits in their defensive positions."

Robert was secretly worried they would leave it too late to be fully prepared. If it were down to him he would give the order now.

Carmen was at odds with herself, not sure what to do next. She had two very good analytical advisors, but what they now offered was mostly guesswork. She had to admit though it was very highly educated guesswork. Ultimately, she had to decide the deadline. Call it too soon and people will be in their spacesuits for far too long, perhaps even running out of air, if the fight raged on for any considerable time. On the other hand, if they were caught out and not ready, it would be an utter disaster.

"What if they don't attack straight away?" She queried, looking to Alex for some sort of answer.

"Oh, I don't think they will hang about for very long. I get the distinct impression they are extremely low on food supplies at the moment. They have travelled a hell of a long way to get here. They will be anxious to start, and end this conflict as soon as is logistically possible."

Carmen considered for a moment before making the decision of her life. She glanced in Robert's direction, looking for some useful input.

"I'd say sooner, rather than later," he offered, guessing Carmen was looking for help from the tortured look on her face. Alex shrugged his indifference at Robert's suggestion.

"Okay, based on what I've heard, the advice I've been given, on what I can physically see, I'm not going to risk waiting any longer." She spoke into her personal communicator. "Toby, start the decompression procedures. Make sure everyone follows the practised drill to the letter."

Tobias Hauss, Chief of Security, was currently occupying his security control room in the next domed building along from the control room. Accompanying him was five of his security guards that had opted to stay. All had some sort of military training from their dim distant past. That experience might come in useful even if a couple of them were not as fit as they once were.

A klaxon alarm sounded twice before Toby's voice announced throughout the complex that all personnel should now suit up. They had fifteen minutes to comply before all the domes would lose their artificial atmosphere.

Robert checked with both the traffic controllers that the information was immediately passed onto *Oceans Dawn,* still out of sight on the blind side of the planet. He also asked they related all recent events to the ice-tugboat crews, currently stationed inside the ice dumping ground storage buildings. They were to follow similar procedures to decompress the ice dump storage control buildings. Finally satisfied that everyone was aware of the current situation, Robert and the two controllers were the last to make their way to the back of the room. It was only now that he noticed his spacesuit had been folded into a neat pile and placed on top of his boots. His helmet sat in front resting on the toecaps. His pile had been positioned next to similar piles for the other occupants of the control room. Now, however, these other piles of spacesuit items were in disarray, scattered on the floor whilst being hastily manipulated by Alex, Carmen, James, Duncan, Josie, both traffic controllers and three of the facility personnel. These three, along with Josie, had been designated as the Space Traffic Control Room guard. All of the room's occupants scrambled to push legs and arms into their spacesuits, now mindful that time was a priority factor.

Before long, Robert was breathing suit air that to him always tasted stale and musty. Being confined in a suit played havoc with his claustrophobia as well, however, the forthcoming events would give him little time to worry about it.

Everyone returned to their posts, the two controllers to their desk, the four-person guard covering the entrance to the room and the rest standing behind the control room console desks. Soon they were greeted by Toby's deep voice once more, this time, from the suit communications units inside their helmets. He was warning them that decompression was imminent.

It wasn't a moment too soon. As they stood listening to Toby's booming voice informing that all domes were now at fifty percent atmosphere and halfway through the decompression cycle, they were just in time to witness a wave of alien Harvester spaceships spewing forth from Nix. Without prompting, the first traffic controller pulled up the telescopic view of the moon onto a quarter of the large viewing screen. There were six Harvester spacecraft in total. They had emerged as two flights of three, from the three spherical holes in the very front of the small moon. Slung below each oblong vessel was a small round cylinder suspended via a small connecting strut.

"That's interesting. Exactly thirty thousand kilometres out, they must be using our metric system," exclaimed Alex excitedly.

"Perhaps they copied the metric system from us for some reason?" Robert said, partially intrigued.

"Ah yes, something else I have only just discovered. Over a substantial period of time they will adapt to using their hosts' weights and measures. Basically they are parasites. Copying our weights, measures and time dimensions for their own guidelines makes logical sense if you think about it," said James, as if he were addressing a convention.

Although these facts appeared to be very interesting for the analysts, it was information that seemed pointless to the Facilities Controller. Carmen was extremely anxious at this precise moment.

"Can we analyse the whys and wherefores later! Right now we need to be focused. Alex, can you inform your army personnel that in about, what shall we say, less than twenty minutes time, all manner of hell is about to be let loose on my facility buildings," her voice was controlled, but underneath, it sounded distinctly contemptuous.

Robert and James thought Alex took the psychological slap on the wrist quite well considering, as he calmly informed his sergeant, corporals and privates of the current situation. Ross Perez and Jacqueline Reilly, wearing their fighting exoskeletons, were dispatched to patrol over by the refinery buildings, their ground vehicle had been adapted with the rocket launcher from Hugh's downed stealth spaceship. Frank Lloyd and Sergio Laurant, also wearing their fighting exoskeleton units, had very bravely volunteered to man the two ground cannons on the valley floor. They had driven out thirty minutes earlier to take up positions manning the weapons. Out of the three main facility domes, Nesrine Ben Ali and Deimos were to be found in the left side dome where,

Toby and his security officers were located. Aban Hossini was in charge of six of what Alex had considered the most military experienced facility personnel to stay. Fully armed with rifles and grenades, they were charged with protecting the right side facility dome. They were joined by Andy with his robot-carrying sphere detector and his adapted mining lance.

Sergeant Paula Alvarez was currently preparing her spacecraft inside hangar three. She was on board, ready to take off at a moment's notice, once the roof retracted. The retraction of the roof started at her command.

"Right, the fire teams are either located or on their way to their designated fire points. All we can do now is wait, possibly pray of course, if you believe in such things. I calculate we have approximately ten minutes until confrontation begins," Alex stated, glaring at Carmen during the delivery of his words. The tension between them was almost visible in the air.

Ignoring his glaring stare, she turned to the second controller who had regained her seat after donning her spacesuit. Carmen tapped her gently on the top of her helmet to gain her attention. The controller swivelled in the chair to face her switching to a one to one comm. link.

"Can you inform Miss Rebecca Jones, Kieron, Leila and the others in the infirmary about the current situation? Can you also give them any updates as events unfold? I shall be busy with other things no doubt, and I did promise to keep that group in the picture at all times."

"Yes ma'am," replied the second controller, turning back to her console to make the connections.

The next ten minutes were nail-biting moments or would have been, if only it were possible for them to chew nails through the spacesuit helmets and gloves they were now all wearing.

—

"So, do we know what's happening yet?" Bjorn asked. He was almost helmet to helmet with the other crew members. The six of them were standing huddled round each other, inside the main depressurised ice dump control and warehouse storage building. They had made a mishmash barricade using the ice-moving machinery. The large hangar-type room was split across the middle by a line of dozers, lifters, cherry pickers and other tracked, heavy vehicles used to shovel the ice. Behind this line of black and yellow striped metal, they would stand their ground. Each was holding or had slung across their backs, a Tesla MKII pulse rifle. There were a couple of opened boxes of fragmentation and flash grenades on top of one of the nearby dozer tracks. Not being military trained, they had no idea what damage they were capable of inflicting.

"Hang on a sec. I'm just receiving a message now. The aliens are en route, ten minutes out from the Mars Facilities," replied Shaun. They had decided that it would be easier if just one of them was in direct touch with the Traffic Control Room, who would then relate status changes to the others. Shaun had been selected for the task.

"Six of the Harvester vessels are heading towards… wait though, the controller is telling me that one of the attacking forces is breaking away from the pack. Yep, it's confirmed. Damn! One of them is headed our way aright. Looks like we are going to have our very own fight on our hands after all," he relayed.

"The ground-based Tesla cannon outside is armed on automatic I hope," quizzed Soren.

"As far as I'm aware it is. That's how the army guys left it," replied Bjorn.

"Let's hope it takes the alien spacecraft out of commission before it gets anywhere near us down here!" Lenka declared.

"Let's hope so, but just in case it doesn't perform as well as we all hope, we know our defensive positions. Spread yourselves out along the barricade. I'm going to the warehouse office to watch the outside monitors and relate events as they unfold. I'll join you back here if they land and attempt a breach of the building."

Shaun ran off towards the back of the building, where a small separated office was located. Leaving the door open he sat down to observe the view from outside the building relayed by four different monitor screens. He glanced at his watch, five minutes to go or thereabouts. It was only then he realised his heart was pounding. He took several deep breaths trying to calm down, at this rate he was going to have a heart attack. That would be most inconvenient and unhelpful at this point in time.

—

"I've warned the ice-tugboat crew members," the first controller declared.

"That leaves the other five headed our way," confirmed Alex. "E.T.A. in two minutes," he added after a quick calculation.

"Paula just reported she has lifted off, they are closing the hangar roof at landing pad three," cut in the second controller.

"But… but, she won't be able to land back inside after…" Carmen stuttered.

"I'm not sure she's even considered 'after' as part of her final flight plan," Alex related unemotionally.

"Don't forget to warn her not to go near those remote Tesla cannons on top of the mesa. They are switched to auto seek and destroy are they not?" James stated, reminding Alex about the possible danger. Alex switched transmission frequencies to speak to the stealth pilot directly, before returning his attention to the control room again.

"Right, I have organised a little surprise for the alien vessels coming in, well, one of them at the very least."

Some of those not occupied in the room turned to look towards Alex expectantly, although all they could actually see was a dark face inside a spacesuit helmet.

"Mentioning the two remote cannons on top of the mesa, I've rigged them to be synchronised, firing as one at the same target. Corporal Lloyd and Private Laurant have been instructed to follow their lead. I am hoping they will all get a couple of thousand rounds off each before they are put out of commission. Combined, they will be devastating," Alex declared, clapping his gloved hands before rubbing them together in anticipation.

For a moment, Carmen had the distinct impression Alex was actually looking forward to the forthcoming conflict, even though there were going to be casualties, mostly his squad members.

To a certain extent she was right. This was the ultimate climax for all the training Alexander Manso had ever undertaken. This conflict, whatever the outcome was his military swansong. A glorious death or instant promotion, either he would willingly accept. Death would make him an immortal figure within the army for eternity. If he managed to survive the upcoming battle, he would make General Analytical Advisor to the European Government in two years.

There was a lull, just before the alien spaceship came into the most operative range for the Tesla cannons. When they eventually opened fire, the lead alien vessel was hit by all four ground weapons simultaneously. The occupants, two black-clad alien pilots on the bridge, did not stand one iota of a chance. The first twenty-five or so metres of the vessel almost disintegrated under the deluge of anion particle pulses. The vessel immediately started a slow dive towards the valley wall to the North. The cylinder underneath the spacecraft detached itself. Appearing to have limited steering abilities, it managed to alter course slightly, before heading straight towards the refinery buildings.

The second and third alien Harvester vessels opened fire on the two cannon at the top of the mesa. Being so open and exposed, they were destroyed immediately. The other two, on the valley floor, took several hits before being put out of commission, but not before crippling another of the attacking spaceships, destroying its under-slung cylinder prior to detaching itself. Corporal Frank Lloyd managed to jump clear of his cannon control seat just in time, landing in a crumpled heap several metres away from the destroyed weapon. Private Sergio Laurant was less fortunate. He had taken the news of the death of his sibling very badly. It had been the main reason he had volunteered for this position. Now was his turn to inflict pain on those assailants who had taken his sister from him. He refused to take his finger off the trigger even when the cannon he sat astride, was neatly sliced lengthways in two equal parts by a combination of the alien laser beam weapons from two of the attacking spaceships.

The almost ineffective pencil laser beams from the Mars defence towers, managed to score weird hieroglyphics on a couple of the alien vessels before they too were sliced to pieces. The alien attackers, now down to three operational vessels, swung round for their second approach.

—

Shaun bit his lip as he observed the monitor screens waiting for any signs, so intense was his concentration, he didn't realise he'd drawn a spot of blood. Suddenly, the Tesla cannon entrenched outside the ice dumping ground storage building, quite still up until that point, sprung into life tracking an object above it. It immediately started firing indiscriminately once the object was within range. Inside the building, they sensed a slight vibration, like someone drumming on the soles of their spacesuit boots. However, it didn't last for very long.

"Shit!" exclaimed Shaun, as he watched the demise of the weapon they had high hopes would save them. "They've cut it up like I would carve a Christmas turkey. You had to see it to believe it," he added, feeling a spasm of intense shock that took his breath away for a split second. Quickly overcoming his personal trauma, Shaun managed to return to his running commentary.

"Right, I can see it now, the alien spacecraft, it's flying right down towards us over the ice mountain, coming in low. Hello, what's that? They seem to have detached something small from underneath the vessel. It must be one of the alien-carrying cylinders we were warned about. It's headed straight for the front of the building. I'm coming out there, take positions! Be ready for an imminent impact!" he shouted, jumping up from the relative comfort of the office chair.

Outside, the alien cylinder barrelled down towards the building after the Harvester spaceship had released the under-slung deadly cargo. On the sled inside the cylinder, standing in two rows three abreast, were six of the alien creatures. They were dressed as usual in their black, tight fitting spacesuits, topped off with their oversized, completely black, helmets. This time, however, there was something else. They carried a long dark-coloured thin spear that was taller than they were themselves, at over three metres in length. One hundred metres from the building's exterior, the sled was skilfully ejected out the back of the cylinder. It touched the ground slowly skidding to a halt. Before it had even stopped, the aliens had already jumped off, running after the cylinder that forged ahead of them.

Inside, they waited with frightened anticipation. Shaun had reached the barricade only to see some of the others backing away, away from the line of machinery. He had to do or say something.

"Take cover everyone, they are coming in right through the front door there," he shouted, pointing to the larger of the two inner airlock doors, the one that was as big as a two storey house.

"All of us have to fire at them as soon as they appear, that's all of us together you understand. That way we stand some sort of chance, if anyone falters, we may all perish. Now, let's take our positions."

His words seemed to have the desired effect. They returned to the makeshift line, finding gaps in between the vehicles, pointing their rifles towards the airlock doors. Lenka, not entirely happy using the rifle, picked out a couple of fragmentation grenades from the nearby box. She was going to push the arming button on one before she thought better of it. She would wait until they were inside she decided, which was just as well. To the left of the airlock the wall gave way as a four-metre circular hole suddenly appeared, the cut out wall section vaporised exposing the outside landscape. The shock of the impact knocked those not holding onto something over, including Lenka who dropped to the floor landing on her backside. She accidentally dropped one of the deadly fragmentation grenades between her legs. It spun slowly round on the floor like a spinning top in front of her. She was dead lucky she hadn't armed it after all.

38

Losing Ground

The remaining three alien vessels from the attack force approached the Mars Facilities once more. This time there was no devastating ground-based Tesla anion particle cannon fire to hinder them. They flew in slow formation assuming they now had total command of the open space above the facility buildings. However, there was a small surprise waiting for them. One diminutive spacecraft, blind to the alien spaceships, was lurking nearby. On their final approach, the Harvester vessels released the cylinder payloads they were carrying, carefully aimed, one for each of the three main facility domes.

Sergeant Paula Alvarez in the military-stealth spacecraft was waiting patiently in the lee of the Hebes Chasma mesa maintaining complete radio silence. She had devised a cunning plan while the alien vessels prepared to make their second approach. The idea was simple really, after she had fired on one of the Harvester spacecraft, she would steer close to one of the downwards travelling cylinders. She concluded they would not dare fire on her for fear of hitting their own kind inside. That's if she could get real close, almost touching if possible. That was the theory anyhow, now she decided to put the plan into action.

The stealth vessel flew straight and fast from its concealment point. Paula let loose two of the chemical rockets aimed directly at the front of the lead alien spacecraft at extremely short range. Immediately slamming on reverse thrust, she turned on a sixpence, spinning the almost electronically invisible vessel round to rub shoulders with the central descending cylinder. This particular one, falling at a steady sedate pace, had been aimed directly towards the Traffic Control Room dome. The launching of her rockets was timed to perfection, with the second rocket flying straight into the hull cavity created by the first. The bridge of the targeted Harvester spaceship erupted, split wide open like a melon hit square on with a baseball bat. The two crew members perished instantly. Now pilotless, it continued flying straight towards the mesa cliff face behind the facility buildings, while the other two vessels peeled off to port.

So far so good, thought Paula, her idea was working. Then, it struck her that she might be able to inflict even more damage, while she was currently trading metal with the cylinder containing the alien warriors. Pulling the controls hard across she forced it to alter course, grinding the outside hull of the stealth spacecraft against the alien alloy. Inside, there was visible concern among the invading occupants. One of the alien invaders was linked telepathically with the feeble steering device. It was more than likely just a simple gliding mechanism. It tried in vain to readjust the angle of approach back to its designated objective, but it was of no use. Paula was now forcing the cylinder down even further to starboard, so they would fall short of their intended target. In fact they were now headed for the landing fields that were covered in dark shadows. That's not so good, she thought, pushing her spaceship harder to its absolute limit for sideways thrust, forcing the cylinder almost at right angles to its original flight path. They were coming down fast now. Paula had to pull away, just in time to see the sled carrying the aliens eject out the back of the cylinder. The empty tube started boring a hole into the Martian surface vaporising the dusty soil in front of it. After a few seconds it halted, leaving a dirty haze in its wake. They were only twenty metres away from the landing fields. With the agility of a leaping salmon, Paula spun the vessel round. She could only imagine what was going through the six alien telepathic minds as she launched a rocket straight for them. They turned to run, but to no avail.

The euphoria of downing the sled and killing the six invaders in the process was short lived, as the stealth spacecraft took a hit from somewhere above. The instrumentation dials projected in front of her eyes went right off the scale. The fusion drive was going reactive. Paula had no choice but to shut it down as the spacecraft hit the soft yielding Martian surface. It slew sideways before sliding down a high slope. Pulling hard on the emergency cockpit canopy release enticed it to be yanked off as gritty Martian soil poured in. She released her full body harness at the same time. Using all her available energy, Paula pushed herself clear of the still moving wreck as it skidded down the ridge of sand and dust. Just in time as the small spacecraft was rifled with the alien weapon fire before exploding, sending pieces in all directions, possibly from the reactive overload of the fusion drive, more than from enemy fire. Thanks to the low gravity Paula's leap landed her well away from the exploding wreck. After what seemed like an age, she eventually stopped tumbling over and over. Everything had happened so fast, she had no time to report back to the control tower. Now might be a good time she thought. "Alex," she said feebly.

"Paula, are you okay?" Alex sounded genuinely concerned.

"Still in one piece, more than can be said for the stealth vessel," she answered.

"Well, at least you survived," he said relieved.

"I'll make my way back to the main complex somehow. I've just got to find my bearings." She signed off before taking a good look around.

Before her, not thirty metres away was the ground-based cannon that had been manned by Corporal Frank Lloyd, now just a melted and partly chopped up mass of mangled metal. A short way off was his body, laying face down. She leaped up, running over to investigate if the corporal was still a functional part of the defending force, or just one more casualty of this badly-progressing conflict.

On the other side of the complex, another skirmish was in progress. The alien cylinder from the first attacking spaceship to be put out of action, made a perfect entrance hole into one of the refinery buildings. It managed to cut out a flawlessly-round section of the wall. The alien force, from the detached sled, stormed down the newly-created tube structure only to find the building inside completely deserted.

As the attacking force vacated the building, they were confronted by Corporal Ross Perez and Private Jacqueline Reilly who were waiting for them. The two soldiers had watched the cylinder descend while racing across from the facility buildings. On the final approach to the remote refinery complex, they witnessed the sled appear from the back of the cylinder. Once the alien attackers landed and then disappeared inside, the ground vehicle raced up the sloping track that led onto a small mound overlooking the spherical breach in the refinery building wall.

"Quick Reilly, we'll get them on the way out. Get on the firing controls for the rocket launcher, while I line us up as best I can," the corporal ordered.

With pinpoint precision, Ross Perez lined up their vehicle.

As the disappointed attack force reappeared and regrouped to decide on their next course of action, Jacqueline Reilly fired two of the chemical rockets from less than one hundred metres. The alien attack force was taken totally by surprise, which was exactly the desired intention.

Five black figures, their suits and helmets ragged by shrapnel, went down immediately, scattered like nine pins. One hovered a second or two before throwing the spear weapon from its grasp towards the ambushers. The alien body now embracing death, toppled forward to join its comrades.

"What the hell is that?" Ross shouted, raising his rifle. They both shot widely at the three metre long projectile with their pulse rifles, but to no avail. It was almost black against black, it was also just too thin an object for them to hit. They shouldered weapons as the corporal barked an order that didn't need verifying.

"Run for it, Reilly!"

First there was an explosion, quickly followed by a shock wave. Perez and Reilly were lifted off their feet. Both tumbled over in the light gravity, luckily they were wearing the protective exoskeleton suits so bounced across the surface like tumbleweeds in the desert. Unfortunately for Private Reilly, her face plate caught a small outcrop of rock in passing. Somehow, the jagged edge avoided the two facial-protection bars, causing the toughened-plastic face plate to smash open. It is quite an agonising death having the air sucked out of your body a few seconds before your face freezes solid. The only consolation is it is relatively quick.

Corporal Ross Perez was more fortunate. At least the protection from the exoskeleton bars kept him from harm as he finally rolled to a stop courtesy of a line of large boulders.

—

Inside the ice dumping ground building, the impact of the incoming cylinder had had the desired effect. It disorientated the ice-tugboat crew defenders long enough for the alien squad to swarm into the building through the newly-created tunnel unopposed. Shaun was the first one who managed to regain his defensive position. He quickly fired in a sweeping motion at the six black clad invaders fast approaching them, managing to down one in the process. One of the other attacking alien humanoids levelled his spear weapon towards him, sending a concentrated shock wave back, knocking Shaun off his feet. The rifle flew from his hands into the air. Luckily, the beam was narrow enough not to affect Lenka, who now launched the two grenades she had been cradling.

Two more aliens went down, their suits torn ragged by blast fragments from the grenades, the pinhead-sized atomic piles exceeding critical mass in a matter of seconds. Chunks of shrapnel ricocheted off the metal barrier of vehicles. Not expecting such devastating resistance, the last three attackers retreated back outside the building. On the way out, they launched from small compartments in the back of their helmets, three small spheres.

The spheres, carrying four inert micro robots, picked Lenka, Maria and Soren as the unfortunate, completely random victims. The two centimetre diameter balls split open as soon as they hit the targeted spacesuits. Now exposed, the insect mimicking robots sprung into immediate action boring into the outer layers of protective spacesuit fabric.

"What the fuck…" Cried Maria.

"It's the micro robots. Quick, get them off them before they can get inside the suits!" Shaun exclaimed, running over to Maria. Thankfully he was quick, quick enough to brush three of them off her. He even removed one of his gloves briefly risking severe frostbite, to grab the last one before it could disappear inside Maria's outer suit membrane, the chewed hole in the outer layer material clearly visible.

"Tread on them!" he screamed. The small robots squirmed like helpless beetles on the floor before they were all smashed underfoot. Pulling a self sealing patch from his pocket, Shaun peeled the back before slapping it over the small puncture in Maria's suit, just as she could feel the freezing air starting to penetrate. After a quick hug, they finally turned to the others only to gasp at what they saw. Soren lay prone on the floor, two small round fissures in the front of his suit. Daniela was sobbing, standing over him.

"He's dead. It happened so fast," she cried.

"Bjorn, how's Lenka? Did you get them all?" Shaun asked, ignoring Daniela for the moment.

"Four of them yes? If there were four, yes, yes I did get them all," he spluttered, surveying the scattered bits of tiny metal at his feet, a little confused by what just occurred.

"Okay, let's get back to the barricade. They may attack again at any time," declared Shaun.

Lenka was in a zombie trance, standing there not moving. She needed a sharp slap to the face Bjorn thought, he slapped both sides of her helmet instead, trying to get a sensible reaction. She acknowledged by nodding her head. Bjorn returned to his position on the barricade.

However, Daniela was far from being in a right state of mind. She slowly picked up her rifle, walked across to the box of grenades to pick one out. Moving with more purpose now, she jumped up onto one of the tractor caterpillar tracks, climbed through the cab before leaping down the other side. It was only then that the others noticed her.

"Daniela, Daniela, wait, stop!" Maria called out. Daniela didn't take any notice. Pushing and holding down the activate button on the grenade, she held the rifle in the other hand and ran towards the opening shouting and swearing obscenities at the alien attackers. The others tried again in vain to call her back, but their voices were drowned out.

Daniela disappeared, rapidly and haphazardly firing her rifle through the short tunnel at everything and anything outside before her. Emerging from the cylinder outside the building, a black-suited arm swung round implanting a half-metre long serrated-edged knife right through her chest. She stopped dead in her tracks as the rifle was snatched from her grasp. In her last dying seconds she saw the Harvester spaceship hovering close by. She counted five aliens, including the one that had been lurking beside the cylinder, waiting to ambush anyone emerging.

"There's five, no, no make that four of them left out here," she rasped with her last breath, for the benefit of those still inside the building. The grenade slipped from her hand dropping next to the black booted foot of her killer, who looked down curiously at the rounded rock that suddenly nudged its foot. With her finger now removed from the activate button, the small nuclear pile inside the fragmentation grenade reached critical mass in approximately three and a half seconds.

—

"What in hell's going on now!" Carmen shouted out loud. "Alex, bring me up to speed please," she added, softening her tone slightly. She'd come to realise Alex didn't respond well to being shouted at. The friction between them had escalated since Nix had moved to within striking distance of the Mars Facilities. It was not helping matters one iota.

"All our Tesla cannons are now defunct. Sergeant Alvarez's stealth spacecraft is now down and out of commission, although she is alive out on the surface somewhere. There are three other squad members that I can no longer raise. I'm assuming they are all K.I.A. There's been no word from *Oceans Dawn*, still maintaining communications blackout no doubt. If they leave it much longer to join in the fight there might not be much left to defend. Finally, we are about to be invaded on both flanks by two of the alien cylinders, presumably with six alien invaders in each one. Things could be better," he replied sarcastically. He raised his eyebrows suggestively to the heavens hoping for some divine inspiration, even though he was a confirmed atheist.

"How many have we put out of action?"

"Three Harvester spaceships and three of the cylinders at the last count," replied Alex without pause.

"And you reckon there are more to come! Our prospects don't look good, not very good at all," Carmen said, shaking her head in dismay.

—

"Nesrine Ben Ali?" Toby enquired, after switching to the close-proximity universal spacesuit communications channel.

He had just emerged from the main corridor that opened into the large high ceiling reception room occupying the front third of the dome-shaped building. This dome was to the left of the main central dome where the traffic control room was situated. The army private, along with two facility personnel and Deimos who was busy waving his scanner about just in case, stood in the large room looking around them completely at a loss.

"Yes Sir!" Private Nesrine Ben Ali retorted, turning round to face him, thankful someone else had joined them.

"No need for all that 'Sir' nonsense. Please, call me Toby," he said.

His subordinate officers noted he had certainly softened his attitude of late.

"These are some of my finest officers. We are at your disposal as part of the defence force for this dome," he said, pointing out the five men in spacesuits armed with Tesla rifles standing behind him.

"I'm so glad you are here! As far as I understand it, the attacking force will penetrate somewhere along the far outer wall from there to there…" She pointed out the large expanse of the inward curving structure. "And, we don't seem to have any cover whatsoever. I was lead to believe there were some old airtight doors we can use. I can't seem to locate where the operational controls are," she added.

"Aha, this is where I come in. If you would all like to all stand behind me over here."

Toby motioned they should make their way back inside the main corridor. Once he was happy they were safely out of the way, he punched open a concealed compartment in the wall that was big enough for a human hand and forearm to enter.

Inside was a double-sided lever, Toby yanked it down with a grunt. At the entrance to the corridor, the disused airtight barriers appeared, simultaneously emerging from previously concealed gaps in both the floor and the ceiling. The doors had interconnecting tabs that looked like giant stained teeth. When they reached approximately a metre apart, he stopped the closing mechanism. Walking over to inspect the horizontal gap, he raised his rifle pushing it through.

"That's seems okay to me, what do you think?"

He turned round to get her opinion, but Nasrine was talking on a private communications circuit to her comrade in arms, Aban Hossini. She was informing him about the protective doors, making sure those in the dome on the other side had access to the same protection.

"Yep, got it, thanks," said Aban, after finding the concealed compartment. He pulled down his lever with satisfying results.

Private Aban Hossini had been allocated to protect the dome that was to the right of the central control room dome. He had six armed military-experienced facility workers with him. Andy Hubbins had joined them, carrying his robot-sphere scanning unit and modified cutting lance. Unlike the dome to the left of the central one, this one had no direct link to the central dome. If they were overcome, they were to fall back to the infirmary to bolster the defences there.

Inside the main central dome control room, they watched in silence. The two approaching cylinders containing the alien attacking forces, were shown as tubular objects, projected onto the glass display in front of them. These images were relayed from outside monitor views. One cylinder was aimed directly for the dome on their left, and the other destined the dome on their right.

"I've just informed those in charge of the domes' defences they are about to be breached," remarked Alex.

Robert turned to James and tapped him gently on the shoulder. "I think you and Duncan can take up your positions now," he suggested.

James nodded grabbing Duncan's arm, pulling him towards the control room's exit.

Those left observed both cylinders perform the procedure that allowed the sled carrying the alien forces to disembark, before the now-empty transport cylinders, crashed into the selected targets creating perfectly round entrance tunnels. There was hardly a murmur as they watched the two sets of six black figures storm into the domes. What they couldn't see from such a distance, was that the black-clad attackers were following several small copper-coloured robot-carrying spheres that preceded them into the domes. The small objects were being controlled by the Harvester spaceship pilots who were looking for one specific item, humans wearing spacesuits.

Carmen closed her eyes. She feared this was the beginning of the end.

39

The Tide Turns

Inside the ice dumping ground storage building, the remaining four pairs of ice-tugboat crew members felt the Martian surface shake beneath their feet. Shaun, Maria and Lenka managed to grab hold of something. Bjorn missed, ending up as a slowly-falling sprawl of arms and legs.

"What the hell was that?" Maria demanded.

"Ah! Sorry about that, one of our microwave-beam weapons missed the proposed target," Captain Edmund Cooper's voice boomed over the suit communications units. He then continued. "Are we ever so glad to hear your voices, I feared we left it too late in our attack to help you. It was imperative the Harvester spaceship put itself in such a position we could take advantage and not leave ourselves vulnerable."

"Hello captain, and are we glad to hear a friendly voice in return," replied a very relieved Shaun.

"How are you holding out down there?" the captain asked.

"We've lost two of our friends," Shaun said, in a sort of regretful, but at the same time brave voice.

"Well, get ready with everything you've got. We have downed the alien vessel outside your building by putting a bloody great big hole through its propulsion unit. Like I said, silly fools let themselves become a sitting target. We think there are possibly four remaining aliens out on the surface now. They are going to rush into you any minute, especially as we are going to flush them out. There will be nowhere for them to hide, except inside the building with you," instructed the captain of *Oceans Dawn*.

"Okay, thanks for the warning. We'll be ready."

Shaun grabbed a few fragmentation grenades and handed them out. "When they are inside the building, all of us throw one of these and then duck," he explained to the others.

They each took one before spreading out along the barricade.

The Captain's voice came through once more loud and clear. "Okay, get ready, there are only three left now, our laser fire is pushing them towards you. They are entering…" The voice of the captain trailed off as Shaun's cut in over the top.

"Three… two… one, throw them now! Throw the grenades!" he shouted at the top of his voice. It was the perfect ambush. The attacking aliens ran into the building and were caught by the multiple blasts. After the explosions and the ricocheting grenade fragments stopped flying over their heads, Shaun stood up and gave each alien a few anion particle rounds from his Tesla pulse rifle, just for good measure.

"Thanks captain, they ran into our trap perfectly. They are positively dead now," Bjorn stated, watching Shaun continuing to fire single rounds into the black covered bodies. He was feeling quite stunned now, a part of him felt like joining in, but he couldn't be bothered to retrieve his rifle that lay a short distance away.

"Okay, we are going to leave you now. We are off to join in the battle over at the Mars Facilities. Things are not going well by all accounts, that's according to the mixed and disjointed messages we have been receiving from the Traffic Controllers. If things go badly for us over there, they will come back for you. Perhaps you should try and make a run for it in the ice tugboats?" Captain Cooper suggested.

"We'll certainly consider it. Thanks again Captain and good luck," replied Bjorn walking over to Shaun. He rested his hand on the top of the rifle barrel to stop him firing any more. Shaun dropped the weapon from his shoulder. As they looked at each other through their visors, Bjorn could see the tears in Shaun's eyes. He understood they would all grieve for their lost friends sooner or later, one way or another.

"Let's all decide what to do next. As the captain said, they may come back yet," declared Lenka. The ice-tugboat crew survivors gathered round in a small group to discuss their options.

—

"Are you two in position yet?" Alex asked James and Duncan.

"All set here Alex," both replied together. Over the past few days Duncan had instructed James the basic operational controls for the VR drone vessels using the VR units. James had sort of mastered the technique. Both of them now lay on the controlling couches ready.

"Nix is now just over fifteen thousand kilometres out. The way the battle is progressing, I expect reserve forces to be deployed at any moment. That's what I'd do, if I were in control over there."

James switched on the headgear and was immediately transported to the small moon Phobos. It felt weird, really weird. His senses, sound and vision were outside his own body. He panicked, where was his spacesuit? He would die outside without one. Duncan came to his rescue, calmed him down. Following Duncan's lead, he inserted himself inside the strange metal realm of the drone spacecraft. This had a calming effect on his nerves. Manipulating the onboard cameras, he could make out the crashed scout spacecraft from *Mother Lode*, also, the other drone spacecraft controlled by Duncan, and further out, the small foreboding moon Nix approaching.

"Right, let's do this Duncan, I'm following you remember," declared James, grabbing hold of the control joystick.

Both drone spacecraft lifted off Phobos before heading straight towards the alien mother ship in tandem. With the moon looming larger and larger James knew they would not be shot at or put out of action as they approached. He knew from his probing of the alien technology that it possessed no outside defensive weaponry. He had discovered the aliens decided they'd never need it, how wrong they had been. However, they had to still watch out for the Harvester vessels, luckily they could not see any at the present time.

"Eenie meenie miny mo, catch an alien by his big fat toe! I'm going straight for the middle entrance James, right down the centre," declared Duncan.

"Your call, I'm right behind you," stated James, desperately trying to control his drone vessel as it attained near top speed.

'Right behind' wasn't strictly true as his spacecraft was wavering back and forth while Duncan was skilfully flying his vessel straight as an arrow. The gap between the two remote-controlled spacecraft steadily widened.

James saw the drone Duncan controlled fly like a bullet into the middle hole on the surface of the approaching moon. His drone vessel, now fifteen seconds behind, managed to clip the roof of the tunnel as it entered, sending out a shower of sparks. Somehow, he kept in control, weaving from side to side like a drunk on a Saturday night staggering home from the pub. Once inside, he switched on the vessel's headlights following Duncan's lead. Luckily, the tunnel was completely level. James knew at their current speed he would not have been quick enough to turn the small powerful spacecraft if they came to any sort of deviation.

Deeper and deeper into the very heart of the moon they continued until, the tunnel opened out into an enormous chamber. James, so overwhelmed by the vastness of the interior, was taken by surprise when all of a sudden there was a gigantic explosion directly in front of him. Temporarily blinded, James automatically turned his spacecraft to avoid a huge ball of flame that appeared out of nowhere.

"Damn, I just flew straight into several Harvester spaceships!" Duncan declared.

"How many exactly?" Alex demanded immediately.

"Four or five I'd guess, it was hard to tell. They were flying straight towards me, making for the exit tunnels."

"Well, I think that rules out the reserve force coming into the fray," interjected Robert excitedly.

"My sentiments entirely," agreed Alex, a wide smile across his face.

The remains of the third and final wave of Harvester spaceships and cylinders crashed into each other, before the mishmash of remains tumbled into the walls of the cavern. None were in any position to continue.

"What shall I do now?" James pleaded, as he flew his drone spacecraft into the immense underground chamber.

"Look for something important. Are there any other Harvester vessels around, on a landing field maybe?" Carmen suggested.

James slowed his vessel down so he could use the cameras to take a closer, more detailed examination of the surroundings. There were what appeared to be accommodation blocks up all the walls, most were in darkness. An odd light here and there glowed faintly. There was one protruding construction that was brightly lit. It stuck out like a sore thumb. Could that be a control centre? As he could see no more of the Harvester vessels about, he made up his mind. Turning the drone to point directly towards the positively-glowing protuberance, he opened up the fusion engine to full throttle and then forced all his logical senses, to ignore desperate mental requests to turn the vessel out of harm's way.

"It's slowing. Bloody hell, I think they did it. Nix is coming to a dead stop. Well done you two," shouted Alex. James didn't hear though, it had been too much for his mind to bear. The shock on his senses of crashing therefore detonating his spaceship, a spaceship controlled by his conscious thought, overcame his mind. It caused him to lapse into a state of unconsciousness.

—

Sergeant Alvarez turned over the body of Corporal Lloyd expecting to see his dead contorted facial features. Instead, she found his face plate intact and he was alive, just about. Knocked out temporarily, but alive. She put him in the passenger seat of the ground vehicle before setting off back towards the facility buildings. Slowly the corporal regained consciousness from being bounced up and down. Racing back in the other direction Corporal Perez could not contact anyone as his communications unit had malfunctioned. He saw the dust cloud kicked up by the vehicle Paula was driving, as she skirted the landing fields. He changed course to intercept her. Above them, the two remaining Harvester vessels circled like vultures. Ross Perez watched them, expecting to be picked off any minute. The alien occupants were in fact in the very last process of hunting down the ground mobile units and ready to open fire, when they received the shock news of the attack on their home and mother ship. The alien pilots were still in a state of disarray when *Oceans Dawn* opened fire on them.

—

Carmen Applegate was a boiling tumultuous sea of terror and confusion inside. She was managing to hide it well.

"What's the latest situation Alex?" she asked. There was a slight dysfunction in her voice, as if she were struggling to keep her sanity under control. It would be so easy to give in, to scream, break down and relinquish command. Let someone else take the strain, but somehow, she held it all together. Being the Facilities Controller she had to set a good example.

"There has been no activity from the moon Nix since encountering the exploding drone spacecraft a while ago. At long last, *Oceans Dawn* has decided to join the fight. It destroyed one of the two attacking Harvester spacecraft before being hit herself in retaliation. Captain Cooper successfully made an emergency landing on pad two. The last Harvester spaceship was about to attack *Oceans Dawn* on the ground, when Duncan, using another one of the explosive drones, managed to ram it. The explosive force cracked it open into two halves just like an egg. The two halves came down way over in the south valley. There is sporadic hand-to-hand fighting going on all over the place. I am trying to gather some Intel on exactly who is fighting who where, but I think I can safely say we now have the upper hand," Alex finished with a flourish.

—

Aban Hossini and Andy were in full retreat. "Where is that damn infirmary?" he shouted, as they ducked round one more corner, narrowly avoiding yet another alien shock wave discharge that reverberated off the far wall. They had not been prepared for the spear-type weapons. He remembered the six alien humanoids rushing into through the newly created hole in the outer-dome wall. Andy skilfully took out three robot-carrying spheres before they could get too close to do any damage. Aban, and the six refinery workers assigned to him, opened fire with their Tesla pulse rifles. He thought they may have downed two aliens before they were knocked backwards by some sort of force field. Only Aban, Andy and two of the other defenders managed to get to their feet, by which time, the remaining invading force had made their way across the hall to the half-closed barricade. There was nothing for it, they ran, and as they ran the remaining two facility personnel were smashed against the wall by the force of another shock wave. They didn't get up a second time. Aban and Andy ran for their lives.

"It should be round the next turn," shouted Andy, desperately trying to recall from memory the building schematics. After the turn they both thought they had run into a dead end, then realised that the last part of the fifty metre passageway was a makeshift barricade of cabinets, beds and mattresses. They ran headlong towards it.

"Infirmary, is anyone there?" Aban grunted half-heartedly.

"Well isn't this your lucky day!" came a reply from a person he assumed was somewhere up ahead, beyond the piled up hospital equipment.

"There are four aliens right behind us," he managed to blurt out whilst they both dived the last few yards towards the makeshift pile of assorted hospital materials with the easily recognisable Tesla MKII pulse rifle muzzles poking through in various positions. He tried to pick a spot to end up where he wouldn't get shot by friendly fire.

"Hello Andy, looks like I'm gonna save your bacon once more," shouted Kieron, as the pursuing alien gang of four rushed headlong round the corner after the fleeing pair.

They were instantly met with a hail of rifle anion particle rounds. Rebecca, Leila, Mei Lien, Nicky and Hugh were in positions to fire upon them through the barricade. Kieron scanned the corridor, but no robot spheres were there for him to dispose of, he almost felt disappointed.

Three aliens went down immediately, their black suits and helmets splattered with anion particle holes. The last one managed to duck back safely into the corridor from whence they came. It was shocked, then confused, and finally a little bemused to be confronted by a smallish human in a marked, tarnished and tatty-looking spacesuit, who didn't appear to be armed, alarmed or even frightened, by its presence.

"This is yours I believe!" Zelda shouted. She lunged forward taking the alien completely by surprise, her left hand swept round from behind her back, the serrated-edged knife she had carefully concealed, thrust upwards, right under the ribs of the startled creature that towered over her. It was a terrific lunge. The alien heart was pierced by the long blade. Those behind the barricade watched in disbelief as a bewildered alien, staggered backwards into their full view, desperately clutching at the haft of one of its own deadly knives almost totally buried into its lower chest. A hail of rifle particle fire put it down for good, alongside its dead comrades.

—

Toby, Private Nesrine Ben Ali, Deimos and the security guards, like Aban, had had a similar confrontation with the alien hoard that burst into their building. However, they were a little better prepared having the airtight doors closed tighter, creating a much narrower gap to fire through. As a direct result, the alien spear weapon shock wave effect was severely reduced. Also, Deimos had used his scanner and mining lance with great skill to defend them against the micro robots. After a brief fire fight, they were currently in a standoff. Toby had closed the shutters down even further to a tiny slit they could just about fire through although they could not see to aim at their adversaries. The shock wave weapons could not penetrate such a small gap. The occasional sphere that had appeared through the gap was quickly dispatched by Deimos before it could reach any of the defenders and release the deadly micro robots inside.

"Ben Ali, what's the situation down there?" Alex Manso enquired.

"We have a couple of people down, but currently we are holding our own. How is it going elsewhere?" Nesrine asked.

"Good, very good. In fact your little skirmish is the last one still on-going," answered the military analyst.

"Wow, that's great, Sir. If only we could get at them to finish it off. I fear if we open the shutters we will be overwhelmed by the shock waves from their spear weapons."

Squad Sergeant Paula Alvarez's voice cut through the chatter. "I think we can help there," she announced.

"Paula!" Alex shouted somewhat elated. "Welcome back. Okay what's your plan of action?" he asked.

"Corporals Perez and Lloyd and I are in our ground vehicles, E.T.A. to the main complex domes in two minutes. I suggest we catch them in a cross fire. We'll drive in through the tunnel created by the alien attack force just as you open the shutters. They won't be expecting us and, as they advance on your position, we'll catch them unawares from behind. How does that sound?"

"Toby, you listening to this?" Alex asked.

"Understood, I'll get on the shutter controls. Just give me the word when you're ready," Toby replied, before switching channels to instruct his officers.

"Good luck everyone." Carmen whispered.

The plan acted out perfectly. As the airlock shutters began to widen the small group of alien invaders emerged from the shadows, beginning to encroach on the defensive position. They fired their spear weapons sending shock waves over the crouching defenders who had ducked down behind the slowly descending lower airlock door.

The two vehicles carrying the three squaddies rushed into the large hall through the short tunnel created by the alien cylinder. With rifles blazing, they dropped two of the alien attackers immediately. The remaining two creatures turned their attention to the newcomers, only to be shot down by Toby and his guards who jumped up from behind the receding shutter at Paula's command.

It was over in seconds, the final skirmish for the Mars Facilities ended when the last alien body slowly hit the floor, its black suit riddled full of holes, dark blood freezing before it had a chance to exit numerous wounds.

Carmen finally sat down on the floor utterly worn out. The two-hour confrontation had all but exhausted her.

"Right…" Was all she could think of to say, before adding with a huge sigh. "That's that then, all over and done with."

—

Except for the two four-metre holes in the main domes created by the large cylinders, the various other rooms and corridors of the facility buildings that could be pressurised were checked and patched where necessary.

"I think we all deserve a stiff drink." Robert declared, once they had disrobed their spacesuits in the traffic control room. The middle dome had somehow managed to avoid sustaining any damage whatsoever, apart from losing the upper control tower in the first attack.

"I could do with a nice shower," remarked Carmen, still somewhat dazed and bemused by the preceding events.

Alex stared at Carmen with slight astonishment. "With what we have just been through, having a shower is the last thing on my mind. Now Carmen, let's go break out the booze just like Robert suggested, please."

The previous tension between the Facilities Controller

and the Military Analyst was fading fast, now the final conflict had passed. Alex even managed a slight grin. Carmen wagged her finger at him in response. Whatever she was going to say went unsaid. Instead, she just laughed out loud, a mixture of emotional relief and released tension.

"Okay. I think I can rustle up some Martian vodka from somewhere to celebrate," she said, finally finding her voice.

Duncan managed to rouse James after removing the VR headgear. It didn't take long for James to recover from the shock of the apparent suicidal VR experience. They were soon en route to be reunited with Carmen, Robert and Alex.

Inside the infirmary, a similar celebration was about to begin with Rebecca dishing out medicinal brandy. However, before they got too carried away, she insisted they remember all those that had fallen during the battle. As one, they raised their glasses in silent salute.

40

Epilogue

James smiled at Jenny. They lay side by side on a large four-poster double bed in the honeymoon suite at the Paradise Moon Resort in the Sea of Tranquillity. A thin silk sheet covered their now slightly flushed perspiring torsos, fresh from the act of human copulation. The two-week stay at the most expensive and personally exclusive resort ever devised by humankind, was a very expensive wedding present awarded to them by the Corporation, a small thank you for the part James played in saving the Mars Facilities.

"Here's to you, my dear husband and, as of now, acting Chief Analyst of The European Space Exploration Travel Corporation!" Jenny proposed, holding up a class of blue-tinted sparkling champagne. James could hardly contain the emotions that were trying to spill out of every orifice in his body. Grinning widely, he touched glasses that softly collided with that distinctive Martian-made crystal chink.

"I can hardly believe my luck! Isn't this just the best thing to ever happen?" he stated rhetorically. "I could not have wished for anything better, this is just heaven," he added, smiling back at his beautiful bride.

It was only then he noticed the communication light

flashing by the side of the bed, no annoying shrill noises here he thought, all very civilised. "Damn," he said, leaning over Jenny's lithe slim body to touch the accept button.

"Yes?" he enquired. A perfect English voice replied without a hint it had been waiting for some time to interject on proceedings.

"So sorry to trouble our most distinguished guests. There is a man who insists on talking to you. I told him you were not to be disturbed, but he is being very persistent. I am sorry to say, this irritating person even used a Corporation priority override code to bypass my protocols. His name is Robert Goodyear, do you wish to speak to him? If you commanded me, I could tell him you don't wish…"

"Put him on, thanks." James interrupted, jumping up from the bed. The three-dimensional communications display in the centre of the room was blank. It had been switched to 'voice only mode' the moment they entered the room some hours previously, the two newlyweds didn't want anybody seeing them, least of all with no clothes on.

"Robert, how is everyone there? Has the crew of *Lode Drifter* spent their large fortunes yet? What about Leila and Blake?" James enquired, unable to contain himself.

"It's a shame you missed the wedding, Leila and Blake were married by Carmen in her official capacity as Facilities Controller. They have taken over *The Lily* and have decided to be ice miners, which I think will suit them, especially since Blake became such a well-known figure thanks to all the recent publicity. There are a few people on Earth in very high places who don't take kindly to industrial spies. I think Jupiter is probably the best, and for the moment, safest place for them." Robert laughed before continuing. "There have been a few wild moments from the crew of *Lode Drifter*, but they have settled down now. They are talking about setting up a hotel and a museum of Martian and alien artefacts in honour of

Teunis Landry, and all those that lost their lives in the Harvester battles. You never know it just might work out. Leastways, they will never have to work again for a living, thanks to the discovery of that gold asteroid."

"So how are you? How's the exploration of Nix proceeding?" James asked anxiously, while simultaneously mouthing 'I'm sorry' to Jenny. Jenny mouthed 'It's okay, honest' in reply, but shrugged as well, to suggest there was not much they could do about it anyway.

"We're great here, although your precise and exact destruction with the explosive drone spacecraft really messed things up inside the alien mother ship, especially the control complex. We're managing to put the pieces back together albeit slowly, that's primarily one of the reasons I wanted to talk to you urgently. I see you have the 3D viewer switched off, is Jenny there with you at the moment?" Robert asked.

"Hi Robert," cut in Jenny, saving James the trouble of replying on her behalf.

"Ah Jenny. Look, I'm really sorry. I have to insist that James rejoins us here as soon as possible. I know you are on your honeymoon. However, it is of the utmost importance. I wouldn't ask otherwise," he trailed off.

Both of them realised that, if it came to it, Robert could actually order James out to Mars, he was just being polite about asking in the first instance.

"Seeing as you asked so nicely, how could I possibly refuse," laughed James rather hollowly. As the laugh subsided, it was instantly replaced by a deep grimace. Jenny's face turned to a stony stare at the same time with apprehension.

"Sorry to break up the party so soon, but it's all been arranged. The Moon shuttle leaves in forty-five minutes returning you back to Gateway. *Stellar Dusk* is waiting to depart and Captain Treadhouse has been ordered to await your arrival. It will add an extra three days onto the interplanetary voyage out to the Mars Facilities. Whether the captain likes it or not, it's not up for discussion, it is the quickest outward transit we could come up with at such short notice. It's entirely up to you if Jenny accompanies you or not, but you have to be here, as soon as is humanly possible." Robert concluded, with a hint of concern in his voice.

"It sounds really serious, any clues?" James enquired, noting the vocal trepidation.

"Sorry James, I can't go into any specific details here. It is very serious I can assure you that. We need you to use the alien head gear equipment for a specific purpose, only you so far have managed to master the alien technology enough to help us. You'd better get dressed and get your skates on, you now have forty minutes to get your gear together and get down to the shuttle bay. Bon voyage." The communication ended abruptly.

"How did he know I have no clothes on?" James commented, looking down at his naked body with a slightly puzzled look.

"Call yourself an analyst, go figure!" Jenny joked jumping up to get dressed. "And yes, before you ask, I am coming with you. We are now married and forever joined at the hip," she said, bouncing her hip off of his as she passed by him heading for the shower room.

—

"Carmen, how nice to see you again, may I introduce my lovely new wife Jenny," James announced, aiming to familiarize his new partner with some sort of panache. Then he suddenly remembered how he was initially attracted to the older Facilities Controller when they first met, he blushed uncontrollably at the memory.

"It's splendid to meet you Jenny, and James, what can I

say, you are as much a hero here as you are on Earth. I have told my personnel to be discreet, but what with all the newscasts, expect to be acknowledged and thanked wherever you may venture inside the facilities," Carmen said, smiling not noticing James's sudden embarrassment. "Once I have settled you into your apartment, I will arrange a meeting with Robert. He is so desperate to see you."

The way she said Robert's name and the following sentence appeared to have acquired an affectionate tone towards his colleague. James wondered if there was something more to it, his analytical perception appeared to be a lot sharper these days. Perhaps it was due to his recent exposure to the alien technology.

"May I ask where the alien equipment has been deposited?" James asked.

"It was transferred from the gear room on *Lode Drifter*, into one of our scientific research buildings. I have to say now, not one of our eminent scientists has yet managed to manipulate the alien headgear like you have. I suspect that's why you were brought back in such a hurry," Carmen suggested, turning to lead the couple to their temporary accommodation.

—

The reunion between James and Robert was emotional to say the least. They hugged, chatted and reminisced for some time about the battle for the Mars Facilities. They were the only two in the Facilities Controller's office that Robert now considered his second home after his small apartment. Robert had asked Carmen to give Jenny a guided tour of the facility buildings to allow the two men complete privacy.

James handed Robert a small bottle of pills. "I took the liberty of obtaining some more of your anxiety pills," he said smiling.

"You knew all along? And I thought I was being so discreet," Robert replied. "Thanks, but no thanks. I don't need them any more. I'm not sure how, but I've been cured of my claustrophobia. Perhaps it was the battle or being out on Mars for so long, who knows. I certainly don't feel hemmed in any more or worried by small spaces. Thanks for the consideration though, very astute of you," he concluded.

James took the bottle back. "That's great news. I'll have to pass these onto Rebecca to dispose off then. Right, before we go any further and discuss the reason you summoned me here, something's still bothering me. I have to ask you if you found anything out about the metallic cylinders discovered in France in the nineteen sixties. Did your data-mining programs find out any facts?" James enquired.

"Yes, I found out a little, but it hasn't been easy. They were definitely hushed up by the governments at the time. The tubes found in Saint-Jean-de-Livet were quite small in length, compared to the resupply cylinders we have been dealing with. They could have been earlier models designed for a specific carrying purpose. Without comparing the metal in the old tubes against ours, we can't be certain they are alien in origin. However, it's the only rational explanation for them to be found in sixty-five million year old Cretaceous chalk. In fact, we conducted an experiment with one of the resupply cylinders found on Nix. The leading edge that would appear to cut though anything does not like powdery substances, especially chalk, which chokes the internals of the cutting devices eventually. That could explain why they ground to a halt within the chalk layer on Earth," concluded Robert.

"That is interesting. Okay, now for the big question, why have you dragged me all the way back out here?" asked James.

"The simple fact is James you are the only one person that can make a telepathic link with the alien technology. The scientific lads have all had a stab at it. They stick their huge, brain-filled heads inside the helmet, but fail to make any sense of what is going on in their conscious minds. You described in detail the roads, the side streets and signposts of information that is available, these guys have not even made it out the front door, let alone onto the pavement! We've even tried using mild hypnotic drugs on some of them," Robert explained. He had a look on his face like being lost in a maze, not knowing which way to turn.

James decided to explain his experiences. "I have to admit it wasn't easy out on Ganymede. I had a few desperate moments near the alien spaceship. Just as well I persisted with my hunch though. We learnt an awful amount of information about our foes as a result of my mind excursions inside the alien artificial intelligence."

"I can only analyse, and now surmise, you had to be in the presence of the original artefacts and alien vessel to get to grips with the whole complete device. With only part of the equipment setup that was removed and transported from the Harvester spaceship down here to the Martian surface, it has resulted in no one else managing to access the alien information stored in the coffin-like structures. Not one of the resident scientists has even come close to operating the device like you have," concluded Robert.

"What about some of the crashed Harvester spacecraft from the final battle, haven't any of those got a bridge room intact?" James asked.

Robert shook his head. "I'm afraid not. Those with control rooms not shot to pieces were severely damaged in the resulting crashes into the Martian surface. Also, you started to decipher the alien language. We here have drawn a complete blank in that respect." Robert affirmed.

"So that's what this is really all about," James started, paused for a second before continuing. "After all the death and destruction within the Mars Facilities and the demise of the last few aliens, all you have left are some communiqués or books you cannot decipher. You dragged me here from honeymooning on the Moon to sort out some alien messages that you cannot translate?" James declared, finally analysing the reason he was summoned back to Mars in such a hurry. "Could it not have waited though?" he added, as an afterthought.

"Yes James, you nailed it, that's exactly what it's all about and no, it couldn't have waited. I now have no doubt you will be my perfect replacement," said Robert. James glared back unflinching.

A heavy silence now descended between them. Robert realised he had to tread carefully. "Look, it's complicated, let me explain. I need you to understand. There are no more aliens in our solar system, that's a foregone conclusion. Our scientists are currently going through the partially-destroyed control complex within Nix, the moon that was once in orbit round Pluto which we know turned out to be the long-time home to the alien species. As far as we are concerned, every local alien threat is now no more. So it should be game over, you agree?"

"What are you saying, the moon is still operative? There are aliens still about somewhere?" James asked with some concern, his frown suddenly disappearing.

Robert continued unperturbed. "Trawling through the debris inside Nix they found an alien instrument for receiving messages. The scientists worked out it was scanning and recording long-range transmissions, and guess what, it was still recording. They tried in vain to understand what the recordings were, but to no avail. That's the reason I need you, we need to know what the transmissions say? And we need to know quickly." Robert almost shouted, thumping the desk in frustration.

"Okay. Okay, let's go now, I'll get your answers then I can

get back to my honeymoon," replied James, pushing his chair back in an attempt to stand up.

"Wait a minute. Don't you see what this means? Work it out, look at this simple fact and work backwards. I'll repeat myself. It was scanning long-range transmissions from other groups of aliens." Robert held out his hands palm upwards suggesting there was more to come.

"So, there may well be many other alien groups out there in the galaxy who were once talking to those on Nix." James answered.

"And, what does that imply?" Robert was getting impatient. He wanted James to come to the same analytical deduction he had without any help from him.

"Oh. Oh my, yes, I see. I see what you're getting at. If other alien groups are out there, it does answer the age old question 'are we alone' in the galaxy. They must be preying on other flesh and blood creatures like us, possibly other human like people elsewhere in other planetary systems throughout the Milky Way," said James, flicking thumb and finger together to make them click and then slumping back in the chair with the realisation.

"Eureka!" Robert shouted out loud, as the penny finally dropped.

—

Jenny and Robert watched James as he lay on the oversized couch that had been extracted from the alien Harvester spacecraft. His head was covered with the enormous, ridiculous looking, alien black helmet. The black coffin structures were stacked up behind him against the wall.

James mind was wandering down what he classified as the roads and side streets inside the alien artificial intelligence machinery. He was looking for a way to connect up with the transmission recording device. There had to be a link to it somewhere in here. He knew quite a few of the symbols now, so it wasn't that hard to find what he considered was a promising avenue to explore. Sure enough, it proved fruitful.

Soon he was reading the streams of data flowing through the recording machine's memory. It didn't take long to understand what the received long-range transmissions were saying. Satisfied he had double checked the message contents, he removed the helmet and jumped down from the couch just as Carmen and Toby entered the small room. The look on James's face must have painted a grim picture.

"What is it James?" Robert enquired.

Jenny grasped his hand to steady him. "Are you okay?" she asked.

"Oh no, not again!" James exclaimed.

"Not what again? Speak some sense man," demanded Toby.

"The aliens on Nix must have sent out some sort of distress signal. They have responded. They are coming..." he trailed off.

"More aliens?" Carmen asked.

James nodded. "Six more to be precise. Six mother ships, converted moons from other solar planetary systems in our galaxy are going to converge here in the near future. They will be full of Harvester spacecraft and full of very hungry three-metre-tall alien humanoids. We may have won the battle for the Mars Facilities. Now... now we will have to go to war for the very survival of the human race!" James declared.

Acknowledgements

Special thanks to Steve Vise, Steve Pile, Derek Edwards, Dale Spence, Colin Sweby, Shirley Percy, Ben Smith and to all those family members and friends who gave me encouragement to complete this novel. Also, I have to thank Wikipedia and the B.B.C. *Focus* magazine for help and inspiration along the way.